SCYTHE

Also by Neal Shusterman

Novels
Bruiser
Challenger Deep
Chasing Forgiveness
The Dark Side of Nowhere
Dissidents
Downsiders
The Eyes of Kid Midas
Full Tilt
The Shadow Club
The Shadow Club Rising
Speeding Bullet

The Accelerati Series
(with Eric Elfman)
Tesla's Attic
Edison's Alley
Hawking's Hallway

The Antsy Bonano Series
The Schwa Was Here
Antsy Does Time
Ship Out of Luck

The Unwind Dystology
Unwind
UnWholly
UnSouled
UnDivided
UnBound

The Skinjacker Trilogy
Everlost
Everwild
Everfound

The Star Shards Chronicles
Scorpion Shards
Thief of Souls
Shattered Sky

The Dark Fusion Series
Dreadlocks
Red Rider's Hood
Duckling Ugly

Story Collections
Darkness Creeping
Kid Heroes
MindQuakes
MindStorms
MindTwisters
MindBenders

Visit the author at storyman.com and
Facebook.com/NealShusterman

ARC OF A SCYTHE BOOK 1

SCYTHE

NEAL SHUSTERMAN

SIMON & SCHUSTER BFYR

NEW YORK · LONDON · TORONTO · SYDNEY · NEW DELHI

SIMON & SCHUSTER BFYR

An imprint of Simon & Schuster Children's Publishing Division

1230 Avenue of the Americas, New York, New York 10020

SIMON & SCHUSTER BFYR is a trademark of Simon & Schuster, Inc.

For information about special discounts for bulk purchases, please contact Simon & Schuster Special Sales at 1-866-506-1949 or business@simonandschuster.com.

The Simon & Schuster Speakers Bureau can bring authors to your live event. For more information or to book an event, contact the Simon & Schuster Speakers Bureau at 1-866-248-3049 or visit our website at www.simonspeakers.com.

Also available in a SIMON & SCHUSTER BFYR hardcover edition

Cover design by Chloë Foglia

Interior design by Hilary Zarycky

The text for this book was set in Bembo Std.

Manufactured in the United States of America

First SIMON & SCHUSTER BFYR paperback edition November 2017

12 14 16 18 20 19 17 15 13 11

Library of Congress Cataloging-in-Publication Data

Names: Shusterman, Neal, author.

Title: Scythe / Neal Shusterman.

Description: First edition. | New York : Simon & Schuster Books for Young Readers, [2016] | Summary: "In a world where disease has been eliminated, the only way to die is to be randomly killed ('gleaned') by professional reapers ('scythes'). Two teens must compete with each other to become a scythe—a position neither of them wants. The one who becomes a scythe must kill the one who doesn't"—Provided by publisher.

Identifiers: LCCN 2016006502 | ISBN 9781442472426 (hardcover) | ISBN 9781442472440 (eBook)

Subjects: | CYAC: Death—Fiction. | Murder—Fiction. | Science fiction. | BISAC: JUVENILE FICTION / Science Fiction. | JUVENILE FICTION / Social Issues / Death & Dying. | JUVENILE FICTION / Action & Adventure / General.

Classification: LCC PZ7.S55987 Scy 2016 | DDC [Fic]—dc23

LC record available at https://lccn.loc.gov/2016006502

ISBN 978-1-4424-7243-3 (pbk)

For Olga (Ludovika) Nødtvedt,
a faraway fan and friend

ACKNOWLEDGMENTS

The creation of a novel is more than just the effort of the writer—there are many people involved in bringing a story to fruition, and every single one of them deserves credit for their contribution.

First and foremost, my editor David Gale and associate editor Liz Kossnar, as well as everyone at Simon & Schuster, who have been, and continue to be amazingly supportive: Justin Chanda, Jon Anderson, Anne Zafian, Katy Hershberger, Michelle Leo, Candace Greene, Krista Vossen, Chrissy Noh, and Katrina Groover to name just a few. Also Chloë Foglia, for what has to be one of my all-time favorite covers!

Thanks to Barb Sobel, my assistant who runs interference and keeps my life organized; and Matt Lurie, who manages my website and has built my social media presence.

Thanks to my book agent, Andrea Brown; my foreign rights agent, Taryn Fagerness, my entertainment industry agents, Steve Fisher & Debbie Deuble-Hill at APA; my manager, Trevor Engelson; my contract attorneys Shep Rosenman and Jennifer Justman, as well as trademark attorneys, Dov Scherzer and Matt Smith.

At the writing of this, *Scythe* is being developed as a feature film, and I'd like to thank everyone involved, including Jay Ireland at Blue Grass Films, as well as Sara Scott and Mika Pryce at Universal.

Forever and always, a special thanks to my kids, Brendan, Jarrod, Joelle and Erin—who keep me on my toes, keep me young, and always have thought-provoking comments and suggestions. And, of course, my aunt Mildred Altman, who is going strong at eighty-eight, and has read every single one of my books!

Thanks everyone! This series promises to be a very exciting journey! I'm glad you're all a part of it!

SCYTHE

Part One

ROBE AND RING

We must, by law, keep a record of the innocents we kill.

And as I see it, they're all innocents. Even the guilty. Everyone is guilty of something, and everyone still harbors a memory of childhood innocence, no matter how many layers of life wrap around it. Humanity is innocent; humanity is guilty, and both states are undeniably true.

We must, by law, keep a record.

It begins on day one of apprenticeship—but we do not officially call it "killing." It's not socially or morally correct to call it such. It is, and has always been, "gleaning," named for the way the poor would trail behind farmers in ancient times, taking the stray stalks of grain left behind. It was the earliest form of charity. A scythe's work is the same. Every child is told from the day he or she is old enough to understand that the scythes provide a crucial service for society. Ours is the closest thing to a sacred mission the modern world knows.

Perhaps that is why we must, by law, keep a record. A public journal, testifying to those who will never die and those who are yet to be born, as to why we human beings do the things we do. We are instructed to write down not just our deeds but our feelings, because it must be known that we do have feelings. Remorse. Regret. Sorrow too great to bear. Because if we didn't feel those things, what monsters would we be?

—From the gleaning journal of H.S. Curie

1

No Dimming of the Sun

The scythe arrived late on a cold November afternoon. Citra was at the dining room table, slaving over a particularly difficult algebra problem, shuffling variables, unable to solve for X or Y, when this new and far more pernicious variable entered her life's equation.

Guests were frequent at the Terranovas' apartment, so when the doorbell rang, there was no sense of foreboding—no dimming of the sun, no foreshadowing of the arrival of death at their door. Perhaps the universe should have deigned to provide such warnings, but scythes were no more supernatural than tax collectors in the grand scheme of things. They showed up, did their unpleasant business, and were gone.

Her mother answered the door. Citra didn't see the visitor, as he was, at first, hidden from her view by the door when it opened. What she saw was how her mother stood there, suddenly immobile, as if her veins had solidified within her. As if, were she tipped over, she would fall to the floor and shatter.

"May I enter, Mrs. Terranova?"

The visitor's tone of voice gave him away. Resonant and inevitable, like the dull toll of an iron bell, confident in the ability of its peal to reach all those who needed reaching. Citra knew before she even saw him that it was a scythe. *My god! A scythe has come to our home!*

"Yes, yes of course, come in." Citra's mother stepped aside to allow him entry—as if she were the visitor and not the other way around.

He stepped over the threshold, his soft slipper-like shoes making no sound on the parquet floor. His multilayered robe was smooth ivory linen, and although it reached so low as to dust the floor, there was not a spot of dirt on it anywhere. A scythe, Citra knew, could choose the color of his or her robe— every color except for black, for it was considered inappropriate for their job. Black was an absence of light, and scythes were the opposite. Luminous and enlightened, they were acknowledged as the very best of humanity—which is why they were chosen for the job.

Some scythe robes were bright, some more muted. They looked like the rich, flowing robes of Renaissance angels, both heavy yet lighter than air. The unique style of scythes' robes, regardless of the fabric and color, made them easy to spot in public, which made them easy to avoid—if avoidance was what a person wanted. Just as many were drawn to them.

The color of the robe often said a lot about a scythe's personality. This scythe's ivory robe was pleasant, and far enough from true white not to assault the eye with its brightness. But none of this changed the fact of who and what he was.

He pulled off his hood to reveal neatly cut gray hair, a mournful face red-cheeked from the chilly day, and dark eyes that seemed themselves almost to be weapons. Citra stood. Not out of respect, but out of fear. Shock. She tried not to hyperventilate. She tried not to let her knees buckle beneath her. They were betraying her by wobbling, so she forced fortitude to her legs, tightening her muscles. Whatever the scythe's purpose here, he would not see her crumble.

"You may close the door," he said to Citra's mother, who did so, although Citra could see how difficult it was for her. A scythe in the foyer could still turn around if the door was open. The moment that door was closed, he was truly, truly inside one's home.

He looked around, spotting Citra immediately. He offered a smile. "Hello, Citra," he said. The fact that he knew her name froze her just as solidly as his appearance had frozen her mother.

"Don't be rude," her mother said, too quickly. "Say hello to our guest."

"Good day, Your Honor."

"Hi," said her younger brother, Ben, who had just come to his bedroom door, having heard the deep peal of the scythe's voice. Ben was barely able to squeak out the one-word greeting. He looked to Citra and to their mother, thinking the same thing they were all thinking, *Who has he come for? Will it be me? Or will I be left to suffer the loss?*

"I smelled something inviting in the hallway," the scythe said, breathing in the aroma. "Now I see I was right in thinking it came from this apartment."

"Just baked ziti, Your Honor. Nothing special." Until this moment, Citra had never known her mother to be so timid.

"That's good," said the scythe, "because I require nothing special." Then he sat on the sofa and waited patiently for dinner.

Was it too much to believe that the man was here for a meal and nothing more? After all, scythes had to eat somewhere. Customarily, restaurants never charged them for food, but that didn't mean a home-cooked meal was not more desirable. There were rumors of scythes who required their victims to prepare them a meal before being gleaned. Is that what was happening here?

Whatever his intentions, he kept them to himself, and they had no choice but to give him whatever he wanted. Will he spare a life here today if the food is to his taste, Citra wondered? No surprise that people bent over backward to please scythes in every possible way. Hope in the shadow of fear is the world's most powerful motivator.

Citra's mother brought him something to drink at his request, and now labored to make sure tonight's dinner was the finest she had ever served. Cooking was not her specialty. Usually she would return home from work just in time to throw something quick together for them. Tonight their lives might just rest on her questionable culinary skills. And their father? Would he be home in time, or would a gleaning in his family take place in his absence?

As terrified as Citra was, she did not want to leave the scythe alone with his own thoughts, so she went into the living room with him. Ben, who was clearly as fascinated as he was fearful, sat with her.

The man finally introduced himself as Honorable Scythe Faraday.

"I . . . uh . . . did a report on Faraday for school once," Ben said, his voice cracking only once. "You picked a pretty cool scientist to name yourself after."

Scythe Faraday smiled. "I like to think I chose an appropriate *Patron Historic*. Like many scientists, Michael Faraday was underappreciated in his life, yet our world would not be what it is without him."

"I think I have you in my scythe card collection," Ben went on. "I have almost all the MidMerican scythes—but you were younger in the picture."

The man seemed perhaps sixty, and although his hair had gone gray, his goatee was still salt-and-pepper. It was rare for a person to let themselves reach such an age before resetting back to a more youthful self. Citra wondered how old he truly was. How long had he been charged with ending lives?

"Do you look your true age, or are you at the far end of time by choice?" Citra asked.

"Citra!" Her mother nearly dropped the casserole she had just taken out of the oven. "What a question to ask!"

"I like direct questions," the scythe said. "They show an honesty of spirit, so I will give an honest answer. I admit to having turned the corner four times. My natural age is somewhere near one hundred eighty, although I forget the exact number. Of late I've chosen this venerable appearance because I find that those I glean take more comfort from it." Then he laughed. "They think me wise."

"Is that why you're here?" Ben blurted. "To glean one of us?"

Scythe Faraday offered an unreadable smile.

"I'm here for dinner."

Citra's father arrived just as dinner was about to be served. Her mom had apparently informed him of the situation, so he was much more emotionally prepared than the rest of them had been. As soon as he entered, he went straight over to Scythe Faraday to shake his hand, and pretended to be far more jovial and inviting than he truly must have been.

The meal was awkward—mostly silence punctuated by the occasional comment by the scythe. "You have a lovely home." "What flavorful lemonade!" "This may be the best baked ziti in all of MidMerica!" Even though everything he said was complimentary, his voice registered like a seismic shock down everyone's spine.

"I haven't seen you in the neighborhood," Citra's father finally said.

"I don't suppose you would have," he answered. "I am not the public figure that some other scythes choose to be. Some scythes prefer the spotlight, but to truly do the job right, it requires a level of anonymity."

"Right?" Citra bristled at the very idea. "There's a right way to glean?"

"Well," he answered, "there are certainly wrong ways," and said nothing more about it. He just ate his ziti.

As the meal neared its close, he said, "Tell me about yourselves." It wasn't a question or a request. It could only be read as a demand. Citra wasn't sure whether this was part of his little dance of death, or if he was genuinely interested. He knew their names before he entered the apartment, so he probably already knew all the things they could tell him. Then why ask?

"I work in historical research," her father said.

"I'm a food synthesis engineer," said her mother.

The scythe raised his eyebrows. "And yet you cooked this from scratch."

She put down her fork. "All from synthesized ingredients."

"Yes, but if we can synthesize anything," he offered, "why do we still need food synthesis engineers?"

Citra could practically see the blood drain from her mother's face. It was her father who rose to defend his wife's existence. "There's always room for improvement."

"Yeah—and Dad's work is important, too!" Ben said.

"What, historical research?" The scythe waved his fork dismissing the notion. "The past never changes—and from what I can see, neither does the future."

While her parents and brother were perplexed and troubled by his comments, Citra understood the point he was making. The growth of civilization was complete. Everyone knew it. When it came to the human race, there was no more left to learn. Nothing about our own existence to decipher. Which meant that no one person was more important than any other. In fact, in the grand scheme of things, everyone was equally useless. That's what he was saying, and it infuriated Citra, because on a certain level, she knew he was right.

Citra was well known for her temper. It often arrived before reason, and left only after the damage was done. Tonight would be no exception.

"Why are you doing this? If you're here to glean one of us, just get it over with and stop torturing us!"

Her mother gasped, and her father pushed back his chair as if ready to get up and physically remove her from the room.

"Citra, what are you doing!" Now her mother's voice was quivering. "Show respect!"

"No! He's here, he's going to do it, so let him do it. It's not like he hasn't decided; I've heard that scythes always make up their mind before they enter a home, isn't that right?"

The scythe was unperturbed by her outburst. "Some do,

some don't," he said gently. "We each have our own way of doing things."

By now Ben was crying. Dad put his arm around him, but the boy was inconsolable.

"Yes, scythes must glean," Faraday said, "but we also must eat, and sleep, and have simple conversation."

Citra grabbed his empty plate away from him. "Well, the meal's done, so you can leave."

Then her father approached him. He fell to his knees. Her father was actually on his knees to this man! "Please, Your Honor, forgive her. I take full responsibility for her behavior."

The scythe stood. "An apology isn't necessary. It's refreshing to be challenged. You have no idea how tedious it gets—the pandering, the obsequious flattery, the endless parade of sycophants. A slap in the face is bracing. It reminds me that I'm human."

Then he went to the kitchen and grabbed the largest, sharpest knife he could find. He swished it back and forth, getting a feel for how it cut through the air.

Ben's wails grew, and his father's grip tightened on him. The scythe approached their mother. Citra was ready to hurl herself in front of her to block the blade, but instead of swinging the knife, the man held out his other hand.

"Kiss my ring."

No one was expecting this, least of all Citra.

Citra's mother stared at him, shaking her head, not willing to believe. "You're . . . you're granting me immunity?"

"For your kindness and the meal you served, I grant you one year immunity from gleaning. No scythe may touch you."

But she hesitated. "Grant it to my children instead."

Still the scythe held out his ring to her. It was a diamond the size of his knuckle, with a dark core. It was the same ring all scythes wore.

"I am offering it to you, not them."

"But—"

"Jenny, just do it!" insisted their father.

And so she did. She knelt and kissed his ring, and her DNA was read and was transmitted to the Scythedom's immunity database. In an instant the world knew that Jenny Terranova was safe from gleaning for the next twelve months. The scythe looked to his ring, which now glowed faintly red, indicating that the person before him had immunity from gleaning. He grinned, satisfied.

And finally he told them the truth.

"I'm here to glean your neighbor, Bridget Chadwell," Scythe Faraday informed them. "But she was not yet home. And I was hungry."

He gently touched Ben on the head, as if delivering some sort of benediction. It seemed to calm him. Then the scythe moved to the door, the knife still in his hand, leaving no question as to the method of their neighbor's gleaning. But before he left, he turned to Citra.

"You see through the facades of the world, Citra Terranova. You'd make a good scythe."

Citra recoiled. "I'd never want to be one."

"That," he said, "is the first requirement."

Then he left to kill their neighbor.

They didn't speak of it that night. No one spoke of gleanings—

as if speaking about it might bring it upon them. There were no sounds from next door. No screams, no pleading wails—or perhaps the Terranovas' TV was turned up too loud to hear it. That was the first thing Citra's father did once the scythe left—turn on the TV and blast it to drown out the gleaning on the other side of the wall. But it was unnecessary, because however the scythe accomplished his task, it was done quietly. Citra found herself straining to hear something—anything. Both she and Ben discovered in themselves a morbid curiosity that made them both secretly ashamed.

An hour later, Honorable Scythe Faraday returned. It was Citra who opened the door. His ivory robe held not a single splatter of blood. Perhaps he had a spare one. Perhaps he had used the neighbor's washing machine after her gleaning. The knife was clean, too, and he handed it to Citra.

"We don't want it," Citra told him, feeling pretty sure she could speak for her parents on the matter. "We'll never use it again."

"But you *must* use it," he insisted, "so that it might remind you."

"Remind us of what?"

"That a scythe is merely the instrument of death, but it is *your* hand that swings me. You and your parents, and everyone else in this world are the wielders of scythes." Then he gently put the knife in her hands. "We are all accomplices. You must share the responsibility."

That may have been true, but after he was gone Citra still dropped the knife into the trash.

It is the most difficult thing a person can be asked to do. And knowing that it is for the greater good doesn't make it any easier. People used to die naturally. Old age used to be a terminal affliction, not a temporary state. There were invisible killers called "diseases" that broke the body down. Aging couldn't be reversed, and there were accidents from which there was no return. Planes fell from the sky. Cars actually crashed. There was pain, misery, despair. It's hard for most of us to imagine a world so unsafe, with dangers lurking in every unseen, unplanned corner. All of that is behind us now, and yet a simple truth remains: People have to die.

It's not as if we can go somewhere else; the disasters on the moon and Mars colonies proved that. We have one very limited world, and although death has been defeated as completely as polio, people still must die. The ending of human life used to be in the hands of nature. But we stole it. Now we have a monopoly on death. We are its sole distributor.

I understand why there are scythes, and how important and how necessary the work is . . . but I often wonder why I had to be chosen. And if there is some eternal world after this one, what fate awaits a taker of lives?

—From the gleaning journal of H.S. Curie

2

.303 %

Tyger Salazar had hurled himself out a thirty-nine-story window, leaving a terrible mess on the marble plaza below. His own parents were so annoyed by it, they didn't come to see him. But Rowan did. Rowan Damisch was just that kind of friend.

He sat by Tyger's bedside in the revival center, waiting for him to awake from speedhealing. Rowan didn't mind. The revival center was quiet. Peaceful. It was a nice break from the turmoil of his home, which lately had been filled with more relatives than any human being should be expected to endure. Cousins, second cousins, siblings, half-siblings. And now his grandmother had returned home after turning the corner for a third time, with a new husband and a baby on the way.

"You're going to have a new aunt, Rowan," she had announced. "Isn't it wonderful?"

The whole thing pissed Rowan's mother off—because this time Grandma had reset all the way down to twenty-five, making her ten years younger than her daughter. Now Mom felt pressured to turn the corner herself, if only to keep up with Grandma. Grandpa was much more sensible. He was off in EuroScandia, charming the ladies and maintaining his age at a respectable thirty-eight.

Rowan, at sixteen, had resolved he would experience

gray hair before he turned his first corner—and even then, he wouldn't reset so far down as to be embarrassing. Some people reset to twenty-one, which was the youngest genetic therapy could take a person. Rumor was, though, that they were working on ways to reset right down into the teens—which Rowan found ridiculous. Why would anyone in their right mind want to be a teenager more than once?

When he glanced back at his friend, Tyger's eyes were open and studying Rowan.

"Hey," Rowan said.

"How long?" Tyger asked.

"Four days."

Tyger pumped his fist in triumph. "Yes! A new record!" He looked at his hands, as if taking stock of the damage. There was, of course, no damage left. One did not wake up from speedhealing until there was nothing left to heal. "Do you think it was jumping from such a high floor that did it, or was it the marble plaza?"

"Probably the marble," Rowan said. "Once you reach terminal velocity, it doesn't matter how high you are when you jump."

"Did I crack it? Did they have to replace the marble?"

"I don't know, Tyger—jeez, enough already."

Tyger leaned back into his pillow, immensely pleased with himself. "Best splat ever!"

Rowan found he had patience to wait for his friend to wake up, but no patience for him now that he was conscious. "Why do you even do it? I mean, it's such a waste of time."

Tyger shrugged. "I like the way it feels on the way down.

Besides, I gotta remind my parents that the lettuce is there."

That made Rowan chuckle. It was Rowan who had coined the term "lettuce-kid" to describe them. Both of them were born sandwiched somewhere in the middle of large families, and were far from being their parents' favorites. "I got a couple of brothers that are the meat, a few sisters that are cheese and tomatoes, so I guess I'm the lettuce." The idea caught on, and Rowan had started a club called the Iceberg Heads at school, which now bragged almost two dozen members . . . although Tyger often teased that he was going to go rogue and start a romaine revolt.

Tyger had started splatting a few months ago. Rowan tried it once, and found it a monumental pain. He ended up behind on all his schoolwork, and his parents levied all forms of punishment—which they promptly forgot to enforce—one of the perks of being the lettuce. Still, the thrill of the drop wasn't worth the cost. Tyger, on the other hand, had become a splatting junkie.

"You gotta find a new hobby, man," Rowan told him. "I know the first revival is free, but the rest must be costing your parents a fortune."

"Yeah . . . and for once they have to spend their money on me."

"Wouldn't you rather they buy you a car?"

"Revival is compulsory," Tyger said. "A car is optional. If they're not forced to spend it, they won't."

Rowan couldn't argue with that. He didn't have a car either, and doubted his parents would ever get him one. The publicars were clean, efficient, and drove themselves, his parents had argued. What would be the point in spending good money on something he didn't need? Meanwhile, they threw money in every direction but his.

"We're roughage," Tyger said. "If we don't cause a little intestinal distress, no one knows we're there."

The following morning, Rowan came face to face with a scythe. It wasn't unheard of to see a scythe in his neighborhood. You couldn't help but run into one once in a while—but they didn't often show up in a high school.

The encounter was Rowan's fault. Punctuality was not his strong point—especially now that he was expected to escort his younger siblings and half-siblings to their school before hopping into a publicar and hurrying to his. He had just arrived and was heading to the attendance window when the scythe came around a corner, his spotless ivory robe flaring behind him.

Once, when hiking with his family, Rowan had gone off on his own and had encountered a mountain lion. The tight feeling in his chest now, as well as the weak feeling in his loins, had been exactly the same. Fight or flight, his biology said. But Rowan had done neither. Back then, he had fought those instincts and calmly raised his arms, as he had read to do, making himself look larger. It had worked, and the animal bounded away, saving him a trip to the local revival center.

Now, at the sudden prospect of a scythe before him, Rowan had an odd urge to do the same—as if raising his hands above his head could frighten the scythe away. The thought made him involuntarily laugh out loud. The last thing you want to do is laugh at a scythe.

"Could you direct me to the main office?" the man asked.

Rowan considered giving him directions and heading the opposite way, but decided that was too cowardly. "I'm going there," Rowan said. "I'll take you." The man would appreciate helpfulness—and getting on the good side of a scythe couldn't hurt.

Rowan led the way, passing other kids in the hall—students who, like him, were late, or were just on an errand. They all gawked and tried to disappear into the wall as he and the scythe passed. Somehow, walking through the hall with a scythe became less frightening when there were others to bear the fear instead—and Rowan couldn't deny that it was a bit heady to be cast as a scythe's trailblazer, riding in the cone of such respect. It wasn't until they reached the office that the truth hit home. The scythe was going to glean one of Rowan's classmates today.

Everyone in the office stood the moment they saw the scythe, and he wasted no time. "Please have Kohl Whitlock called to the office immediately."

"Kohl Whitlock?" said the secretary.

The scythe didn't repeat himself, because he knew she had heard—she just wasn't willing to believe.

"Yes, Your Honor, I'll do it right away."

Rowan knew Kohl. Hell, everyone knew Kohl Whitlock. Just a junior, he had already risen to be the school's quarterback. He was going to take them all the way to a league championship for the first time in forever.

The secretary's voice shook powerfully when she made the call into the intercom. She coughed as she said his name, choking up.

And the scythe patiently awaited Kohl's arrival.

The last thing Rowan wanted to do was antagonize a scythe. He should have just slunk off to the attendance window, gotten his readmit, and gone to class. But as with the mountain lion, he just had to stand his ground. It was a moment that would change his life.

"You're gleaning our star quarterback—I hope you know that."

The scythe's demeanor, so cordial a moment before, took a turn toward tombstone. "I can't see how it's any of your business."

"You're in my school," Rowan said. "I guess that makes it my business." Then self-preservation kicked in, and he strode to the attendance window, just out of the scythe's line of sight. He handed in his forged tardy note, all the while muttering *Stupid stupid stupid* under his breath. He was lucky he wasn't born in a time when death was natural, because he'd probably never survive to adulthood.

As he turned to leave the office, he saw a bleak-eyed Kohl Whitlock being led into the principal's office by the scythe. The principal voluntarily ejected himself from his own office, then looked to the staff for an explanation, but only received the teary-eyed shaking of their heads.

No one seemed to notice Rowan still lingering there. Who cared about the lettuce when the beef was being devoured?

He slipped past the principal, who saw him just in time to put a hand on his shoulder. "Son, you don't want to go in there."

He was right; Rowan didn't want to go in there. But he went anyway, closing the door behind him.

There were two chairs in front of the principal's well-organized desk. The scythe sat in one, Kohl in the other, hunched and sobbing. The scythe burned Rowan a glare. *The mountain lion,* thought Rowan. Only this one actually had the power to end a human life.

"His parents aren't here," Rowan said. "He should have someone with him."

"Are you family?"

"Does it matter?"

Then Kohl raised his head. "Please don't make Ronald go," he pleaded.

"It's Rowan."

Kohl's expression shot to higher horror, as if this error somehow sealed the deal. "I knew that! I did! I really did!" For all his bulk and bravado, Kohl Whitlock was just a scared little kid. Is that what everyone became in the end? Rowan supposed only a scythe could know.

Rather than forcing Rowan to leave, the scythe said, "Grab a chair then. Make yourself comfortable."

As Rowan went around to pull out the principal's desk chair, he wondered if the scythe was being ironic, or sarcastic, or if he didn't even know that making oneself comfortable was impossible in his presence.

"You can't do this to me," Kohl begged. "My parents will die! They'll just die!"

"No they won't," the scythe corrected. "They'll live on."

"Can you at least give him a few minutes to prepare?" Rowan asked.

"Are you telling me how to do my job?"

"I'm asking you for some mercy!"

The scythe glared at him again, but this time it was somehow different. He wasn't just delivering intimidation, he was extracting something. Studying something in Rowan. "I've done this for many years," the scythe said. "In my experience, a quick and painless gleaning is the greatest mercy I can show."

"Then at least give him a reason! Tell him why it has to be him!"

"It's random, Rowan!" Kohl said. "Everyone knows that! It's just freaking random!"

But there was something in the scythe's eyes that said otherwise. So Rowan pressed.

"There's more to it, isn't there?"

The scythe sighed. He didn't have to say anything—he was, after all, a scythe, above the law in every way. He owed no one an explanation. But he chose to give one anyway.

"Removing old age from the equation, statistics from the Age of Mortality cite 7 percent of deaths as being automobile-related. Of those, 31 percent involved the use of alcohol, and of those, 14 percent were teenagers." Then he tossed Rowan a small calculator from the principal's desk. "Figure it out yourself."

Rowan took his time crunching the numbers, knowing that every second taken was a second of life he bought for Kohl.

".303 percent," Rowan finally said.

"Which means," said the scythe, "that about three out of every thousand souls I glean will fit that profile. One out of every three hundred thirty-three. Your friend here just got a new car and has a record of drinking to excess. So, of the teens who fit that profile, I made a random choice."

Kohl buried his head in his hands, his tears intensifying. "I'm such an IDIOT!" He pressed his palms against his eyes as if trying to push them deep within his head.

"So tell me," the scythe said calmly to Rowan. "Has the explanation eased his gleaning, or made his suffering worse?"

Rowan shrunk a bit in his chair.

"Enough," said the scythe. "It's time." Then he produced from a pocket in his robe a small paddle that was shaped to fit over his hand. It had a cloth back and a shiny metallic palm. "Kohl, I have chosen for you a shock that will induce cardiac arrest. Death will be quick, painless, and nowhere near as brutal as the car accident you would have suffered in the Age of Mortality."

Suddenly Kohl thrust his hand out, grabbing Rowan's and holding it tightly. Rowan allowed it. He wasn't family; he wasn't even Kohl's friend before today—but what was the saying? *Death makes the whole world kin.* Rowan wondered if a world without death would then make everyone strangers. He squeezed Kohl's hand tighter—a silent promise that he wouldn't let go.

"Is there anything you want me to tell people?" Rowan asked.

"A million things," said Kohl, "but I can't think of any of 'em."

Rowan resolved that he would make up Kohl's last words to share with his loved ones. And they would be fine words. Comforting ones. Rowan would find a way to make sense of the senseless.

"I'm afraid you'll have to let go of his hand for the procedure," the scythe said.

"No," Rowan told him.

"The shock could stop your heart, too," the scythe warned.

"So what?" said Rowan. "They'll revive me." Then he added, "Unless you've decided to glean me, too."

Rowan was aware that he had just dared a scythe to kill him. In spite of the risk, he was glad he had done it.

"Very well." And without waiting an instant longer, the scythe pressed the paddle to Kohl's chest.

Rowan's vision went white, then dark. His entire body convulsed. He flew backward out of his chair and hit the wall behind him. It might have been painless for Kohl, but not for Rowan. It hurt. It hurt more than anything—more pain than a person is supposed to feel—but then the microscopic pain-killing nanites in his blood released their numbing opiates. The pain subsided as those opiates took effect, and when his vision cleared, he saw Kohl slumped in his chair and the scythe reaching over to close his sightless eyes. The gleaning was complete. Kohl Whitlock was dead.

The scythe stood and reached out to offer Rowan his hand, but Rowan didn't take it. He rose from the floor on his own, and although Rowan felt not an ounce of gratitude, he said, "Thank you for letting me stay."

The scythe regarded him a little too long, then said, "You stood your ground for a boy you barely knew. You comforted him at the moment of his death, bearing the pain of the jolt. You bore witness, even though no one called you to do so."

Rowan shrugged. "I did what anyone would do."

"Did anyone else offer?" the scythe put to him. "Your principal? The office staff? Any of the dozen students we passed in the hall?"

"No . . . ," Rowan had to admit. "But what does it matter what I did? He's still dead. And you know what they say about good intentions."

The scythe nodded, and glanced down at his ring, sitting so fat on his finger. "I suppose now you'll ask me for immunity."

Rowan shook his head. "I don't want anything from you."

"Fair enough." The scythe turned to go, but hesitated before he opened the door. "Be warned that you will not receive kindness from anyone but me for what you did here today," he said. "But remember that good intentions pave many roads. Not all of them lead to hell."

The slap was just as jarring as the electric shock—even more so because Rowan wasn't expecting it. It came just before lunch, as he was standing at his locker, and flew in with such force it knocked him back, making the row of lockers resound like a steel drum.

"You were there and you didn't stop it!" Marah Pavlik's eyes flared with grief and righteous indignation. She looked ready to reach up his nostrils with her long nails and extract his brain. "You just let him die!"

Marah had been Kohl's girlfriend for over a year. Like Kohl, she was a highly popular junior, and as such would actively avoid any interaction with sophomore rabble such as Rowan. But these were extraordinary circumstances.

"It wasn't like that," Rowan managed to blurt out before she swung again. This time he deflected her hand. She broke a nail but didn't seem to care. If nothing else, Kohl's gleaning had given her perspective.

"It was *exactly* like that! You went in there to watch him die!"

Others had begun to gather, drawn, as most are, to the scent of conflict. He looked to the crowd for a sympathetic face—

someone who might take his side—but all he saw in the faces of his classmates was communal disdain. Marah was speaking, and slapping, for all of them.

This is not what Rowan had expected. Not that he wanted pats on the back for coming to Kohl's aid in his last moments—but he wasn't expecting such an unthinkable accusation.

"What, are you nuts?" Rowan shouted at her—at all of them. "You can't stop a scythe from gleaning!"

"I don't care!" she wailed. "You could have done something, but all you did was watch!"

"I did do something! I . . . I held his hand."

She slammed him back into the locker with more strength than he thought she could possibly have. "You're lying! He'd *never* hold your hand. He'd never touch any part of you!" And then, "*I* should have held his hand!"

Around them the other kids scowled, and whispered things that they clearly wanted him to hear.

"I saw him walking in the hall with the scythe like they were best buddies."

"They came into school together this morning."

"I heard he gave the scythe Kohl's name."

"Someone told me he actually helped."

He stormed to the obnoxious kid who made the last accusation—Ralphy something or other. "Heard from who? No one else was in the room, you moron!"

But it didn't matter. Rumors adhered to no logic but their own.

"Don't you get it? I didn't help the scythe, I helped *Kohl*!" Rowan insisted.

"Yeah, helped him into the grave," someone said, and everyone else grumbled in agreement.

It was no use—he had been tried and convicted—and the more he denied it, the more convinced they'd be of his guilt. They didn't need his act of courage; what they needed was someone to blame. Someone to hate. They couldn't take their wrath out on the scythe, but Rowan Damisch was the perfect candidate.

"I'll bet he got immunity for helping," a kid said—a kid who'd always been his friend.

"I didn't!"

"Good," said Marah with absolute contempt. "Then I hope the next scythe comes for you."

He knew she meant it—not just in the moment, but forever—and if the next scythe did come for him, she would relish the knowledge of his death. It was a darkly sobering thought, that there were now people in this world who actively wished him dead. It was one thing not to be noticed. It was something else entirely to be the repository of an entire school's enmity.

Only then did the scythe's warning come back to him: that he would receive no kindness for what he had done for Kohl. The man had been right—and he hated the scythe for it, just as the others hated Rowan.

2042. It's a year that every schoolchild knows. It was the year when computational power became infinite—or so close to infinite that it could no longer be measured. It was the year we knew . . . everything. "The cloud" evolved into "the Thunderhead," and now all there is to know about everything resides in the near-infinite memory of the Thunderhead for anyone who wants to access it.

But like so many things, once we had possession of infinite knowledge, it suddenly seemed less important. Less urgent. Yes, we know everything, but I often wonder if anyone bothers to look at all that knowledge. There are academics, of course, who study what we already know, but to what end? The very idea of schooling used to be about learning so that we could improve our lives and the world. But a perfect world needs no improvement. Like most everything else we do, education, from grade school through the highest of universities, is just a way to keep us busy.

2042 is the year we conquered death, and also the year we stopped counting. Sure, we still numbered years for a few more decades, but at the moment of immortality, passing time ceased to matter.

I don't know exactly when things switched over to the Chinese calendar—Year of the Dog, Year of the Goat, the Dragon, and so on. And I can't exactly say when animal activists around the world began calling for equal billing for their own favorite species, adding in Year of the Otter, and the Whale, and the Penguin. And I couldn't tell you when they stopped repeating, and when it was decreed that every year henceforth would be named after a different species. All I know for sure is that this is the Year of the Ocelot.

As for the things I don't know, I'm sure they're all up there in the Thunderhead for anyone with the motivation to look.

—From the gleaning journal of H.S. Curie

3

The Force of Destiny

The invitation came to Citra in early January. It arrived by post—which was the first indication that it was out of the ordinary. There were only three types of communications that arrived by post: packages, official business, or letters from the eccentric—the only type of people who still wrote letters. This appeared to be of the third variety.

"Well, open it," Ben said, more excited by the envelope than Citra was. It had been handwritten, making it even odder. True, handwriting was still offered as an elective, but, aside from herself, she knew few people who had taken it. She tore the envelope open and pulled out a card that was the same eggshell color as the envelope, then read to herself before reading it aloud.

The pleasure of your company is requested at the Grand Civic Opera, January ninth, seven p.m.

There was no signature, no return address. There was, however, a single ticket in the envelope.

"The opera?" said Ben. "Ew."

Citra couldn't agree more.

"Could it be some sort of school event?" their mother asked.

Citra shook her head. "If it was, it would say so."

She took the invitation and envelope from Citra to study them herself. "Well, whatever it is, it sounds interesting."

"It's probably some loser's way of asking me on a date because he's too afraid to ask me to my face."

"Do you think you'll go?" her mother asked.

"Mom . . . a boy who invites me to the opera is either joking or delusional."

"Or he's trying to impress you."

Citra grunted and left the room, annoyed by her own curiosity. "I'm not going!" she called out from her room, knowing full well that she would.

The Grand Civic Opera was one of several places where anyone who was anyone went to be seen. At any given performance, only half the patrons were there for the actual opera. The rest were there to participate in the great melodrama of social climbing and career advancement. Even Citra, who moved in none of those circles, knew the drill.

She wore the dress she had bought for the previous year's homecoming dance, when she was sure that Hunter Morrison would invite her. Instead, Hunter had invited Zachary Swain, which apparently everyone but Citra knew would happen. They were still a couple, and Citra, until today, hadn't had any use for the dress.

When she put it on, she was far more pleased with it than she thought she'd be. Teenage girls change in a year, but now the dress—which was more about wishful thinking last year—actually fit her perfectly.

In her mind, she had narrowed down the possibilities of her secret admirer. It could be one of five, only two of whom she would enjoy spending an evening alone with. The other three she would endure for the sake of novelty. There was, after all, some fun to be had spending an evening pretending to be pretentious.

Her father insisted on dropping her off. "Call when you're ready to be picked up."

"I'll take a publicar home."

"Call anyway," he said. He told her she looked beautiful for the tenth time, then she got out and he drove off to make room for the limousines and Bentleys in the drop-off queue. She took a deep breath and went up the marble steps, feeling as awkward and out of place as Cinderella at the ball.

Upon entering, she was not directed toward either the orchestra or the central staircase leading to the balcony. Instead, the usher looked at the ticket, looked at her, then looked at the ticket again before calling over a second usher to personally escort her.

"What's all this about?" she asked. Her first thought was that it was a forged ticket and she was being escorted to the exit. Perhaps it had been a joke after all, and she was already running a list of suspects through her mind.

But then the second usher said, "A personal escort is customary for a box seat, miss."

Box seats, Citra recalled, were the ultimate in exclusivity. They were usually reserved for people too elite to sit among the masses. Normal people couldn't afford them, and even if they could, they weren't allowed access. As she followed the usher up the narrow stairs to the left boxes, Citra began to get scared. She knew no one with that kind of money. What if this invitation came to her by mistake? Or if there actually was some sort of big, important person waiting for Citra, what on earth were his or her intentions?

"Here we are!"The usher pulled back the curtain of the box to reveal a boy her age already sitting there. He had dark hair and light freckled skin. He stood up when he saw her, and Citra could see that his suit revealed a little too much of his socks.

"Hi."

"Hello."

And the usher left them alone.

"I left you the seat closer to the stage," he said.

"Thanks." She sat down, trying to figure out who this was and why he had invited her here. He didn't appear familiar. Should she know him? She didn't want to let on that she didn't recognize him.

Then out of nowhere, he said, "Thank you."

"For what?"

He held up an invitation that looked exactly like hers. "I'm not much into opera, but hey, it's better than doing nothing at home. So . . . should I, like, know you?"

Citra laughed out loud. She didn't have a mysterious admirer; it appeared they both had a mysterious matchmaker, which set Citra working on another mental list—at the top of which were her own parents. Perhaps this was the son of one of their friends—but this kind of subterfuge was pretty obtuse, even for them.

"What's so funny?" the boy asked, and she showed him her identical invitation. It didn't make him laugh. Instead he seemed a bit troubled, but didn't share why.

He introduced himself as Rowan, and they shook hands

just as the lights dimmed, the curtain went up, and the music exploded too lush and loud for them to be able to hold a conversation. The opera was Verdi's *La Forza del Destino*, The Force of Destiny, but it clearly wasn't destiny that had hurled these two together; it was a very deliberate hand.

The music was rich and pretty, until it became too much for Citra's ears. And the story, while easy to follow even without a knowledge of Italian, had little resonance for either of them. It was, after all, a work from the Age of Mortality. War, vengeance, murder—all the themes on which the tale was strung—were so removed from modern reality, few could relate. Catharsis could only gather around the theme of love, which, considering that they were strangers trapped in an opera box, was far more uncomfortable than cathartic.

"So, who do you think invited us?" Citra asked as soon as the lights came up for the first act intermission. Rowan had no more clue than she did, so they shared whatever they could that might help them generate a theory. Aside from them both being sixteen, they had very little in common. She was from the city, he the suburbs. She had a small family, his was large, and their parents' professions couldn't have been further apart.

"What's your genetic index?" he asked—a rather personal question, but perhaps it could have some relevance.

"22-37-12-14-15."

He smiled. "Thirty-seven percent Afric descent. Good for you! That's pretty high!"

"Thanks."

He told her that his was 33-13-12-22-20. She thought to ask him if he knew the subindex of his "other" component, because

20 percent was pretty high, but if he didn't know, the question would embarrass him.

"We both have twelve percent PanAsian ancestry," he pointed out. "Could that have something to do with it?" But he was grasping at straws—it was merely coincidence.

Then, toward the end of intermission, the answer stepped into the box behind them.

"Good to see you're getting acquainted."

Although it had been a few months since their encounter, Citra recognized him immediately. Honorable Scythe Faraday was not a figure you soon forgot.

"You?" Rowan said with such severity, it was clear that he had a history with the scythe as well.

"I would have arrived sooner, but I had . . . other business." He didn't elaborate, for which Citra was glad. Still, his presence here could not be a good thing.

"You invited us here to glean us." It wasn't a question, it was a statement of fact, because Citra was convinced it was true—until Rowan said, "I don't think that's what this is about."

Scythe Faraday did not make any move to end their lives. Instead, he grabbed an empty chair and sat beside them. "I was given this box by the theater director. People always think making offerings to scythes will prevent them from being gleaned. I had no intention of gleaning her, but now she thinks her gift played a part."

"People believe what they want to believe," Rowan said, with a sort of authority that told Citra he knew the truth of it.

Faraday gestured toward the stage. "Tonight we witness the spectacle of human folly and tragedy," he said. "Tomorrow, we shall live it."

The curtain went up on the second act before he could explain his meaning.

For two months, Rowan had been the school pariah—an outcast of the highest order. Although that sort of thing usually ran its course and diminished over time, it was not the case when it came to the gleaning of Kohl Whitlock. Every football game rubbed a healthy dose of salt in the communal wound—and since all of those games were lost, it doubled the pain. Rowan was never particularly popular, nor was he ever the target of derision before, but now he was cornered and beaten on a regular basis. He was shunned, and even his friends actively avoided him. Tyger was no exception.

"Guilt by association, man," Tyger had said. "I feel your pain, but I don't want to live it."

"It's an unfortunate situation," the principal told Rowan when he turned up in the nurse's office, waiting out during lunch for some newly inflicted bruises to heal. "You may want to consider switching schools."

Then one day, Rowan gave in to the pressure. He stood on a table in the cafeteria and told everyone the lies they wanted to hear.

"That scythe was my uncle," he proclaimed. "I *told* him to glean Kohl Whitlock."

Of course they believed every word of it. Kids began to boo and throw food at him, until he said:

"I want you all to know that my uncle's coming back— and he asked me to choose who gets gleaned next."

Suddenly the food stopped flying, the glares ceased,

and the beatings miraculously stopped. What filled the void was . . . well . . . a void. Not a single eye would meet his anymore. Not even his teachers would look at him—a few actually started giving him As when he was doing B and C work. He began to feel like a ghost in his own life, existing in a forced blind spot of the world.

At home things were normal. His stepfather stayed entirely out of his business, and his mother was preoccupied with too many other things to give much attention to his troubles. They knew what had happened at school, and what was happening now, but they dismissed it in that self-serving way parents often had of pretending anything they can't solve is not really a problem.

"I want to transfer to a different high school," he told his mother, finally taking his principal's advice, and her response was achingly neutral.

"If you think that's best."

He was half convinced if he told her he was dropping out of society and joining a tone cult, she'd say, *If you think that's best.*

So when the opera invitation arrived, he hadn't cared who sent it. Whatever it meant, it was salvation—at least for an evening.

The girl he met in the box seat was nice enough. Pretty, confident—the kind of girl who probably already had a boyfriend, although she never mentioned one. Then the scythe showed up and Rowan's world shifted back into a dark place. This was the man responsible for his misery. If he could have gotten away with it, Rowan would have pushed him over the railing—but attacks against scythes were not tolerated. The punishment was the gleaning of the offender's entire family. It was a consequence that ensured the safety of the revered bringers of death.

At the close of the opera, Scythe Faraday gave them a card and very clear instructions.

"You will meet me at this address tomorrow morning, precisely at nine."

"What should we tell our parents about tonight?" Citra asked. Apparently she had parents who might care.

"Tell them whatever you like. It doesn't matter, as long as you're there tomorrow morning."

The address turned out to be the Museum of World Art, the finest museum in the city. It didn't open until ten, but the moment the security guard saw a scythe coming up the steps of the main entrance, he unlocked the doors and let the three of them in without even having to be asked.

"More perks of the position," Scythe Faraday told them.

They strolled through galleries of the old masters in silence, punctuated only by the sound of their footfalls and the scythe's occasional commentaries. "See how El Greco uses contrast to evoke emotional yearning." "Look at the fluidity of motion in this Raphael—how it brings intensity to the visual story he tells." "Ah! Seurat! Prophetic pointillism a century before the pixel!"

Rowan was the first to ask the necessary question.

"What does any of this have to do with us?"

Scythe Faraday sighed in mild irritation, although he probably anticipated the question. "I am supplying you with lessons you won't receive in school."

"So," said Citra, "you pulled us out of our lives for some

random art lesson? Isn't that a waste of your valuable time?"

The scythe laughed, and Rowan found himself wishing he had been the one to make him laugh.

"What have you learned so far?" Scythe Faraday asked.

Neither had a response, so he asked a different question.

"What do you think our conversation would have been like had I brought you to the post-mortality galleries instead of these older ones?"

Rowan ventured an answer. "Probably about how much easier on the eye post-mortal art is. "Easier and . . . untroubled."

"How about uninspired?" prompted the scythe.

"That's a matter of opinion," said Citra.

"Perhaps. But now that you know what you're looking for in this art of the dying, I want you to try to feel it." And he led them to the next gallery.

Although Rowan was sure he'd feel nothing, he was wrong.

The next room was a large gallery with paintings hanging floor to ceiling. He didn't recognize the artists, but that didn't matter. There was a coherence to the work, as if it had been painted by the same soul, if not the same hand. Some works had a religious theme, others were portraits, and others simply captured the elusive light of daily life with a vibrancy that was missing in post-mortal art. Longing and elation, anguish and joy—they were all there, sometimes commingling in the same canvas. It was in some ways unsettling, but compelling as well.

"Can we stay in this room a little longer?" Rowan asked, which made the scythe smile.

"Of course we can."

The museum had opened by the time they were done. Other patrons gave them a wide berth. It reminded Rowan of the way they treated him in school. Citra still seemed to have no clue why Scythe Faraday had called them—but Rowan was beginning to have an idea.

He took the kids to a diner, where the waitress sat them immediately and brought them menus, ignoring other customers to give them priority. Perk of the position. Rowan noticed that no one came in once they were seated. The restaurant would probably be empty by the time they left.

"If you want us to provide you with information on people we know," Citra said, as her food came, "I'm not interested."

"I gather my own information," Scythe Faraday told her. "I don't need a couple of kids to be my informants."

"But you do need us, don't you?" Rowan said.

He didn't answer. Instead, he talked about world population and the task of the world's scythes, if not to level it, then to wrangle it to a reasonable ratio.

"The ratio of population growth to the Thunderhead's ability to provide for humanity requires that a certain number of people be gleaned each year," he told them. "For that to happen, we're going to need more scythes."

Then he produced from one of the many pockets hidden in his robe a scythe's ring identical to the one he already wore. It caught the light in the room, reflecting it, refracting it, but never bending light into the heart of its dark core.

"Three times a year, scythes meet at a great assembly called a conclave. We discuss the business of gleaning, and whether or not more scythes are needed in our region."

Citra now seemed to shrink in her chair. She finally got it. Although Rowan had suspected this, to actually see the ring made him shrink a bit, too.

"The gems on scythe rings were made in those first post-mortal days by the early scythes," Faraday said, "when society deemed that unnatural death needed to take the place of natural death. There were many more gems made than were needed at the time, for the founders of the Scythedom were wise enough to anticipate a need. When a new scythe is required, a gem is placed into a gold setting and is bestowed upon the chosen candidate." He turned the ring in his fingers, pondering it, sending refracted light dancing around the room. Then he looked them in the eye—first Citra, then Rowan. "I just returned from Winter Conclave and have been given this ring so that I might take on an apprentice."

Citra backed away. "Rowan can do it. I'm not interested."

Rowan turned to her, wishing he had spoken. "What makes you think I am?"

"I have chosen *both* of you!" Faraday said, raising his voice. "You will both learn the trade. But in the end, only one of you will receive the ring. The other may return home to his or her old life."

"Why would we compete for something that neither of us wants?" Citra asked.

"Therein lies the paradox of the profession," Faraday said. "Those who wish to have the job should not have it . . . and those who would most refuse to kill are the only ones who should."

He put the ring away, and Rowan let out his breath, not even realizing he had been holding it.

"You are both made of the highest moral fiber," Faraday told them, "and I believe the high ground on which you stand will compel you into my apprenticeship—not because I force it upon you, but because you choose it."

Then he left without paying the bill, because no bill was, or would ever be, brought to a scythe.

The nerve! To think he could impress them with airs of culture, and then reel them into his sick little scheme. There was no way Citra would ever, under any circumstances, throw away her life by becoming a taker of other people's lives.

She told her parents what had happened when they got home that evening. Her father embraced her and she cried into his arms for being given the terrible proposition. Then her mother said something that Citra was not expecting.

"Will you do it?" she asked.

The fact that she could even ask that question was more of a shock than seeing the ring held out to her that morning.

"What?"

"It's a difficult choice, I know," her father said. "We'll support you either way."

She looked at them as if she had never truly seen them before that moment. How could her parents know her so little that they would think she'd become a scythe's apprentice? She didn't even know what to say to them.

"Would you . . . want me to?" She found herself terrified of their answer.

"We want what you want, honey," her mother said. "But look at it in perspective: A scythe wants for nothing in this world. All of your needs and desires would be met, and you'd never have to fear being gleaned."

And then something occurred to Citra. "*You'd* never have worry about being gleaned either....A scythe's family is immune from gleaning for as long as that scythe's alive."

Her father shook his head. "It's not about *our* immunity."

And she realized he was telling the truth. "It's not about yours . . . it's about Ben's . . . ," Citra said.

To that, they didn't have an answer. The memory of Scythe Faraday's unexpected intrusion into their home was still a dark specter haunting them. At the time, they hadn't known why he was there. He could very well have been there to glean Citra or Ben. But if Citra became a scythe, they never needed to fear an unexpected visitor again.

"You want me to spend my life killing people?"

Her mother looked away. "Please, Citra, it's not killing, it's *gleaning*. It's important. It's necessary. Sure, nobody likes it, but everyone agrees it has to happen and that someone has to do it. Why not you?"

Citra went to bed early that night, before supper, because her appetite was a casualty of the day. Her parents came to her door several times, but she told them to go away.

She had never been sure what path her life would take. She assumed she would go to college, get a degree in something pleasant, then settle into a comfortable job, meet a comfortable guy, and have a nice, unremarkable life. It's not that she longed for such an existence, but it was expected. Not just of her, but of everyone. With nothing to really aspire to, life had become about maintenance. Eternal maintenance.

Could she possibly find greater purpose in the gleaning of human life? The answer was still a resolute "No!"

But if that were the case, then why did she find it so hard to sleep?

For Rowan, the decision wasn't quite so difficult. Yes, he hated the thought of being a scythe—it sickened him—but what sickened him more was the thought of just about anyone else he knew doing it. He didn't see himself as morally superior to anyone—but he did have a keener sense of empathy. He felt for people, sometimes more than he felt for himself. It's what drove him into Kohl's gleaning. It's what brought him to Tyger's side each and every time he splat.

And Rowan already knew what it was like to be a scythe— to be treated separate and apart from the rest of the world. He was living that now, but could he bear to live it forever? Maybe he wouldn't have to. Scythes got together, didn't they? They had conclaves three times a year and must befriend one another. It was the world's most elite club. No, he didn't want to be a part of it, but he had been called to it. It would be a burden, but also the ultimate honor.

He didn't tell his family that day, because he didn't want them to sway his decision. Immunity for all of them? Of course they'd want him to accept. He was loved, but only as one among a group of other beloved things. If his sacrifice could save the rest, the greater familial good would be served.

In the end it was the art that did it. The canvases haunted his dreams that night. What must life have been like in the Age of Mortality? Full of passions, both good and bad. Fear giving rise to faith. Despair giving meaning to elation. They say even the winters were colder and the summers were warmer in those days.

To live between the prospects of an unknown eternal sky and a dark, enveloping Earth must have been glorious—for how else could it have given rise to such magnificent expression? No one created anything of value anymore—but if, by gleaning, he could bring back a hint of what once was, it might be worth it.

Could he find it in himself to kill another human being? Not just one, but many, day after day, year after year, until he reached his own eternity? Scythe Faraday believed he could.

The following morning, before he left for school, he told his mother that a scythe had invited him to become his apprentice and that he'd be dropping out of school to accept the position.

"If you think that's best," she said.

I had my cultural audit today. It happens only once a year, but it's never any less stressful. This year, when they crunched each cultural index from those I gleaned over the past twelve months, I, thankfully, came up well within accepted parameters:

20 percent Caucasoid

18 percent Afric

20 percent PanAsian

19 percent Mesolatino

23 percent Other

Sometimes it's hard to know. A person's index is considered private, so we can only go by visible traits, which are no longer as obvious as they had been in past generations. When scythes' numbers become lopsided, they are disciplined by the High Blade, and are assigned their gleanings for the next year rather than being allowed to choose for themselves. It is a sign of shame.

The index is supposed to keep the world free from cultural and genetic bias, but aren't there underlying factors that we can't escape? For instance, who decided that the first number of one's genetic index would be Caucasoid?

—From the gleaning journal of H.S. Curie

4

Learner's Permit to Kill

Forget what you think you know about scythes. Leave behind your preconceived notions. Your education begins today.

Citra could not believe she was actually going through with this. What secret, self-destructive part of herself had asserted its will over her? What had possessed her to accept the apprenticeship? Now there was no backing out. Yesterday—on the third day of the new year—Scythe Faraday had come to her apartment and had given a year's immunity to her father and brother. He added several months to her mother's so their immunity would all expire at the same time. Of course, if Citra was chosen to be a full scythe, their immunity would become permanent.

Her parents were tearful when she left. Citra wondered whether they were tears of sorrow, joy, or relief. Perhaps a combination of all three.

"We know you'll do great things in this world," her father had said. And she wondered what about bringing death could be considered great.

Do not be so arrogant as to think you have a license to glean. The license is mine and mine alone. At most you have . . . shall we say . . . a learner's permit. I will, however, require at least one of you to be present at each of my gleanings. And if I ask you to assist, you will.

Citra unceremoniously withdrew from school and said good-bye to friends in awkward little conversations.

"It's not like I won't be around, I just won't be at school anymore." But who was she kidding? Accepting this apprenticeship put her on the outside of an impenetrable wall. It was both demoralizing yet heartening to know that life would go on without her. And it occurred to her that being a scythe was like being the living dead. In the world, but apart from it. Just a witness to the comings and goings of others.

We are above the law, but that does not mean we live in defiance of it. Our position demands a level of morality beyond the rule of law. We must strive for incorruptibility, and must assess our motives on a daily basis.

While she did not wear a ring, Citra was given an armband to identify her as a scythe's apprentice. Rowan had one, too—bright green bands bearing the curved blade of a farmer's scythe above an unblinking eye—the double symbol of the scythehood. That symbol would become a tattoo on the arm of the chosen apprentice. Not that anyone would ever see the tattoo, for scythes are never seen in public without their robes.

Citra had to tell herself that there was an out. She could fail to perform. She could be a lousy apprentice. She could sabotage herself so completely that Honorable Scythe Faraday would be forced to choose Rowan and return her to her family at the end of the year. The problem was that Citra was very bad at doing things half-assed. It would be much harder for her to fail than to succeed.

I will not tolerate any romantic notions between the two of you, so banish the thought from your mind now.

Citra had looked over at Rowan when the scythe said that, and Rowan had shrugged.

"Not a problem," he said, which irritated Citra. At the very least he could have voiced some minor disappointment.

"Yeah," Citra said. "No hope of that, with or without the rule."

Rowan just grinned at that, which made her even more annoyed.

You shall study history, the great philosophers, the sciences. You will come to understand the nature of life and what it means to be human before you are permanently charged with the taking of life. You will also study all forms of killcraft and become experts.

Like Citra, Rowan found himself unsettled by his decision to take this on, but he was not going to show it. Especially not to Citra. And in spite of the blasé attitude he showed her, he was, in fact, attracted to her. But he knew even before the scythe forbade them that such a pursuit could not end well. They were adversaries, after all.

Like Citra, Rowan had stood beside Scythe Faraday as the man held out his ring to each member of his family, offering them immunity. His brothers, sisters, half-siblings, grandma, and her all-too-perfect husband, who Rowan suspected might actually be a bot. Each in turn knelt respectfully and kissed the ring, transmitting their DNA to the worldwide immunity database in the Scythedom's own special cloud separate and apart from the Thunderhead.

The rule was that all members of an apprentice's household would receive immunity for one year, and there were nineteen people in Rowan's sprawling household. His mother had mixed feelings, because now no one would move out for at least a year, to make sure their immunity would become permanent once Rowan received his scythe's ring—*if* he got the ring.

The only glitch had been when the ring vibrated, giving off a little alarm, refusing immunity to his grandmother's new husband because he was a bot after all.

You shall live as I do. Modestly, and subsisting on the goodwill of others. You will take no more than you need, and waste nothing. People will attempt to buy your friendship. They will lavish things upon you. Accept nothing but the barest of human necessities.

Faraday had brought Rowan and Citra to his home to begin their new lives. It was a small bungalow in a run-down part of the city that Rowan hadn't even known existed. "People playing at poverty," he had told them, because no one was impoverished anymore. Austerity was a choice, for there were always those who shunned the plenty of the post-mortal world.

Faraday's home was Spartan. Little decoration. Unimpressive furniture. Rowan's room had space for only a bed and a small dresser. Citra, at least, had a window, but the view was of a brick wall.

I will not tolerate childish pastimes or vapid communications with friends. Commitment to this life means leaving behind your old life as fully as possible. When, a year from now, I choose between you, the unchosen one can return to his or her former life easily enough. But for now, consider that life a part of your past.

Once they were settled in, he didn't allow them to brood over their circumstances. As soon as Rowan had unpacked his bags, the scythe announced that they were going to the market.

"To glean?" Rowan asked, more than a little sick at the prospect.

"No, to get food for the two of you," Faraday told them. "Unless you'd prefer to eat my leftovers."

Citra smirked at Rowan for asking—as if she hadn't been worrying about that herself.

"I liked you a lot more before I knew you," he told her.

"You still don't know me," she answered, which was true. Then she sighed, and for the first time since their night at the opera, she offered up something more than attitude. "We're being forced to live together and forced to compete at something neither of us wants to compete over. I know it's not your fault, but it doesn't exactly put us in a friendly place."

"I know," Rowan admitted. After all, Citra didn't own all the tension between them. "But that still doesn't mean we can't have each other's backs."

She didn't answer him. He didn't expect her to. It was just a seed he wanted to plant. Over the past two months he had learned that no one had his back anymore. Perhaps no one ever did. His friends had pulled away. He was a footnote in his own family. There was only one person now who shared his plight. That was Citra. If they couldn't find a way to trust each other, then what did they have beyond a learner's permit to kill?

The greatest achievement of the human race was not conquering death. It was ending government.

Back in the days when the world's digital network was called "the cloud," people thought giving too much power to an artificial intelligence would be a very bad idea. Cautionary tales abounded in every form of media. The machines were always the enemy. But then the cloud evolved into the Thunderhead, sparking with consciousness, or at least a remarkable facsimile. In stark contrast to people's fears, the Thunderhead did not seize power. Instead, it was people who came to realize that it was far better suited to run things than politicians.

In those days before the Thunderhead, human arrogance, self-interest, and endless infighting determined the rule of law. Inefficient. Imperfect. Vulnerable to all forms of corruption.

But the Thunderhead was incorruptible. Not only that, but its algorithms were built on the full sum of human knowledge. All the time and money wasted on political posturing, the lives lost in wars, the populations abused by despots—all gone the moment the Thunderhead was handed power. Of course, the politicians, dictators, and warmongers weren't happy, but their voices, which had always seemed so loud and intimidating, were suddenly insignificant. The emperor not only had no clothes— turns out he had no testicles either.

The Thunderhead quite literally knew everything. When and where to build roads; how to eliminate waste in food distribution and thus end hunger; how to protect the environment from the ever-growing human popula-tion. It created jobs, it clothed the poor, and it established the World Code. Now, for the first time in history, law was no longer the shadow of justice, it *was* justice.

The Thunderhead gave us a perfect world. The utopia that our ancestors could only dream of is our reality.

There was only one thing the Thunderhead was not given authority over.

The Scythedom.

When it was decided that people needed to die in order to ease the tide of population growth, it was also decided that this must be the responsibility of humans. Bridge repair and urban planning could be handled by the Thunderhead, but taking a life was an act of conscience and consciousness. Since it could not be proven that the Thunderhead had either, the Scythedom was born.

I do not regret the decision, but I often wonder if the Thunderhead would have done a better job.

—From the gleaning journal of H.S. Curie

5

"But I'm Only Ninety-Six . . ."

While a trip to the market should be an ordinary, everyday occurrence, Citra found that food shopping with a scythe carried its own basket of crazy.

The moment the market doors parted for them and the three of them stepped in, the dread around them was enough to raise gooseflesh on Citra's arms. Nothing so blatant as gasps or screams—people were used to scythes passing through their daily lives. It was silent, but pervasive, as if they had just accidentally strolled onto some theatrical stage and fouled the performance.

Citra noticed that, in general, there were three types of people.

1) The Deniers: These were the people who forged on and pretended the scythe wasn't there. It wasn't just a matter of ignoring him—it was actively, willfully denying his presence. It reminded Citra of the way very small children would play hide-and-seek, covering their own eyes to hide, thinking that if they couldn't see you, then you couldn't see them.

2) The Escape Artists: These were the people who ran away but tried to make it look as if they weren't. They suddenly remembered they forgot to get eggs, or began chasing after a running child that didn't actually exist. One shopper abandoned a cart, mumbling about a wallet he must have left at home,

---

despite an obvious bulge in his back pocket. He hurried out and didn't come back.

3) The Scythe's Pets: These were the people who went out of their way to engage the scythe and offer him something, with the secret (not so secret) hope that he might grant them immunity, or at least glean the person to their right instead of them some day. "Here, Your Honor, take my melon, it's bigger. I insist." Did these people know that such sycophantic behavior would make a scythe want to glean them even more? Not that Citra would want to level a death penalty for such a thing, but if she were given a choice between some innocent bystander and someone who was being nauseatingly obsequious about their produce, she'd choose the melon-giver.

There was one shopper who didn't seem to fit the other three profiles. A woman who actually seemed pleased to see him.

"Good morning, Scythe Faraday," she said as they passed her near the deli counter, then looked at Citra and Rowan, curious. "Your niece and nephew?"

"Hardly," he said, with a bit of disdain in his voice for relatives Citra had no interest in knowing about. "I've taken apprentices."

Her eyes widened a bit. "Such a thing!" she said in a way that made it unclear whether she thought it a good or bad idea. "Do they have a penchant for the work?"

"Not the slightest."

She nodded. "Well then, I guess it's all right. You know what they say: 'Have not a hand in the blade with abandon.'"

The scythe smiled. "I hope I can introduce them to your strudel sometime."

She nodded at the two of them. "Well, that goes without saying."

After she had moved on, Scythe Faraday explained that she was a longtime friend. "She cooks for me from time to time—and she works in the coroner's office. In my line of work it's always good to have a friend there."

"Do you grant her immunity?" Citra asked. Rowan thought the scythe might be indignant at the question, but instead he answered:

"The Scythedom frowns upon those who play favorites, but I've found I can grant her immunity on alternate years without raising a red flag."

"What if another scythe gleans her during the off years?"

"Then I shall attend her funeral with heartfelt grief," he told them.

As they shopped, Citra chose some snacks that the scythe eyed dubiously. "Are these really necessary?" he asked.

"Is anything really necessary?" Citra responded.

Rowan found it amusing how Citra gave the scythe attitude—but it worked. He let her keep the chips.

Rowan tried to be more practical, picking out staples like eggs, flour, and various proteins and side dishes to go with them.

"Don't get chickenoid tenders," Citra said, looking at his choices. "Trust me, my mother's a food synthesis engineer. That stuff's not actual chicken—they grow it in a petri dish."

Rowan held up another bag of frozen protein. "How about this?"

"SeaSteak? Sure, if you like plankton pressed into meat shapes."

"Well then, maybe you should pick your own meals instead of grabbing sweets and snacks."

"Are you always this boring?" she asked.

"Didn't he say we have to live as he lives? I don't think cookie dough ice cream is a part of his lifestyle."

She sneered at him, but switched out the flavor for vanilla.

As they continued to shop, it was Citra who first noticed two suspicious-looking teens who seemed to be tracking them through the store, lingering behind them, trying to look like they were just shopping. They were probably unsavories—people who found enjoyment in activities that bordered on the fringe of the law. Sometimes unsavories actually broke the law in minor ways, although most lost interest eventually, because they were always caught by the Thunderhead and reprimanded by peace officers. The more troublesome offenders were tweaked with shock nanites in their blood, just powerful enough to deter any scoffing of the law. And if that didn't work, you got your own personal peace officer 24/7. Citra had an uncle like that. He called his officer his guardian angel, and eventually married her.

She tugged on Rowan's sleeve, bringing the unsavories to his attention but not to Scythe Faraday's.

"Why do you think they're following us?"

"They probably think there's going to be a gleaning and they want to watch," suggested Rowan, which seemed a likely theory. As it turned out, however, they had other motives.

As the three of them waited in the checkout line, one of the unsavories grabbed Scythe Faraday's hand and kissed his ring before he could stop him. The ring began to glow red, indicating his immunity.

"Ha!" said the unsavory, puffing up at his strategic triumph. "I've got immunity for a year—and you can't undo it! I know the rules!"

Scythe Faraday was unfazed. "Yes, good for you," he said. "You have three hundred sixty-five days of immunity." And then, looking him in the eye, said, "And I'll be seeing you on day three hundred sixty-six."

Suddenly the teen's smug expression dropped, as if all the muscles that held up his face failed. He stuttered a bit, and his friend pulled him away. They ran out of the store as fast as they could.

"Well played," said another man in line. He offered to pay for the scythe's groceries—which was pointless, because scythes got their groceries for free anyway.

"Will you really track him down a year from now?" Rowan asked.

The scythe grabbed a roll of breath mints from the rack. "Not worth my time. Besides, I've already meted out his punishment. He'll be worried about being gleaned all year. A lesson for both of you: A scythe doesn't have to follow through on a threat for it to be effective."

Then, a few minutes later, as they were loading the grocery bags into a publicar, the scythe looked across the parking lot.

"There," he said, "you see that woman? The one who just dropped her purse?"

"Yeah," said Rowan.

Scythe Faraday pulled out his phone, aimed the camera at the woman, and in an instant information about her began to scroll on screen. Naturally ninety-six years of age, physically thirty-four. Mother of nine. Data management technician for a small shipping company. "She's off to work after she puts away her groceries," the scythe told them. "This afternoon we will go to her place of business and glean her."

Citra drew in an audible breath. Not quite a gasp, but close. Rowan focused on his own breathing so he didn't telegraph his emotions the way Citra had.

"Why?" he asked. "Why her?"

The scythe gave him a cool look. "Why not her?"

"You had a reason for gleaning Kohl Whitlock. . . ."

"Who?" Citra asked.

"A kid I knew at school. When I first met our honorable scythe, here."

Faraday sighed. "Fatalities in parking lots made up 1.25 percent of all accidental deaths during the last days of the Age of Mortality. Last night I decided I would choose today's subject from a parking lot."

"So all this time while we were shopping, you knew it would end with this?" Rowan said.

"I feel bad for you," said Citra. "Even when you're food shopping, death is hiding right behind the milk."

"It never hides," the scythe told them with a world-weariness that was hard to describe. "Nor does it sleep. You'll learn that soon enough."

But it wasn't something either of them was eager to learn.

That afternoon, just as the scythe had said, they went to the shipping company where the woman worked, and they watched—just as Rowan had watched Kohl's gleaning. But today it was a little more than mere observation.

"I have chosen for you a life-terminating pill," Scythe Faraday told the speechless, tremulous woman. He reached into his robe and produced a small pill in a little glass vial.

"It will not activate until you bite it, so you can choose the moment. You need not swallow it, just bite it. Death will be instantaneous and painless."

Her head shook like a bobblehead doll. "May I . . . may I call my children?"

Scythe Faraday sadly shook his head. "No, I'm sorry. But we shall pass on any message you have to them."

"What would it hurt to allow her to say good-bye?" Citra asked.

He put up his hand to silence her, and handed the woman a pen and piece of paper.

"Say all you need to say in a letter. I promise we shall deliver it."

They waited outside her office. Scythe Faraday seemed to have infinite patience.

"What if she opens a window and decides to splat?" Rowan asked.

"Then her life will end on schedule. It would be a more unpleasant choice, but the ultimate result is the same."

The woman didn't choose to splat. Instead, she let them back into the room, politely handed the envelope to Scythe Faraday, and sat down at her desk.

"I'm ready."

Then Scythe Faraday did something they didn't expect. He turned to Rowan and handed him the vial. "Please place the pill in Mrs. Becker's mouth."

"Who, me?"

Scythe Faraday didn't answer. He simply held the vial out, waiting for Rowan to take it. Rowan knew he wasn't officially performing the gleaning, but to be an intermediary . . . the thought was debilitating. He swallowed, tasting bitterness as if the pill were in his own mouth. He refused to take it.

Scythe Faraday gave him a moment more, then turned to Citra. "You, then."

Citra just shook her head.

Scythe Faraday smiled. "Very good," he told them. "I was testing you. I would not have been pleased if either of you were eager to administer death."

At the word "death," the woman took a shuddering breath.

Scythe Faraday opened the vial and carefully removed the pill. It was triangular with a dark green coating. Who knew death could arrive so small?

"But . . . but I'm only ninety-six," the woman said.

"We know," the scythe told her. "Now please . . . open your mouth. Remember, it's not to swallow; you must bite it."

She opened her mouth as she was told, and Scythe Faraday placed the pill on her tongue. She closed her mouth, but didn't bite it right away. She looked at each of them in turn. Rowan, then Citra, then finally settled her gaze on Scythe Faraday. Then the slightest crunch. And she went limp. Simple as that. But not so simple at all.

Citra's eyes were moist. She pressed her lips together. As much as Rowan tried to control his emotions, his breath came out uneasily and he felt light-headed.

And then Scythe Faraday turned to Citra. "Check for a pulse, please."

"Who, me?"

The scythe was patient. He didn't ask again. The man never asked a thing twice. When she continued to hesitate, he finally said, "This time it's not a test. I actually want you to confirm for me that she has no pulse."

Citra reached up a hand to the woman's neck.

"Other side," the scythe told her.

She pressed her fingers to the woman's carotid artery, just beneath her ear. "No pulse."

Satisfied, Scythe Faraday stood.

"So that's it?" Citra asked.

"What were you expecting?" said Rowan. "A chorus of angels?"

Citra threw him a halfhearted glare. "But I mean . . . it's so . . . uneventful."

Rowan knew what she meant. Rowan had experienced the electrical jolt that had taken his schoolmate's life. It was awful, but somehow this was worse. "What now? Do we just leave her like this?"

"Best not to linger," Scythe Faraday said, tapping something out on his phone. "I've notified the coroner to come collect Mrs. Becker's body." Then he took the letter she had written and slipped it into one of the many pockets of his robe. "You two shall present the letter to her family at the funeral."

"Wait," said Citra. "We're going to her *funeral*?"

"I thought you said it was best not to linger," said Rowan.

"Lingering and paying respects are two different things. I attend the funerals of all the people I glean."

"Is that a scythe rule?" Rowan asked, having never been to a funeral.

"No, it's my rule," he told them. "It's called 'common decency.'"

Then they left, Rowan and Citra both avoiding eye contact with the dead woman's coworkers. This, both of them realized, was their first initiation rite. This was the moment their apprenticeship had truly begun.

Part Two

NO LAWS
BEYOND THESE

The Scythe Commandments

1) Thou shalt kill.

2) Thou shalt kill with no bias, bigotry, or malice aforethought.

3) Thou shalt grant an annum of immunity to the beloved of those who accept your coming, and to anyone else you deem worthy.

4) Thou shalt kill the beloved of those who resist.

5) Thou shalt serve humanity for the full span of thy days, and thy family shall have immunity as recompense for as long as you live.

6) Thou shalt lead an exemplary life in word and deed, and keep a journal of each and every day.

7) Thou shalt kill no scythe beyond thyself.

8) Thou shalt claim no earthly possessions, save thy robes, ring, and journal.

9) Thou shalt have neither spouse nor spawn.

10) Thou shalt be beholden to no laws beyond these.

Once a year I fast and ponder the commandments. In truth, I ponder them daily, but once a year I allow them to be my sole sustenance. There is genius in their simplicity. Before the Thunderhead, governments had constitutions and massive tomes of laws—yet even then, they were forever debated and challenged and manipulated. Wars were fought over the different interpretations of the same doctrine.

When I was much more naive, I thought that the simplicity of the scythe commandments made them impervious to scrutiny. From whatever angle you approached them, they looked the same. Over my many years, I've been both bemused and horrified by how malleable and elastic they can be. The things we scythes attempt to justify. The things that we excuse.

In my early days, there were several scythes still alive who were present when the commandments were formed. Now none remain, all having invoked commandment number seven. I wish I would have asked them how the commandments came about. What led to each one? How did they decide upon the wording? Were there any that were jettisoned before the final ten were written in stone?

And why number ten?

Of all the commandments, number ten gives me the greatest pause for thought. For to put oneself above all other laws is a fundamental recipe for disaster.

—From the gleaning journal of H.S. Curie

6

An Elegy of Scythes

The flight was on time. As usual. While weather couldn't entirely be controlled, it was easily diverted away from airports and out of flight paths. Most airlines boasted 99.9 percent on-time service.

It was a full flight, but with the lavishly appointed seats of modern air travel, it didn't feel crowded at all. These days flying was as comfortable as sitting in one's own living room, with the added perk of live entertainment. String quartets and vocal stylists soared across the skies with a cabin full of contented passengers. Air travel these days was far more civilized than in the Age of Mortality. It was now an exceptionally pleasant way to reach one's destination. Today, however, the passengers of BigSky Air flight 922 were on their way to a different destination than the one on which they had planned.

The businessman was seated comfortably in seat 15C—an aisle seat. He always requested that seat, not out of superstition but out of habit. When he didn't get 15C, he was cranky, and resentful of whoever did. The company he ran, which was developing hibernation technology, would someday make the longest journeys seem to pass in a matter of minutes, but for now he would be happy with BigSky Air, as long as he got seat 15C.

People were still filing on, taking their seats. He eyed the passengers moving down the aisle with mild disinterest, but only to make sure they didn't hit his shoulder with their purses and carry-ons as they passed.

"Are you heading out or heading home?" asked the woman sitting beside him in 15A. There was no 15B—the concept of the B seat, where one had to sit between two other passengers, had been eliminated along with other unpleasant things, like disease and government.

"Out," he told her. "And you?"

"Home," she told him with a heavy but relieved sigh.

At five minutes to departure, a commotion up front caught his attention. A scythe had entered the plane and was talking to a flight attendant. When a scythe wants to travel, any seat is fair game. The scythe could displace a passenger, forcing them to take a different seat, or even a different flight if there were no other available seats. More unnerving, however, were tales of scythes who gleaned the passenger from the seat they took.

The businessman could only hope that this particular scythe didn't have his sights set on seat 15C.

The scythe's robe was unusual. Royal blue, speckled with glittering jewels that appeared to be diamonds. Rather ostentatious for a scythe. The businessman didn't know what to make of it. The age the scythe presented was late thirties, although that meant nothing. No one looked their true age anymore; he could have been anywhere from thirty-something to two-hundred-thirty-something. His hair was dark and well-groomed. His eyes were invasive. The businessman tried not to catch his gaze as the scythe looked down the aisle into the cabin.

Then three more scythes appeared behind the first. They

were younger—perhaps in their early twenties. Their robes, each in a different bright color, were also decorated with gems. There was a dark-haired woman in apple green speckled with emeralds, a man in orange speckled with rubies, and another man in yellow speckled with golden citrines.

What was the collective word for a group of scythes? An "elegy," wasn't it? Odd that there'd be a word for something so rare. In his experience, scythes were always solitary, never traveling together. A flight attendant greeted the elegy of scythes, and then the second they were past her, she turned, left the plane, and ran down the jetway.

She's escaping, thought the businessman. But then he banished the thought. She couldn't be. She was probably just hurrying to let the gate agent know of the added passengers. That's all. She couldn't be panicking—flight attendants were trained not to panic. But then the remaining flight attendant closed the door, and the look on her face was anything but reassuring.

The passengers began talking to one another. Mumbling. A little bit of nervous laughter.

Then the lead scythe addressed the passengers. "Your attention, please," he said with an unnerving smile. "I regret to inform you that this entire flight has been selected for gleaning."

The businessman heard it, but his brain told him that he could not have possibly heard correctly. Or maybe this was scythe humor, if such a thing even existed. *This entire flight has been selected for gleaning.* That couldn't be possible. It couldn't be allowed. Could it?

In a few moments passengers began to wrap their minds around what the scythe had said. Then came the gasps, the wails, the whimpers, and finally uncontrolled sobs. The misery could not have been worse had they lost an engine in flight, as planes did back in the mortal days, when technology occasionally failed.

The businessman was a quick study, and excelled at split-second decisions in crisis. He knew what he had to do. Perhaps others were thinking the same thing, but he was the one who took action first. He left his seat and hurled himself down the aisle toward the back of the plane. Others followed him, but he was first to the back door. He quickly scanned its operation, then pulled the red lever and swung the door open into a bright sunny morning.

A jump from this height to the tarmac might have broken a bone or twisted an ankle, but the healing nanites in his blood would quickly release opiates and deaden the pain. He'd be able to escape in spite of any injury. But before he could leap, he heard the lead scythe say:

"I suggest you all return to your seats if you value the lives of your loved ones."

It was standard procedure for scythes to glean the families of those who resist or run from being gleaned. Familial gleaning was a remarkable deterrent. But this was a full plane—if he jumped and ran, how would they know who he was?

As if reading his mind, the lead scythe said:

"We have the manifest from this plane. We know the names of everyone on board. Including the name of the flight attendant who displayed cowardice unbecoming to her position and left. Her entire family will pay the price, along with her."

The businessman slid down to his knees and put his head in his hands. A man behind him pushed past and jumped anyway.

He hit the ground and ran, more worried by what was happening in the moment than what might happen tomorrow. Perhaps he had no family he cared about, or perhaps he'd rather they journey with him into oblivion. But as for the businessman, he could not bear the thought of his wife and children gleaned because of him.

Gleaning is necessary, he told himself. Everyone knows, everyone has agreed this is a crucial necessity. Who was he to go against it? It only seemed terrible now that he was the one lined up in the cold crosshairs of death.

Then the lead scythe raised an arm and pointed at him. His fingernails seemed just the slightest bit too long.

"You," he said, "the bold one. Come here."

Others in the aisle stepped aside and the businessman found himself moving forward. He couldn't even feel his legs doing it. It was as if the scythe were pulling him with an invisible string. His presence was that commanding.

"We should glean him first," said the blond, brutish scythe in a bright orange robe, wielding what appeared to be a flame-thrower. "Glean him first to set an example."

But the lead scythe shook his head. "First of all, put that thing away; we will not play with fire on a plane. Secondly, setting an example presupposes that someone will be left to learn from it. It's pointless when there's no one to set an example for."

He lowered his weapon and looked down, chastised. The other two scythes remained silent.

"You were so quick to leave your seat," the lead scythe said to the businessman. "Clearly you're the alpha of this plane, and as alpha I will allow you to choose the order in which these good folks shall be gleaned. You can be last if you choose, but first you must select the order of the others."

"I . . . I . . ."

"Come now, no indecisiveness. You were decisive enough when you ran to the back of the plane. Bring that formidable will to bear on this moment."

Clearly the scythe was enjoying this. He shouldn't enjoy it—that's one of the basic precepts of Scythedom. A random part of his mind thought, *I should lodge a complaint.* Which he realized would be very difficult to do if he was dead.

He looked to the terrified people around him—now they were terrified of him. He was the enemy too, now.

"We're waiting," said the woman in green, impatient to begin.

"How?" The man asked, trying to control his breathing, stalling for time. "How will you glean us?"

The lead scythe pulled back a fold of his robe to display an entire collection of weapons neatly concealed beneath. Knives of various lengths. Guns. Other objects that the man didn't even recognize. "Our method will be as our mood suits us. Sans incendiary devices, of course. Now please start choosing people so we may begin."

The female scythe tightened her grip on the handle of a machete and brushed back her dark hair with her free hand. Did she just actually lick her lips? This would not be a gleaning, it would be a bloodbath, and the businessman realized he wanted no part of it. Yes, his fate was sealed—nothing could change that. Which meant he didn't have to play the scythe's twisted game. Suddenly he found himself sublimating his fear, rising to a place where he could look the scythe in his dark eyes, the same deep shade of blue as his robe.

"No," the man said, "I will not choose and I will not give you the pleasure of watching me squirm." Then he turned to the other passengers. "I advise everyone here to end your own lives before these scythes get their hands on you. They take too much pleasure in it. They don't deserve their rank any more than they deserve the honor of gleaning you."

The lead scythe glared at him, but only for a moment. Then he turned to his three compatriots. "Begin!" he ordered. The others drew weapons and began the awful gleaning.

"I am your completion," the lead scythe said loudly to the dying. "I am the last word of your lives well lived. Give thanks. And thus farewell."

The lead scythe pulled out his own blade, but the businessman was ready. The moment the blade was drawn, he thrust himself forward onto it—a final willful act, making death his own choice, rather than the scythe's. Denying the scythe; if not his method, then his madness.

In my early years, I wondered why it was so rare to catch a scythe out of his or her robes and in common street clothes. It's a rule in some places, but not in MidMerica. Here it is just an accepted practice, although rarely violated. Then, as I settled in, it occurred to me why it must be. For our own peace of mind, we scythes must retain a certain level of separation from the rest of humanity. Even in the privacy of my own home I find myself wearing only the simple lavender frock that I wear beneath my robes.

Some would call this behavior aloof. I suppose on some level it is, but for me it's more the need to remind myself that I am "other."

Certainly, most uniformed positions allow the wearers to have a separate life. Peace officers and firefighters, for instance, are only partially defined by their job. In the off-hours they wear jeans and T-shirts. They have barbecues for neighbors and coach their children in sports. But to be a scythe means you are a scythe every hour of every day. It defines you to the core of your being, and only in dreams is one free of the yoke.

Yet even in dreams I often find myself gleaning. . . .

—From the gleaning journal of H.S. Curie

7

Killcraft

"During your year with me," Scythe Faraday told Rowan and Citra, "you will learn the proper way to wield various blades, you will become marksmen in more than a dozen types of firearms, you will have a working knowledge of toxicology, and you will train in the deadliest of martial arts. You will not become masters in these things—that takes many years—but will have the basic skills upon which you will build."

"Skills that will be useless for the one you don't choose," Citra pointed out.

"Nothing we learn is useless," he told her.

While the scythe's house was modest and unadorned, it had one impressive feature: the weapons den. It had once been the garage of the old house, but now was lined with the scythe's extensive weapons collection. One wall was hung with blades, another firearms. A third wall looked like a pharmacist's shelf, and the fourth wall held more archaic objects. Elaborately carved bows, a quiver of obsidian-tipped arrows, frighteningly muscular crossbows—even a mace, although it was hard for them to imagine Scythe Faraday taking someone out with a mace. The fourth wall was more of a museum, they supposed, but the fact that they weren't sure was unsettling.

The daily regimen was rigorous. Rowan and Citra trained

with blades and staffs, sparring against the scythe, who was surprisingly strong and limber for a man of his apparent age. They learned to shoot at a special firing range for scythes and apprentices, where weapons that were banned for public use were not only allowed, but encouraged. They learned the basics of Black Widow Bokator—a deadly version of the ancient Cambodian martial art developed specifically for the Scythedom. It left them exhausted, but stronger than either of them had ever been.

Physical training, however, was only half their regimen. There was an old oak table in the center of the weapons den, clearly a relic from the Age of Mortality. This is where Scythe Faraday spent several hours a day schooling them in the ways of a scythe.

Studies in mental acuity, history, and the chemistry of poisons—as well as daily entries in their apprentice journals. There was more to learn about death than either of them had ever considered.

"History, chemistry, writing—this is like school," Rowan grumbled to Citra, because he wouldn't dare complain to Scythe Faraday.

And then there was the gleaning.

"Each scythe must perform a quota of two hundred sixty gleanings per year," Scythe Faraday told them, "which averages to five per week."

"So you get weekends off," joked Rowan—trying to add a little nervous levity to the discussion. But Faraday was not amused. For him nothing about gleaning was a laughing matter. "On days that I don't glean, I attend funerals and do research for future gleanings. Scythes . . . or should I say *good* scythes . . . don't often have days off."

The idea that not all scythes were good was something neither Rowan or Citra had ever considered. It was widely accepted that scythes adhered to the highest moral and ethical standards. They were wise in their dealings and fair in their choices. Even the ones who sought celebrity were seen to deserve it. The idea that some scythes might not be as honorable as Scythe Faraday did not sit well with either of his new apprentices.

The raw shock of gleaning never left Citra. Although Scythe Faraday had not, since that first day, asked them to be the life-taking hand, being an accomplice was difficult enough. Each untimely end came draped in its own shroud of dread, like a recurring nightmare that never lost its potency. She had thought she would grow numb—that she would become used to the work. But it didn't happen.

"It means I chose wisely," Scythe Faraday told her. "If you do not cry yourself to sleep on a regular basis, you are not compassionate enough to be a scythe."

She doubted Rowan cried himself to sleep. He was the type of kid who kept his emotions very much to himself. She couldn't read him. He was opaque, and it bothered her. Or perhaps he was so transparent, she was seeing through him to the other side. She couldn't be sure.

They quickly learned that Scythe Faraday was very creative in his gleaning methods. He never repeated the exact same method twice.

"But aren't there scythes who are ritualistic in their work," Citra asked him, "performing each gleaning exactly the same?"

"Yes, but we must each find our own way," he told her.

"Our own code of conduct. I prefer to see each person I glean as an individual deserving of an end that is unique."

He outlined for them the seven basic methods of killcraft. "Most common are the three Bs: blade, bullet, and blunt force. The next three are asphyxiation, poison, and catastrophic induction, such as electrocution or fire—although I find fire a horrific way to glean and would never use it. The final method is weaponless force, which is why we train you in Bokator."

To be a scythe, he explained, meant that one had to be well versed in all methods. Citra realized that being "well versed" meant she would have to participate in various types of gleaning. Would he have her pull the trigger? Thrust the knife? Swing the club? She wanted to believe she wasn't capable of it. She desperately wanted to believe she wasn't scythe material. It was the first time in her life that she aspired to fail.

Rowan's feelings on the matter were mixed. He found that Scythe Faraday's moral imperative and ethical high ground infused Rowan with purpose—but only in the scythe's presence. When left to his own thoughts, Rowan doubted everything. Burned into his mind was the look on that woman's face as she fearfully yet obediently opened her mouth to be poisoned. The look on her face the moment before she bit down. *I am an accomplice to the world's oldest crime,* he told himself in his loneliest moments. *And it will only get worse.*

While the journals of scythes were public record, an apprentice still had the luxury of privacy. Scythe Faraday gave Rowan and Citra pale leather-bound volumes of rough-edged parchment. To Rowan it looked like a relic from the dark ages. He wouldn't have been surprised if Faraday gave them a feather quill to go with it. Mercifully, however, they were allowed to use normal writing utensils.

"A scythe's journal is traditionally made of lambskin parchment and kid leather."

"I assume you mean 'kid' as in 'goat,'" Rowan said, "and not 'kid' as in 'kid.'"

That finally made the scythe laugh. Citra seemed to be annoyed that he had made Faraday laugh—as if it put him a point ahead of her. Rowan knew that as much as she hated the idea of being a scythe, she would jockey for position over him because that's how she was hardwired. Competition was in her very nature; she couldn't help herself.

Rowan was much better at picking his battles. He could compete when necessary, but rarely got caught up in petty one-upsmanship. He wondered if that would give him an advantage over Citra. He wondered if he wanted one.

Being a scythe would not have been his life choice. He had not made any life choices yet, so he had no real clue what he would do with his eternal future. But now that he was being mentored by a scythe, he began to feel he might have the mettle to be one. If Scythe Faraday had selected him as morally capable of the job, perhaps he was.

As for the journal, Rowan hated it. In a large family where no one particularly cared to hear his thoughts on anything, he had become accustomed to keeping his thoughts to himself.

"I don't see what the big deal is," Citra said as they worked in their journals after dinner one evening. "No one will ever read it but you."

"So why write it?" Rowan snapped back.

Citra sighed as if talking to a child. "It's to prepare you for writing an official scythe's journal. Whichever one of us gets the ring will be legally obligated by commandment six to keep a journal every day of our lives."

"Which I'm sure no one will read," added Rowan.

"But people *could* read it. The Scythe Archive is open to everyone."

"Yeah," said Rowan, "like the Thunderhead. People can read anything, but no one does. All they do is play games and watch cat holograms."

Citra shrugged. "All the more reason not to worry about writing one. If it's lost among a gazillion pages, you can write your grocery list and what you ate for breakfast. No one will care."

But Rowan cared. If he was going to put pen to paper—if he was going to do what a scythe does—he would do it right or not at all. And so far, as he looked at his painfully blank page, he was leaning toward "not at all."

He watched Citra as she wrote, completely absorbed in her journal. From where he sat, he couldn't read what she had written, but he could tell it was in fine penmanship. It figures she would take penmanship in school. It was one of those classes people took just to be superior. Like Latin. He supposed he'd have to learn to write in cursive if he became a scythe, but right now he'd be stuck with inelegant, sloppy printing.

He wondered, had Citra and he been in the same school, would they have gotten along? They probably wouldn't have even known each other. She was the type of girl who participates, and Rowan was the kind of kid who avoids. Their circles were about as far from intersecting as Jupiter and Mars in the night sky. Now, however, they had been pulled into convergence. They were not exactly friends—they were never given the opportunity to develop a friendship before being thrust into apprenticeship together. They were partners; they were adversaries—and Rowan found it increasingly hard to parse his feelings about her. All he knew was that he liked watching her write.

Scythe Faraday was strict on his no-family policy. "It is ill-advised for you to have contact with your family during your apprenticeship." It was difficult for Citra. She missed her parents, but more than that, she missed her brother, Ben—which surprised her, because at home, she never had much patience for him.

Rowan seemed to have no problem with being separated from his family.

"They'd much rather have their immunity than have me around, anyway," he told Citra.

"Boo hoo," Citra said. "Am I supposed to feel sorry for you?"

"Not at all. Envious maybe. It makes it easier for me to leave it all behind."

Scythe Faraday did bend his own rule once, however. About a month in, he allowed Citra to attend her aunt's wedding.

While everyone else was dressed in gowns and tuxedos, Scythe Faraday did not allow Citra to dress up, "Lest you feel yourself a part of that world." It worked. Wearing simple street clothes amid the pageantry made her feel even more the outsider—and the apprentice armband made it worse. Perhaps this was the reason Faraday allowed her to attend—to make crystal clear the distinction between who she had been and who she was now.

"So, what's it like?" asked her cousin Amanda. "Gleaning and stuff. Is it, like, gross?"

"We're not allowed to talk about it," Citra told her. Which was not true, but she had no interest in discussing gleaning like it was school gossip.

She should have nurtured that conversation, however, instead of shutting it down, because Amanda was one of the few people who spoke to her. There were plenty of sideways glances and people talking *about* her when they thought she wasn't watching, but most everyone avoided her like she carried a mortal-age disease. Perhaps if she already had her ring they might try to curry favor in hopes of receiving immunity, but apparently as an apprentice she offered them nothing but the creeps.

Her brother was standoffish, and even speaking to her mother was awkward. She asked standard questions like "Are you eating?" and "Are you getting enough sleep?"

"I understand there's a boy living with you," her father said.

"He has his own room and he's not interested in me at all," she told him, which she found oddly embarrassing to admit.

Citra sat through the wedding ceremony, but excused herself before the reception and took a publicar back to Scythe Faraday's house, unable to bear another minute of it.

"You're back early," Scythe Faraday commented when she returned. And although he feigned surprise, he had set her place for dinner.

Scythes are supposed to have a keen appreciation of death, yet there are some things that are beyond even our comprehension.

The woman I gleaned today asked me the oddest question.

"Where do I go now?" she asked.

"Well," I explained calmly, "your memories and life recording are already stored in the Thunderhead, so it won't be lost. Your body is returned to the earth in a manner determined by your next of kin."

"Yes, I know all that," she said. "But what about me?"

The question perplexed me. "As I said, your memory construct will exist in the Thunderhead. Loved ones will be able to talk to it, and your construct will respond."

"Yes," she said, getting a bit agitated, "but what about *me?*"

I gleaned her then. Only after she was gone did I say, "I don't know."

—From the gleaning journal of H.S. Curie

8

A Matter of Choice

"I will glean alone today," Scythe Faraday told Rowan and Citra
one day in February, the second month of their apprenticeship. "While I am gone I have a task for each of you." He took
Citra into the weapons den. "You, Citra, shall polish each of my
blades."

She had been in the weapons den nearly every day for lessons, but to be there alone, nothing but her and instruments of
death, was entirely different.

The scythe went to the blade wall, which had everything
from swords to switchblades. "Some are merely dusty, others tar-
nished. You shall decide what type of care each one needs."

She watched the way his eyes moved from one blade to
another, lingering long enough, perhaps, to recall a memory.

"You've used them all?" she asked

"Only about half of them—and even then, for only one
gleaning." He reached up and pulled a rapier from the fourth
wall—the one with the older-looking weapons. This one
looked like the kind one of the Three Musketeers might have
used. "When I was young, I had much more of a flair for drama.
I went to glean a man who fancied himself a fencer. So I challenged him to a duel."

"And you won?"

"No, I lost. Twice. He skewered me through the neck the first time and tore open my femoral artery the second—he was very good. Each time, after I woke up in the revival center, I returned to challenge him. His wins bought him time—but he was chosen to be gleaned, and I would not relent. Some scythes will change their minds, but that leads to compromise, and it favors the persuasive. I make my decisions firm.

"In the fourth bout, I pierced his heart with the tip of my blade. As he breathed his last, he thanked me for allowing him to die fighting. It was the only time in all my years as a scythe that I had been thanked for what I do."

He sighed, and put the rapier back in what Citra realized was a place of honor.

"If you have all these weapons, why did you take *our* knife that day you came to glean my neighbor?" Citra had to ask.

The scythe grinned. "To gauge your reaction."

"I threw it away," she told him.

"I suspected as much," he said. "But these you will polish." Then he left her there.

When he was gone, Citra studied the weapons. She was not particularly morbid, but she found herself wanting to know which blades had been used, and how. It seemed to her that a noble weapon deserved to have its story passed down, and if not to her and Rowan, then to whom?

She pulled a scimitar from the wall. A heavy beast that could decapitate you with a single swing. Had Scythe Faraday used it for a beheading? It was, in a way, his style: swift, painless, efficient. As she moved it clumsily through the air, she wondered if she had the strength to behead someone.

My god, what am I becoming?

She put the weapon on the table, grabbed the rag, and rubbed polish on it, and when she finished she went to the next, and the next, trying not to see her reflection in each of the gleaming blades.

Rowan's task was not as visceral, but was even more troubling.

"Today, you shall lay the groundwork for my next gleaning," Scythe Faraday told him, then gave him a list of parameters that tomorrow's subject should have. "All the information you need is in the Thunderhead, if you're clever enough to find it." Then he left for the day's gleaning.

Rowan almost made the mistake of giving the list of parameters to the Thunderhead and asking it for a subject—until he remembered that asking the Thunderhead for assistance was strictly forbidden for scythes. They had full access to the great cloud's wealth of information, but could not access its algorithmic "conscious" mind. Scythe Faraday had told them of a scythe who tried to do so. The Thunderhead itself reported him to the High Blade, and he was "severely disciplined."

"How is a scythe disciplined?" Rowan had asked.

"He was put to death twelvefold by a jury of scythes, then revived each time. After the twelfth revival, he was on probation for a year."

Rowan imagined a jury of scythes would be very creative in their methods of punishment. He suspected that dying twelve times at the hands of scythes would be a lot worse than splatting.

He began to enter search parameters. He was instructed to have his search include not just their city, but all of MidMerica—which stretched nearly a thousand miles across the middle of the continent. Then he narrowed the search to towns with populations under ten thousand that were also on the banks of rivers. Then to homes or apartments that were within one hundred feet of the river bank. Then he searched for people twenty and older who lived in those residences.

That gave him more than forty thousand people.

He had done that in five minutes. The next few requirements were not going to be as easy to nail down.

The subject must be a strong swimmer.

He got a list of every high school and university in each river town, and cross-referenced everyone who had been on a swim team for the past twenty years or had registered for a triathlon. About eight hundred people.

The subject must be a dog lover.

Using Scythe Faraday's access code, he found the subscription lists of every publication and blog dealing with dogs. He accessed pet store databases to get a list of anyone who made regular purchases of dog food over the past few years. That brought the number down to one hundred twelve names.

The subject must have a history of heroism in a nonprofessional capacity.

He painstakingly searched for words like "hero," "bravery," and "rescue," for all one hundred twelve names. He thought he'd be lucky if a single one came up—but to his surprise, four of them were noted as having done something heroic at some point in their lives.

He clicked on each name and brought up four pictures. He immediately regretted it, because the moment those names had faces, they became people instead of parameters.

A man with a round face and a winning smile.

A woman who could have been anyone's mother.

A guy with a bad case of bed-hair.

A man who looked like he hadn't shaved in three days.

Four people. And Rowan was about to decide which one would die tomorrow.

He immediately found himself leaning toward the unshaven man, but realized he was showing a bias. A person shouldn't be discriminated against because he hadn't shaved for a picture. And was he ruling out the woman just because she was a woman?

Okay then, the guy with the smile. But was Rowan overcompensating now by choosing the most pleasant looking of them?

He decided to learn more about each of them, using Faraday's access code to dig up more personal information than he really should have been allowed to; but this was a person's life he was dealing with—shouldn't he use any means necessary to make his decision fair?

This one had run into a burning building in his youth to save a family member. But this one has three young kids. But this one volunteers at an animal shelter. But this one's brother was gleaned just two years ago. . . .

He thought each fact would help him, but the more he came to know about each of them, the harder the decision became. He kept digging into their lives, getting more and more desperate, until the front door opened and Scythe Faraday returned. It was dark out. When had night fallen?

The scythe looked weary, and his robes were splattered with blood.

"Today's gleaning was . . . more troublesome than expected," he said. Citra came out of the weapons den. "All blades are now polished to a perfect shine!" she announced.

Faraday gave her his nod of approval. Then he turned to Rowan, who still sat at the computer. "And who do we glean next?"

"I . . . uh . . . narrowed it down to four."

"And?" said the scythe.

"All four fit the profile."

"And?" said the scythe again.

"Well, this one just got married, and this one just bought a house—"

"Pick one," said the scythe.

"—and this one received a humanitarian award last year—"

"PICK ONE!" yelled the scythe with a ferocity Rowan had never heard from the man. The very walls seemed to recoil from his voice. Rowan thought he might get a reprieve, as he had when Faraday asked him to hand that woman the cyanide pill. But no; today's test was very different. Rowan looked to Citra, who still stood in the doorway of the weapons den, frozen like a bystander at an accident. He was truly alone in this awful decision.

Rowan looked to the screen, grimacing, and pointed to the man with bed-hair. "Him," Rowan said. "Glean him."

Rowan closed his eyes. He had just condemned a man to death because he'd had a bad hair day.

Then he felt Faraday put a firm hand on his shoulder. He thought he'd get a reprimand, but instead, the scythe said, "Well done."

Rowan opened his eyes. "Thank you, sir."

"Were this not the hardest thing you've ever done, I'd be concerned."

"Does it ever get easier?" Rowan asked.

"I certainly hope not," the scythe said.

The following afternoon, Bradford Ziller returned from work to find a scythe sitting in his living room. The scythe stood up as Bradford entered. His instincts told him to turn and run, but before he did, a teenage boy with a green armband, who had been standing off to the side, closed the door behind him.

He waited with increasing dread for the scythe to speak, but instead the scythe gestured to the boy, who cleared his throat and said, "Mr. Ziller, you have been chosen for gleaning."

"Tell him the rest, Rowan," said the scythe patiently.

"I mean to say that . . . that I chose you for gleaning."

Bradford looked between the two of them, suddenly deeply relieved, because this was clearly some sort of joke. "Okay, who the hell are you? Who put you up to this?"

Then the scythe held up his hand, showing his ring. And Bradford's spirits fell again like the second drop of a roller coaster. That was no fake—it was the real thing. "The boy is one of my apprentices," the scythe said.

"I'm sorry," said the boy. "It's not personal—you just fit a certain profile. Back in the Age of Mortality lots of people died trying to perform rescues. A lot of them were people who jumped into flooded rivers to save their pets. Most of them were good swimmers, but that doesn't matter in a flood."

The dogs! thought Bradford. That's right, the dogs! "You can't

hurt me!" he said. "You do, and my dogs'll rip you to pieces."
But where were they?

Then a girl came out of his bedroom, wearing the same armband as the boy. "I sedated all three," she said. "They'll be fine, but
they won't be bothering anyone." There was blood on her arm.
Not the dogs' but her own. They had bitten her. Good for them.

"It's not personal," the boy said again. "I'm sorry."

"One apology is enough," the scythe told the boy. "Especially when it's genuine."

Bradford guffawed, even though he knew this was real. He
just somehow found this funny. His knees weak, he settled onto
the sofa and his laughter resolved into misery. How was this fair?
How was any of this fair?"

But then the boy knelt down before him, and when Bradford
looked up, he was caught by the boy's gaze. It was as if he were
looking into the eyes of a much older soul.

"Listen to me, Mr. Ziller," the boy said. "I know you saved
your sister from a fire when you were my age. I know how hard
you struggled to save your marriage. And I know you think that
your daughter doesn't love you, but she does."

Bradford stared at him, incredulous. "How do you know all
this?"

The boy pursed his lips. "It's our job to know. Your gleaning
won't change any of that. You lived a good life. Scythe Faraday is
here to complete it for you."

Bradford begged to make a phone call, pleaded for just one
more day, but of course, those things were not granted. They
said he could write a note, but he couldn't bring himself to find
anything to write.

"I know how that feels," the boy told him.

"How will you do it?" he finally asked them.

The scythe responded. "'I have chosen for you a traditional drowning. We shall take you to the river. I shall submerge you until your life leaves you."

Bradford clenched his eyes. "I've heard that drowning is a bad way to go."

"Can I give him some of the stuff I gave the dogs?" the girl asked. "Knock him out so that he'll already be unconscious?"

The scythe considered it and nodded. "If you choose, we can spare you the suffering."

But Bradford shook his head, realizing he wanted every second he had left. "No, I want to be awake." If drowning was to be his last experience, then let him experience it. He could feel his heart beating faster, his body trembling with the surge of adrenaline. He was afraid, but fear meant he was still alive.

"Come then," the scythe told him gently. "We'll all go down to the river together."

Citra was awed by how Rowan handled himself. Although he began a little shaky when he first spoke to the man, he took charge. He took the reigns of that man's fear and gave him peace. Citra only hoped that when it came her turn to make a choice, she could keep her composure as well as Rowan had. All she had done today was tranquilize a few dogs. Sure, she got bitten in the process, but it was nothing, really. She tried to convince Faraday to take the dogs to a shelter, but he wouldn't have it. He did allow her to call the shelter to come for the dogs. And the coroner to come for the man. The scythe offered to take her to a hospital for some speedhealing of the dog bite on her arm, but she declined. Her own nanites would heal it by morning, and besides, there was something compelling about the discomfort. She owed it to the dead man to hurt a little for him.

"That was impressive," she told Rowan on the long ride home.

"Yeah, right until I puked on the riverbank."

"But that was only after he was gleaned," Citra pointed out. "You gave that man strength to face death."

Rowan shrugged. "I guess."

Citra found it both maddening and endearing how modest he could be.

There's a poem by Honorable Scythe Socrates—one of the first scythes. He wrote many poems, but this one has grown to be my personal favorite.

Have not a hand in the blade with abandon,
Cull from the fold all the brazen and bold,
For a dog who just might,
Love the bark and the bite,
Is a carrion raven, the craven of old.

It reminds me that in spite of our lofty ideals and the many safeguards to protect the Scythedom from corruption and depravity, we must always be vigilant, because power comes infected with the only disease left to us: the virus called human nature. I fear for us all if scythes begin to love what they do.

—From the gleaning journal of H.S. Curie

9

Esme

Esme ate far too much pizza. Her mother told her pizza would be the death of her. She never imagined it might actually be true.

The scythe attack came less than a minute after she was given her slice, piping hot from the oven. It was the end of the school day, and the daily trials of fourth grade had exhausted her. Lunch had sucked. The tuna salad her mother had given her was warm and mildly fermented by the time lunch rolled around. Not exactly appetizing. In fact, none of the food her mother packed for her hit high on the flavor scale. She was trying to get Esme to eat healthier, because Esme had a bit of a weight problem. And although her nanites could be programmed to speed up her metabolism, her mother wouldn't hear of it. She claimed it would be treating the symptom, not the problem.

"You can't solve everything by tweaking your nanites," her mother told her. "You need to learn self-control."

Well, she could learn self-control tomorrow. Today she wanted pizza.

Her favorite pizza place, Luigi's, was in the food court of the Fulcrum City Galleria—which was on her way home from school. Sort of. She was negotiating the cheese, trying to figure out how to take that first bite without burning the roof of her mouth, when the scythes arrived. Her back was to them, so she didn't see them at first. But she heard them—or at least one of them.

"Good afternoon, good people," he said. "Your lives are about to change in a fundamental way."

Esme turned to see them. Four of them. They were clad in bright robes that glittered. They looked like no one Esme had ever seen. She had never met a scythe. She was fascinated. Until three of them pulled out weapons that glistened even more than their bejeweled robes, and the fourth pulled out a flamethrower.

"This food court has been selected for gleaning," their leader said. And they began their terrible mission.

Esme knew what she had to do. Forgetting her pizza, she dropped beneath the table and crawled away. But she wasn't the only one. It seemed everyone had dropped and was scrambling on the floor. It didn't seem to faze the scythes. She could see their feet through the crawling crowd. The fact that their victims were on all fours did not slow them down in the least.

Now Esme began to panic. She had heard stories of scythes who did mass gleanings, but until now she thought they were nothing but stories.

Before her she could see the robes of the scythe in yellow, so she doubled back, only to find the scythe in green closing in. Esme crawled through a gap in the tables and between two potted palms that the scythe in orange had set on fire, and when she emerged on the other side of the large pots, she found herself with no cover.

She was at the food concessions now. The man who had served her pizza was slumped over the counter, dead. There was a gap between a trash can and the wall. She was not a slim girl, so she thought the skinniest thoughts she could, and squeezed her way into the gap. It was not much of a hiding space, but if she left it, she would be right in the line of fire. She had already seen two people trying to dart across the walkway and both were taken down by steel crossbow arrows. She didn't dare move. So instead, she buried her face in her hands. She stayed that way, sobbing, listening to the terrible sounds around her, until silence fell. Still she refused to open her eyes until she heard a man say, "Hello there."

Esme opened her eyes to see the lead scythe—the one in blue—standing over her.

"Please . . ." she begged, "please, don't glean me."

The man held out his hand to her. "The gleaning is over," he said. "There's no one left but you. Now, take my hand."

Afraid to refuse, Esme reached out and placed her hand in his, and rose from her hiding place.

"I've been looking for you, Esme," he said.

Esme gasped when she heard him say her name. Why would a scythe be looking for her?

The other three scythes gathered round. None of them raised a weapon at her.

"You'll be coming with us now," the scythe in blue said.

"But . . . but my mother."

"Your mother knows. I've granted her immunity."

"Really?"

"Yes, really."

Then the girl scythe, in emerald green, handed Esme a plate. "I believe this was your pizza."

Esme took it. It was cool enough to eat now. "Thank you."

"Come with us," said the scythe in blue, "and I promise you from this moment on, your life will be everything you've ever dreamed it could be."

And so Esme left with the four scythes, thankful to be alive, and trying not to think of the many around her who weren't. This was certainly not the way she imagined her day would go—but who was she to fight against something that rang so clearly of destiny?

Was there ever a time when people weren't plagued with boredom? A time when motivation wasn't so hard to come by? When I look at news archives from the Age of Mortality, it seems people had more reasons to do the things they did. Life was about forging time, not just passing time.

And those news reports—how exciting they were. Filled with all nature of criminal activity. Your neighbor could be a salesperson of illegal chemicals of recreation. Ordinary people would take life without the permission of society. Angry individuals would take possession of vehicles they didn't own, then lead law enforcement officers in dangerous pursuits on uncontrolled roadways.

We do have the unsavories nowadays, but they do little more than drop occasional pieces of litter and move shop items to places they don't belong. No one rages against the system anymore. At most, they just glare at it a bit.

Perhaps this is why the Thunderhead still allows a measured amount of economic inequality. It could certainly make sure that everyone had equal wealth—but that would just add to the plague of boredom that afflicts the immortal. Although we all have what we need, we're still allowed to strive for the things we want. Of course, no one strives like they did in mortal days, when the inequality was so great people would actually steal from one another—sometimes ending lives in the process.

I wouldn't want the return of crime, but I do tire of we scythes being the sole purveyors of fear. It would be nice to have competition.

—From the gleaning journal of H.S. Curie

10

Forbidden Responses

"Dude, I'm telling you, it's all anyone can talk about. Everyone thinks you're becoming a scythe to take revenge on the school!"

On a mild day in March—on one of the rare afternoons that Scythe Faraday allowed Rowan downtime—Rowan had gone to visit his friend Tyger, who had not splatted once in the past three months. Now they shot hoops at a park just a few blocks away from Rowan's home—where he wasn't allowed to visit, and might not have even if he were allowed.

Rowan threw Tyger the ball. "That's *not* why I accepted the apprenticeship."

"*I* know that, and *you* know that, but people will believe whatever they want to believe." He grinned. "Suddenly I got all sorts of game because I'm your friend. They think I can get them access to your ring. Immunity talks; death walks."

The thought of Tyger playing intercessor on his behalf almost made Rowan laugh. He could see Tyger milking that for all it was worth. Probably charging people for the service.

Rowan stole the ball and took a shot. He hadn't played since before moving in with the scythe, but he found his arm, if not his aim. He was stronger than ever—and had endless stamina, all thanks to his Bokator training.

"So when you get your ring, you *are* gonna give me immunity, right?" Tyger took a shot and missed. It was clearly intentional. He was letting Rowan win.

"First of all, I don't know that he'll choose me to get the ring. And secondly, I can't give you immunity."

Tyger looked genuinely shocked. "What? Why not?"

"That's playing favorites."

"Isn't that what friends are for?"

A few other kids came to the court and asked if maybe they wanted to play a pickup game—but the second they saw Rowan's armband, they had a change of heart.

"No worries," the oldest one said. "It's all yours."

It was exasperating. "No, we can all play. . . ."

"Naah . . . we'll go somewhere else."

"I said we can all play!" Rowan insisted—and he saw such fear in the other kid's eyes, he felt ashamed for pushing.

"Yeah, yeah, sure," said the other kid. He turned to his friends. "You heard the man! Play!"

They took to the court in earnest, and in earnest played to lose, just as Tyger had. Was this how it would always be? Was he now such an intimidating presence that even his own friends would be afraid to truly challenge him? The only one who ever challenged him in any way now was Citra.

Rowan quickly lost interest in the game and left with Tyger, who found it all amusing. "Dude, you're not lettuce anymore, you're deadly nightshade. You're the mean greens now!"

Tyger was right. If Rowan had told those other kids to get down on all fours and lick the pavement, they would have. It was heady, and horrible, and he didn't want to think about it.

Rowan didn't know what possessed him to do what he did

next. Frustration at his isolation maybe—or maybe just wanting to bring a sliver of his old life into his new one.

"Wanna come over and see the scythe's place?"

Tyger was a little dubious. "Will he mind?"

"He's not there," Rowan told him. "He's gleaning in another city today. He won't be home till late." He knew that Scythe Faraday would blow a brain stem if he found out Rowan had someone over. It made the desire to do it even more enticing. He had been so good, so obedient; it was about time he did something that *he* wanted to do.

When they arrived, the house was empty. Citra, who also was granted a free afternoon by Scythe Faraday, was out. He had wanted Tyger to meet her, but then thought, *What if they happen to like each other? What if Tyger charms her?* He always had a way with girls. He had even convinced a girl to splat with him once, just so he could say, "Girls fall for me—literally."

"It'll be like Romeo and Juliet," he had told her. "Except we get to come back."

Needless to say, the girl's parents were livid, and after she was revived, they forbade her to see Tyger ever again.

Tyger shrugged it off. "What can I say? Her life is a tale told by idiots," which, Rowan believed, was a very bad Shakespeare misquote.

The thought of Citra falling for Tyger—even just figuratively—made Rowan a bit nauseated.

"This is it?" Tyger said as he looked around the place. "It's just a house."

"What did you expect? A secret underground lair?"

"Actually, yeah. Or something like it. I mean, look at this

furniture—I can't believe he makes you live in this hellhole."

"It's not so bad. C'mon, I'll show you something cool."

He took Tyger to the weapons den, which, as expected, Tyger found truly impressive.

"This is so edge! I've never seen so many knives—and are those guns? I've only seen pictures!" He took a pistol off the wall and looked in the barrel.

"Don't do that!"

"Calm down—I'm a splatter, not a blaster."

Rowan took it away from him anyway, and in the time it took to put it back on the wall, Tyger had taken down a machete and was swishing it through the air.

"Think I could borrow this?"

"Absolutely not!"

"C'mon—he's got so many, he'll never miss it."

Tyger, Rowan knew, was the very definition of "bad idea." That had always been part of the fun of being his friend. But now that was a major liability. Rowan grabbed Tyger's arm, kicked him behind the knee to buckle his leg, and spun him to the ground—all in a single Bokator move. Then he held Tyger's arm at an unnatural angle, with just enough leverage for it to hurt.

"What the hell!" Tyger said through gritted teeth.

"Drop the machete. Now!"

Tyger did—and just then, they heard the front door being opened. Rowan let go. "Be quiet," he said in a power-whisper.

He peeked out the door, but couldn't see who had come in. "Stay here," he told Tyger, then he slipped out to find Citra closing the front door behind her. She must have been running, because she wore a workout outfit that was much more revealing than Rowan needed at the moment—it drained far too much blood from his brain. So he focused on her apprentice armband to remind himself that hormonal responses were strictly forbidden. Citra looked up and gave him an obligatory greeting.

"Hey, Rowan."

"Hey."

"Something wrong?"

"No."

"Why are you just standing there?"

"Where should I be standing?"

She rolled her eyes and went into the bathroom, closing the door. Rowan slipped back into the weapons den.

"Who is it?" asked Tyger. "Is it what's-her-name? I want to meet your competition. Maybe *she'll* give me immunity. Or something else."

"No," Rowan told him. "It's Scythe Faraday, and he'll glean you on the spot if he finds you here."

Suddenly Tyger's bravado evaporated. "Oh crap! What are we gonna do?"

"Calm down. He's taking a shower. As long as you're quiet I can get you out."

They came out into the hallway. Sure enough, the sound of a shower hissed behind the closed bathroom door.

"He's washing off the blood?"

"Yeah. There was a lot of it." He led Tyger to the front door, and did everything short of pushing him out.

After being an apprentice for nearly three months, Citra couldn't deny that she wanted to be chosen by Scythe Faraday to receive the ring. As much as she resisted, as much as she told herself this was not the life for her, she had come to see its importance, and how good a scythe she would be. She had always wanted to live a life of substance and to make a difference. As a scythe, she would. Yes, she would have blood on her hands, but blood can be a cleansing thing.

It was certainly treated as such in Bokator.

Citra found Black Widow Bokator to be the most physically demanding thing she had ever done. Their trainer was Scythe Yingxing, who used no weapons but his own hands and feet to glean. He had taken a vow of silence. It seemed every scythe had surrendered something of themselves—not because they had to but because they chose to—as a way to pay for the lives they took.

"What would *you* give up?" Rowan once asked Citra. The question made her uncomfortable.

"If I become a scythe, I'm giving up my life, aren't I? I think that's enough."

"You're also giving up a family." Rowan reminded her.

She nodded, not wanting to speak to it. The idea of having a family was so far off to her, the idea of *not* having one felt equally distant. It was hard to have feelings about something she was years away from even considering. Besides, such things had to be kept far from her mind during Bokator. One's mind had to be clear.

Citra had never taken any sort of martial art before. She had always been a non-contact-sport kind of girl. Track, swimming, tennis—any sport that had a clear lane line or net between her and her opponent. Bokator was the antithesis of that. Hand-to-hand, body-to-body combat. Even communication was entirely physical in the class, as their mute instructor would correct their positions as if they were action figures. It was all mind and body, without the brash mediation of words.

There were eight in their class, and although their instructor was a scythe, Citra and Rowan were the only apprentices. The others were junior scythes, in the first years of their scythehood. There was one other girl, who made no overtures of friendship to Citra. The girls were given no special treatment, and were expected to be every bit the equal of the boys.

Sparring was punishing in Bokator. Each match began simply enough, with a ritualistic strutting around the circle, the two combatants physically taunting each other in a sort of aggressive dance. Then things got serious, and brutal. All nature of kicks and punches and body slams.

Today she sparred against Rowan. He had more finesse to his moves, but she had the advantage of speed. He was stronger, but he was also taller, which was not an asset. Citra's lower center of gravity made her more stable. All taken into account, they were evenly matched.

She spun and gave Rowan a powerful kick to the chest that almost took him down.

"Good one," Rowan said. Scythe Yingxing zipped his own lip to remind them that there was no cross talk during combat.

She came at him from his left, and he countered so quickly, she had no idea where his hand had come from. It was as if he suddenly had three. She was thrown off-balance, but only for an instant. She felt heat where his hand had connected with her side. *There'll be a bruise.* She grinned. *He'll pay for that!*

She feinted left again, then came at him from the right with the full force of her body. She took him down and had him pinned—but it was as if gravity reversed, and suddenly she realized he had turned the tables. Now he was on top, pinning her. She could have flipped him again—she had the leverage—but she didn't do it. She could feel his heartbeat now as if it were beating in her own chest . . . and she realized she wanted to feel that a little longer. She wanted to feel it more than she wanted to win the match.

That made her angry. Angry enough to pull away from his grip and put some space between them. There was no lane line, no net, nothing to keep them apart but the wall of her will. But that wall kept losing bricks.

Scythe Yingxing signaled the end of the match. Citra and Rowan bowed to each other, then took their places on opposite sides of the circle as two others were called up to spar. Citra watched intently, determined not to give Rowan a single glance.

We are not the same beings we once were.

Consider our inability to grasp literature and most entertainment from the mortal age. To us, the things that stirred mortal human emotions are incomprehensible. Only stories of love pass through our post-mortal filter, yet even then, we are baffled by the intensity of longing and loss that threatens those mortal tales of love.

We could blame it on our emo-nanites limiting our despair, but it runs far deeper than that. Mortals fantasized that love was eternal and its loss unimaginable. Now we know that neither is true. Love remained mortal, while we became eternal. Only scythes can equalize that, but everyone knows the chance of being gleaned in this, or even the next, millennium is so low as to be ignored.

We are not the same beings we once were.

So then, if we are no longer human, what are we?

—From the gleaning journal of H.S. Curie

11

Indiscretions

Citra and Rowan were not always together at gleanings. Sometimes Scythe Faraday took just one of them. The worst gleaning Citra witnessed took place in early May, just a week before Vernal Conclave—the first of three conclaves she and Rowan would attend during their apprenticeship.

Their quarry was a man who had just turned the corner and reset his age to twenty-four. He was at home having dinner with his wife and two kids, who seemed to be around Citra's age. When Scythe Faraday announced who they had come for, the family wept, and the man slipped off into a bedroom.

Scythe Faraday had chosen a peaceful bloodletting for the man, but that was not what happened. When Citra and the scythe entered the room, he ambushed them. The man was in peak condition, and in the arrogance of his new rejuvenation, he rejected his gleaning and fought the scythe, breaking his jaw with a vicious punch. Citra came to his aid, trying some Bokator moves she had learned from Scythe Yingxing—and quickly learned that applying a martial art is much different from practice in a dojo. The man swatted her away and advanced on Faraday, who was still reeling from his injury.

Citra leaped on him again, clinging to him, for the moment giving up on anything beyond eye gouging and hair pulling. It distracted him just long enough for Scythe Faraday to pull out a hunting knife he had concealed in his robe and slit the man's throat. He began gasping for air, his hands to his neck trying futilely to hold back the flow of blood.

And Scythe Faraday, holding a hand to his own swelling jaw, spoke to him—not with malice but with great sorrow. "Do you understand the consequences of what you've done?"

The man could not answer. He fell to the ground quivering, gasping. Citra thought death from such a wound would be instantaneous, but apparently not. She had never seen so much blood.

"Stay here," the scythe told her. "Look upon him kindly and be the last thing he sees."

Then he left the room. Citra knew what he was going to do. The law was very clear as to the consequences of running from or resisting one's gleaning. She couldn't close her eyes, because she was instructed not to, but if there was a way, she wished she could have closed her ears, because she knew what she was about to hear from the living room.

It began with pleas from the woman begging for the lives of her children, and the children sobbing in despair.

"Do not beg!" Citra heard the scythe say sharply. "Show these children more courage than your husband did."

Citra kept her gaze fixed on the dying man's until his eyes finally emptied of life. Then she went to join Scythe Faraday, steeling herself for what was to come.

The two children were on the sofa, their sobs having degraded into tearful whimpers. The woman was on her knees whispering to them, comforting them.

"Are you quite done?" the scythe said impatiently.

At last the woman rose. Her eyes were tearful, but they no longer seemed pleading. "Do what you have to do," she said.

"Good," said the scythe. "I applaud your fortitude. Now, as it happens, your husband did not resist his gleaning." Then he touched his swelling face. "However, my apprentice and I had an altercation, resulting in these wounds."

The woman just stared at him, her jaw slightly unhinged. So was Citra's. The scythe turned to Citra and glared at her. "My apprentice shall be severely disciplined for fighting with me." Then he turned back to the woman. "Please kneel."

The woman fell to her knees, not so much a kneel as a collapse.

Scythe Faraday held out his ring to her. "As is customary, you and your children shall receive immunity from gleaning for one year henceforth. Each of you, please kiss my ring."

The woman kissed it again, and again, and again.

The scythe said little after they left. They rode a bus, because whenever possible the scythe avoided the use of a publicar. He saw it as an extravagance.

When they got off at their stop, Citra dared to speak.

"Shall I be disciplined for breaking your jaw?" Citra knew it would be healed by morning, but the healing nanites were not spontaneous. He still looked pretty awful.

"You will speak to no one of this," he told her sternly. "You will not even comment on it in your journal, is that clear? The man's indiscretion shall never be known."

"Yes, Your Honor."

She wanted to tell him how much she admired him for what he had done. Choosing compassion over obligation. There was a lesson to be learned in every gleaning, and today's was one she would not soon forget. The sanctity of the law . . . and the wisdom to know when it must be broken.

Citra, try as she might to be a stellar apprentice, was not immune to indiscretion herself. One of Citra's nightly chores was to bring Scythe Faraday a glass of warm milk before bed. "As in my childhood, warm milk smooths the edges of the day," the scythe had told her. "I have, however, dispensed with the cookie that once came with it."

The thought of a scythe having milk and cookies before bed bordered on absurd to Citra. But she supposed even an agent of death would have guilty pleasures.

Quite often, however, when a gleaning had been difficult, he would fall asleep before she came into his room at the appointed time with the milk. In those cases she would drink it herself, or give it to Rowan, because Scythe Faraday made it clear that nothing in his household was ever wasted.

On the night of that awful gleaning, she lingered in his room a bit longer.

"Scythe Faraday," she said gently. Then said it again. No response. She could tell by his breathing he was out.

There was an object on the nightstand. In fact, it was there every night.

His ring.

It caught the oblique light spilling in from the hallway. Even in the dim room it glittered.

She downed the glass of milk and set it on the nightstand, so that in the morning the scythe would see she had brought it and that it hadn't been wasted. Then she knelt there, her eyes fixed on the ring. She wondered why he never slept with it, but felt that asking would be some sort of intrusion.

When she received hers—if she received hers—would it retain the solemn mystery that it held for her now, or would it become ordinary to her? Would she come to take it for granted?

She reached forward, then drew her hand back. Then reached forward again and gently took the ring. She turned it in her fingers so that it caught the light. The stone was big, about the size of an acorn. It was said to be a diamond, but there was a darkness in its core that made it different from a simple diamond ring. There was something in the core of that ring, but no one knew what it was. She wondered if even the scythes themselves knew. The center wasn't exactly black—it was a deep discoloration that looked different depending on the light—the way a person's eyes sometimes do.

Then, when she glanced at the scythe, she could see that his eyes were open and watching her.

She froze, knowing she was caught, knowing that putting the ring down now wouldn't change that.

"Would you like to try it on?" Scythe Faraday asked.

"No," she said. "I'm sorry. I shouldn't have touched it."

"You shouldn't have, but you did."

She wondered if he had been awake this whole time.

"Go ahead," he told her. "Try it on. I insist."

She was dubious, but did as she was told, because in spite of what she told him, she did want to try it on.

It felt warm on her finger. It was sized for the scythe, so it was too large for her. It was also heavier than she imagined.

"Do you worry that it will ever be stolen?" she asked.

"Not really. Anyone foolish enough to steal a scythe's ring is quickly removed from the world, so they cease to be a problem."

The ring was getting noticeably cooler.

"It is a covetable object, though, don't you agree?" the scythe said.

Suddenly Citra realized the ring wasn't just cool, it was freezing. The metal, in a matter of seconds, had grown white with frost, and her finger was in such intense pain from the cold, she cried out and pulled the ring from her hand. It flew across the room.

Not only was her ring finger severely frostbitten, so were the fingers that had pulled it free. She bit back a whimper. She could now feel warmth flowing through her body as her healing nanites released morphine. She became woozy, but forced herself to stay alert.

"A security measure I installed myself," the scythe said. "A micro-coolant chip in the setting. Let me see." He turned on his nightstand light and grabbed her hand, looking at her ring finger. The flesh at the joint was pale blue and frozen solid. "In the Age of Mortality, you might have lost the finger, but I trust your nanites are already mending the damage." He let go of her hand. "You'll be fine by morning. Perhaps next time you'll think before touching things that don't belong to you." He retrieved his ring, set it back on the nightstand, then handed her the empty glass. "From now on Rowan will bring me my evening milk," he said.

Citra deflated. "I'm sorry I disappointed you, Your Honor. You're right; I don't deserve to bring you your milk."

He raised an eyebrow. "You misunderstand. This is not a punishment. Curiosity is human; I merely allowed you to get it out of your system. I have to say, it took you long enough." Then he gave her a little conspiratorial grin. "Now let's see how long it takes Rowan to go for the ring."

Sometimes, when the weight of my job becomes over-whelming, I begin to lament all the things lost when we conquered death. I think about religion and how, once we became our own saviors, our own gods, most faiths became irrelevant. What must it have been like to believe in something greater than oneself? To accept imperfection and look to a rising vision of all we could never be? It must have been comforting. It must have been frightening. It must have lifted people from the mundane, but also justified all sorts of evil. I often wonder if the bright benefit of belief outweighed the darkness its abuse could bring.

There are the tone cults, of course, dressing in sackcloth and worshiping sonic vibrations—but like so many things in our world, they seek to imitate what once was. Their rituals are not to be taken seriously. They exist merely to make the passing time feel meaningful and profound.

Lately I've been preoccupied with a tone cult in my neighborhood. I went into their gathering place the other day. I was there to glean one of the cult's congregants—a man who had not yet turned his first corner. They were intoning what they called "the resonant frequency of the universe." One of them told me that the sound is alive and that harmonizing with it brings inner peace. I wonder, when they look at the great tuning fork that stands as the symbol of their faith, if they truly believe it to be a symbol of power or are they just joining in a communal joke?

—From the gleaning journal of H.S. Curie

12

No Room for Mediocrity

"The Scythedom is the world's only self-governing body," said Scythe Faraday. "While the rest of the world is under Thunderhead rule, the Scythedom is not. Which is why we hold conclaves three times a year to resolve disputes, review policy, and mourn the lives we've taken."

Vernal Conclave, which was to take place during the first week of May, was less than a week away. Rowan and Citra had studied enough of the structure of the Scythedom to know that all twenty-five regions of the world held their conclaves on the same day, and that there were currently three hundred twenty-one scythes in their region, which encompassed the heart of the North Merican continent.

"The MidMerican Conclave is an important one," Scythe Faraday told them, "because we tend to set the trend for much of the world. There's an expression, 'As goes MidMerica, so goes the planet.' The Grandslayer scythes of the Global Conclave always have their eyes on us."

Scythe Faraday explained that at each conclave they would be tested. "I do not know the nature of this first test, which is why you need to be as prepared as possible in all aspects of your training."

Rowan found he had a million questions about conclave,

but kept them to himself. He let Citra do all the asking—mainly because the questions irritated Scythe Faraday, and he never answered them.

"You'll find out all you need to know when you get there," the scythe told them. "For now all your attention must be on your training and your studies."

Rowan had never been an exceptional student—but that was by design. To be either too good or too bad drew attention. As much as he hated being the lettuce, it was his comfort zone.

"If you apply yourself, I have no doubt you could be at the top of your class," his science teacher had told him after getting the highest grade on his midterm last year. He had done it just to see if he could. Now that he knew, he saw no great need to do it again. There were many reasons, not the least of which was his own ignorance about scythes in those days before his apprenticeship. He assumed that being a stellar student would make him a target. Supposedly, a friend of a friend was gleaned at eleven because he was the smartest kid in fifth grade. It was nothing more than an urban myth, but Rowan believed it just enough that it kept him from wanting to stand out. He wondered if other kids held back for fear of being gleaned.

He had little experience with being so studious. He found it exhausting, and there was more than just poison chemistry, post-mortal history, and journaling. There was metallurgy as it applies to weapons, the philosophy of mortality, the psychology of immortality, and the literature of the Scythedom, from poetry to the wisdom found in famous scythes' journals. And of course, the mathematical statistics that Scythe Faraday relied upon so heavily.

There was no room for mediocrity, especially now with conclave coming up.

Rowan did ask him one question about conclave. "Will we be disqualified if we fail the test?"

Faraday took a moment before answering. "No," he told them, "but there *is* a consequence." Although he would not tell them what that consequence was. Rowan concluded that not knowing was more terrifying than knowing.

With just a few days before conclave, he and Citra stayed up late studying in the weapons den. Rowan found himself dozing, but was quickly awakened when Citra slammed a book.

"I hate this!" she announced. "Cerberin, aconite, conium, polonium—the poisons are all running together in my head."

"That would sure make a person die faster," Rowan said with a smirk.

She crossed her arms. "Do *you* know your poisons?"

"We're only supposed to know forty by conclave," he pointed out.

"And do you know them?"

"I will," he told her.

"What's the molecular formula for tetrodotoxin?"

He wanted to ignore her, but found he couldn't back away from the challenge. Perhaps a bit of her competitive nature was rubbing off on him. "$C_{11}H_{17}N_3O_6$."

"Wrong!" she said, pointing a finger at him. "It's O_8, not O_6. You fail!"

She was trying to rile him up, so she wouldn't be the only one riled. He wasn't going to oblige. "Guess so," he said, and tried to return to his studies.

"Aren't you the least bit worried?"

He took a breath and closed his book. When Faraday first began teaching them, Rowan found the use of actual old-school books very off-putting, but over time, he'd learned there was something very satisfying to the turning of pages, and—as Citra had already discovered—the emotional catharsis of slamming a book shut.

"Of course I'm worried, but here's the way I look at it. We know they won't disqualify us, and we already know we can't be gleaned, and we'll have two more chances to make up for any screw-ups before one of us is chosen. Whatever the consequence of failing the first round of tests, if either of us fail, we'll deal with it."

Citra slumped in her chair. "I don't fail," she said, but didn't sound too convinced of it. There was this pouty look on her face that made Rowan want to smile, but he didn't because he knew that would infuriate her. He actually liked how she would get infuriated—but they had too much work to do to indulge in emotional distraction.

Rowan put away his toxicology book and pulled out his volume on weapons identification. They were required to be able to identify thirty different weapons, how to wield them, and their detailed history. Rowan was more worried about that than the poisons. He spared a glance at Citra, who noticed the glance, so he tried not to look at her again.

Then out of nowhere she said, "I would miss you."

He looked up, and she looked away. "How do you mean?"

"I mean that if disqualification was part of the rules, I'd miss having you around."

He considered reaching out to take her hand, which rested gently on the table. But the table was big, and her hand was too far away for it to be anything other than insanely awkward. Then again, even if they sat closer, it would be an insane thing to do.

"But it's not part of the rules," he said. "Which means that no matter what, you're stuck with me for eight more months."

She grinned. "Yeah. I'm sure I'll really be sick of you by then."

It was the first time it occurred to Rowan that she might not hate him as much as he thought she did.

The quota system has worked for over two hundred years, and although it fluctuates region to region, it makes it crystal clear what each scythe's responsibility to the world is. Of course it's all based on averages—we can go days or even weeks without gleaning—but we must meet our quota before the next conclave. There are those eager ones who glean early, and find themselves with little to do as conclave draws near. There are those who procrastinate and have to hurry toward the end. Both those approaches lead to sloppiness and unintentional bias.

I often wonder if the quota will ever change, and if so, how much. Population growth is still off the charts, but it's balanced by the Thunderhead's ability to provide for an ever-increasing population. Renewable resources, subsurface dwellings, artificial islands, and all without there ever being any less green or a sense of overcrowding. We have mastered this world, and yet protected it in a way that our forefathers could scarcely have dreamed.

But all things are limited. While the Thunderhead does not interfere with the Scythedom, it does suggest the number of scythes there should be in the world. Currently there are approximately five million people gleaned per year worldwide—a tiny fraction of the death rate in the Age of Mortality, and nowhere near enough to balance population growth. I shudder to think how many more scythes it would take, and how many gleanings would be required, if we ever need to curb population growth altogether.

—From the gleaning journal of H.S. Curie

13

Vernal Conclave

Fulcrum City was a post-mortal metropolis toward the very center of MidMerica. There, by the river, set low between the skysoaring spires of graceful city living, was a venerable structure of stone, impressive if not in height then in solidity. Marble columns and arches supported a great copper dome. It was an unyielding homage to ancient Greece and Imperial Rome, the birthing grounds of civilization. It was still called the Capitol Building, for it was once a state capital, back when there were still states—in those days before government became obsolete. Now it had the honor of holding the administrative offices of the MidMerican Scythedom, as well as hosting its conclave three times a year.

It was pouring rain the day of the Vernal Conclave.

Citra rarely minded the rain, but a day of gloom coupled with a day of pure tension did not sit well with her. But then, a bright sunny day would feel mocking. Citra realized there was no good day to be presented to an intimidating elegy of scythes.

Fulcrum City was only an hour away by hypertrain, but of course, Scythe Faraday saw hypertrains as an unnecessary extravagance. "Besides, I want scenery rather than a windowless subterranean tunnel. I'm a human being, not a mole."

A standard train took six hours, and Citra did enjoy the scenery along the way, although she spent most of the trip studying.

Fulcrum City was on the Mississippi River. She recalled that there was once a giant silver arch on the riverbank, but it was gone now. Destroyed back in the Age of Mortality by something called "terrorism." She'd have learned more about the city if she weren't so focused on her poisons and weapons.

They had arrived the evening before conclave, and stayed in a downtown hotel. Morning came much too quickly.

As Citra, Rowan, and Scythe Faraday walked from their hotel at the awful hour of six thirty a.m., people in the streets ran to them and handed them umbrellas, choosing to get wet rather than see a scythe and his apprentices go without one.

"Do they know you've taken two apprentices instead of just one?" Citra asked.

"Of course they know," said Rowan. "Why wouldn't they?"

But Scythe Faraday's silence on the matter was a clear red flag to Citra.

"You did clear it with the High Blade, didn't you, Scythe Faraday?"

"I have found that with the Scythedom, it is better to ask forgiveness than permission," he told them.

Citra gave Rowan an I-told-you-so look, and he cocked his umbrella slightly so he didn't have to see it.

"It will not be a problem," Faraday said, but he didn't sound very convincing.

Citra looked to Rowan again, who was no longer eclipsed by his umbrella. "Am I the only one who's worried about that?"

Rowan shrugged. "We have immunity until Winter Conclave, and it can't be revoked—everyone knows that. What's the worst they could do?"

Some scythes arrived at the Capitol Building on foot, as they had; others in publicars, some in private cars, and several in limousines. There were ropes to hold back spectators on either side of the wide marble staircase leading up to the building, as well as peace officers and members of the BladeGuard—the Scythedom's elite security force. The arriving scythes were protected from their adoring public, even if the public was not protected from them.

"I despise 'running the gauntlet.'" Scythe Faraday said, referring to climbing the steps to conclave. "It's even worse when it's not raining. The crowd on either side is a dozen people deep."

Now it was only half that. It never occurred to Citra that people would come out to see scythes arriving at conclave, but then, all celebrity events drew onlookers, so why not a gathering of scythes?

Some of the arriving scythes gave obligatory waves, others played to the crowd, kissing babies and randomly granting immunity. Citra and Rowan followed Faraday's lead, which was to ignore the crowd completely.

There were dozens of other scythes in the entry vestibule. They removed their raincoats to reveal robes of all colors, all textures. It was a rainbow that summoned forth anything but thoughts of death. This, Citra realized, was intentional. Scythes wished to be seen as the many facets of light, not of darkness.

Through a grand arch lay a grander chamber beneath the

central dome—a rotunda where hundreds of scythes greeted one another, engaging in casual conversation around an elaborate breakfast spread in the center. Citra wondered what it was that scythes talked about. The tools of gleaning? The weather? The chafing of their robes? It was intimidating enough to be in the presence of a single scythe. To be surrounded by hundreds was enough to make one crumble.

Scythe Faraday leaned over and spoke to them in a hushed voice. "See there?" He pointed to a bald, heavily bearded man. "Scythe Archimedes—one of the world's oldest living scythes. He'll tell you he was there in the Year of the Condor, when the Scythedom was first formed, but it's a lie. He's not *that* old! And over there . . ." He pointed to a woman with long silver hair in a pale lavender robe. "That's Scythe Curie."

Citra gasped. "The Grande Dame of Death?"

"So they say."

"Is it true she gleaned the last president, before the Thunderhead was given control?" Citra asked.

"And his cabinet, yes." He looked at her—perhaps a bit wistfully, Citra thought. "Her actions were quite controversial back in the day."

The woman caught them glancing her way and turned to them. Citra chilled when her piercing gray eyes zeroed in on her. Then the woman smiled at the three of them, nodded, and returned to her conversation.

There was a group of four or five scythes closer to the assembly chamber entrance, the doors of which were still closed. They wore bright robes studded with gems. The center of their attention was a scythe in royal blue whose robe contained what appeared to be diamonds. He said something and the others laughed a little too heartily for it to be anything but sycophantic.

"Who's that?" Citra asked.

Scythe Faraday's expression took a turn toward sour.

"That," he said, not even trying to hide his distaste, "is Scythe Goddard, and his company is best avoided."

"Goddard . . . isn't he the master of mass gleanings?" Rowan asked.

Faraday looked at him a bit concerned. "Where did you hear that?"

Rowan shrugged. "I have a friend who's obsessed with that kind of stuff, and he hears things."

Citra gasped, realizing she had heard of Goddard, not by name, just by deed. Or, more accurately, rumor because there was never any official report. But like Rowan said, you hear things. "Is he the one who gleaned an entire airplane?"

"Why?" asked Faraday, giving her a cold, accusing eye. "Does that impress you?"

Citra shook her head. "No, the opposite." But she couldn't help but be a bit dazzled by the way the man's robe caught the light. Everyone was—which must have been his intent.

And yet his was not the most ostentatious robe on display. Moving through the crowd was a scythe in a lavishly gilded robe. The man was so large, his robe seemed a bit like a golden tent.

"Who's the fat guy?" Citra asked.

"He looks important," said Rowan.

"Indeed," said Scythe Faraday. "'The fat guy,' as you call him, is the High Blade. The most powerful man in the MidMerican Scythedom. He presides over conclave."

The High Blade worked the crowd like a great gaseous planet bending space around it. He could have tweaked his nanites to eliminate at least some of his girth, but clearly he had chosen not to. The choice was a bold statement and his size made him an imposing figure. When he saw Faraday, he excused himself from his current conversation and made his way toward them.

"Honorable Scythe Faraday, always a pleasure to see you." He used both his hands to grip Faraday's in what was meant to be a heartfelt greeting, but felt forced and artificial.

"Citra, Rowan, I'd like you to meet High Blade Xenocrates," Faraday said, then turned back to the large man. "These are my new apprentices."

He took a moment to appraise them. "A double apprenticeship," he said jovially. "I believe that's a first. Most scythes have trouble with just one."

"The better of the two shall receive my blessing for the ring."

"And the other," said the High Blade, "will be sorely disappointed, I'm sure." Then he moved on to greet other scythes that were just now coming in from the rain.

"See?" Rowan said. "And you were worried."

But to Citra, nothing about the man seemed sincere.

Rowan *was* nervous, he just didn't want to admit it. He knew admitting it would make Citra more worried, which would make him more worried. So he bit back his fears and misgivings, and kept his eyes and ears open, taking in everything that happened around him. There were other apprentices there. He overheard two talking about how this was the "big day." A boy and a girl—both older than him, maybe eighteen or nineteen, would be getting their rings today and become junior scythes. The girl lamented about how, for the first four years, they would have to get approval from the selection committee for their gleanings.

"Every single one," she complained. "Like we're babies."

"At least the apprenticeship isn't four years long," Rowan interjected, as a way to get into the conversation. The two looked at him with mild disgust.

"I mean, it takes four years to get a college degree, right?" Rowan knew he was just digging himself deeper, but he had already committed. "At least it doesn't take that long to get a license to glean."

"Who the hell are you?" the girl asked.

"Ignore him, he's just a *spat*."

"A what?" Rowan had been called many things, but never that.

They both smirked at him. "Don't you know anything?" said the girl. "'Spat,' as in 'spatula.' It's what they call new apprentices, because you're not good for anything but flipping your scythe's burgers."

Rowan laughed at that, which just irritated them.

Then Citra came up next to them. "So if we're spatulas, what does that make you? Safety scissors? Or are you just a couple of tools?"

The boy looked like he might slug Citra. "Who's your mentor scythe?" he asked her. "He should be told of this disrespect."

"I am," said Faraday, putting his hand on Citra's shoulder.

"And you don't warrant anyone's respect until after you receive your ring."

The boy seemed to shrink by about three inches. "Honorable Scythe Faraday! I'm sorry, I didn't know." The girl took a step away as if to distance herself from him.

"Best of luck today," he told them with a magnanimous gesture that they didn't deserve.

"Thank you," said the girl, "but if I may say, luck plays no part. We've both trained long and have been taught well by our scythes."

"Very true," Faraday said. They nodded respectful good-byes that bordered on bows, and left.

After they were gone, Faraday turned to Rowan and Citra. "The girl will get her ring today," he said. "The boy will be denied."

"How do you know?" asked Rowan.

"I have friends on the bejeweling committee. The boy is smart, but too quick to anger. It's a fatal flaw that cannot be tolerated."

As annoying as Rowan found the kid, he couldn't help but feel a twinge of pity. "What happens to the apprentices that get denied?"

"They are returned to their families to take up life where they left off."

"But life can never be the same after a year of training to be a scythe," Rowan pointed out.

"True," said Faraday, "but only good can come from a keen understanding of what it takes to be a scythe."

Rowan nodded, but thought, for a man of such wisdom,

that seemed very naive. Scythe training was a scarring endeavor. Purposefully so, but it was scarring nonetheless.

The rotunda became increasingly crowded with scythes, and the marble walls, floor, and dome made voices echo into a cacophony. Rowan tried to hear more individual conversations, but they were lost in the din. Faraday had told them that the great bronze doors to the assembly room would open promptly at seven a.m., and the scythes would be dismissed at the stroke of seven p.m. Twelve hours to accomplish any and all business. Anything left undone would have to wait four months until the next conclave.

"In the early days," Scythe Faraday told them as the doors opened to admit the throng, "a conclave would last for three days. But they discovered that after the first day, it became little more than arguments and posturing. There's still plenty of that, but it's curtailed. It behooves us all to move through the agenda quickly."

The chamber was a huge semicircle with a large wooden rostrum at the front where the High Blade sat, and slightly lower seats on either side for the Conclave Clerk, who kept records, and the Parliamentarian, who interpreted rules and procedures if any questions arose. Scythe Faraday had told them enough about the power structure of the Scythedom for Rowan to know that much.

The first order of business, once everyone was settled, was the Tolling of the Names. One by one, in no particular order, the scythes came to the front to recite various names of people they had gleaned over the past four months.

"We can't recite them all," Scythe Faraday told them. "With

over three hundred scythes, it would be more than twenty-six thousand names. We are to choose ten. The ones we most remember, the ones who died most valiantly, the ones whose lives were the most notable."

After each name spoken, an iron bell was rung, solemn and resonant. Rowan was pleased to hear Scythe Faraday reciting Kohl Whitlock's name as one of his chosen ten.

The Tolling of the Names got old very quickly for Citra. Even reduced to ten names each, the recitation lasted for almost two hours. It was noble that the scythes saw fit to pay homage to the gleaned, but if they only had twelve hours to complete three months worth of business, she didn't see the sense of it.

There was no written agenda, so there was no way for her and Rowan to know what came next, and Scythe Faraday only explained things as they happened.

"When is our test? Will we be taken somewhere else for it?" Citra asked, but Faraday shushed her.

After the Tolling of the Names, the next order of business was a ceremonial washing of the hands. The scythes all rose and lined up before two basins, one on either side of the rostrum. Again, Citra didn't see the point. "All this ritual—it's like something you'd see in a tone cult," she said when Faraday returned to his seat, hands still damp.

Faraday leaned over to her and whispered, "Don't let any of the other scythes hear you say that."

"Do you feel clean after sticking your hands in water that a hundred other hands have been in?"

Faraday sighed. "It brings solace. It binds us as a community. Do not belittle our traditions because one day they may be yours."

"Or not," goaded Rowan.

Citra shifted uncomfortably and grumbled. "It just seems like a waste of time."

Faraday must have known her real gripe was with not knowing when they would be presented to the conclave and taken away for their test. Citra was not a girl who could endure being in the dark for long. Perhaps that's why Faraday made sure that she was. He was constantly poking at their weaknesses.

Next, a number of scythes were singled out for showing bias in their gleanings. This held some interest for Citra, and gave her some insight as to how it all worked behind the scenes.

One scythe had gleaned too few wealthy people. She was reprimanded and assigned to only glean the rich between now and the next conclave.

Another scythe was found to have racial ratio issues. High on the Spanic, low on the Afric.

"It's due to the demographic where I live," he pleaded. "People have a higher percentage of Spanic in their personal ratios."

High Blade Xenocrates was not swayed. "Then cast a wider net," he said. "Glean elsewhere."

He was charged with bringing his ratios back into line or face being disciplined—which consisted of having future gleanings preapproved by the selection committee. Having one's freedom to glean taken away was a humiliation that no scythe wanted.

Sixteen scythes were taken to task. Ten were warned, six were disciplined. The oddest situation was a scythe who was far too pretty for his own good. He got called out for gleaning too many unattractive people.

"What an idea," one of the other scythes shouted out. "Imagine what a world it would be if we gleaned only ugly people!"

That brought a round of laughter from the rest of the room.

The scythe tried to defend himself, claiming the old adage, "Beauty is in the eye of the beholder," but the High Blade wasn't buying it. This was apparently his third such offense, so he was given permanent probation. He could live as a scythe but could not glean, "Until the next reptilian year," the High Blade proclaimed.

"That's crazy," Citra commented just loud enough for Rowan and Faraday to hear. "No one knows what animals future years will be named after. I mean, the last reptilian year was the Year of the Gecko and that was before I was born."

"Precisely!" said Faraday with a little bit of guilty glee. "Which means his punishment could end next year or never. Now he'll spend his time lobbying the office of the Calendaria to name a year after the skink, or Gila monster, or some other reptile that has not yet been used."

Before they moved on from the disciplinary portion of the morning, there was one more scythe to be called out. It wasn't a matter of bias, however.

"I have before me an anonymous note," the High Blade said, "which accuses Honorable Scythe Goddard of malfeasance."

A rumble throughout the room. Citra saw Scythe Goddard whisper to his inner circle of companions, then stood. "Of what sort of malfeasance am I being accused?"

"Unnecessary cruelty in your gleaning."

"And yet this accusation comes anonymously!" said Goddard. "I cannot believe that a fellow scythe would show such cowardice. I demand that the accuser reveal his or herself."

More rumbles around the room. No one stood up, no one took responsibility.

"Well then," said Goddard, "I refuse to answer to an invisible accuser."

Citra expected High Blade Xenocrates to press the issue. After all, an accusation from a fellow scythe should be taken seriously—but the High Blade put the paper down and said, "Well, if there's nothing more, we'll take our midmorning break."

And the scythes, Earth's grand bringers of death, began to file out into the rotunda for donuts and coffee.

Once they were in the rotunda, Faraday leaned close to Citra and Rowan and said, "There was no anonymous accuser. I'm sure that Scythe Goddard accused himself."

"Why would he do that?" asked Citra.

"To take the steam out of his enemies. It's the oldest trick in the book. Now anyone who accuses him will be assumed to be the cowardly anonymous accuser. No one will go after him now."

Rowan found himself less interested in the stagecraft and parrying within the assembly room as he was in the things that went on outside of it. He was already getting a feeling for the Scythedom and how it truly worked. The most important business did not occur within the bronze doors, but in the rotunda and dim alcoves of the building—of which there were many, probably for this exact purpose.

The early morning conversations had been just small talk, but now, as the day progressed, Rowan could see a number of scythes congregating during break into small klatches, doing side deals, building alliances, pushing secret agendas.

He overheard one group that was planning to propose a ban on remote detonators as a method of gleaning—not for any ethical reason, but because the gun lobby had made a sizeable contribution to a particular scythe. Another group was trying to groom one of the younger scythes for a position on the selection committee, so that he might sway gleaning choices when they needed those choices swayed.

Power politics might have been a thing of the past elsewhere, but it was alive and seething in the Scythedom.

Their mentor did not join any of the plotters. Faraday remained solitary and above petty politics, as did perhaps half of the scythes.

"We know the schemes of the schemers," he told Rowan and Citra as he negotiated a jelly donut. "They only get their way when the rest of us want them to."

Rowan made a point to observe Scythe Goddard. Many scythes approached him to talk. Others grumbled about him under their breath. His entourage of junior scythes was a multicultural bunch, in the old-school meaning of the word. While no one had pristine ethno-genetics anymore, his inner circle showed traits that leaned toward one ethnos or another. The girl in green seemed mildly PanAsian, the man in yellow had Afric leanings, the one in fiery orange was as Caucasoid as could be, and he himself leaned slightly toward the Spanic. He was clearly a scythe who wanted high visibility—even his grand gesture of ethnic balance was a visible one.

Although Goddard never turned to look, Rowan had the distinct feeling that he knew Rowan was watching him.

For the rest of the morning, proposals were made and hotly debated in the assembly room. As Scythe Faraday had said, the schemers only prevailed when the more high-minded body of the Scythedom allowed. The ban on remote detonators was adopted—not because of bribes from the gun lobby, but because blowing people up was determined to be crude, cruel, and beneath the Scythedom. And the young scythe put forth for membership on the selection committee was voted down, because no one on that committee should be in anyone's pocket.

"I should like to be on a scythe committee one day," Rowan said.

Citra looked at him oddly. "Why are you talking like Faraday?"

Rowan shrugged. "When in Rome . . ."

"We're not in Rome," she reminded him. "If we were, we'd have a much cooler place for conclave."

Local restaurants vied for the chance to cater the conclave, so lunch was a buffet out in the rotunda even more sumptuous than the one at breakfast—and Faraday packed his plate, which was out of character for him.

"Don't think ill of him," Scythe Curie told Rowan and Citra, her voice mellifluous, yet sharp at the same time. "For those of us who take our vow of austerity seriously, conclave is the only time we allow ourselves the luxury of fine food and drink. It reminds us that we're human."

Citra, who had a one-track mind, took this as her opportunity to get information.

"When will the apprentices be tested?" she asked.

Scythe Curie smirked and brushed back her silky silver hair. "The ones who are hoping to receive their ring today were tested last night. As for all the others, you'll be tested soon enough," she said. Citra's frustration made Rowan snicker, which earned him a glare from Citra.

"Just shut up and stuff your face," she said. Rowan was happy to oblige.

As focused as Citra was on the upcoming test, she began to wonder what in conclave she would miss when the apprentices were taken for testing. Like Rowan, she found conclave to be an education like none other. There were few people beyond scythes and their apprentices who ever witnessed this. And those others who did caught only a glimpse—such as the string of salespeople after lunch, who were each given ten minutes to expound the virtues of some weapon or poison they were trying to sell to the Scythedom, and more importantly the Weaponsmaster, who had the final decision over what the Scythedom purchased. They sounded like those awful people on info-holograms. "It dices, it slices! But wait! There's more!"

One salesperson was selling a digital poison that would turn the healing nanites in a person's bloodstream into hungry little bastards that would devour the victim from the inside out in less than a minute. He actually used the word "victim," which immediately soured the scythes. He was flatly dismissed by the Weaponsmaster.

The most successful salesperson was offering a product called Touch of Quietude, which sounded more like a feminine hygiene product than a death delivery system. The woman selling it displayed a small pill—but not to give to the subject. The pill was for the scythe. "Take with water and within seconds your fingers will secrete a transdermal poison. Anyone you touch for the next hour will be instantly and painlessly gleaned."

The Weaponsmaster was so impressed, he came up to the stage to take a dose, then, in the ultimate demonstration, proceeded to glean the saleswoman. She sold fifty vials of the stuff to the Scythedom posthumously.

The rest of the afternoon consisted of more discussion, arguments, and votes about policy. Scythe Faraday only found fit to voice his opinion once—when it came to forming an immunity committee.

"It seems clear to me that there should be oversight for the granting of immunity, just as the selection committee provides oversight for gleaning."

Rowan and Citra were pleased to see that his opinion carried a great deal of weight. Several scythes who had initially voted against the forming of an immunity committee switched their vote. However, before a final tally was taken, High Blade Xenocrates announced that time had run out for legislative issues.

"The subject will be at the top of our agenda for the next conclave," he announced.

A number of scythes applauded, but several rose up and shouted their grievous discontent at the issue being tabled. Scythe Faraday did not voice his own displeasure. He took a long breath in and out. "Interesting . . ." was all he said.

This might have all pinged loudly on Rowan and Citra's

radar, had the High Blade not immediately announced that the next order of business was the apprentices.

Citra found herself wanting to grip Rowan's hand in anticipation and squeeze it until it was bloodless, but she restrained herself.

Rowan, on the other hand, followed his mentor's lead. He took a deep breath in, then out, and tried to let his anxiety wash from him. He had studied all he could study, learned all he could learn. He would do the best he could do. If he failed today there would be more than enough chances to redeem himself.

"Good luck," Rowan said to Citra.

"You too," she returned. "Let's make Scythe Faraday proud!"

Rowan smiled, and thought that Faraday might smile at Citra as well, but he didn't. He just kept his gaze on Xenocrates.

First, the candidates for Scythedom were called up. There were four whose apprenticeships were now complete. Having had their final test the evening before, there was nothing left but to ordain them. Or not, as the case may be. Word was there was a fifth candidate who had failed the final test last night. He or she wasn't even invited to conclave.

Three rings were brought out, resting on red velvet pillows. The four looked to one another now, aware that even though they had passed their final test, one of them would not be ordained and would be sent home in shame.

Scythe Faraday turned to the scythe beside him and said, "Only one scythe gleaned himself since last conclave, and yet three are being confirmed today. . . . Has the population grown so drastically in three months that we need two additional scythes?"

The three chosen apprentices were called one by one by Scythe Mandela, who presided over the bejeweling committee. As each knelt before him, he said something about each of them in turn, and then handed them their rings, which they slipped on their fingers and held to show the conclave— which responded for each of them with obligatory applause. Then they announced their Patron Historic, the luminary from history whom they would name themselves after. The conclave applauded with each announcement, accepting Scythes Goodall, Schrödinger, and Colbert into the MidMerican Scythedom.

When the three had left the stage, the hot-tempered boy remained, just as Scythe Faraday had said earlier in the day. He stood alone after the applause died down. Then Scythe Mandela said, "Ransom Paladini, we have chosen not to ordain you as a scythe. Wherever life leads you, we wish you well. You are dismissed."

He lingered for a few moments, as if thinking it might be a joke—or maybe one final test. Then, his lips pursed, his face turned red and he strode quickly up the center aisle in silence, pushing through the heavy bronze doors, their hinges complaining at his exit.

"How awful," said Citra. "At least they could applaud him for trying."

"There are no accolades for the unworthy," Faraday said.

"One of us will exit that way," Rowan pointed out to her. He resolved that if it was him, he would take his time going down that aisle. He'd make eye contact and nod to as many scythes as he could on his way out. Were he to be ejected, he would leave that final conclave with dignity.

"The remaining apprentices may now come forward," said Xenocrates. Rowan and Citra rose, ready to face whatever the Scythedom had in store for them.

I do believe people still fear death, but only one one-hundredth as much as they used to. I say that because, based on current quotas, a person's chance of being gleaned within the next one hundred years is only 1 percent. Which means the chance that a child born today will be gleaned between now and their five thousandth year on Earth is only 50 percent.

Of course, since we no longer count the years numerically, aside from children and adolescents, no one knows how old anyone is anymore—sometimes not even themselves. These days people roughly know within a decade or two. At the writing of this, I can tell you that I am somewhere between one hundred sixty and one hundred eighty years old, although I don't enjoy looking my age. Like everyone else, I turn the corner on occasion and set my biological age back substantially—but like many scythes, I don't set it back past the age of forty. Only scythes that are actually young like to look young.

To date, the oldest living human being is somewhere around three hundred, but only because we are still so close to the Age of Mortality. I wonder what life will be like a millennium from now, when the average age will be nearer to one thousand. Will we all be renaissance children, skilled at every art and science, because we've had the time to master them? Or will boredom and slavish routine plague us even more than it does today, giving us less of a reason to live limitless lives? I dream of the former, but suspect the latter.

—From the gleaning journal of H.S. Curie

14

A Slight Stipulation

Rowan stepped on Citra's toes on his way to the aisle. She grunted slightly, but didn't wisecrack about it.

That was because Citra was too busy going over her weapons and poisons in her head. Rowan's clumsiness was the least of her concerns.

She thought they would be led to a room elsewhere in the building—a quiet place for their exam—but other apprentices who had been to conclave before were heading down the aisle toward the open space in front of the rostrum. They lined up in what seemed like no particular order, facing the conclave like a chorus line, so Citra joined the line next to Rowan.

"What is this?" she whispered.

"Not sure," he whispered back.

There were eight in total. Some stood with hard expressions, in control of their emotions, others were trying not to look terrified. Citra wasn't sure what image she projected, and found herself annoyed that Rowan looked as casual as if he were waiting for a bus.

"Honorable Scythe Curie will be the examiner today," Xenocrates said.

A hush fell over the chamber as Scythe Curie, the Grande Dame of Death, came forward. She walked down the line of apprentices twice, sizing them up. Then she said, "Each of you will be asked one question. You will have one opportunity to give an acceptable answer."

One question? What kind of exam could possibly consist of one question? How could they test anyone's knowledge that way? Citra's heart beat so violently, she imagined it bursting out of her chest. Then she would find herself waking up in a revival center tomorrow, a laughingstock.

Scythe Curie began at the left end of the line. It meant Citra would be fourth to be questioned.

"Jacory Zimmerman," Scythe Curie said to the gangly boy on the end. "A woman hurls herself on your blade, offering herself as a sacrifice to prevent you from gleaning her child, and dies. What do you do?"

The boy hesitated for just an instant, then said, "By resisting the gleaning, she has violated the third commandment. I therefore am obliged to glean the rest of her family."

Scythe Curie was silent for a moment, then said, "Not an acceptable answer!"

"But . . . but . . . ," said Jacory, "she resisted! The rule says—"

"The rule says if one resists one's *own* gleaning. Were she the chosen one, the third commandment would most certainly apply. But if we are ever unsure, we are obliged to err on the side of compassion. In this case you would glean the child and arrange for the woman to be brought to a revival center, granting her a year of immunity along with the rest of the family." Then she gestured toward the assembly. "Step down. Your sponsoring scythe will choose your punishment."

Citra swallowed. Shouldn't the punishment for failure be

the awful knowledge of that failure? What sorts of punishments would scythes devise for their disgraced disciples?

Scythe Curie moved on to a strong-looking girl with high cheekbones on a face that looked like it could weather a hurricane.

"Claudette Catalino," Scythe Curie said, "you have made a mistake in your poison—"

"That would never happen," Claudette said.

"Do not interrupt me."

"But your premise is flawed, Honorable Scythe Curie. I know my poisons so well, I could never make a mistake. Ever."

"Well," said Curie, with deadpan irony, "how proud your sponsoring scythe must be to have the first perfect pupil in human history."

It brought forth a smattering of chuckles from the room.

"All right then," continued Scythe Curie. "Let us say that someone irritated by your arrogance has sabotaged your poison. Your subject, a man who offered you no resistance, begins to convulse and it appears that his end will be slow and likely filled with much more pain than his nanites can suppress. What do you do?"

And without hesitation Claudette said, "I draw the pistol that I always keep for emergencies, and end the subject's suffering with a single well-placed bullet. But first I would order any family members to leave the room, sparing them the trauma of witnessing a ballistic gleaning."

Scythe Curie raised her eyebrows, considering the response, and said, "Acceptable. And thinking of the family is a nice touch—even in a hypothetical." Then she grinned. "I'm disappointed I couldn't prove you imperfect."

Next was a boy whose gaze was fixed on a spot on the back wall, clearly trying to find his happy place.

"Noah Zbarsky," said Curie.

"Yes, Your Honor." His voice quivered. Citra wondered what sort of response that might evoke from Curie. What sort of question might she ask a boy so frightened?

"Name for me five species that generate neurotoxins powerful enough to be effective on a poison-tipped dart."

The boy, who had been holding his breath, exhaled with loud relief.

"Well, Phyllobates aurotaenia, of course, better known as the poison dart frog," he said. "The blue-ringed octopus, the marbled cone snail, the inland taipan snake, and . . . uh . . . the deathstalker scorpion."

"Excellent," Scythe Curie said. "Can you name any more?"

"Yes," Noah told her, "but you said one question."

"And what if I tell you I've changed my mind, and I want six instead of five?"

Noah took a deep breath, but didn't hold it. "Then I would tell you in a most respectful way that you were not honoring your word, and a scythe is duty bound to honor their word."

Scythe Curie smiled. "Acceptable answer! Very good!"

And then she moved on to Citra.

"Citra Terranova."

She had realized the scythe knew everyone's name, and yet it came as a shock to hear her say it.

"Yes, Honorable Scythe Curie."

The woman leaned in close, peering deeply into Citra's eyes. "What is the worst thing you have ever done?"

Citra was prepared for just about any question. Any question but that one.

"Excuse me?"

"It's a simple question, dear. What is the worst thing you've ever done?"

Citra's jaw clenched. Her mouth went dry. She knew the answer. She didn't even have to think about it.

"Can I have a moment?"

"Take your time."

Then some random scythe in the audience heckled. "She's done so many terrible things, she's having trouble selecting just one."

Laughter everywhere. In that moment she hated them all.

Citra held eye contact with Scythe Curie. Those all-seeing gray eyes. She knew she couldn't back away from the question.

"When I was eight," she began, "I tripped a girl down the stairs. She broke her neck, and had to spend three days at a revival center. I never told her that it was me. That's the worst thing I ever did."

Scythe Curie nodded and offered a sympathetic grin, then said, "You're lying, dear." She turned to the crowd, shaking her head perhaps a little bit sadly. "Unacceptable answer." Then she turned back to Citra. "Step down," she said. "Scythe Faraday will choose your punishment."

She didn't argue, she didn't insist that she was telling the truth. Because she wasn't. She had no idea how Scythe Curie knew.

Citra went back to her place, unable to look at Scythe Faraday, and he said nothing to her.

Then Scythe Curie moved on to Rowan, who seemed so smug, Citra just wanted to hit him.

"Rowan Damisch," Scythe Curie asked. "What do you fear? What do you fear above all else?"

Rowan did not hesitate in his response. He shrugged and said, "I don't fear anything."

Citra wasn't sure she heard him right. Did he say he didn't fear anything? Had he lost his mind?

"Perhaps you want to take some time before answering," Scythe Curie prompted, but Rowan just shook his head.

"I don't need any more time. That's my answer. Not gonna change it."

Absolute silence in the room. Citra found herself involuntarily shaking her head. And then she realized . . . he was doing this for her. So she wouldn't have to suffer alone through whatever punishment was in store. So she wouldn't feel she had fallen behind him. Although she still wanted to smack him, now it was for an entirely different reason.

"So," said Scythe Curie, "today we have one perfect apprentice and one fearless one." She sighed. "But I'm afraid that no one is entirely fearless, so your answer, as I'm sure you must know, is unacceptable."

She waited, perhaps thinking Rowan might respond to that, but he did not. He just waited for her to say, "Step down. Scythe Faraday will choose your punishment."

Rowan returned to his place next to Citra as nonchalant as could be.

"You're an idiot!" she whispered to him.

He gave her the same shrug he gave Scythe Curie. "Guess so."

"You think I don't know why you did that?"

"Maybe I did it so that I'll look better at the next conclave. Maybe if I gave too good an answer today, my next question would be harder."

But Citra knew it was false, faulty logic. Rowan didn't think that way. And then Scythe Faraday spoke up—his voice quiet and measured, but somehow carrying an intensity that was chilling.

"You shouldn't have done that."

"I'll accept whatever punishment you see fit," Rowan said.

"It's not about the punishment," he snapped.

By now Scythe Curie had questioned a few more apprentices. One was sent to sit, two others stayed.

"Maybe Scythe Curie will see what I did as noble," Rowan suggested.

"Yes, and so will everyone else," Faraday said. "Motives can easily be beaten into weapons."

"Which proves," Citra said to Rowan, "that you're an idiot." But he only grinned idiotically.

She thought she had the last word on the matter and that it was over until they returned home, where, no doubt Scythe Faraday would inflict some annoying but fair punishment that fit the crime. She was mistaken.

After the apprentices were done being traumatized, the focus of the scythes began to wear down. There was now a constant murmur as scythes discussed dinner plans as the hour approached seven. The remaining business was of little interest to anyone. Issues of building maintenance, and whether or not scythes should be required to announce the turning of a corner so it wasn't so shocking when they looked thirty years younger at the next conclave.

It was as things were wrapping up that one scythe stood up and loudly addressed Xenocrates. She was the one dressed in green with emeralds embroidered into her robe. One of Scythe Goddard's bunch.

"Excuse me, Your Excellency," she began, although clearly she was speaking to the entire assembly, not just the High Blade. "I'm finding myself troubled by this set of new apprentices. More specifically the apprentices taken on by Honorable Scythe Faraday."

Both Citra and Rowan looked up. Faraday did not. He seemed frozen, looking downward almost in meditation. Or perhaps steeling himself for what was to come.

"To the best of my knowledge, a scythe has never taken on two apprentices and set them in competition for the ring," she continued.

Xenocrates looked over to the Parliamentarian, who had jurisdiction in such matters. "There's no law against it, Scythe Rand," said the Parliamentarian.

"Yes," Scythe Rand continued, "but clearly the competition has turned into camaraderie. How will we ever know which is the better candidate if they continue to aid each other?"

"Your complaint is duly noted," said Xenocrates, but Scythe Rand was not done.

"I propose that, to ensure this competition is *truly* a competition, we add a slight stipulation."

Scythe Faraday rose to his feet as if launched from his chair. "I object!" he shouted. "This conclave cannot stipulate how I train my apprentices! It is my sole right to teach them, train them, and discipline them!"

Rand held up her hands in a gesture of mock magnanimity. "I merely seek to make your ultimate choice fair and honest."

"Do you think you can beguile this conclave with your baubles and vanity? We are not so base as to be dazzled by shiny things."

"What is your proposal, Scythe Rand?" asked Xenocrates.

"I object!" shouted Faraday.

"You can't object to something she has not yet said!"

Faraday bit down his objection, and waited.

Citra watched, feeling almost detached, as if this were a tennis match and it was match point. But she wasn't an observer, was she? She was the ball. And so was Rowan.

"I propose," said Scythe Rand, with the slickness of a deathstalker scorpion, "that upon the confirmation of the winner, the first order of business will be for that winner to glean the loser."

Gasps and grumbles from around the room. And—Citra couldn't believe it—some laughter and affirmations as well. She wanted to believe the woman in green could not be serious. That this was yet another level of the test.

Faraday was so beside himself, he said nothing at first. He couldn't even find the words to object. Finally he thundered his fury, like a force of nature. A wave pounding the shore. "This flies in the face of everything we are! Everything we do! We are in the business of gleaning, but you and Scythe Goddard and all of his disciples—you would turn this into a blood sport!"

"Nonsense," said Rand. "It makes perfect sense. The threat of gleaning will ensure that the best applicant comes out on top."

And then rather than striking it down as ridiculous, to Citra's horror, Xenocrates turned to the Parliamentarian.

"Is there a rule against it?"

The Parliamentarian considered and said, "Since there is no precedent for the treatment of a double apprenticeship, there are no rules as to how it should be dealt with. The proposal is within our guidelines."

"Guidelines?" shouted Scythe Faraday. "Guidelines? The moral fabric of the Scythedom should be our guidelines! To even consider this is barbaric!"

"Oh, please," said Xenocrates with an exaggerated sweep of his hand. "Spare us all the melodrama, Faraday. This is, after all, the consequence of your decision to take on two apprentices when one would have been sufficient."

Then the clock began to strike seven o'clock.

"I demand a full debate and vote on this!" Scythe Faraday pleaded, but three bells had already rung, and Xenocrates ignored him.

"As is my prerogative as High Blade, I so stipulate that in the matter of Rowan Damisch and Citra Terranova, whosoever shall prevail will be required to glean the other upon receipt of his or her ring."

Then he banged his gavel heavily upon the rostrum, adjourning conclave and sealing their fate.

There are times I long for a relationship with the Thunderhead. I suppose we always want what we can't have. Others can call on the Thunderhead for advice, ask it to resolve disputes. Some rely on it as a confidant, for it's known to have a compassionate, impartial ear, and never gossips. The Thunderhead is the world's best listener.

But not for scythes. For us, the Thunderhead is eternally silent.

We have full access to its wealth of knowledge, of course. The Scythedom uses the Thunderhead for countless tasks—but to us, it's simply a database. A tool, nothing more. As an entity—as a mind—the Thunderhead does not exist for us.

And yet it does, and we know it.

Estrangement from the collective consciousness of humanity's wisdom is just one more thing that sets scythes apart from others.

The Thunderhead must see us. It must be aware of the Scythedom's petty bickering, and growing corruption, even though it has pledged noninterference. Does it despise us scythes, but abides us because it has to? Or does it simply choose not to think of us at all? And which is worse—to be despised, or to be ignored?

—From the gleaning journal of H.S. Curie

15

The Space Between

The night was bleak and rain streaked the windows of the train, distorting the lights beyond, until the lights were gone. Rowan knew they were slicing through the countryside now, but the darkness could have been the airless expanse of space.

"I won't do it," Citra finally said, breaking the silence that had engulfed them since leaving conclave. "They can't make me do it."

Faraday didn't say a word—didn't even look at her—so Rowan took it upon himself to answer.

"Yes, they can."

Finally Faraday looked to them. "Rowan is right," he said. "They will find whatever button will make you dance, and dance you will, no matter how hideous the tune."

Citra kicked the empty seat in front of her. "How could they be so awful, and why do they hate us so much?"

"It's not all of them," Rowan said, "and I don't think it's really about us. . . ." Clearly, Faraday was a respected scythe—and although he didn't come out against Goddard today, his feelings about the man were clear. Goddard must see Faraday as a threat; attacking Rowan and Citra was a warning shot.

"What if we *both* fail?" Citra suggested. "If we're lousy apprentices, then they can't choose either of us."

"And yet they will," Faraday told her with an authority and finality that left little room for doubt. "No matter how poorly you perform, they will still choose one of you, for the spectacle alone." Then he scowled in disgust. "And to set the precedent."

"I'll bet Goddard has enough friends to make sure it happens," said Rowan. "I think he has the High Blade on his side, too."

"Indeed," Faraday said with a world-weary sigh. "Never before have there been so many wheels within wheels in the Scythedom."

Rowan closed his eyes, wishing he could close his mind as well and hide from his own thoughts. *In eight months I will be killed by Citra,* he thought. *Or I will kill her.* And calling it "gleaning" didn't change the fact of what it was. He cared for Citra, but enough to surrender his life and let her win? Citra certainly wouldn't back down to let him earn the ring.

When he opened his eyes, he caught her staring at him. She didn't look away.

"Rowan," she said, "whatever happens, I want you to know—"

"Don't," Rowan told her. "Just don't."

And the rest of the ride was silence.

Citra, who was not the heaviest sleeper, found herself awake all night after they arrived home. Images of the scythes she saw at conclave filled even the hint of dreams, jarring her back to unwanted wakefulness. The wise ones, the schemers, the compassionate, and those who did not seem to care. Such a delicate charge as pruning the human race should not be subject to the quirks of personality. Scythes were supposed to be above the petty, just as they were above the law. Faraday certainly was. If she became a scythe, she would follow his lead. And if she didn't become one, it wouldn't matter because she'd be dead.

Perhaps there was some sort of twisted wisdom in the decision to have one of them gleaned by the other. Whoever wins will begin their life as a scythe in abject sorrow, never to forget the cost of that ring.

Morning came with no great fanfare. It was just an ordinary day, like any other. The rain had passed, and the sun peeked from behind shifting clouds. It was Rowan's turn to make breakfast. Eggs and hash browns. He never cooked the potatoes long enough. "Hash pales" Citra always called them. Faraday never complained when the meals they made were subpar. He ate what they served, and didn't tolerate complaints from either of them. The punishment for making something barely edible was having to eat it yourself.

Citra ate, even though she didn't have an appetite. Even though the whole world had slid off its axis. Breakfast was breakfast. How dare it be?

When Faraday broke the silence, it felt like a brick flying through the window.

"I will go out alone today. The two of you will attend to your studies."

"Yes, Scythe Faraday," Citra said, with Rowan saying the same in a half-second echo.

"For you nothing has changed."

Citra looked down into her cereal. It was Rowan who dared to state the obvious.

"Everything has changed, sir."

And then Faraday said something enigmatic that would only resonate with them much later.

"Perhaps everything will change again."

Then he left them.

The space between Rowan and Citra had quickly become a minefield. A dangerous no-man's-land that promised nothing but misery. It was hard enough to negotiate with Scythe Faraday there, but his absence left the two of them with no one to mediate the space between.

Rowan stayed in his room, studying there rather than going into the weapons room, which would feel painfully wrong without Citra sitting with him. Still, he kept his door cracked on the faint hope that she'd want to bridge the distance. He heard her leave, probably for a run, and she was gone for a good long time. Her way of dealing with the dark discomfort of their new situation was to remove herself from it even more completely than Rowan had.

After she returned, Rowan knew there would be no peace between them, or within himself, unless he took the first step into that minefield.

He stood outside her closed door for at least a full minute before he worked up the nerve to knock.

"What do you want?" she asked, her voice muffled by the closed door.

"Can I come in?"

"It's not locked."

He turned the knob and slowly opened the door. She was

in the middle of the room with a hunting knife, practicing bladecraft against the empty air, as if battling ghosts.

"Nice technique," Rowan said, then added, "if you're planning on gleaning a pack of angry wolves."

"Skill is skill, whether you use it or not." She sheathed the blade, tossed it on her desk, and put her hands on her hips. "So what do you want?"

"I just wanted to say I'm sorry for shutting you down before. On the train, I mean."

Citra shrugged. "I was babbling. You were right to shut me up."

The moment began to get awkward, so Rowan just went for it. "Should we talk about this?"

She turned away from him and sat on her bed, picking up a book on anatomy and opening it as if she were about to start studying. She hadn't yet realized she was holding it upside down. "What's to talk about? I kill you, or you kill me. Either way, I don't want to think about it until I have to." She glanced at the open book, turned it right side up, and then gave up the charade completely, closing it and tossing it to the floor. "I just want to be left alone, okay?"

Even so, Rowan sat on the edge of her bed. And when she didn't tell him to go, he shifted a little bit closer. She watched him, but said nothing.

He wanted to reach for her, maybe touch her cheek. But thinking about that made him think of the saleswoman who was gleaned by a touch. What a perverse poison that was. Rowan wanted to kiss her. There was no denying that anymore. He had suppressed the urge for weeks because he knew it would not be tolerated by the scythe. But Faraday wasn't here, and the turmoil they had both been hurled into had washed all bets off the table.

Then, to his surprise, she suddenly lurched forward and kissed him, catching him completely off guard.

"There," she said. "We've done it. Now it's out of the way and you can leave."

"What if I don't want to?"

And she hesitated. Long enough to make it clear that staying was a distinct possibility. But in the end she said, "What good would it do, really? For either of us."

She moved farther away on the bed, bringing her knees to her chest. "I haven't fallen in love with you, Rowan. And now I want to keep it that way."

Rowan got up and moved to the safety of the threshold before turning back to her. "It's all right, Citra," he told her. "I haven't fallen in love with you, either."

I am not a man easily brought to fury, but how dare the old-guard scythes presume to dictate my behavior? Let every last one of them glean themselves, and we can be done with their self-loathing, sanctimonious ways. I am a man who chooses to glean with pride, not shame. I choose to embrace life, even as I deal death. Make no mistake—we scythes are above the law because we deserve to be. I see a day when new scythes will be chosen not because of some esoteric moral high ground, but because they enjoy the taking of life. After all, this is a perfect world—and in a perfect world, don't we all have the right to love what we do?

—From the gleaning journal of H.S. Goddard

16

Pool Boy

There was a scythe at the door of the executive's mansion. Actually a quartet of them, although the other three stood back, allowing the one in the royal blue to be the point man.

The executive was frightened—terrified actually—but he hadn't risen to this level of success by wearing his emotions on his sleeve. He had a keen mind, and a consummate poker face. He would not be intimidated by death on his doorstep—even when death's robe was studded with diamonds.

"I'm surprised you got to the front door without my gate guards alerting me," the executive said, as nonchalant as could be.

"They would have alerted you, but we gleaned them," one of the other scythes said—a woman in green with PanAsian leanings.

The executive would not allow this news to daunt him. "Ah, so you need me to give you their personal information, in order for you to alert their families."

"Not exactly," said the lead scythe. "May we come in?"

And since the executive knew he didn't have the right to refuse, he stepped aside.

The diamond-studded scythe and his rainbow of subordinates followed, looking around at the understated opulence of the mansion.

"I am Honorable Scythe Goddard. These are my junior associates, Scythes Volta, Chomsky, and Rand."

"Sharp robes," commented the executive, still successfully capping his fear.

"Thank you," said Scythe Goddard. "I can see you are a man of taste. My compliments to your decorator."

"That would be my wife," he said, then inwardly grimaced to have brought her, in any way, to the attention of the life-takers.

Scythe Volta—the one in yellow, with an Afric look about him—strolled around the grand foyer, peering through the archways that led to other areas of the mansion. "Excellent feng shui," he said. "Energy flow is very important in a home so large."

"I imagine there's a good-size pool," said the one in the flame-colored robe embedded with rubies. Scythe Chomsky. He was blond, pale, and brutish.

The executive wondered if they were enjoying prolonging this encounter. The more he played along, the more power they had, so he cut through the small talk before they could see him crack.

"May I ask your business here?"

Scythe Goddard glanced at him but ignored the question. He gestured to his subordinates, and two of the three left. The one in yellow took the winding stairs, the woman in green went to explore the rest of the first floor. The pale one in orange stayed nearby. He was the largest of them, and perhaps a bodyguard for their leader—as if anyone would actually be stupid enough to strike a scythe.

The executive wondered where his children were at the moment. Out back with the nanny? Upstairs? He wasn't sure, and the last thing he wanted was to have scythes in the house out of his sight.

"Wait!" he said. "Whatever your purpose, I'm sure we could reach some sort of arrangement. You do know who I am, don't you?"

Scythe Goddard took in a piece of artwork on display in the foyer, instead of looking at him. "Someone wealthy enough to own a Cézanne."

Could it be that he didn't know? That their presence here was not planned, but random? Scythes were supposed to be random in their choices, but *this* random? He found the dam that held back his fear was fracturing.

"Please," the executive said, "I'm Maxim Easley—surely the name means something to you?"

The scythe looked at him without a hint of recognition. It was the flame-clad one who reacted. "The guy who runs Regenesis?"

Finally there came recognition from Goddard. "Oh, right—your company is number two in the turncorner industry."

"Soon to be number one," Easley reflexively bragged. "Once we release our technology that allows cellular regression beyond the twenty-first year."

"I have friends who've used your services. I myself have yet to turn a corner."

"You could be the first to officially use our new process."

Goddard laughed and turned to his associate. "Could you imagine me as a teenager?"

"Not a chance."

The more amused they were, the more horrified Easley

became. No sense in hiding his desperation anymore. "There must be something you want—something of value I can offer you. . . ."

And finally Goddard laid his cards on the table.

"I want your estate."

Easley resisted the urge to say "Excuse me?" because the statement was not ambiguous in any way. It was an audacious demand. But Maxim Easley was nothing if not a negotiator.

"I have a garage with more than a dozen mortal-age motor vehicles. Priceless, every last one of them. You can have any of them. You can have them all."

The scythe stepped closer, and Easley suddenly found a blade pressed to his neck, to the right of his Adam's apple. He never saw the scythe draw it. So quick was he that it seemed to just appear at his jugular.

"Let's clarify," Goddard said calmly. "We are not here to barter and bargain. We are scythes—which means that by law, anything we want we can take. Any life we wish to end, we will. Simple as that. You have no power here. Do I make myself clear?"

Easley nodded, feeling the blade almost but not quite cut his skin as he did. Satisfied, Goddard removed the blade from his neck.

"An estate like this must require a sizable staff. House-keepers, gardeners, perhaps even stable personnel. How many do you employ?"

Easley tried to speak, but nothing came out. He cleared his throat and tried again. "Twelve," he said. "Twelve full-time employees."

Then the woman in green—Scythe Rand—emerged from the kitchen, bringing with her a man Easley's wife had recently hired. He was in his early twenties, or appeared so. Easley couldn't remember his name.

"And who is this?" Goddard asked.

"The pool boy."

"Pool boy," mimicked Scythe Rand.

Goddard nodded to the muscle-bound Scythe in orange, who then approached the young man, reached up, and touched his cheek. The pool boy collapsed to the ground, his head hitting the marble. His eyes stayed open, but no life remained in them. He had been gleaned.

"It works!" said Scythe Chomsky, looking at his hand. "Definitely worth what the Weaponsmaster paid."

"Now then," said Goddard. "While we are within our rights to take anything we choose, I am a fair man. In exchange for this lovely estate, I will offer you, your family, and your surviving staff full immunity for every year that we choose to remain here."

Easley's relief was intense and immediate. How odd, he thought, to have his home stolen, and yet feel relieved.

"On your knees," Goddard said, and Easley obeyed.

"Kiss it."

Easley did not hesitate. He planted his lips on the ring, pressing hard, feeling the edge of the setting catch on his lip.

"Now you will go to your office and resign your position, effective immediately."

This time Easley did say, "Excuse me?"

"Someone else can do your job—I'm sure there are others itching for the opportunity."

Easley rose, his legs still a bit shaky. "But . . . but why? Can't you just let me and my family leave? We won't bother you. We'll take nothing but the clothes on our backs. You'll never see us again."

"But alas, I can't let you leave," said Scythe Goddard. "I need a new pool boy."

I think it's wise that scythes may not glean one another. It was clearly implemented to prevent Byzantine grabs at power; but where power is concerned there are always those who find ways to grasp for it.

I think it's also wise that we are allowed to glean ourselves. I will admit there were times when I considered it. When the weight of responsibility felt so heavy, leaving the yoke of the world behind seemed a better alternative. But one thought always stayed my hand from committing that final act.

If not me, who?

Will the scythe who replaces me be as compassionate and fair?

I can accept a world without me in it . . . but I can't bear the thought of other scythes gleaning in my absence.

—From the gleaning journal of H.S. Curie

17

The Seventh Commandment

Citra and Rowan were awakened sometime after midnight by someone pounding on the front door. They left their rooms, meeting in the hallway, and both reflexively glanced toward Scythe Faraday's closed door. Citra turned the knob, finding it unlocked, and pushed it open just enough to see that the scythe wasn't there. His bed had not yet been slept in tonight.

It was unusual but not unheard of for him to stay out this late. They had no idea what his occasional late nights were about, and they didn't want to ask. Curiosity was one of the first casualties of apprenticeship. They had long since learned there were many things they'd rather not know in the life of a scythe.

The relentless pounding continued—not the rapping of knuckles, but the full-fisted heel of a hand.

"So?" said Rowan. "He forgot his keys. So?"

It was the most sensible explanation, and didn't the most sensible explanation tend to be correct? They approached the door, steeling themselves for admonishment.

How could you not hear me knocking? he would chide. *Last I heard, no one's been deaf for two hundred years.*

But when they opened the door, they were faced not with Scythe Faraday, but with a pair of officers. Not common peace officers, but members of the BladeGuard, the sign of the

Scythedom clearly emblazoned on the breast of their uniforms.

"Citra Terranova and Rowan Damisch?" one of the guards-men asked.

"Yes?" answered Rowan. He stepped slightly forward, put-ting a shoulder in front of Citra in a sort of protective stance. He felt it gallant, but Citra found it irritating.

"You'll need to come with us."

"Why?" asked Rowan. "What's going on?"

"It's not our place to say," the second guardsman told them.

Citra pushed Rowan's protective shoulder to the side. "We're scythe's apprentices," she said, "which means the BladeGuard serves us, and not the other way around. You have no right to take us against our will." Which was probably untrue, but it gave the guards pause.

And then came a voice from the shadows.

"I'll handle this."

Out of the darkness swelled a familiar figure, wholly out of place in Faraday's neighborhood. The High Blade's gilded robe did not shine in the dimness of the doorstep. It seemed dull, almost brown.

"Please . . . you must come with me immediately. Someone will be sent for your things."

As Rowan was in pajamas and Citra a bathrobe, neither was too keen to obey, but they both sensed that their nightclothes were the least of their concerns.

"Where's Scythe Faraday?" Rowan asked.

The High Blade took a deep breath in, and sighed. "He invoked the seventh commandment," Xenocrates said. "Scythe Faraday has gleaned himself."

• • •

High Blade Xenocrates was a bloated bundle of contradictions. He wore a robe of rich baroque brocades, yet on his feet were frayed, treadworn slippers. He lived in a simple log cabin—yet the cabin had been reassembled on the rooftop of Fulcrum City's tallest building. His furniture was mismatched and thrift-store shabby, yet on the floor beneath them were museum-quality tapestries that could have been priceless.

"I can't tell you how sorry I am," he told Rowan and Citra, who were still too shell-shocked to wrap their minds around what had happened. It was morning now, the three of them having ridden in a private hypertrain to Fulcrum City, and they were now out on a small wooden deck that overlooked a well-tended lawn that ended in a sheer ledge and a seventy-story drop. The High Blade did not want anything to obstruct his view—and anyone stupid enough to trip over the edge would deserve the time and cost of revival.

"It's always a terrible thing when a scythe leaves us," the High Blade lamented, "especially one as well-respected as Scythe Faraday."

Xenocrates had a full retinue of assistants and flunkies in the outside world to help him go about his business, but here in his home, he didn't have as much as a single servant. Yet another contradiction. He had brewed them tea, and now poured it for them, offering cream but no sugar.

Rowan sipped his, but Citra refused the slightest kindness from the man.

"He was a fine scythe and a good friend," Xenocrates said. "He will be sorely missed."

It was impossible to guess at Xenocrates' sincerity. Like everything else about him, his words seemed both sincere—and not—at the same time.

He had told them the details of Scythe Faraday's demise on the way here. At about ten fifteen the evening before, Faraday was on a local train platform. Then, as a train approached, he hurled himself in front of it. There were several witnesses—all probably relieved that the scythe had gleaned himself and not any of them.

Had it been anyone but a scythe, his broken body would have been rushed to the nearest revival center, but rules for scythes were very clear. There would be no revival.

"But it doesn't make sense," Citra said, fighting tears with little success. "He wasn't the kind of man who would *do* something like that. He took his responsibility as a scythe—and training us—very seriously. I can't believe he would just give up like that. . . ."

Rowan held his silence on the subject, waiting for the High Blade's response.

"Actually," Xenocrates said, "it makes perfect sense." He took an excruciatingly long sip of tea before he spoke again. "Traditionally, when a mentor scythe self-gleans, anyone bound to an apprenticeship is unbound."

Citra gasped, realizing the implication.

"He did it," said Xenocrates, "to spare one of you from having to glean the other."

"Which means," said Rowan, "that this is your fault." And then he added with a little bit of derision, "Your Excellency."

Xenocrates stiffened. "If you are referring to the decision to set the two of you in mortal competition, that was not my suggestion. I was merely carrying out the will of the Scythedom, and frankly, I find your insinuation offensive."

"We never heard the will of the Scythedom," Rowan reminded him, "because there was never a vote."

Xenocrates stood, ending the conversation with, "I'm sorry for your loss." It was more than just Rowan's and Citra's loss, though; it was a loss to the entire Scythedom, and Xenocrates knew it, whether he said so or not.

"So . . . that's it then?" said Citra. "We go home now?"

"Not exactly," said Xenocrates, this time not looking either of them in the eye. "While it's traditional for the apprentices of dead scythes to go free, another scythe can come forward and take over the training. It's rare, but it does happen.

"You?" Citra asked. "You've volunteered to train us now?"

It was Rowan who saw the truth of it in his eyes. "No, it's not him," Rowan said. "It's someone else. . . ."

"My responsibilities as High Blade would make it far too difficult to take on apprentices. You should be flattered, however; not just one, but two scythes have come forward—one for each of you."

Citra shook her head. "No! We were pledged to Scythe Faraday and no one else! He died to free us, so we should be freed!"

"I'm afraid I've already given my blessing, so the matter is settled." Then he turned to each of them in turn. "You, Citra, will now be the apprentice of Honorable Scythe Curie. . . ."

Rowan closed his eyes. He knew what was coming next, even before Xenocrates said the words.

"And you, Rowan, will complete your training in the capable hands of Honorable Scythe Goddard."

Part Three

THE OLD GUARD AND THE NEW ORDER

I have never taken an apprentice. I simply never felt compelled to subject another human being to our way of life. I often wonder what motivates other scythes to do so. For some it is a form of vanity: "Learn from me and be awed because I am so wise." For others perhaps it is compensation for not being allowed to have children: "Be my son or my daughter for a year, and I will give you power over life and death." Yet for others, I imagine it is to prepare for their own self-gleaning. "Be the new me, so that the old me can leave this world satisfied."

I suspect, however, if I ever take on an apprentice, it will be for a different reason entirely.

—From the gleaning journal of H.S. Curie

18

Falling Water

At the far eastern edge of MidMerica, near the EastMerica border, was a home with a river running beneath it, spilling from its foundations into a waterfall.

"It was designed by a very well-known mortal age architect," Scythe Curie told Citra as she led the way across a footbridge to the front door. "The place had fallen into disrepair; as you can imagine, a home such as this couldn't survive without constant attention. It was in a horrible state, and no one cared enough to preserve it. Only the presence of a scythe would bring forth the kind of donations required to save it. Now it's been returned to its former glory."

The Scythe opened the door and let Citra step in first. "Welcome to Falling Water," Scythe Curie said.

The main floor was a huge open room with a polished stone floor, wooden furniture, a large fireplace, and windows. Lots and lots of windows. The waterfall was right beneath an expansive terrace. The sound of the river running beneath the home and over the falls was a constant but calming white noise.

"I've never been in a house with a name," Citra said as she looked around, doing her best to be unimpressed. "But it's a bit much, isn't it? Especially for a scythe. Aren't you all supposed to live simple lives?"

Citra knew such a comment could bring forth the scythe's temper, but she didn't care. Her presence here meant that Scythe Faraday died for nothing. A beautiful home was no consolation.

Scythe Curie did not respond in anger. She just said, "I live here not because of its extravagance, but because my presence here is the only way to preserve it."

The decor seemed to be frozen in the twentieth century, when the place was built. The only hints of modernization were a few simple computer interfaces in unobtrusive corners. Even the kitchen was a throwback to an earlier time.

"Come, I'll show you to your room."

They climbed a staircase that was lined on the left by layered sheets of granite and echoed on the right by rows and rows of shelved books. The second floor was the scythe's bedroom suite. The third floor held a smaller bedroom and a study. The bedroom was simply furnished, and, like the rest of the home, had huge windows framed in polished cedar, wrapping around two entire walls. The view of the forest made Citra feel as if she were perched in a tree house. She liked it. And she hated that she did.

"You know that I don't want to be here," Citra said.

"At last some honesty from you," Scythe Curie said with the slightest of grins.

"And," added Citra, "I know you don't like me—so why did you take me on?"

The scythe looked at her with those cold, inscrutable gray eyes. "Whether or not I like you is irrelevant," she said. "I have my reasons."

Then she left Citra alone in her room without as much as a good-bye.

. . .

Citra didn't remember falling asleep. She hadn't even considered how exhausted she was. She recalled lying down on the comforter, looking out at the trees, listening to the river roaring endlessly below, wondering if the noise would eventually go from soothing to unbearable. And then she opened her eyes to stark incandescence, squinting at Scythe Curie, who was standing in the doorway, by the light switch. It was dark outside now. Not just dark but lightless, like space. She could still hear the river, but couldn't see even a hint of the trees.

"Did you forget about dinner?" Scythe Curie asked.

Citra rose, ignoring the sudden vertigo when she stood. "You could have woken me."

Scythe Curie smirked. "I thought I just did."

Citra made her way down toward the kitchen—but the scythe let her go first, and she couldn't quite remember the way. The house was a maze. She took a few wrong turns, and Scythe Curie didn't correct her. She just waited for Citra to find her way.

What, Citra wondered, would this woman want to eat? Would she silently accept anything that Citra prepared, as Scythe Faraday had? The thought of the man brought a wave of sorrow chased by anger, but she didn't know who exactly to be angry at, so it just festered.

Citra arrived on the main floor ready to assess the contents of the pantry and refrigerator, but to her surprise she found the dinner table set for two, and steaming plates of food already there.

"I had a hankering for hasenpfeffer," the scythe said. "I think you'll like it."

"I don't even know what hasenpfeffer is."

"Best if you don't." Scythe Curie sat down, and bade Citra to do the same. But Citra wasn't quite ready, still wondering if this might be a trick.

Scythe Curie dug a spoon into the rich stew, but paused when she saw Citra still standing. "Are you waiting for a formal invitation?" she asked.

Citra couldn't tell if she was irritated or amused. "I'm an apprentice. Why would you cook for me?"

"I didn't. I cooked for *me*. Your grumbling stomach just happened to be in the vicinity."

Finally Citra sat and tasted the stew. Flavorful. A little gamey, but not bad. The sweetness of honey-glazed carrots cut the gaminess.

"The life of a scythe would be dreadful if we didn't allow ourselves the guilty pleasure of a hobby. Mine is cooking."

"This is good," Citra admitted. Then added, "Thank you."

They ate mostly in silence. Citra felt odd not being of service at the table, so she got up to refill the scythe's glass of water. Scythe Faraday did not have any hobbies—or at least none that he shared with Citra and Rowan.

The thought of Rowan made her hand tremble as she poured, and she sloshed some water on the table.

"I'm sorry, Scythe Curie." She grabbed her own napkin and blotted the spill before it could spread.

"You'll need a steadier hand than that if you're going to be a scythe." Again, Citra couldn't tell if she was being serious or sardonic. The woman was even harder for Citra to read than Faraday—and reading people was not her forte by any means. Of course, she never realized that until she spent time with Rowan, who, in his own unobtrusive way, was a master of observation. Citra had to remind herself that she had other skills. Speed and decisiveness of action. Coordination. Those things would have to come into play if she was going to . . .

She couldn't finish the thought—wouldn't allow herself to. The territory where that thought led was still too terrible to consider.

In the morning, Scythe Curie made blueberry pancakes, and then they went out gleaning.

While Scythe Faraday always reviewed his notes on his chosen subject and used public transportation, Scythe Curie had an old-school sports car that required substantial skill to drive—especially on a winding mountain road.

"This Porsche was a gift from an antique car dealer," Scythe Curie explained to her.

"He wanted immunity?" Citra asked, assuming the man's motive.

"On the contrary. I had just gleaned his father, so he already had immunity."

"Wait," said Citra. "You gleaned his father, and he gave you a car?"

"Yes."

"So he hated his father?"

"No, he loved his father very much."

"Am I missing something?"

The road ahead of them straightened out, Scythe Curie shifted gears, and they accelerated. "He appreciated the solace

I afforded him in the aftermath of the gleaning," she told Citra. "True solace can be worth its weight in gold."

Still, Citra didn't quite understand—and wouldn't until much later that evening.

They went to a town that was hundreds of miles away, arriving around lunchtime. "Some scythes prefer big cities; I prefer smaller towns," Scythe Curie said. "Towns that perhaps haven't seen a gleaning in over a year."

"Who are we gleaning?" Citra asked as they looked for a parking place—one of the liabilities of taking a car that was off-grid.

"You'll find out when it's time to know."

They parked on a main street, then walked—no, strolled—down the street, which was busy but not bustling. Scythe Curie's leisurely pace made Citra uncomfortable, and she wasn't sure why. Then it occurred to her that when she went gleaning with Scythe Faraday, his focus was always on the destination, and that destination wasn't a place, but a person. The subject. The soul to be gleaned. As awful as that was, it had somehow made Citra feel more secure. With Scythe Faraday, there was always a tangible end to their endeavor. But nothing about Scythe Curie's manner suggested premeditation at all. And there was a reason for that.

"Be a student of observation," Curie told Citra.

"If you want a student of observation, you should have chosen Rowan."

Scythe Curie ignored that. "Look at people's faces, their eyes, the way they move."

"What am I looking for?"

"A sense that they've been here too long. A sense that they're ready to . . . *conclude*, whether they know it or not."

"I thought we weren't allowed to discriminate by age."

"It's not about age, it's about stagnation. Some people grow stagnant before they turn their first corner. For others it could take hundreds of years."

Citra looked at the people moving around them—all trying to avoid eye contact and get away from the scythe and her apprentice as quickly as possible, all the while trying not to be obvious about it. A couple stepping out of a café; a businessman on his phone; a woman beginning to cross the street against the light, then coming back, perhaps fearing that jaywalking would get her gleaned.

"I don't see anything in anyone," Citra said, irritated at both the task and her inability to rise to it.

A group of people came out of an office building—perhaps the tallest one in town at about ten stories. Scythe Curie zeroed in on one man. Her eyes looked almost predatory as she and Citra began to follow him at a distance.

"Do you see how he holds his shoulders, as if there is an invisible weight upon them?"

"No."

"Can you see how he walks—a little less intently than those around him?"

"No."

"Do you notice how scuffed his shoes are, as if he doesn't care anymore?"

"Maybe he's just having a bad day," suggested Citra.

"Yes, maybe," admitted Scythe Curie, "but I choose to believe otherwise."

They closed in on the man, who never seemed to be aware that he was being stalked.

"All that remains is to see his eyes," the scythe said. "To be sure."

Scythe Curie touched him on the shoulder, he turned, and their eyes met, but only for the slightest moment. Then he suddenly gasped—

—because Scythe Curie's blade had already been thrust up beneath his rib cage and into his heart. So quick was Scythe Curie that Citra never saw her do it. She never even saw the scythe pull out her blade.

The scythe offered no response to the man's awful surprise; she said nothing to him at all. She just withdrew the blade, and the man fell. He was dead before he hit the pavement. Around them people gasped and hurried away, but not so far away that they couldn't watch the aftermath. Death was unfamiliar to most of them. It needed to exist in its own bubble, as long as they could stay just beyond its outer edge, peering in.

The scythe wiped her blade on a chamois cloth the same pale lavender as her robe, and that's when Citra lost control.

"You gave him no warning!" she blurted. "How could you do that? You don't even know him! You didn't even let him prepare!"

The cloud of rage that billowed forth from Scythe Curie was so powerful it was almost a visible thing, and Citra knew she had made a terrible mistake.

"ON THE GROUND!" yelled the scythe, with such volume it echoed back and forth between the brick buildings of the street.

Citra immediately got to her knees.

"FACE TO THE PAVEMENT! NOW!"

Citra complied, fear overcoming her fury. She splayed herself, prostrate on the ground, her right cheek pressed against the pavement, which was searingly hot from the midday sun. Her view was now of the dead man, just a foot away, whose eyes were empty, and yet staring into Citra's at the same time. How could dead eyes still stare?

"YOU DARE PRESUME TO TELL ME HOW TO ACCOMPLISH MY TASK?"

It seemed the world had frozen around them.

"YOU WILL APOLOGIZE FOR YOUR INSOLENCE, AND BE DISCIPLINED."

"I'm sorry, Scythe Curie." At the mention of Scythe Curie's name, a murmur erupted among the bystanders. She was legendary everywhere.

"CONVINCE ME!"

"I'm truly sorry, Scythe Curie," Citra said louder, screaming it into the face of the dead man. "I will never disrespect you again."

"Get up."

The scythe was no longer raging with earthshaking wrath. Citra rose, furious at the weakness of her own legs, which shook beneath her, and the incontinence of her eyes, which spewed tears she wished would evaporate before Scythe Curie or any of the bystanders could see.

The world-renowned Grande Dame of Death turned to stride away, and Citra followed in her wake, humbled, hobbled, wishing she could take the scythe's blade and stab it into the woman's back—and then furious at herself for wishing such a thing.

They got into the car and pulled away from the curb. Only when they were about a block away did the scythe speak to Citra.

"Now then, it will be your task to identify the man, find his immediate family, and invite them to Falling Water so that I may grant them immunity." She spoke without the slightest hint of the fury of just a few moments ago.

"Wh . . . what?" It was as if the scene on the street had never happened. Citra was caught completely off guard—a bit dizzy, as if all the air had been sucked out of the car.

"I have forty-eight hours to grant them immunity. I'd like them to gather at my home this evening."

"But . . . but back there . . . when you had me on the ground . . ."

"Yes?"

"And you were so angry . . ."

Scythe Curie sighed. "There is an image to uphold, dear," she said. "You defied me in public, so I had no choice but to publicly put you in your place. In the future, you need to hold your opinions until we are alone."

"So you're not angry?"

The scythe considered the question. "I'm annoyed," she said. "But then, I should have warned you what I was about to do. Your response was . . . justified. And so was the consequence I levied."

Even at this end of the emotional roller coaster, Citra had to admit that the scythe was right. There was a certain amount of decorum required of an apprentice. Another scythe might have exacted a punishment far worse.

They circled back, and Scythe Curie let Citra off on a side street just a block from where the gleaning had occurred. She would have an hour to find the family and extend them the invitation.

"And if he lives alone, both our jobs will be easy today," the scythe said.

Citra wondered what about gleaning could possibly be easy.

The man's name was Barton Breen. He had turned the corner many times, had fathered more than twenty children over the years, some of whom were now over a century old themselves. His current household consisted of his most recent wife and his three youngest children. These were the ones who would receive immunity from gleaning for one year.

"What if they don't come?" Citra asked Scythe Curie on the way home.

"They always come," the scythe told her.

And she was right. They arrived a little after eight in the evening, somber and shell-shocked. Scythe Curie had them kneel right at the door to kiss her ring, granting them immunity. Then she and Citra served them dinner, which the scythe had prepared. Comfort food: pot roast, green beans, and garlic mashed potatoes. Clearly the family had no appetite, but they ate out of obligation.

"Tell me about your husband," Scythe Curie asked, her voice gentle and sincere.

The woman was reluctant to say much at first, but soon she couldn't stop telling the tale of her husband's life. Soon the kids joined in with their memories. The man quickly went from an anonymous subject on the street to an individual whose life even Citra now missed, although she had never known him.

And Scythe Curie listened—*truly* listened—as if she were intent on memorizing everything they said. More than once her eyes moistened, reflecting the tears of the family.

And then the scythe did the oddest thing. She produced from her robe the blade that had taken the man's life, and set it down on the table.

"You may take my life, if you like," she told the woman.

The woman just stared at her, not understanding.

"It's only fair," the scythe said. "I've taken away your husband, robbed your children of their father. You must despise me for it."

The woman looked to Citra, as if she might know what to do, but Citra only shrugged, equally surprised by the offer.

"But . . . attacking a scythe is punishable by gleaning."

"Not if you have the scythe's permission. Besides, you've already received immunity. I promise there will be no retribution."

The knife lay on the table between them, and Citra suddenly felt like the pedestrians at the gleaning: frozen just on the other side of some unthinkable event horizon.

Scythe Curie smiled at the woman with genuine warmth. "It's all right. If you strike me down, my apprentice will simply bring me to the nearest revival center, and in a day or two I'll be as good as new."

The woman contemplated the blade, the children contemplated their mother. Finally the woman said, "No, that won't be necessary."

Scythe Curie removed the blade from sight. "Well, in that case, on to dessert."

And the family devoured the chocolate cake with a passion they hadn't shown for the rest of the meal, as if a great pall had been lifted.

After they were gone, Scythe Curie helped Citra with the dishes. "When *you're* a scythe," she told Citra, "I'm sure you won't do things my way. You won't do things the way Scythe Faraday did, either. You'll find your own path. It may not bring you redemption, it might not even bring you peace, but it will keep you from despising yourself."

Then Citra asked a question she had asked before—but this time she suspected she might get an answer.

"Why did you take me on, Your Honor?"

The scythe washed a dish, Citra dried it, and finally Scythe Curie said the oddest thing. "Have you ever heard of a 'sport' called cockfighting?"

Citra shook her head.

"Back in the mortal age, unsavories would take two roosters, put them in a small arena, and watch them battle to the death, wagering on the outcome."

"That was legal?"

"No, but people did it anyway. Life before the Thunderhead was a blend of bizarre atrocities. You weren't told this—but Scythe Goddard had offered to take both you and Rowan on."

"He offered to take both of us?"

"Yes. And I knew it would be only so he could pit the two of you against each other day after day for his own amusement, like a cockfight. So I intervened and offered to take you, in order to spare you both Scythe Goddard's bloody arena."

Citra nodded in understanding. She chose not to point out that they hadn't been spared the arena at all. They were still facing a mortal struggle. Nothing could change that.

She tried to imagine what it might have been like had Scythe Curie not stepped forward. The thought of not being separated from Rowan was tempered by the knowledge of whose hand they'd be under. She didn't even want to imagine how he was faring with Goddard.

As this had turned into an evening of answers, Citra dared to ask the question she had asked so inappropriately on the street, before the man's body had even gone cold.

"Why did you glean that man today without warning? Didn't he deserve at least a moment of understanding before your blade?"

This time Scythe Curie was not offended by the question. "Every scythe has his or her method. That happens to be mine. In the Age of Mortality, death would often come with no warning. It is our task to mimic what we've stolen from nature—and so that is the face of death I've chosen to recreate. My gleanings are always instantaneous and always public, lest people forget what we do, and why we must do it."

"But what happened to the scythe who gleaned the president? The hero who went after corporate corruption that not even the Thunderhead could rout. I thought the Grande Dame of Death would always glean with greater purpose."

A shadow seemed to pass over Scythe Curie's face. A ghost of some sorrow Citra couldn't even guess at.

"You thought wrong."

If you've ever studied mortal age cartoons, you'll remember this one. A coyote was always plotting the demise of a smirking long-necked bird. The coyote never succeeded; instead, his plans always backfired. He would blow up, or get shot, or splat from a ridiculous height.

And it was funny.

Because no matter how deadly his failure, he was always back in the next scene, as if there were a revival center just beyond the edge of the animation cell.

I've seen human foibles that have resulted in temporary maiming or momentary loss of life. People stumble into manholes, are hit by falling objects, trip into the paths of speeding vehicles.

And when it happens, people laugh, because no matter how gruesome the event, that person, just like the coyote, will be back in a day or two, as good as new, and no worse—or wiser—for the wear.

Immortality has turned us all into cartoons.

     —From the gleaning journal of H.S. Curie

Grande Dame of Death sees you as a monster, what a monster you must truly be.

"What a terrible thing to do," said the scythe, but her voice was even, not shocked. "Was she killed?"

"Instantly," Citra admitted. "Of course, she was back in school three days later, but it didn't change what I had done. . . . And the worst thing was, no one knew. People thought she had tripped, and all the other kids were laughing—because you know how funny it is when someone gets deadish by accident—but it wasn't an accident, and no one knew. No one saw me do it. And when she came back, *she* didn't even know."

Citra forced herself to look at the Grande Dame of Death, who now sat in a chair across the room from her, gazing at Citra with those invasive gray eyes.

"You asked me the worst thing I've ever done." Citra said. "Now you know."

Scythe Curie didn't speak right away. She just sat there, letting the moment linger. "Well," Scythe Curie finally said, "we're going to have to do something about that."

Rhonda Flowers was in the middle of a midafternoon snack when the doorbell rang. She didn't think anything of it until a few moments later, when she looked up to see her mother standing at the kitchen threshold with a look of such abject pain on her face, it was clear that something was very wrong.

"They . . . they want to see *you*," her mother announced.

Rhonda slurped the ramen noodles that were dangling from her mouth and got up. "Who's *they*?"

Her mother didn't answer. Instead she threw her arms

19

A Terrible Thing to Do

Citra wasn't sure what possessed her to bring up the question she had been asked at conclave. Perhaps it was the unexpected closeness she felt to Scythe Curie after seeing her feed the grieving family and listen—truly listen—to their stories about the man she had gleaned.

That night, Scythe Curie came into Citra's room with clean sheets. They made her bed together, and just as they finished, Citra said, "In conclave you accused me of lying."

"You were," Scythe Curie said.

"How did you know?"

Scythe Curie didn't offer a smile, but she didn't offer any judgment either. "When you've lived nearly two hundred years, some things are obvious." She tossed Citra a pillow and Citra stuffed it into a pillowcase.

"I didn't push that girl down the stairs," Citra said.

"I suspected as much."

Citra now clutched the pillow. If it were alive, she would have suffocated it. "I didn't push her down the stairs," Citra repeated. "I pushed her in front of a speeding truck."

Citra sat down, turning away from Scythe Curie. She couldn't look the woman in the face, and now she regretted having confessed this dark secret from her childhood. If the around Rhonda, giving her a bone-crushing hug, and melted into sobs. Then over her mother's shoulder, Rhonda saw them. A girl about her age, and a woman in a lavender garment— clearly in the style of a scythe's robe.

"Be brave . . . ," her mother whispered desperately into Rhonda's ear.

But bravery was about as far away as terror. There simply wasn't enough time to summon either fortitude or fear. All Rhonda felt was a sudden tingling in her extremities and a dreamy disconnect, as if she were watching a scene from someone else's life. She left her mother and moved toward the door, where the two figures waited.

"You want to see *me*?"

The scythe, a woman with silky silver hair and a steely gaze, smiled. Rhonda never considered that a scythe might smile. On the rare occasions she'd encountered them, they always seemed so somber.

"I don't, but my apprentice does," the woman said, indicating the girl. But Rhonda couldn't take her eyes off of the scythe.

"Your apprentice is going to glean me?"

"We're not here for gleaning," said the girl.

Only after hearing that did the terror Rhonda should have felt finally blossom. Her eyes filled with tears that she quickly wiped away, as relief followed on terror's tail. "You could have told my mother that." She turned and called to her mother. "It's okay, they're not here to glean." Then she stepped outside, pulling the door closed behind her, knowing if she didn't, her mother would eavesdrop on whatever this was about. She had heard that traveling scythes would show up at people's doors asking for shelter and food for the night. Or sometimes they needed information from people for reasons she could only guess at. But why would they specifically want to speak to her?

"You probably don't remember me," said the girl, "but we used to go to school together years ago—before you moved here."

As Rhonda studied the girl's face, she pulled forth the vaguest memory, and tried to grasp at a name. "Cindy something, right?"

"Citra. Citra Terranova."

"Oh, right."

And then the moment became awkward. As if standing on your porch with a scythe and her apprentice wasn't awkward enough already.

"So . . . what can I do for . . . Your Honors?" She wasn't sure if an apprentice warranted the title of "Your Honor," but it couldn't hurt to err on the side of respect. Now that she had time to let her face and name sink in, Rhonda did remember Citra. As she recalled, they didn't like each other very much.

"Well, here's the thing," said Citra. "Do you remember that day when you fell in front of that truck?"

Rhonda gave an involuntary shift of her shoulders. "Like I could possibly forget it. After I got back from the revival center, everybody called me Rhonda Roadkill for months."

Getting run over by a truck was perhaps the most annoying thing that had ever happened to her. She was deadish for three whole days, and ended up missing every last performance of her dance recital. The other girls said they did fine without her, which just made it worse. The only good thing about it was the food at the revival center on the day she regained consciousness. They had the best homemade ice cream—so good that she once splatted just to get another taste of it. But of course, leave it to her parents to send her to a cheapo revival center with sucky food.

"So you were there when it happened?"

"Well, here's the thing," Citra said for the second time. Then she took a deep breath and said, "It wasn't an accident. I pushed you."

"Ha!" said Rhonda, "I knew it! I knew someone pushed me!" At the time her parents had tried to convince her that it was unintentional. That someone had bumped her. Eventually she came to believe it, but in the back of her mind she always held on to a little bit of doubt. "So it was you!" Rhonda found herself smiling. There was victory in knowing that she hadn't been crazy all these years.

"Anyway, I'm sorry," Citra said. "I'm really, really sorry."

"So why are you telling me now?"

"Well, here's the thing," Citra repeated, like it was a nervous tick. "Being a scythe's apprentice means I have to make amends for my . . . well, for my past bad choices. And so . . . I want to give you the chance to do the same thing to me." She cleared her throat. "I want you to push me in front of a truck."

Rhonda guffawed at the suggestion. She didn't mean to; it just came out. "Really? You want me to throw you in front of a speeding truck?"

"Yes."

"Right now?"

"Yes."

"And your scythe is okay with that?"

The scythe nodded. "I support Citra entirely."

Rhonda considered the proposal. She supposed she could. How many times had there been someone in her life she wanted to dispose of—even just temporarily? Just last year she had come remarkably close to "accidentally" electrocuting her lab partner in science because he was such an ass. But in the end she realized that he'd get a few days vacation, and she'd have to finish the lab alone. This situation was different. It was a free revenge ticket. The question was, how badly did she want revenge?

"Listen, it's tempting and all," said Rhonda, "but I've got homework, and dance class later."

"So . . . you don't want to?"

"It's not that I don't want to, I'm just busy today. Can I throw you under a truck some other time?"

Citra hesitated. "Okay . . ."

"Or better yet, maybe you can just take me out to lunch or something."

"Okay . . ."

"Just next time, please give us some warning so you don't freak out my mother." Then she said good-bye, stepped inside, and closed the door.

"How bizarre . . . ," said Rhonda.

"What was that all about?" her mother asked.

And since she didn't want to get into it, Rhonda said, "Nothing important," which irritated her mother, just as it was intended to.

Then she went back to the kitchen, where she found her ramen had gotten cold. Great.

• • •

Citra felt both relieved and humiliated at once. For years she had held on to this secret crime. Her gripe with Rhonda had been petty, as most childhood resentments are. It was the way Rhonda always spoke of her dancing as if she were the most talented ballerina in the world. Citra was in the same dance class, back in that magical childhood time when little girls nurtured the delusion that they were as graceful as they were cute.

Rhonda had led the pack in disabusing Citra of that delusion through eyeball rolls and exasperated exhales each time Citra took an imperfect step.

The push wasn't premeditated. It was a crime of opportunity, and that one act had cast a shadow over Citra that she hadn't even realized until she faced the girl today.

And Rhonda didn't even care. It was water under a very old bridge. Citra felt stupid about the whole thing now.

"You realize that in the Age of Mortality, you would have been treated much differently." Scythe Curie didn't look at her as she spoke—she never looked away from the road when she was driving. Citra was still getting used to the odd habit. How strange to actually have to see the path of your journey in order to make it.

"If it was the Age of Mortality, I wouldn't have done it," Citra told her with confidence, "because I'd know she wouldn't be back. Pushing her then would have been more like gleaning."

"They had a word for it. 'Murder.'"

Citra chuckled at the archaic word. "That's funny. Like a bunch of crows."

"I'm sure it wasn't funny at the time." She did a quick maneuver to avoid a squirrel on the winding road. Then Scythe Curie took a rare moment to glance over at Citra, when the road ahead straightened. "So now the penance you've given your-self is to be a scythe, forever doomed to take lives as punishment for that one childhood act."

"I didn't give it to myself."

"Didn't you?"

Citra opened her mouth to answer, but then stopped. Because what if Scythe Curie was right? What if, deep down, Citra had accepted the apprenticeship with Scythe Faraday to punish herself for the crime only she cared about. If so, it was an unusually harsh judgment. Had she been caught, or had she confessed, her punishment would have been a short suspension from school, at most, plus a fine for her parents, and a stern reprimand. It would even have had an upside: Her schoolmates would have been afraid to cross her.

"The difference between you and most other people, Citra, is that another person would not have cared once that girl was revived. They would have simply forgotten about it. Scythe Faraday saw something in you when he chose you—perhaps the weight of your conscience." And then she added, "It was that same weight that let me know you were lying in conclave."

"I'm actually surprised the Thunderhead didn't see me push her," Citra said offhandedly. Then the scythe said something that began a chain reaction in Citra's mind that changed everything.

"I'm sure it did," she said. "The Thunderhead sees just about everything, what with cameras everywhere. But it also decides what infractions are worth the effort to address and which ones are not."

The Thunderhead sees just about everything.

It had a record of practically every human interaction

since the moment it became aware—but unlike in mortal days, that knowledge was never abused. Before the Thunderhead achieved consciousness, when it was merely known as "the cloud," criminals—and even public agencies—would find ways into people's private doings, against the law, and exploit that information. Every schoolchild knew of the information abuses that nearly brought down civilization before the Thunderhead condensed into power. Since that time there had not been a single breach of personal information. People waited for it. People prophesized doom at the hands of a soulless machine. But apparently the machine had a purer soul than any human.

It watched the world from millions of eyes, listened from millions of ears. It either acted, or chose not to act on, the countless things it perceived.

Which meant that somewhere in its memory lurked a record of Scythe Faraday's movements on the day his life ended.

Citra knew it was probably a pointless endeavor to track those movements, but what if Faraday's demise was not an act of self-gleaning at all? What if he was pushed, just as Citra had pushed Rhonda all those years ago? But this wouldn't have been a childish crime of the moment. It would have been cruelly premeditated. What if Faraday's death was, to use the word Scythe Curie had taught her, murder?

As a young man, I marveled at the stupidity and hypocrisy of the mortal age. In those days, the purposeful act of ending human life was considered the most heinous of crimes. How ridiculous! I know how hard it is to imagine that what is now humanity's highest calling was once considered a crime. How small-minded and hypocritical mortal man was, for even as they despised the enders of life, they loved nature—which, in those days, took every human life ever conceived. Nature deemed that to be born was an automatic sentence to death, and then brought about that death with vicious consistency.

We changed that.

We are now a force greater than nature.

For this reason, scythes must be as loved as a glorious mountain vista, as revered as a redwood forest, and as respected as an approaching storm.

—From the gleaning journal of H.S. Goddard

20

Guest of Honor

I am going to die.

Rowan had begun repeating this to himself like a mantra, hoping it would make it easier to digest. Yet he seemed no closer to accepting it. Even under different scythes, the edict pronounced at conclave still stood. He would kill Citra at the end of their apprenticeship, or she would kill him. It was too juicy a bit of drama for the scythes to cancel just because they were no longer apprentices of Scythe Faraday. Rowan knew he could not kill Citra. And the only way to avoid the possibility would be to throw the competition; to perform so poorly between now and the final conclave that they had no choice but to grant scythehood to Citra. Then, her first honor-bound duty would be to glean Rowan. He trusted she would make it quick, and that she would be merciful. The trick would be to not make his failure obvious. He must appear to be doing his best. No one must know his true plan. He was up to the task.

I am going to die.

Before that fateful day in the principal's office with Kohl Whitlock, Rowan hadn't even known anyone who died. Gleaning had always been at least three degrees removed. The relative of someone who knew someone he knew. But over the past four months, he'd witnessed dozens upon dozens of gleanings firsthand.

I am going to die.

Eight more months. He would see his seventeenth birthday, but not much more. Even though it would be his choice, the thought of being just another statistic for the scythes' records infuriated him. His life had been a whole lot of nothing. Lettuce-kid. He had thought the label was funny—a badge of honor—but now it was an indictment. His was a life without substance, and now it would end. He should never have accepted Scythe Faraday's invitation to be a scythe's apprentice. He should have just gone on with his unremarkable life—because then, maybe, just maybe, he might have had the chance to do something remarkable with it in time.

"You've barely said a word since you got into the car."

"I'll talk when I have something to say."

He rode with Scythe Volta in an off-grid Rolls Royce perfectly maintained since the Age of Mortality, the scythe's yellow robe in stark contrast to the dark earth tones of the vehicle's interior. Volta didn't do the driving; there was a chauffeur. They wove through a neighborhood where the homes became increasingly larger and the grounds more vast, until the residences disappeared entirely behind gates and ivy-covered walls.

Volta, one of Goddard's disciples, had golden citrine gems embedded in his yellow robe. He was clearly a junior scythe, just a few years out of apprenticeship, in his early twenties perhaps—still an age where numbering one's years felt important. His features and skin tone had an Afric leaning, which made the yellow of his garment seem even brighter.

"So is there a reason why you chose your robes to be the color of piss?"

Volta laughed. "I think you'll fit in just fine. Scythe Goddard likes those close to him to be as sharp as his blades."

"Why do you follow him?"

The honest question seemed to bother him more than the urinary barb. Volta became the tiniest bit defensive. "Scythe Goddard is a visionary. He sees our future. I'm much more interested in being a part of the Scythedom's future than its past."

Rowan turned back to the window. The day was bright but the tinted windows dimmed it, as if they were in the midst of a partial eclipse. "You glean people by the hundreds. Is that the future you mean?"

"We have the same quota as all other scythes," was all Volta said on the matter.

Rowan turned back to look at Volta, who now seemed to have trouble keeping eye contact. "Who did you train under?" Rowan asked.

"Scythe Nehru."

Rowan seemed to recall Scythe Faraday chatting with Scythe Nehru during conclave. They appeared to be on good terms.

"How does he feel about you hanging around with Goddard?"

"To you, he's *Honorable Scythe* Goddard," Volta said, a bit indignant. "And I couldn't care less how Scythe Nehru feels. Old-guard scythes have obsolete ideas. They're too set in their ways to see the wisdom of the Change."

He spoke of "the Change" as if it were a tangible thing. A thing that, by its very weight, could make a person strong simply by pushing it.

They stopped at a pair of wrought iron gates, which slowly swung open to admit them. "Here we are," said Volta.

A quarter-mile driveway ended at a palatial estate. A servant greeted them and led them into the mansion.

Rowan was immediately assaulted by loud dance music. There were people everywhere, reveling as if it were New Year's Eve. The whole estate seemed to undulate in the throes of the relentless beat. People laughing, drinking, and laughing some more. Some of the guests were scythes—and not just Goddard's obvious disciples, other scythes as well. There were also some minor celebrities. The rest seemed to be beautiful people who were probably professional party guests. His friend Tyger aspired to be one of those. A lot of kids said that, but Tyger really meant it.

The servant led them out back to a huge pool that seemed more suited to a resort than a home. There were waterfalls and a swim-up bar, and more beautiful people happily bobbing. Scythe Goddard was in a cabana beyond the deep end, its front open to the festivities before him. He was attended by more than one fawning bimbotech. He wore his signature royal blue robe, but as Rowan got closer, he could see it was a sheerer variation than the one he had worn at conclave. His leisure robe. Rowan wondered if the man had a diamond-studded bathing suit in his wardrobe as well.

"Rowan Damisch!" said Scythe Goddard as they approached. He told a servant passing with a tray of drinks to give Rowan a glass of champagne. When Rowan didn't take it, Scythe Volta grabbed one and put it in Rowan's hand before disappearing into the throng, leaving Rowan to fend for himself.

"Please—enjoy," said Goddard. "I serve only Dom Pérignon."

Rowan took a sip, wondering if an underage scythe's apprentice could get marked down for drinking. Then he remembered that such rules didn't apply to him anymore. So he took another sip.

"I arranged this little bacchanal in your honor," the scythe said, gesturing to the party around them.

"What do you mean, in my honor?"

"Exactly that. This is *your* party. Do you like it?"

The surreal display of excess was even more intoxicating than the champagne, but did he like it? Mostly he just felt weird, and weirder still to know that he was the guest of honor.

"I don't know. I've never had a party before," Rowan told him. It was true—his parents had seen so many birthdays by the time Rowan was born, they had stopped celebrating them. He was lucky if they even remembered to get him a gift.

"Well then," said Scythe Goddard, "let this be the first of many."

Rowan had to remind himself that this man with the perfect smile, secreting charisma instead of sweat, was the man who had manipulated him and Citra into mortal competition. But it was hard not to be dazzled by his style. And as distasteful as all this spectacle was, it still made his adrenaline flow.

The scythe patted the seat beside him for Rowan to sit, and Rowan took his place at the scythe's right hand.

"Doesn't the eighth commandment say that a scythe can't own anything but his robe, ring, and journal?"

"Correct," said Scythe Goddard brightly. "And I own none of this. The food is donated by generous benefactors, the guests are here by choice, and this fine estate has been graciously loaned to me for as long as I choose to grace its halls."

Upon the mention of the estate, a man cleaning the pool looked up at them for a moment before returning to his labors.

"You should reread the commandments," Scythe Goddard said. "You'll find that nothing in them demands that scythes shun the creature comforts that make life worth living. That bleak interpretation by old-guard scythes is a relic from another time."

Rowan did not offer any further opinion on the subject. It was Scythe Faraday's humble and serious "old-guard" nature that had made an impression on Rowan. Had he been approached by Scythe Goddard with enticements of rock star glamour in exchange for the taking of lives, he would have declined. But Faraday was dead, and Rowan was here, looking out on strangers that were here for his benefit.

"If it's my party, shouldn't it have people I know?"

"A scythe is a friend to the world. Open your arms and embrace it." It seemed Scythe Goddard had an answer for everything. "Your life is about to change, Rowan Damisch," he said, waving his arm to indicate the pool and the partiers and the servants and the elaborate spread of food just past the shallow end that kept being replenished. "In fact, it already has."

Among the party guests was a girl who seemed markedly out of place. She was young—nine or ten at the most, and completely oblivious to the party around her as she frolicked in the shallow end of the pool.

"It looks like one of your guests brought their kid to the party," Rowan commented.

"That," said Goddard, "is Esme, and you would be wise to treat her well. She is the most important person you will meet today."

"How so?"

"That chubby little girl is the key to the future. So you'd better hope she likes you."

Rowan would have continued picking at Goddard's enigmatic responses, but his attention was grabbed by a beautiful party girl approaching in a bikini that seemed almost painted on. Rowan realized a moment too late that he was staring. She grinned and he blushed, looking away.

"Ariadne, would you be so kind as to give my apprentice a massage?"

"Yes, Your Honor," said the girl.

"Uh . . . maybe later," Rowan said.

"Nonsense," said the scythe. "You need to loosen up, and Ariadne has magical hands skilled in Swedish technique. Your body will thank you."

She took Rowan by the hand, and that killed any resistance. He rose and let himself be led away.

"If our young man is pleased by your efforts," Scythe Goddard called after them, "I will allow you to kiss my ring."

As Ariadne led him to the massage tent, Rowan thought, *In eight months I am going to die.* So perhaps he could allow himself a little indulgence on the way.

I am disturbed by those who revere us far more than those who disdain us. Too many put us on a pedestal. Too many long to be one of us—and knowing that they can never be makes their longing even greater, for all scythes are apprenticed in their youth.

It is either naivete in thinking that we are somehow of a higher order of being, or it is the product of a depraved heart—for who but the depraved would revel in the taking of life?

For a time years ago, there were groups who would emulate and imitate us. They would fashion robes like those of scythes. They would wear rings that looked similar to ours. For many it was just costume play, but some would actually pretend to be scythes, fooling others, granting false immunity. Everything short of gleaning.

There are laws against impersonating workers in any profession, but no law preventing anyone from impersonating a scythe. Since the Thunderhead has no jurisdiction over the Scythedom, it cannot pass any laws concerning us. It was an unforeseen glitch in the separation of Scythe and State.

However, it wasn't a glitch for long. In the Year of the Stingray, at the Sixty-Third World Conclave, it was decided that all such imposters shall be gleaned on sight, publicly, and most violently. While one might expect such an edict to produce a bloodbath, very few gleanings ever took place. Once word got out, the posers shed their false robes and vanished into the woodwork of the world. To this day the edict remains, but rarely needs to be invoked, because few are foolish enough to impersonate a scythe.

And yet now and again, I hear at conclave the rare tale of a scythe coming face to face with an imposter and having to glean them. Usually the conversation is about the inconvenience of it. How the scythe must then track down the imposter's family to grant immunity and such.

But I wonder more about the imposter. What was it they hoped to achieve? Was it the lure of the forbidden? Were they enticed by the danger of being caught? Or did they simply wish to leave this life so badly that they chose one of the few direct paths to annihilation?

—From the gleaning journal of H.S. Curie

21

Branded

The party continued for another day. A festival of excess on all levels. Rowan joined in the revelry, but it was more out of obligation than anything. He was the center of attention, the celebrity of the moment. In the pool beautiful people bobbed toward him, at the buffet guests cleared the way so he could always be at the front of the line. It was awkward, yet heady. He couldn't deny that there was a part of him that enjoyed the surreal nature of celebratory attention. The lettuce elevated to a place of honor.

It was only when the other scythes in attendance shook his hand and wished him luck in his mortal competition against Citra that he sobered and remembered what was at stake.

He borrowed brief snippets of sleep in the cabana, always awakened by music, or raucous laughter, or fireworks. Then, late in the afternoon of the second day, when Scythe Goddard had enough, he merely whispered so and word spread quickly. In less than an hour the guests had left, and servants began to clean the detritus of revelry from the eerily silent grounds. Now only the other residents of the estate remained: Scythe Goddard, his three junior scythes, the servants, and the girl, Esme, who peered out of her bedroom window at Rowan like a wraith, as he sat in Goddard's cabana, awaiting whatever came next.

Scythe Volta approached, his yellow robes rippling in the breeze. "What are you still doing out here?" he asked.

"I have nowhere else to be," Rowan told him.

"Come with me," Volta said. "It's time to begin your training."

There was a wine cellar in the basement of the main house. Hundreds, perhaps thousands of bottles of wine rested in brick alcoves. A bare minimum of bulbs lit the space, casting long shadows and making the alcoves seem like portals to undisclosed hells.

Scythe Volta led Rowan to the central chamber of the cellar, where Goddard and the other scythes waited. Scythe Rand produced a device from her green robe. It looked like a cross between a gun and a flashlight.

"Do you know what this is?" she asked.

"It's a tweaker," Rowan told her. He'd had the occasion several years ago to have his nanites tweaked when his teachers decided his moodiness had crossed the line into depression. That was five or six years ago. The tweaking was painless, and the effect subtle. He hadn't noticed much of a change, but everyone agreed that he had begun to smile more.

"Arms out, legs spread," said Scythe Rand. Rowan did as he was told and Scythe Rand passed the tweaker all over his body like some sort of magic wand. Rowan felt a mild tingling in his extremities that quickly faded. She stepped back, and Scythe Goddard approached.

"Have you ever heard the expression 'being made'?" asked Scythe Goddard. "Or being 'jumped in'?"

Rowan shook his head, noticing that the other scythes had

positioned themselves around him, leaving Rowan at the center of their circle.

"Well, you are about to find out what it means."

The other scythes then removed their cumbersome outer robes. Now down to their tunics and knickers, they took aggressive stances. There was a look of determination on each of their faces, and maybe a little bit of joyous anticipation. Rowan knew what was about to happen an instant before it began.

Scythe Chomsky, the largest of them, stepped forward and, without warning, swung his fist, connecting with Rowan's cheek so hard, he spun around, lost his footing, and fell to the dusty floor.

Rowan felt the shock of the punch, the jagged bolt of pain, and waited for the telltale warmth of his nanites releasing painkilling opiates into his bloodstream. But relief didn't come. Instead the pain swelled.

It was horrible.

Overwhelming.

Rowan had never experienced such pain—he never knew such pain could even exist.

"What did you do?" he wailed. *"What did you do to me?"*

"We turned off your nanites," Scythe Volta said calmly, "so you could experience what our ancestors once did."

"There's a very old expression," Scythe Goddard told him. "'To be painless is to be gainless.'" He gripped Rowan warmly on the shoulder. "And I wish you to gain much."

Then he stood back, signaled the others to advance, and they began to beat Rowan to a pulp.

• • •

Recovery without the aid of healing nanites was a slow, miserable process that seemed to get worse before it got better. The first day Rowan longed to die. The second day he thought he actually might. His head pounded, his thoughts swam. He slipped in and out of consciousness with little warning. It was hard to breathe, and he knew he had several broken ribs. And although Scythe Chomsky had painfully popped his dislocated shoulder back into place at the end of his beating, it still ached with each heartbeat.

Scythe Volta visited him several times a day. He sat with Rowan, spoon-feeding him soup, and blotting where it spilled from his split, swollen lips. There seemed to be a halo around him, but Rowan knew it was just optical damage that caused the effect. He wouldn't be surprised if he had detached retinas.

"It burns," he told Volta as the salty soup spilled over his lips.

"It does for now," Volta told him with genuine compassion. "But it will pass, and you'll be better for it."

"How could I be better for any of this?" he asked, horrified at how distorted and liquid his words sounded, as if he were speaking through the blowhole of a whale.

Volta fed him another spoonful of soup. "Six months from now, you tell me if I was right."

He thanked Volta for taking the time to visit him when no one else did.

"You can call me Alessandro," Volta said.

"Is that your real name?" Rowan asked.

"No, idiot, it's Volta's first name."

Rowan supposed that's as close as anyone got to knowing anyone else in the Scythedom.

"Thank you, Alessandro."

. . .

On the evening of the second day, the girl—the one who Goddard said was so important—came into his room in between deliriums. What was her name again? Amy? Emmy? Oh yes—Esme.

"I hate that they did this to you," she said with tears in her eyes. "But you'll get better."

Of course he'd get better. He didn't have any choice in the matter. In mortal days, one died or recovered. Now there was only one option.

"Why are you here?"

"To see how you were getting on," she said.

"No . . . I mean here, in this place?"

She hesitated before she spoke. Then she looked away. "Scythe Goddard and his friends came to a mall near where I lived. They gleaned everyone in the food court except for me. Then he told me to come with him. So I did."

It didn't explain anything, but it was the only explanation she offered—perhaps the only one she knew. From what Rowan could see, this girl served no discernible function at the estate. Yet Goddard gave orders that anyone who ran afoul of her would be severely disciplined. She was not to be bothered in any way, and was allowed free run of the estate. She was the biggest mystery he'd encountered yet in Scythe Goddard's world.

"I think you'll be a better scythe than the others," she told him, but gave no explanation as to why she thought so. Perhaps it was a gut feeling, but she couldn't be more wrong.

"I won't be a scythe," he told her. She was the first person he confessed it to.

"You will if you want to," she said. "And I think you'll want to."

Then she left him to ponder the pain and the possibility.

Scythe Goddard didn't show his face in Rowan's room until day three.

"How are you feeling?" he asked. Rowan wanted to spit at him, but knew it would hurt too much, and might even bring about a second beating.

"How do you think I'm feeling?" Rowan answered.

He sat on the edge of the bed and studied Rowan's face. "Come see yourself." Then he helped Rowan out of the bed, and Rowan hobbled to an ornate wardrobe on which was a full-length mirror.

Rowan barely recognized himself. His face was so swollen it was pumpkin-like. Purple bruises all over his face and body were mottling to all shades of the spectrum.

"Here is where your life begins," Goddard told him. "What you see is the boy dying. The man will emerge."

"That's such a load of crap." Rowan said, not even caring what response it might evoke.

Goddard merely raised an eyebrow "Perhaps . . . but you can't deny this is a turning point in your life, and every turning point must be marked by an event—one that burns itself into you as indelibly as a brand."

So now he was branded. Yet he suspected this was just the beginning of a much larger trial by fire.

"The world longs to be like us," Goddard told Rowan. "Taking and doing what we choose, with neither consequence nor remorse. They would steal our robes and wear them if they could. You have been given an opportunity to become greater than royalty, so at the very least it requires this rite of passage that I have provided for you."

Goddard stood there, studying Rowan a few moments more. Then he pulled out the tweaker from his robes. "Arms up, legs spread."

Rowan took as deep a breath as he could, and did as he was told. Goddard wanded him. Rowan felt tingling in his extremities, but when it was done, he didn't feel the warmth of opiates or the deadening of his pain.

"It still hurts," Rowan told him.

"Of course it does. I didn't activate your painkillers, just your healing nanites. You'll be good as new by morning, and ready to begin your training. But from this moment on, you'll feel every measure of your body's pain."

"Why?" Rowan dared to ask. "What person in their right mind would want to feel that kind of pain?"

"Rightmindedness is overrated," Goddard said. "I'd rather have a mind that's clear than one that's 'right.'"

In the business of death, we scythes have no competition. Unless, of course, you consider fire. Fire kills just as swiftly and completely as a scythe's blade. It's frightening, but also somehow comforting to know that there's one thing the Thunderhead can't fix. One type of damage that revival centers are powerless to undo. Once one's goose is cooked, it is truly and permanently cooked.

Death by fire is the only natural death left. It almost never happens, though. The Thunderhead monitors heat on every inch of the planet, and the fighting of fires often begins before one can even smell smoke. There are safety systems in every home and every office building, with multiple levels of redundancy, just in case. The more extreme tone cults try to burn their deadish, to make it permanent, but ambudrones usually get to them first.

Isn't it good to know that we are all safe from the threat of the inferno? Except, of course, when we're not.

—From the gleaning journal of H.S. Curie

22

Sign of the Bident

Citra's days were filled with training and gleaning.

Each day Citra would go out with Scythe Curie to towns that were selected completely at random. She would watch as the scythe prowled the streets and malls and parks, becoming like a lioness in search of vulnerable prey. Citra learned to see the signs of the "stagnant," as Scythe Curie called them—although Citra was not as convinced as she about their readiness to be gleaned. Citra wondered how many of her own days had been filled with world-weariness before becoming an apprentice to death. If Scythe Curie had come across Citra on one of those days, would the woman have gleaned her?

They passed an elementary school one day as it was letting out, and Citra had a sinking feeling that she would glean one of the students.

"I never glean children," Scythe Curie told her. "I've never found a child who seemed stagnant, but even if I did, I wouldn't do it. I've been admonished in conclave about it, but they've never taken disciplinary action against me."

Scythe Faraday had no such rule. He had been strictly about statistics from the Age of Mortality. Fewer preadolescents died in those days, but they did die on occasion. In their time together, Citra had known him to only do one such gleaning. He did not invite Rowan or her, and at dinner that night he broke into uncontrollable sobbing and had to excuse himself. If Citra was ordained, she vowed to follow a policy like Scythe Curie, even if it got her in trouble with the selection committee.

Almost every night, she and the scythe would prepare dinner for mourning family members. Most would leave with their spirits lifted. Some would remain inconsolable, resentful, hateful, but they were in the minority. Such was life and death for Citra in the days before the Harvest Conclave. She couldn't help but think of Rowan and wonder how he was faring. She longed to see him, but she dreaded it at the same time, because she knew in a few short months she'd be seeing him for the last time, one way or another.

And she held on to the narrow hope that if she could prove Scythe Faraday was taken out by a fellow scythe, perhaps that could be a monkey wrench hurled into the relentless gearworks of the Scythedom. A monkey wrench that would free Citra from having to glean or be gleaned by Rowan.

Most of the bereaved that Citra had to notify were the same: husbands, wives, children, parents. At first she had resented that Scythe Curie made her the front line for these heartbroken people, but soon she came to understand why. It wasn't so that Scythe Curie could avoid it, but so that Citra could experience it and learn how to show compassion in the face of tragedy. It was emotionally exhausting, but rewarding. It was preparing her to be a scythe.

Only one time did her post-gleaning experience differ. The first part of her job was tracking down the immediate family of the gleaned. There was one woman who seemed to have no immediate family; just one estranged brother. It was odd in this time when extended families were more often than not a convoluted web that spanned six living generations or more. Yet this poor woman had only a brother. Citra mapped out the address, went there, but wasn't paying all that much attention. She didn't know where she was until she was right in front of the place.

It wasn't a home—not in the traditional sense—it was a monastery. A walled adobe compound styled after the historical missions. But unlike those ancient structures, the symbol at the apex of the central steeple was not a cross, but a two-pronged tuning fork. The bident. It was a sign of the tone cults.

This was a Tonist monastery.

Citra shivered in the way anyone shivers at the prospect of something vaguely alien and darkly mystic.

"Stay away from those lunatics," her father once told her. "People get sucked in and are never seen again." Which was a ridiculous thing to say. No one truly disappears in this day and age. The Thunderhead knows exactly where everyone is at all times. Of course, it doesn't have to tell.

Under other circumstances, Citra might have heeded her father's advice. But she was making a bereavement call, and that trumped any trepidation.

She entered the compound through a gated arch. The gate wasn't locked. She found herself in a garden full of white, rich-smelling flowers. Gardenias. Tone cults were all about aroma and sounds. They gave little value to the sense of sight. In fact, the more extreme Tonist groups actually blinded themselves, and the Thunderhead reluctantly allowed it, preventing their healing nanites from restoring sight. It was awful, and yet was one of the few expressions of religious freedom left in a world that had laid its various gods to rest.

Citra followed a stone path through the garden to the church on which stood the sign of the fork, and she pushed her way through the heavy oak doors into a chapel lined with pews. It was dim, even though there were stained glass windows on either side. They were not from the mortal age, but were Tonist in nature. They depicted various strange scenes: a shirtless man carrying a huge tuning fork on his burdened back; a stone fracturing and shooting forth bolts of lightning; crowds running from a nasty vermiform creature in the form of a double helix that spiraled out of the ground.

She didn't like the images and didn't know what these people believed, only that it was laughable. Ludicrous. Everyone knew that this so-called religion was just a hodgepodge of mortal age faiths slapped together into a troubling mosaic. Yet somehow there were people who found that strange ideological mosaic to be enticing.

A priest, or monk, or whatever you call a cult clergyman, was at the altar, chanting in monotone and dousing lit candles one by one.

"Excuse me," Citra said. Her voice was much louder than she meant it to be. A trick of the chapel's acoustics.

The man wasn't startled by her. He put out one more candle, then set down his silver snuffer and hobbled toward her with a pronounced limp. She wondered if it was affected, or if his religious freedom allowed him to retain whatever scarring caused the limp. By the wrinkles on his face she could tell that he was long overdue to turn a corner.

"I am Curate Beauregard," he said. "Have you come for atonement?"

"No," she told him, showing her armband that bore the seal of scythes. "I need to speak to Robert Ferguson."

"Brother Ferguson is in afternoon repose. I shouldn't disturb him."

"It's important," she told him.

The curate sighed. "Very well. That which comes can't be avoided." Then he hobbled off, leaving Citra alone.

She looked around, taking in the strange surroundings. The altar in the front contained a granite basin filled with water—but the water was cloudy and foul-smelling. Just behind that was the focal point of the entire church: a steel two-pronged fork similar to the one on the roof outside. This bident was six feet tall and protruded from an obsidian base. Beside it, on its own little platform, sat a rubber mallet resting on a black velvet pillow. But it was the bident that held her attention. The huge tuning fork was cylindrical, silvery smooth, and cold to the touch.

"You want to strike it, don't you? Go on—it's not forbidden."

Citra jumped and silently chided herself for being caught off guard.

"I am Brother Ferguson," said the man as he approached. "You wanted to see me?"

"I'm the apprentice of Honorable Scythe Marie Curie," Citra told him.

"I've heard of her."

"I'm here on a bereavement mission."

"Go on."

"I'm afraid that your sister, Marissa Ferguson, was gleaned by

Scythe Curie today at one fifteen p.m. I'm very sorry for your loss."

The man didn't seem upset or shocked, merely resigned. "Is that all?"

"Is that all? Didn't you hear me? I just told you that your sister was gleaned today."

The man sighed. "That which comes can't be avoided."

If she didn't already dislike the Tonists, she certainly did now. "Is that it?" she asked. "Is that your people's 'holy' line?"

"It's not a line; it's just a simple truth we live by."

"Yeah, whatever you say. You'll need to make arrangements for your sister's body—because that's coming and can't be avoided either."

"But if I don't step forward, won't the Thunderhead provide a funeral?"

"Don't you care at all?"

The man took a moment before answering. "Death by scythe is not a natural death. We Tonists do not acknowledge it."

Citra cleared her throat, biting back the verbal reaming she wanted to give him, and did her best to remain professional. "There's one more thing. Although you didn't live with her, you are her only documented relative. That entitles you to a year of immunity from gleaning."

"I don't want immunity," he said.

"Why am I not surprised." This was the first time she had ever encountered anyone who refused immunity. Even the most downhearted would kiss the ring.

"You've done your job. You may go now," Brother Ferguson said.

There was only so long Citra could restrain her frustration.

She couldn't yell at the man. She couldn't use her Bokator moves to kick him in the neck or take him down with an elbow slam. So she did the only thing she could do. She picked up the mallet and put all of her anger into a single, powerful strike at the tuning fork.

The fork resounded so powerfully, she could feel it in her teeth and her bones. It rang not like a bell, which was a hollow sound. This tone was full and dense. It shocked the anger right out of her. Diffused it. It made her muscles loosen, her jaw unclench. It echoed in her brain, her gut, and her spine. The tone rang much longer than such a thing should, then slowly began to fade. She had never experienced anything that was quite so jarring and soothing at the same time. All she could say was, "What was that?"

"G-sharp," said Brother Ferguson. "Although there's a standing argument among the brethren that it's actually A-flat."

The fork was still ringing faintly. Citra could see it vibrating, making its edge look blurry. She touched it, and the moment she did it fell silent.

"You have questions," said Brother Ferguson. "I'll answer what I can."

Citra wanted to deny that she had any questions whatsoever, but suddenly she found that she did.

"What do you people believe?"

"We believe many things."

"Tell me one."

"We believe that flames were not meant to burn forever."

Citra looked to the candles by the altar. "Is that why the curate was dousing candles?"

"Part of our ritual, yes."

"So you worship darkness."

"No," he said. "That's a common misconception. People use that to vilify us. What we worship are the wavelengths and vibrations that are beyond the limits of human sight. We believe in the Great Vibration, and that it will free us from being stagnant."

Stagnant.

It was the word Scythe Curie used to describe the people she chose to glean. Brother Ferguson smiled. "Indeed, something resonates in you now, doesn't it?"

She looked away, not wanting to meet his intrusive gaze, and found her eyes settling on the stone basin. She pointed to it. "What's with the dirty water?"

"That's primordial ooze! It's brimming with microbes! Back in the Age of Mortality, this single basin could have wiped out entire populations. It was called 'disease.'"

"I know what it was called."

He dipped his finger in the slimy water and swirled it around. "Smallpox, polio, Ebola, anthrax—they're all in there, but it's harmless to us now. We couldn't get sick if we wanted to." He raised his finger from the foul sludge and licked it off. "I could drink down the whole bowl and it wouldn't even give me indigestion. Alas, we can no longer turn water into worm."

Citra left without another word, and without turning back . . . but for the rest of the day she couldn't get the stench of that foul-smelling water out of her nostrils.

The business of the Thunderhead is no business of mine. The Thunderhead's purpose is to sustain humanity. Mine is to mold it. The Thunderhead is the root, and I am the shears, pruning the limbs into fine form, keeping the tree vital. We are both necessary. And we are mutually exclusive.

I do not miss my so-called relationship with the Thunderhead—nor do the junior scythes I've come to see as disciples. The absence of the Thunderhead's uninvited intrusions into our lives is a blessing, for it allows us to live without a safety net. Without the crutch of a higher power. I am the highest power I know, and I like it that way.

And as for my gleaning methods, which, now and then, have been brought under scrutiny, I say merely this: Is it not the job of the gardener to shape the tree as much as possible? And shouldn't branches that begin to reach unreasonably high be the first to be pruned?

—From the gleaning journal of H.S. Goddard

23

The Virtual Rabbit Hole

Just down the hall from Citra's room was a study. Like every other room in the residence, it had windows on multiple sides, and like everything else in Scythe Curie's life, was kept in perfect order. There was a computer interface there, which Citra used for her studies because unlike Faraday, Scythe Curie did not shun the digital when it came to learning. As a scythe's apprentice, Citra had access to databases and information that most people didn't. The "backbrain" it was called—all the raw data within the Thunderhead's memory that was not organized for human consumption.

Before her apprenticeship, when she did a standard search for things, the Thunderhead would invariably intrude, saying something like, *I see you are searching for a gift. May I ask for whom? Perhaps I can help you find something appropriate.* Sometimes she would let the Thunderhead help her, other times she enjoyed searching alone. But since becoming a scythe's apprentice, the Thunderhead had gone disturbingly mute, as if it were nothing more than its data.

"You'll have to get used to that," Scythe Faraday had told her early on. "Scythes cannot speak to the Thunderhead, and it will not speak to us. But in time you'll come to appreciate the silence and self-reliance that comes from its absence."

Now more than ever she could have used the Thunderhead's
AI guidance as she browsed through its data files, because the
worldwide public camera system seemed designed to thwart her
efforts. Her attempts to track Scythe Faraday's movements on the
day he died was proving harder than she thought. Video records
in the backbrain were not organized by camera, or even by location. It seemed the Thunderhead linked them by concept. A
moment of identical traffic patterns in completely different parts
of the world were linked. Footage featuring people with similar strides were linked. One strand of associations led to images
of increasingly spectacular sunsets, all caught by streetcams. The
Thunderhead's digital memory, Citra came to realize, was struc-
tured like a biological brain. Every moment of every video record
was connected to a hundred others by different criteria—which
meant that every connection Citra followed led her down a rabbit
hole of virtual neurons. It was like trying to read someone's mind
by dissecting their cerebral cortex. It was maddening.

The Scythedom, she knew, had created its own algorithms
for searching the unsearchable contents of the backbrain—but
Citra couldn't ask Scythe Curie without making her suspicious.
The woman had already proven that she could see through any
lie Citra put forth, so best not to be in a position where Citra
would have to lie.

The search began as a project, quickly evolved into a challenge, and now was an obsession. Citra would secretly spend an
hour or two each day trying to find footage of Scythe Faraday's
final movements, but to no avail.

She wondered if, even in its silence, the Thunderhead was
watching what she did. *My, oh my, you've been picking through*

my brain, it would say if it were allowed, with a virtual wink. *Naughty, naughty.*

Then, after many weeks, Citra had an epiphany. If everything uploaded to the Thunderhead was stored in the backbrain, then not just public records were there, but personal as well. She couldn't access other people's private records, but anything *she* uploaded would be available to her. Which meant she could seed the search with data of her own. . . .

"There is no actual law that says I can't visit my family while I'm an apprentice."

Citra brought it up in the middle of dinner one night, with neither warning nor context of conversation. It was her intent to blindside Scythe Curie with it. She could tell it worked because of the length of time it took Scythe Curie to respond. She took two whole spoonfuls of soup before saying a thing.

"It's our standard practice—and a wise one, if you ask me."

"It's cruel."

"Didn't you already attend a family wedding?"

Citra wondered how Scythe Curie knew that, but wasn't about to let herself be derailed. "In a few months I might die. I think I should have a right to see my family a few times before then."

Scythe Curie took two more spoonfuls of soup before saying, "I'll consider it."

In the end, she agreed, as Citra knew she would; after all, Scythe Curie was a fair woman. And Citra had not lied—she did want to see her family—so the scythe could not read deceit in Citra's face because there was none. But, of course, seeing her family wasn't Citra's only reason for going home.

. . .

Everything on Citra's street looked the same as she and Scythe Curie strode down it, yet everything was different. A faint sense of longing tugged at her, but she couldn't be sure what she longed for. All she knew was that walking down her street suddenly felt like she was walking in some foreign land where the people spoke a language she didn't know. They rode the elevator up to Citra's apartment with a pudgy woman with a pudgier pug, who was positively terrified. The woman, not the dog. The dog couldn't care less. Mrs. Yeltner—that was her name. Before Citra left home, Mrs. Yeltner had reset her lipid point to svelte. But apparently the procedure was struggling against a gluttonous appetite, because she was bulging in all the wrong places.

"Hello, Mrs. Yeltner," Citra said, guilty to be enjoying the woman's thinly veiled terror.

"G . . . good to see you," she said, clearly not remembering Citra's name. "Wasn't there just a gleaning on your floor earlier this year? I didn't think it was allowed to hit the same building so soon."

"It's allowed," Citra said. "But we're not here to glean today."

"Although," added Scythe Curie, "anything's possible."

When the elevator reached her floor, Mrs. Yeltner actually tripped over her dog in her hurry to get out.

It was a Sunday—both of Citra's parents and her brother were home, waiting. The visit wasn't a surprise, but there was surprise on her father's face when he opened the door.

"Hi, Dad," Citra said. He took her into his arms in a hug that felt warm, but yet obligatory as well.

"We've missed you, honey," said her mother, hugging her as

well. Ben kept his distance and just stared at the scythe.

"We were expecting Scythe Faraday," her father said to the lavender-clad woman.

"Long story," said Citra. "I have a new mentor now."

And Ben blurted out, "You're Scythe Curie!"

"Ben," chided their mother, "don't be rude."

"But you are, aren't you? I've seen pictures. You're famous."

The scythe offered a modest grin. "'Infamous' is more accurate."

Mr. Terranova gestured to the living room. "Please, come in."

But Scythe Curie never crossed the threshold. "I have business elsewhere," she said, "but I'll return for Citra at dusk." She nodded to Citra's parents, winked at Ben, then turned to leave. The moment the door was closed both her parents seemed to fold just a bit, as if they had been holding their breath.

"I can't believe you're being taught by *the* Scythe Curie. The Grandma of Death!"

"Grande Dame, not grandma."

"I didn't even know she still existed," said Citra's mom. "Don't all scythes have to glean themselves eventually?"

"We don't *have* to do anything," Citra said, a little surprised at how little her parents really knew about how the Scythedom worked. "Scythes only self-glean if they want to." *Or if they're murdered,* thought Citra.

Her room was the way she had left it, just cleaner.

"And if you're not ordained, you can come home and it will be like you never left," her mother said. Citra didn't tell her that either way, she would not be coming home. If she achieved scythehood, she would probably live with other junior scythes, and if she did not become an ordained scythe, she would not live at all. Her parents didn't need to know that.

"It's your day," her father said. "What would you like to do?"

Citra rummaged through her desk drawer until she found her camera. "Let's go for a walk."

The small talk was of the microscopic variety, and although it was good to be with her family, never had the barrier between them felt denser. There were so many things she wished she could talk about, but they'd never understand. Never be able to relate. She couldn't talk to her mother about the intricacies of killcraft. She couldn't commiserate with her father about that moment when life left a person's eyes. Her brother was the only one she felt remotely comfortable talking to.

"I had a dream that you came to my school and gleaned all the jerks," he told her.

"Really?" Citra said. "What color were my robes?"

He hesitated. "Turquoise, I think."

"Then that will be the color I'll choose."

Ben beamed.

"What will we call you once you're ordained?" her father said, treating it as if it were a certainty.

Citra hadn't even considered the question. She never heard a scythe referred to by anything but their Patron Historic or "Your Honor." Were family members bound to that as well? She hadn't even chosen her Patron yet. She dodged the question by saying, "You're my family, you can call me whatever you like," hoping that was true.

They strolled around town. Although she didn't tell them,

they passed the small home where she had lived with Rowan and Scythe Faraday. They passed the train station nearest the home. And everywhere they went, Citra made a point to take a family picture . . . each from an angle very close to that of the nearest public camera.

The day was emotionally exhausting. Citra wanted to stay longer, and yet a big part of her couldn't wait for Scythe Curie to arrive. She resolved not to feel guilty about that. She'd had more than her share of guilt. "Guilt is the idiot cousin of remorse," Scythe Faraday had been fond of saying.

Scythe Curie didn't ask Citra any questions about her visit on the way home, and Citra was content not to share. She did ask the scythe something, though.

"Does anyone ever call you by your name?"

"Other scythes—ones I'm friendly with—will call me Marie."

"As in Marie Curie?"

"My Patron Historic was a great woman. She coined the term 'radioactivity,' and was the first woman to win the Nobel Prize, back when such things were awarded."

"But what about your real name? The one you were born with?"

Scythe Curie took her time in answering. Finally she said, "There's no one in my life who knows me by that name."

"What about your family? They must be still around— after all, they have immunity from gleaning as long as you're alive."

She sighed. "I haven't been in touch with my family for more than a hundred years."

Citra wondered if that would happen to her. Do all scythes lose the ties to everyone they had known—everything they had been before they were chosen?

"Susan," Scythe Curie finally said. "When I was a little girl, they called me Susan. Suzy. Sue."

"It's a pleasure to meet you, Susan."

Citra found it next to impossible to imagine Scythe Curie as a little girl.

When they got home, Citra uploaded her pictures to the Thunderhead without worrying if the scythe saw, because there was nothing unusual or suspicious about that—everyone uploaded their photos. It would have been suspicious if she hadn't.

Then, later that night, when Citra was sure Scythe Curie was asleep, she went to the study, got online, and retrieved the pics—which was easy to do since they were tagged. Then she dove into the backbrain, following all the links the Thunderhead had forged to her images. She was led to other pictures of her family, as well as other families that resembled hers in some way. Expected. But there were also links to videos taken by streetcams in the same locations. That's just what she was looking for. Once she created her own algorithm to sort out the irrelevant photos from the streetcams, she had a full complement of surveillance videos. Of course, she was still left with millions of randomly accessed, unordered files, but at least now they were all streetcam records of Scythe Faraday's neighborhood.

She uploaded an image of Scythe Faraday to see if she could isolate videos in which he appeared, but as she suspected, nothing came back. The Thunderhead's hands-off policy when it came to scythes meant that scythe's images were not tagged in any way. Still, she had successfully narrowed the field from billions of records to millions. However, tracking Scythe Faraday's movements on the day he died was like trying to find a needle in a field of haystacks that stretched to the horizon. Even so, she was determined to find what she was looking for, no matter how long it took.

Gleanings should be iconic. They should be memorable. They should have the legendary power of the greatest battles of the mortal age, passed down by word of mouth, becoming as immortal as we are. That is, after all, why we scythes are here. To keep us connected to our past. Tethered to mortality. Yes, most of us will live forever, but some of us, thanks to the Scythedom, will not. For those who will be gleaned, do we not, at the very least, owe them a spectacular end?

—From the gleaning journal of H.S. Goddard

24

An Embarrassment to Who and What We Are

Numb. Rowan could feel himself growing numb—and while it might have been a good thing for his beleaguered sanity, it was not a good thing for his soul.

"Never lose your humanity," Scythe Faraday had told him, "or you'll be nothing more than a killing machine." He had used the word "killing" rather than "gleaning." Rowan hadn't thought much of it at the time, but now he understood; it stopped being gleaning the moment one became desensitized to the act.

Yet this great plain of numbness was not the worst place to be. Numbness was a mere purgatory of gray. No, there was a much worse place. Darkness masquerading as enlightenment. It was a place of royal blue studded with diamonds that glistened like stars.

"No no no!" chided Scythe Goddard as he watched Rowan practice bladecraft with a samurai sword on cotton-stuffed dummies. "Have you learned nothing?"

Rowan was exasperated, but he kept it just beneath a simmer, counting to ten in his head before turning to face the scythe, who approached across the expanse of the estate's front lawn, now littered with fluff and cottony remains.

"What did I do wrong this time, Your Honor?" To Rowan, the phrase "Your Honor" had become a profanity, and he couldn't help but spit it out like one. "I cleanly decapitated five of them, eviscerated three, and I severed the aortas of the rest. If any of them had actually been alive, they would be dead now. I did just what you wanted."

"That's the problem," said the scythe. "It's not what *I* want, it's what *you* want. Where is your passion? You attack like a bot!"

Rowan sighed, sheathing his blade. Now would come a lecture, or more accurately, an oration, because Scythe Goddard loved nothing more than performing to the gallery, even if it was just a gallery of one.

"Human beings are predatory by nature," he began. "That nature may have been bleached out of us by the sanitizing force of civilization, but it can never be taken from us completely. Embrace it, Rowan. Suckle at its transformative breast. You may think gleaning is an acquired taste, but it's not. The thrill of the hunt and the joy of the kill simmers in all of us. Bring it to the surface and then you'll be the kind of scythe this world needs."

Rowan wanted to despise all of this, but there was something about honing one's skill, no matter the nature of that skill, that was rewarding. What he hated was the fact that he didn't hate it.

Servants replaced the dummies with fresh effigies. Scarecrows with extremely short life spans. Then Goddard took the samurai blade from him and handed him a nasty-looking hunting knife instead, for a more intimate delivery of death.

"It's a bowie knife, like Texan scythes use," Goddard told

him. "Take great satisfaction and pleasure in this, Rowan," said Scythe Goddard, "or you'll be nothing more than a killing machine."

Each day was the same: a morning run with Scythe Rand, weight training with Scythe Chomsky, and a nutritionally precise breakfast prepared by a master chef. Then would come killcraft administered by Scythe Goddard himself. Blades, bows, ballistics, or the use of his own body as a weapon of death. Never poisons unless they were on the tips of weapons.

"Gleaning is *performed*, not *administered*," Scythe Goddard told him. "It is a willful action. To slip into passivity and allow a poison to do all the work is an embarrassment to who and what we are."

Goddard's pontifications were constant, and although Rowan often disagreed, he didn't argue or voice his dissent. In this way, Goddard's voice began to supplant his own internal moderator. It became the voice of judgment in his own head. Rowan didn't know why this would be so. Yet Goddard was now there in his head, passing judgment on everything he did.

The afternoons would be filled with mental training with Scythe Volta. Memory exercises, and games to increase cognitive acuity. The smallest part of Rowan's day, just before dinner, was spent in book learning—but Rowan found that the mental training helped him retain the things he learned without the repetition of study.

"You will know your history, your biochemistry, and your toxins ad nauseam to impress at conclave," Goddard told Rowan with a disgusted wave of his hand. "I've always found it pointless, but one must impress the academics in the Scythedom as well as the pragmatists."

"Is that what you are?" Rowan asked. "A pragmatist?"

It was Volta who answered him. "Scythe Goddard is a visionary. That puts him on a level above every other scythe in MidMerica. Maybe even the world."

Goddard didn't disagree.

And then there were the parties. They came upon the estate like seizures. Everything else stopped. They even took precedence over Rowan's training. He had no idea who organized them, or where the revelers came from, but they always came, along with food enough to feed armies, and every sort of decadence.

Rowan didn't know if it was his imagination, but there seemed to be more scythes and known celebrities frequenting Goddard's parties than when he first arrived.

In three months, the change in Rowan's physique was obvious, and he spent more time than he would want anyone to know studying the change in the tall mirror in his bedroom. There was definition everywhere—his abs, his pecs. Biceps seemed to inflate out of nowhere, and Scythe Rand constantly slapped his glutes, threatening all sorts of lewd liaisons with him once he was of age.

He had finally gotten the hang of his journal, writing things that bordered on thoughtful—but it was still just a sham. He never wrote what he truly felt, for he knew that his "private" journal was not private at all, and that Scythe Goddard read every last word. So he wrote only things that Goddard would want to read.

Although Rowan did not forget his secret pledge to throw the scythehood to Citra, there were moments when he willfully suppressed it in his mind, allowing himself to imagine what it would be like to be an ordained scythe. Would he be the type of scythe Faraday was, or would he accept the teachings of Goddard? As much as Rowan tried to deny it, there was logic to Goddard's approach. After all, what creature in nature despised its own existence and felt shame for its means of survival?

We became unnatural the moment we conquered death, Scythe Faraday would say—but couldn't that be a reason to seek whatever nature we could find within ourselves? If he learned to enjoy gleaning, would it be such a tragedy?

He kept these thoughts to himself, but Scythe Volta could read, if not the specifics, then the general nature of his thoughts.

"I know you were first brought on as an apprentice for very different traits than the ones Scythe Goddard admires," Volta told him. "He sees compassion and forbearance as weakness. But you have other traits that are beginning to awaken. You'll be a new-order scythe yet!"

Of all of Goddard's junior scythes, Volta was the most admirable and the one Rowan most related to. He imagined they might be friends, once they were equals.

"Do you remember the pain when we beat you down?" Volta asked one afternoon, at the end of memory training.

"How could I ever forget?"

"There are three reasons for it," Volta told him. "The first is to connect you with our ancestors, reliving the pain, and the fear of pain, because that's what led to civilization and humanity's advancement beyond its own mortality. The second is a rite of passage—something sorely missing in our passive world. But the third reason may be the most important: Being made to suffer pain frees us to feel the joy of being human."

To Rowan it sounded like more empty platitudes—but Volta wasn't like Goddard that way. He didn't usually speak in lofty, meaningless ideas.

"I felt plenty of joy in my life without having to be beaten to a pulp," Rowan told him.

Volta nodded. "You felt some—but just a shadow of what it can be. Without the threat of suffering, we can't experience true joy. The best we get is pleasantness."

Rowan had no response to that, because it struck him as true. He had led a pleasant life. His biggest complaint was being marginalized. But didn't everyone feel marginalized? They lived in a world where nothing anyone did really mattered. Survival was guaranteed. Income was guaranteed. Food was plentiful, and comfort was a given. The Thunderhead saw to everyone's needs. When you need nothing, what else can life be but pleasant?

"You'll get it eventually," Scythe Volta told him. "Now that your pain nanites are dialed to zero, it's inevitable."

Esme remained a mystery. Sometimes she came down to eat with them, sometimes she didn't. Sometimes Rowan would catch her reading in various places around the mansion: mortal age books made of paper that had apparently been collected by the owner before he surrendered it all to Scythe Goddard. She would always hide from him whatever it was she was reading, as if embarrassed by it.

"When you become a scythe, are you going to stay?" she asked him.

"Maybe," he told her. "And maybe not. Maybe I won't get to be a scythe. So maybe I'll be nowhere."

She ignored that last part of his answer. "You should stay," she told him.

The fact that this nine-year-old girl seemed to have a crush on him was one more complication Rowan didn't need. She seemed to get everything she wanted. So did that mean she got him if she wanted that, too?

"My name's Esmerelda, but everyone calls me Esme," she told him when she followed him into the weight room one morning. Usually he'd be nice to younger kids—but since he was told he *had* to be nice, he suddenly found he didn't want to be.

"I know, Scythe Goddard told me. You really shouldn't be here—these weights can be dangerous."

"And you're not supposed to be here without Scythe Chomsky to spot you," she pointed out, then sat down on a bench press showing no sign of leaving. "If you like, we could play a game or something when you're done with your training."

"I really don't play games."

"Not even cards?"

"Not even cards."

"It must have been boring to be you."

"Yeah, well, it's not boring anymore."

"I'll teach you to play cards after dinner tomorrow," she

announced. And since Esme got what she wanted, Rowan was there at the appointed time, whether he wanted to be there or not.

"Esme must be kept happy," Scythe Volta reminded him after Rowan's card game with her.

"Why?" Rowan asked. "Goddard doesn't seem to care about anyone who doesn't wear scythe robes, so why does he care about her?"

"Just be decent to her."

"I'm decent to everyone," Rowan pointed out. "In case you haven't noticed, I'm a decent person."

Volta laughed. "Hold on to that for as long as you can," he said, as if doing so would be a very difficult thing.

Then came the day Scythe Goddard threw a new wrinkle into the taut fabric of Rowan's life. It came without warning, as did all things Scythe Goddard threw at him. It was during killcraft. Today Rowan was working with two blades—daggers in each hand. Two blades were difficult for him; he favored his right and had little dexterity with his left. Scythe Goddard loved to make it difficult for Rowan in these training sessions and always judged him harshly when he didn't rise to some imaginary level of perfection. Yet Rowan had been surprising himself. He had been getting better at wielding weaponry, and had even drawn forth mild admissions of approval from Goddard.

"Adequate," Goddard would say, or, "That wasn't entirely dismal." High praise from the man.

And in spite of himself, Rowan felt satisfaction each time Goddard gave him approval. And he had to admit he was beginning to like wielding deadly weapons. It had grown on him like any other sport. Skill for the sake of skill, and then a sense of accomplishment when he did well.

On this particular day, things took a severe turn. It was evident from the moment he stepped out onto the lawn that something was up, because the dummies had not yet been put out. Instead, there were at least a dozen people milling about the lawn. He didn't get it at first. He should have known that something was different because all the junior scythes were there today to watch his training. Usually it was just Goddard.

"What's going on here?" Rowan asked. "I can't do my training with people in the way—tell them to clear out."

Scythe Rand laughed at him. "You're charmingly dense," she said.

"This ought to be fun," said Scythe Chomsky, folding his arms, ready to relish what was to come.

And then Rowan finally understood. On the lawn the people weren't milling around, they were standing, evenly spaced. They were waiting for him. There were to be no more dummies. Now his practice would be the real thing. Killcraft would now truly be killcraft.

"No," Rowan said, shaking his head. "No, I can't do this!"

"Oh, but you will," Scythe Goddard said calmly.

"But . . . but I'm not ordained yet, I can't glean!"

"You won't be gleaning," Scythe Volta said, putting a comforting hand on Rowan's shoulder. "There are ambudrones waiting for each of them. As soon as you're done with them, they'll be rushed to the nearest revival center, and be as good as new in a day or two."

"But . . . but . . ." Rowan found he had no viable argument except to say, "It isn't right!"

"Listen here," Scythe Goddard said, stepping forward. "There are thirteen people out on that lawn. Every single one of them is here by choice, and every single one of them is being well paid for the service provided. They all know why they're here, they know what their job is, they are more than happy to do it, and I expect the same from you. So do your job."

Rowan pulled out his blades and looked at them. Those blades would not be cutting into cotton today, but into flesh.

"Hearts and jugulars," Scythe Goddard told him. "Dispatch your subjects with speed. You will be timed."

Rowan wanted to protest—insist that he couldn't do it—but as much as his heart told him he couldn't, his mind knew the truth.

Yes, he could.

He had been training for precisely this. All he had to do was dial his conscience down to zero. He knew he was capable of that, and it terrified him.

"You are to take down twelve of them," Scythe Goddard told him, "and leave the last one alive."

"Why leave the last?"

"Because I said so."

"C'mon, we don't have all day," grumbled Chomsky. Volta threw Chomsky a withering glare, then spoke to Rowan with far more patience. "It's just like jumping into a cold pool. The anticipation is much worse than the reality. Take the leap, and I promise all will be well."

Rowan could leave.

He could drop his blades and go into the house. He could prove himself to be a failure here and now, and perhaps not have to endure any more of this. But Volta believed in him. And so did Goddard, even if he wouldn't admit it aloud—for why would Goddard set this challenge before him if he didn't believe Rowan would rise to it?

Rowan took a deep breath, gripped his blades tightly in both hands, and with a guttural war cry that drowned the alarms blaring in his soul, he launched himself forward.

There were men and there were women. The subjects represented different ages, ethnic mixes, and body types, from muscular to obese to gaunt. He yelled and screamed and grunted with every thrust, slice, and twist. He had trained well. The blades sunk in with perfect precision. Once he began, he found he couldn't stop. Bodies fell, and he was on to the next, and the next. They didn't fight back, they didn't run in fear, they just stood there and took it. They were no different from the dummies. He was covered in blood. It stung his eyes; the smell was thick in his nostrils. Finally he came to the last one. It was a girl his age, and there was a look on her face of resignation bordering on sorrow. He wanted to end that sorrow. He wanted to complete what he had begun, but he overrode the brutal imperative of the hunter in him. He forced himself not to swing his blades.

"Do it," she whispered. "Do it or I won't get paid."

But he dropped his blades to the grass. Twelve deadish, one left alive. He turned to the scythes, and they all began to applaud.

"Well done!" Scythe Goddard said, more pleased than Rowan had ever seen him. "Very well done!"

Ambudrones began to descend from above, grasping his victims and spiriting them away to the nearest revival center. And Rowan found himself smiling. Something had torn loose inside of him. He didn't know whether it was a good thing or not. And while part of him felt like falling to his knees and hurling up breakfast, another part of him wanted to howl to the moon like a wolf.

A year ago if you'd told me that I'd know how to wield more than two dozen types of blades, that I would become an expert at firearms, and that I would know at least ten ways to end a life with my bare hands—I would have laughed and suggested that you ought to get your brain chemistry tweaked. Amazing what can happen in just a few short months.

Training under Scythe Goddard is different from under Scythe Faraday. It's intense, physical, and I can't deny that I'm getting better at everything I do. If I am a weapon, then I'm being sharpened against a grindstone every day.

My second conclave is coming up in a few weeks. The first trial was nothing more than a simple question. I'm told it will be different this next time. There's no telling what the apprentices will be expected to do. One thing's for sure, there will be serious consequences for me if I don't perform to Goddard's liking.

I have every confidence that I will.

—From the journal of Rowan Damisch, scythe apprentice

25

Proxy of Death

The engineer liked to believe that his work at Magnetic Propulsion Laboratories was useful, even though it had always appeared pointless. Magnetic trains were already moving as efficiently as they could. Applications for private transportation needed little more than tweaking. There was no more "new and improved," there was just the trick of *different*—new styles, and advertisements to convince that stylishness was all the rage—but the basic technology remained exactly the same.

In theory, however, there were new uses that were yet to be tapped—or else why would the Thunderhead put them to work?

There were project managers who knew more about the ultimate goal of the work they did, but no one had all the pieces. Still, there was speculation. It had long been believed that a combination of solar wind and magnetic propulsion would be required to move about in space with any efficiency. True, the prospect of space travel had been out of favor for many years, but that didn't mean it would always be.

There had once been missions to colonize Mars, to explore Jupiter's moons, and even to launch to the stars beyond, but every mission had ended in utter and disastrous failure. Ships blew up. Colonists died—and in deep space, death meant death, just as completely as if they had been gleaned. The idea of irrevocable death without the controlled hand of a scythe was too much to bear for a world that had conquered mortality. The public outcry shut down all space exploration. Earth was our sole home, and would remain so.

Which is why, the engineer suspected, the Thunderhead moved forward on these projects so carefully and so slowly as not to draw the public's attention. It was by no means underhanded, because the Thunderhead was incapable of underhandedness. It was merely discreet. Wisely discreet.

One day, perhaps the Thunderhead would announce that while everyone was looking the other way, humanity had achieved a sustainable presence beyond the bounds of planet Earth. The engineer looked forward to that day, and fully expected he'd live to see it. He had no reason to expect that he wouldn't.

Until the day a team of scythes laid siege to his research facility.

Rowan was awakened at dawn by a towel hurled at his face.

"Get up, sleeping beauty," Scythe Volta said. "Shower and get dressed. Today's the day."

"Today's what day?" Rowan said, still too groggy to sit up.

"Gleaning day!" said Volta.

"You mean you guys actually glean? I thought you just partied and spent other people's money."

"Just get yourself ready, smart-ass."

When Rowan turned off his shower, he heard the chop of helicopter blades, and when he came out onto the lawn, it was waiting for them. It was no surprise to Rowan that it was painted royal blue and studded with glistening stars. Everything in Scythe Goddard's life was a testament to his ego.

The other three scythes were already out front, practicing their best kill moves. Their robes were bulky, and clearly loaded down with all nature of weaponry sheathed within the folds. Chomsky torched a potted shrub with a flamethrower.

"Really?" said Rowan, "A flamethrower?"

Chomsky shrugged. "No law against it. And anyway, what business is it of yours?"

Goddard strode out of the mansion. "What are you waiting for? Let's go!" As if they hadn't all been waiting on him.

The moment was charged with the adrenaline of anticipation, and as they strode toward the waiting helicopter, Rowan, for an instant, had an image of them as superheroes . . . until he remembered what their true purpose was, and the image shattered.

"How many are you going to glean?" he asked Scythe Volta, but Volta just shook his head and pointed to his ear. Too loud to hear Rowan over the chopper blades, which made the scythes' robes flail like flags in a storm as they crossed the lawn.

Rowan did some calculations. Scythes were charged with five gleanings per week, and to the best of his knowledge, these four hadn't taken a life in the three months that Rowan had been there. That meant they could glean about two hundred fifty today and still be within their quota. This wasn't going to be a gleaning, it was going to be a massacre.

Rowan hesitated, falling back as the others got in. Volta noticed.

"IS THERE A PROBLEM?" Volta shouted over the deafening chop of the blades.

But even if Rowan could make himself heard, he would never be understood. This is what Goddard and his disciples did. It was how they operated. This was business as usual. Could this ever be that way for him? He thought to his latest training sessions. The ones with living targets. The feeling he had when he had rendered all but one deadish, revulsion fighting a primal sense of victory. He felt that now as he stood at the entrance to the helicopter. With each step deeper into Goddard's world, it became harder and harder to retreat.

All four scythes were looking at him now. They were ready to go on their mission. The only thing holding them back was Rowan.

I am not one of them, he told himself. *I will not be gleaning. I will only be there to observe.*

He willed himself to step up into the helicopter, pulled the door closed, and they rose skyward.

"Never been up in one of these, have you?" Volta asked, misreading Rowan's apprehension.

"No, never."

"It's the only way to travel," Scythe Rand said.

"We are angels of death," said Scythe Goddard. "It is only fitting that we swoop in from the heavens."

They flew south, over Fulcrum City, to the suburbs beyond. All the way Rowan silently hoped the helicopter would crash—but realized what a pointless exercise that would be. Because even if it did, they'd all be revived by the weekend.

• • •

A helicopter landed on the main building's rooftop heliport. It was unexpected, unannounced—which never happened. The Thunderhead piloted just about everything airborne, and even if it was an off-grid chopper, someone onboard would always announce their approach and request clearance.

This thing just dropped from the sky and onto the roof.

The closest security guard bounded up the stairs from the sixth floor and onto the roof, in time to see the scythes stepping out. Four of them—blue, green, yellow, and orange—and a boy with an apprentice armband.

The guard stood there slackjawed, unsure what to do. He thought to call this in to the main office, but realized that doing so might get him gleaned.

The female scythe, in green with witchy dark hair and a PanAsian leaning to her, approached him, grinning.

"Knock, knock," she said.

He was too stunned to respond.

"I said, knock, knock."

"Wh . . . who's there?" he finally responded.

She reached into her robe, producing the most awful looking knife the man had ever seen, but her arm was grabbed by the scythe in blue before she could use it.

"Don't waste it on him, Ayn," he said to her.

The scythe in green put her knife away and shrugged. "Guess you'll miss the punch line." Then she stormed past him with the others, and down the stairs into the building.

He caught the gaze of the apprentice, who lagged a few yards behind the others.

"What should I do?" he asked the boy.

"Get out," the boy told him. "And don't look back."

So the guard did what he was told. He crossed to the far stairwell, bounded all the way down, burst out of the emergency exit, and didn't stop running until he was too far away to hear the screams.

"We'll start up here on the sixth floor and work our way down," Goddard told the others. They came out of the stairwell to see a woman waiting for the elevator. She gasped and froze.

"Boo!" said Scythe Chomsky. The woman flinched, dropping the folders she carried. Rowan knew that any of the scythes, on a whim, could have taken her out. She must have known that too, because she braced for it.

"How high is your security clearance?" Goddard asked her.

"Level one," she told him.

"Is that good?"

She nodded, and he took her security badge. "Thank you," he said. "You get to live."

And he moved toward a locked door, swiping the card to gain entrance.

Rowan found himself getting light-headed, and realized he was beginning to hyperventilate.

"I should wait here," he told them. "I can't glean, I should wait here."

"No way," said Chomsky. "You come with us."

"But . . . but what use will I be? I'll just be in the way."

Then Scythe Rand kicked in the glass of an emergency case, pulled out a fire hatchet, and handed it to him. "Here," she said. "Break stuff."

"Why?"

She winked at him. "Because you can."

The employees in suite 601—which took up the entire north half of the floor, had no warning. Scythe Goddard and his scythes strode to the center of activity.

"Attention!" he announced in full theatrical voice. "Attention, all! You have been selected for gleaning today. You are commanded to step forward and meet your demise."

Murmurs, gasps, and cries of shock. No one stepped forward. No one ever did. Goddard nodded to Chomsky, Volta, and Rand, and the four advanced through the maze of cubicles and offices, leaving nothing living in their wake.

"I am your completion!" intoned Goddard. "I am your deliverance! I am your portal to the mysteries beyond this life!"

Blades and bullets and flames. The office was catching fire. Alarms began to blare, sprinklers gushed forth icy water from the ceiling. The doomed were caught between fire and water, and the deadly sights of four master hunters. No one stood a chance.

"I am your final word! Your omega! Your bringer of peace and rest. Embrace me!"

No one embraced him. Mostly people cowered and pleaded for mercy, but the only mercy shown was the speed at which they were dispatched.

"Yesterday you were gods. Today you are mortal. Your death is my gift to you. Accept it with grace and humility."

So focused were the scythes that none of them noticed Rowan slipping out behind them and crossing to suite 602, where he pounded on the glass door until someone came and Rowan could warn him what was coming.

"Take the back stairs," he told the man. "Get as many out as you can. Don't ask questions—just go!" If the man had any doubts, they were chased away by the sounds of desperation and despair coming from just across the hall.

A few minutes later, when Goddard, Volta, and Chomsky were done with suite 601, they crossed the hall to find suite 602 empty, save for Rowan, swinging his fire hatchet at computers and desks and everything in his path, doing exactly as he was told to do.

The scythes moved faster than the flames—faster than the flow of workers trying to escape. Volta and Chomsky blocked two of the three stairwells. Rand made her way to the main entrance and stood like a goalie, taking out anyone trying to escape through the front doors. Goddard spouted his ritualistic litany as he moved through the panicked mob, switching his weapons as it suited him, and Rowan swung his hatchet at anything that would shatter, then secretly directed whoever he could toward the one unguarded stairwell.

It was over in less than fifteen minutes. The building was in flames, the helicopter was now hovering above, and the scythes strode out of the front entrance, like the four horsemen of the post-mortal apocalypse.

Rowan brought up the rear, dragging his hatchet on the marble, until he dropped it with a clatter.

Before them were half a dozen fire trucks and ambudrones, and behind that hordes of survivors. Some ran when they saw the scythes come out, but just as many stayed, their fascination overcoming their terror.

"You see?" Goddard told Rowan. "The firefighters can't interfere with a scythe action. They'll let the whole thing burn down. And as for the survivors, we have a wonderful public relations opportunity."

Then he stepped forward and spoke loudly to those who hadn't fled. "Our gleaning is complete," he announced. "To those who survive, we grant immunity. Come forward to claim it." He held out his hand—the one that bore his ring. The other scythes followed his lead and did the same.

No one moved at first, probably thinking it was a trick. But in a few moments, one ash-stained employee stumbled forward, followed by another and another, and then the entire mob was apprehensively coming toward them. The first few knelt and kissed the scythes' rings—and once the others saw that this was for real, they surged forward, mobbing the scythes.

"Easy!" shouted Volta. "One at a time!"

But the same mob mentality that propelled their escape now pushed them toward those lifesaving rings. All of a sudden, no one seemed to remember their dead coworkers.

Then, as the crowd around them got denser and more agitated, Goddard pulled back his hand, removed his ring, and handed it to Rowan.

"I tire of this," Goddard said. "Take it. Share in the adoration."

"But . . . I can't. I'm not ordained."

"You can use it if I give you permission as a proxy," Goddard told him. "And right now you have my permission."

Rowan put it on, but it wouldn't stay, so he switched it to his index finger, where it was a bit more snug. Then he held out his hand as the other scythes did.

The crush of people didn't care which finger the ring was on, or even whose hand it was on. They practically climbed over one another to kiss it, and to thank him for his justice, his love, and his mercy, calling him "Your Honor," not even noticing he wasn't a scythe.

"Welcome to life as a god," Scythe Volta said to him. While behind them the building burned to the ground.

We are wise but not perfect, insightful but not all-seeing. We know that by establishing the Scythedom, we will be doing something very necessary, but we, the first scythes, still have our misgivings. Human nature is both predictable and mysterious; prone to great and sudden advances, yet still mired in despicable self-interest. Our hope is that by a set of ten simple, straightforward laws, we can avoid the pitfalls of human fallibility. My greatest hope is that, in time, our wisdom will become as perfect as is our knowledge. And if this experiment of ours fails, we have also embedded a way to escape it.

May the Thunderhead help us all, if we ever need that escape.

—From the gleaning journal of H.S. Prometheus, the first World Supreme Blade

26

Not Like the Others

That night they feasted, although Rowan could not dig up an appetite, no matter how deep he mined. Goddard ate enough for everyone. He was invigorated by the day's hunt, like a vampire sucking in the life force of its victims. He was more charming, more suave than ever, saying things to make everyone laugh. *How easy,* thought Rowan, *to fall in with him. To be stroked into his elite club, just as the others had been.*

Clearly, Chomsky and Rand were cut from a similar cloth as Goddard. They held not the slightest illusion of conscience. But unlike Goddard, they held no delusions of grandeur. They gleaned for sport—for the joy of it—and as Scythe Rand so accurately put it, *because they can.* They were more than happy to wield their weapons while Goddard inhabited his role as the Angel of Death. Rowan couldn't be sure if the man believed it, or if it was all artifice. Theatricality to add flair to the show.

Scythe Volta, though, was different. Yes, he stormed the office building and gleaned his share, just as the others had, but he said little as their god-machine carried them home across the sky. And now at dinner, he barely touched the food on his plate. He kept getting up to wash his hands. He probably thought nobody noticed, but Rowan did. And so did Esme.

"Scythe Volta is always cranky after a gleaning," Esme leaned over to tell Rowan. "Don't stare at him, or he'll throw something at you."

Halfway through dinner, Goddard asked for a final count.

"We gleaned two hundred sixty-three," Rand told him. "We're ahead of our quota now. We'll have to glean fewer next time."

Goddard slammed his fist down on the table in disgust. "The damn quota hobbles us all! If it weren't for the quota, every day could be like today." Then Goddard turned to Scythe Volta and asked how his task was coming. It was Volta's job to set appointments with the families of the deceased, so that they could be granted the obligatory immunity.

"I've spent the whole day reaching out to each family," Volta said. "They'll be lining up at the outer gate first thing tomorrow morning."

"We should let them onto the grounds," Goddard said with a smirk. "They can watch Rowan train on the lawn."

"I hate the bereaved," Rand said, as she stabbed a fresh piece of meat with her fork and dragged it to her plate. "They always have such awful oral hygiene—my ring always reeks after an hour of granting bereavement immunity."

Unable to stomach any more, Rowan excused himself. "I promised Esme I'd play cards with her after dinner, and it's getting late." There was no truth in that, but he threw a glance to Esme and she nodded, pleased to be part of an impromptu conspiracy.

"But you'll miss the crème brûlée," said Goddard.

"More for us," said Chomsky, shoving a forkful of prime rib into his maw.

Rowan and Esme went to the game room and played gin rummy, mercifully undisturbed by talk of gleaning and quotas and the kissing of rings. Rowan was thankful that the suicide king held the monopoly on misery in this room.

"We should get others to join us," Esme suggested. "Then we can play hearts or spades. You can't play those games with just two."

"I have no interest in playing cards with the scythes," Rowan told her flatly.

"Not them, silly—I mean the servants." She picked up his discarded nine—the second one he fed to her, as if he didn't know she was collecting them. Letting her win today was payment for helping him escape the dining room.

"I play cards with the pool man's sons sometimes," she told him. "But they don't like me very much on account of this used to be their house. Now they all share a room in the servant's quarters." Then she added, "You're sleeping in one of their rooms, you know. So I'll bet they don't like you much, either."

"I'm sure they don't like any of us."

"Probably not."

Maybe it was because Esme was young, but she seemed entirely oblivious to the things that weighed so heavily on Rowan. Perhaps she knew better than to question things, or to pass judgment on what she saw. She accepted her situation at face value, and never spoke ill of her benefactor—or more accurately, her captor, for she was clearly Goddard's prisoner, even though she might not see it that way. Hers was a gilded cage, but it was a cage nonetheless. Still, her ignorance was her bliss, and Rowan decided not to shatter her illusion that she was free.

Rowan picked up an ace, which he needed for his hand, but discarded it anyway. "Does Goddard ever talk to you?" he asked Esme.

"Of course he talks to me," she said. "He's always asking me how I am, and if there's anything I need. And if there is, he always makes sure I get it. Just last week I asked for a—"

"No, not that kind of talking," said Rowan, cutting her off. "I mean *real* talking. Has he ever hinted as to why you matter so much to him?"

Esme didn't answer. Instead she lay down her cards. Nines over threes. "Rummy," she said. "Loser shuffles."

Rowan gathered the cards. "Scythe Goddard must have had a good reason to let you live, and to grant you immunity. Aren't you at all curious?"

Esme shrugged, and stayed tight-lipped. It was only after Rowan dealt the next hand that she said, "Actually, Scythe Goddard didn't grant me immunity. He can glean me any time he wants, but he doesn't." Then she smiled. "That makes me even more special, don't you think?"

They played four games. One Esme won fair and square, two Rowan let her win, and one Rowan won, so it wouldn't be as obvious that he had thrown the others. By the time they were done, dinner had broken up and the others were going about their particular evening routines. Rowan avoided everyone and tried to go straight to his room, but on his way he heard something that gave him pause. There was faint sobbing coming from Scythe Volta's room. He listened at the door to make sure it wasn't his imagination, then turned the knob. The door wasn't locked. He pushed it open slightly and peered inside.

Scythe Volta was there, sitting on his bed, head in hands. His body heaved with sobs that he tried to stifle, but could not. It was a few moments before he looked up and saw Rowan.

Volta's sorrow instantly turned to fury. "Who the hell said you could come in here? Get out!" He grabbed the nearest object—a glass paperweight—and hurled it at Rowan, just as Esme had suggested he might. It would have left a pretty nasty gash on Rowan's head had it connected, but Rowan ducked and the thing hit the door, leaving a substantial dent in the wood instead of in Rowan's skull. Rowan could have retreated. That probably would have been the most judicious course of action, but leaving well enough alone was not Rowan's strong point. He was notoriously skilled at sticking his nose where it didn't belong.

He stepped into the room and closed the door behind him, preparing to dodge the next blunt object hurled his way. "You have to be quieter if you don't want anyone to hear you," he told Volta.

"If you tell *anyone,* I will make your life a living hell."

Rowan laughed at that, because it implied his life wasn't already that.

"You think that's funny? I'll show you funny."

"Sorry, I didn't mean to laugh. I wasn't laughing at you, if that's what you think."

Since Volta was no longer throwing things and wasn't chasing him out, Rowan grabbed a chair and sat down, far enough away to give Volta some space.

"Today was hard," Rowan said. "I don't blame you."

"What do you know about it?" snapped Volta.

"I know you're not like the others," said Rowan. "Not really."

Volta looked up at him then, his eyes red from tears that he didn't try to hide anymore. "There's something wrong with me, you mean." Volta looked down again, clenching his fists, but Rowan didn't move because he didn't expect to get a beating. He suspected that Volta would use his own fists against himself if he could.

"Scythe Goddard is the future," Volta said. "I don't want to be part of the past. Don't you understand?"

"But you hated today, didn't you? Even more than me, because you weren't just watching, you were a part of it."

"And you'll be part of it soon, too."

"Maybe not," said Rowan.

"Oh, you will be. The moment you get your ring and kill that pretty little girlfriend of yours, you'll know there's no turning back for you, either."

Rowan swallowed, trying to fight down what little bit of dinner he had eaten. Citra's face bloomed in his mind, but he pushed the image away. He couldn't let himself think about her now.

Rowan knew he was out on a limb with Volta. The only thing to do was shimmy to its precarious end. "You only pretend to like gleaning," he said to Volta. "But you hate it more than you've ever hated anything. Your mentor was Scythe Nehru, right? He's very old-school, which means he chose you for your conscience. You don't want to take life—and you definitely don't want to take dozens upon dozens at a time."

Volta leaped up, moving faster than seemed possible. He

lifted Rowan up and pushed him against the wall with a bruising slam that made Rowan sorely miss his painkilling nanites.

"You will never repeat that to anyone, do you hear me? I've come too far to have my position jeopardized! I won't be blackmailed by a snot-nosed apprentice!"

"Is that what you think I'm doing? Blackmailing you?"

"Don't toy with me!" growled Volta "I know why you're here!"

Rowan was genuinely disappointed. "I thought you knew me."

A moment more and Volta loosened his grip. "Nobody knows anyone, do they?" he said.

"I promise I won't tell anyone. And I don't want anything from you."

Volta finally backed off. "I'm sorry. After you've been surrounded by so much scheming, you start to think that's how everyone plays." He sat back down on the bed. "I believe you, because I know you're better than that. In fact, I knew from the moment Goddard brought you in. He sees you as a challenge—because if he can turn one of Faraday's apprentices to his way of thinking, it proves he can turn anyone."

Then it occurred to Rowan that Volta wasn't all that much older than him. He had always feigned a confidence that made him seem older, but now his vulnerability revealed the truth. He was twenty at most. Which meant he'd only been a scythe for a couple of years. Rowan didn't know the path that led him from an old-guard scythe to Goddard, but he could imagine. He could see how a junior scythe might gravitate toward Goddard's flash and charisma. After all, Goddard promised his disciples anything a human heart could desire, in exchange for the complete abdication of one's conscience. In a profession where a conscience was a liability, who would want one?

Rowan sat down again and pulled his chair close enough to Volta to whisper. "I'll tell you what I think," Rowan said. "Goddard isn't a scythe. He's a killer." It was the first time Rowan dared to say it out loud. "There's a lot written about killers from the mortal age—monsters like Jack the Ripper, or Charlie Manson, or Cyber Sally—and the only difference between them and Goddard is that people let Goddard get away with it. The mortals knew how wrong it was, but somehow we've forgotten."

"Yeah, but even if that's true, what can anyone do about it?" asked Volta. "The future comes whether we want it to or not. Rand, and Chomsky, and the dozens of other sick, twisted bastards longing to be in Goddard's inner circle are going to dominate that future. I'm sure the founding scythes must be rolling in their graves—but the point is, they *are* in their graves, and they're not coming back any time soon." Volta took a deep breath, and wiped the last of his tears. "For your sake, Rowan, I hope you come to love killing as much as Goddard does. It would make your life so much easier. So much more rewarding."

The suggestion weighed heavily on him. A month ago, Rowan would have denied that he could ever become such a monster, but now he wasn't so sure. The pressure to surrender was greater every day. He had to hope that if Volta had never truly surrendered to the darkness, then maybe he might stand a chance as well.

There is no official media coverage of gleanings, much to the chagrin of the more publicity-minded scythes. Not even large-scale gleanings get on the news. Even so, plenty of personal pictures and videos of gleanings are uploaded to the Thunderhead, providing a guerilla record—which is so much more exciting and enticing than anything official.

Notoriety and infamy quickly evolve into celebrity and fame for scythes—and the most brazen acts harden further into legend. Some scythes find the fame addictive, and seek greater and greater celebrity. Others would rather remain anonymous.

I cannot deny that I am legend. Not for the simple gleanings I do now, but for the audacious ones I did more than a hundred and fifty years ago. As if I weren't already immortal enough, I am further immortalized on collectible cards. The newer ones are prized by schoolchildren. The older ones are worth a fortune to hard-core collectors, regardless of the condition.

I am legend. Yet every day I wish that I was not.

—From the gleaning journal of H.S. Curie

27

Harvest Conclave

Citra's secret investigation led to some surprises she couldn't wait to share with Rowan when she finally saw him at Harvest Conclave. She certainly couldn't share them with Scythe Curie. The two had come to trust each other, and the scythe would have seen Citra secretly using her online credentials as a flagrant violation of that trust.

Citra's life had taken a very different turn from Rowan's. She did not attend loud, lavish parties, nor did she train against live subjects. She helped cook quiet meals for heartbroken families, and sparred with a black belt Bokator bot. She created tinctures and studied the practical use of deadly poisons in Scythe Curie's personal apothecary and toxic herb garden. She learned about all the infamous acts of both the best and the worst scythes in history.

In the past it was usually laziness, prejudice, or lack of foresight that made a bad scythe, Citra had discovered. There were those who seemed to glean too many neighbors because they couldn't be bothered to look farther. There were those who, in spite of repeated disciplinary action, would glean people with specific ethnic traits. As for poor judgment, there were plenty of examples there as well. Such as Scythe Sartre, who thought it was a good idea to do all of his gleanings at rodeos, thereby destroying the sport entirely, since no one would attend a rodeo for fear of being gleaned.

Of course, the bad scythes weren't all in the past. But instead of "bad" they were now called "innovative" and "forward-thinking."

Like the innovative bloodbaths of Scythe Goddard and his killer cronies.

The mass gleaning at Magnetic Propulsion Laboratory, although never reported officially, was big news. And there were plenty of private videos uploaded to the Thunderhead, showing Goddard and his disciples doling out immunity like bread to the poor. Rowan was right there in the middle of it. Citra didn't know what to think about that.

"The world has a talent for rewarding bad behavior with stardom," Scythe Curie said, as she viewed some of the videos that had been uploaded. Then she got a bit pensive. "I know the pitfalls of being a celebrity scythe," she confessed, although Citra already knew. "I was headstrong and stupid in my early days. I thought that by gleaning just the right people at just the right time, I could change the world for the better. I believed, in my arrogance, that I had a keen grasp of the big picture that others lacked. But of course, I was just as limited as anyone else. When I gleaned the president and his cabinet, it shook the world— but the world was already shaking just fine without me. They called me 'Miss Massacre,' and as time went on that changed to 'the Grande Dame of Death.' I spent more than a hundred years trying to fade into anonymity, but even the youngest of children know of me. I am the boogeyman parents use to get their children to behave. *Be good or the Grande Dame will get you.*" Scythe Curie shook her head sadly. "Most celebrity is fleeting, but when you're a scythe, your defining deeds stand forever. Take my advice, Citra, and remain undefined."

"You might be a celebrity scythe," Citra pointed out, "but even at your worst, you were nothing like Goddard."

"No, I wasn't, thank goodness," Scythe Curie said. "I never took life for sport. You see, there are some who seek celebrity to change the world, and others who seek it to ensnare the world. Goddard is of the second kind." And then she said something that guaranteed Citra many a sleepless night.

"I wouldn't trust your friend Rowan anymore. Goddard is as corrosive as acid hurled in the eye. The kindest thing you can do is win that ring when Winter Conclave comes, and glean the boy quickly, before that acid burns any deeper than it already has."

Citra was glad that Winter Conclave was still months away. It was Harvest Conclave she had to worry about. At first, Citra had looked forward to September and the Harvest Conclave, but as it approached, she began to dread it. It wasn't the upcoming test that troubled her. She felt she was prepared for whatever trials would be thrown at the apprentices. What she dreaded was seeing Rowan, because she had no idea what all these months with Goddard had done to him. *Win that ring and glean him quickly,* Scythe Curie had said. Well, Citra didn't have to worry about that now. She had four months until *that* decision would be made. But the clock never stopped ticking. It moved inexorably toward one of their deaths.

Harvest Conclave took place on a clear but blustery September day. While a storm had kept many spectators away from the last conclave, they gathered in force today on the street before the Fulcrum City Capitol Building. Even more peace officers than before were posted to keep the gawking crowds back. Some scythes—mostly the old-guard ones—arrived on foot, choosing a humble walk from their hotels over a more flashy arrival. Others pulled up in high-end cars, choosing to make the most of their celebrity status. News crews aimed their cameras but mostly kept their distance. This was, after all, not a red carpet. No questions, no interviews—but there was certainly a lot of preening. Scythes waved to the cameras and squared their shoulders, standing tall so they'd look their best on screen.

Scythe Goddard and his crew showed up in a limousine— royal blue studded with mock diamonds, just in case there was any question as to who was inside. As Goddard and his entourage emerged, the crowd *ooh*ed and *aah*ed, as if their dazzling appearance rivaled a display of fireworks.

"There he is!"

"It's him!"

"He's so handsome!"

"He's so scary!"

"He's so well-groomed!"

Goddard took a moment to turn to the crowd and sweep his hand in a royal wave. Then he focused on one girl from the audience, held her gaze, pointed at her, then continued on up the stairs, saying nothing.

"He's so strange!"

"He's so mysterious!"

"He's so charming."

As for the girl he singled out, she was left impressed and

terrified and confused by his momentary attention—which was precisely the intent.

So focused was the crowd on Goddard and his colorful entourage, no one much noticed Rowan bringing up the rear as they climbed the steps to the entrance.

Goddard's crew weren't the only scythes up for the show. Scythe Kierkegaard had a crossbow slung over his shoulder. Not that he had any intention of using it today—it was merely a part of the spectacle. Still, he could have aimed at just about anyone in the audience and taken them out. The knowledge of that made the crowd all the more excited. No one had ever been gleaned on the Capitol steps before a conclave, but that didn't mean that it *couldn't* happen.

While most scythes approached down the main avenue, Scythe Curie and Citra made their entrance from a side street, to avoid being the focus of the crowd's attention for as long as possible. As the stately scythe pushed through the crowd of onlookers, a rumble erupted from the people closest to her as they realized who it was moving among them. People reached out to touch her silky lavender robe. She endured this as a matter of course, but one man actually grabbed the fabric and she had to slap his hand away.

"Careful," she said, meeting his eye. "I don't take kindly to the violation of my person."

"I apologize, Your Honor," said the man. Then he reached for her hand, intent on touching her ring, but she pulled her hand away from him.

"Don't even think about it."

Citra pushed her way in front of Scythe Curie to help clear

a path for her. "Maybe we should have taken a limo," Citra said. "At least that way we wouldn't have to fight our way through."

"That's always been a little too elitist for me," Curie said.

As they cleared the crowd, a sudden gust came down the wide Capitol steps, catching Scythe Curie's long silver hair and blowing it back like a bridal train, making her look almost mystical.

"I knew I should have braided it today," she said.

As she and Citra climbed the white marble steps, someone to their left shouted, "We love you!"

Scythe Curie stopped and turned, unable to find the speaker, so she addressed them all.

"Why?" she demanded, but now, under her cool scrutiny, no one responded. "I could end your existence at any moment; why love me?"

Still no one answered—but the exchange attracted a cameraman who moved forward, getting a little too close. Scythe Curie smacked the camera so hard, it wrenched the man's whole body around, and he nearly dropped it. "Mind your manners," said the scythe.

"Yes, Your Honor. Sorry, Your Honor."

She continued up the steps with Citra behind her. "Hard to imagine that I used to love this attention. Now I'd avoid it entirely if I could."

"You didn't seem this tense at the last conclave," Citra noted.

"That's because I didn't have an apprentice being tested. Instead, I was the one testing other scythes' apprentices."

A test that Citra had failed spectacularly. But she didn't feel like bringing that up.

"Do you know what today's test will be?" Citra asked as they reached the top of the stairs and stepped into the entry vestibule.

"No—but I do know that it's being administered by Scythe Cervantes, and he tends to be very physically minded. For all I know, he'll have you tilting at windmills."

As before, the scythes greeted one another in the grand rotunda, waiting for the assembly room doors to open. Breakfast was set out on tables in the center of the rotunda, featuring a pyramid of Danish that must have taken hours to assemble but seconds to fall as scythes carelessly took the lower Danish without regard to the ones above. The waitstaff scrambled to gather the fallen pastries before they could be ground underfoot. Scythe Curie found it all very amusing. "It was foolhardy of the caterer to think that scythes would leave anything in a state of order."

Citra spotted Junior Scythe Goodall—the girl who had been ordained at the last conclave. She had her robes made by Claude DeGlasse, one of the world's preeminent fashion designers. It had been a monumental mistake, because today's designers were all about shocking people out of their happy place. Scythe Goodall's orange-and-blue-striped robe made her look more like a circus clown than a scythe.

Citra couldn't help but notice how Goddard and his junior scythes were the center of even more attention than at the Vernal Conclave. Although there were a number of scythes who turned a cold shoulder, even more crowded them, seeking to ingratiate themselves.

"There are more and more scythes who think like Goddard,"

Scythe Curie said quietly to Citra. "They've slipped between the cracks like snakes. Infiltrating our ranks. Supplanting the best of us like weeds."

Citra thought about Faraday, a decent scythe most certainly choked out by the weeds.

"The killers are rising to power," Scythe Curie said. "And if they do, the days of this world will be very dark indeed. It is left to the truly honorable scythes to stand firm against it. I look forward to the day you join in that fight."

"Thank you, Your Honor." Citra had no problem fighting the good fight if she became a scythe. It was the events that would lead up to it that she couldn't bear to consider.

Scythe Curie went off to greet several of the old-guard scythes who held true to the founders' ideals. That's when Citra finally spotted Rowan. He didn't bask in the false glow of Goddard. Instead, he was his own little center of attention. He was surrounded by other apprentices, and even a few junior scythes. They chatted, they laughed, and Citra found herself feeling slighted that Rowan hadn't even sought her out.

Rowan had, in fact, tried to find her, but by the time Citra entered the rotunda, Rowan had already been set upon by unexpected admirers. Some were envious of his position with Goddard, others were just curious, and others were clearly hoping to attach themselves to his rising star. Political positioning started young in the Scythedom.

"You were there at that office building, weren't you?" one of the other apprentices said—a "spat," one of the new ones, at conclave for the first time. "I saw you in the videos!"

"He wasn't just there," said another spat. "He had Goddard's freaking ring, handing out immunity!"

"Wow! Is that even allowed?"

Rowan shrugged. "Goddard said it was, and anyway, it wasn't like I asked him to give me his ring. He just did it."

One of the junior scythes sighed wistfully. "Man, he must really like you if he let you do that."

The thought that Goddard might actually like him made Rowan uncomfortable—because the things that Goddard liked, Rowan categorically despised.

"So what's he like?" one girl asked.

"Like . . . no one I've ever met," Rowan told her.

"I wish I was his apprentice," said one of the spats, then grimaced like he had just bitten into a rancid cheese Danish. "I was taken on by Scythe Mao."

Scythe Mao, Rowan knew, was another showboater, enjoying the celebrity of his public image. He was notoriously independent and didn't align himself with the old guard or the new. Rowan didn't know if he was a man who voted his own conscience or sold his vote to the highest bidder. Faraday would have known. There were so many things Rowan missed about being Faraday's apprentice. The inside scoop was one of them.

"Goddard and his junior scythes totally owned the Capitol steps when they came up," said an apprentice Rowan remembered from last conclave—the one who knew his poisons. "They looked so good."

"Have you decided what color you'll be? And what jewels you'll have on your robe?" a girl asked, suddenly hanging on his arm like a fast-growing vine. He didn't know which would be more awkward, pulling out of her grip or not.

"Invisible," Rowan said. "I'll come up the statehouse steps naked."

"Those'll be some jewels," quipped one of the junior scythes, and everyone laughed.

Then Citra pushed her way through, and Rowan felt as if he was caught doing something he shouldn't. "Citra, hi!" he said. It felt so forced, he just wanted to take it back and find another way to say it. He shrugged out of the vine girl's grip, but it was too late, because Citra had seen it.

"Looks like you've made a lot of friends," Citra said.

"No, not really," he said, then realized he'd just insulted them all. "I mean, we're all friends, right? We're in the same boat."

"Same boat," repeated Citra with deadpan dullness but daggers in her eyes as sharp as the ones that used to hang in Faraday's weapons den. "Good to see you too, Rowan." Then she strode away.

"Let her go," said the vine girl. "She'll be history after the next conclave anyway, right?"

Rowan didn't even excuse himself as he left them.

He caught up with Citra quickly, which told him she really wasn't trying all that hard to get away. This was a good sign.

He gently grabbed her arm and she turned to him.

"Hey," he said. "I'm sorry about back there."

"No, I get it," she said. "You're a big deal now. You have to flaunt it."

"It's not like that. Do you think I wanted them fawning all over me like that? C'mon, you know me better."

Citra hesitated. "It's been four months," she said. "Four months can change a person."

That much was true. But some things hadn't changed. Rowan knew what she wanted to hear, but that would just be another dance. Another bit of posturing. So he told her the truth.

"It's good to see you, Citra," he said. "But it hurts to see you. It hurts a lot, and I don't know what to do about it."

He could tell that reached her, because her eyes began to glisten with tears that she blinked away before they could spill. "I know. I hate that it has to be this way."

"I'll tell you what," said Rowan. "Let's not even think about Winter Conclave right now. Let's be in the here and now, and let Winter Conclave take care of itself."

Citra nodded. "Agreed." Then she took a deep breath. "Let's take a walk. There's something I have to show you."

They walked along the outer edge of the rotunda, passing the archways where scythes wheeled and dealed.

Citra pulled out her phone and projected a series of holograms into her palm, cupping it so no one but Rowan could see. "I dug these out of the Thunderhead's backbrain."

"How did you do that?"

"Never mind how. What's important is that I did—and what I found."

The holograms were of Scythe Faraday on the streets near his home.

"These are from his last day," Citra said. "I was able to retrace at least some of his steps that day."

"But why?"

"Just watch." The hologram showed him being let into

someone's home. "That's the house of the woman he introduced us to at the market. He spent a few hours there. Then he went to this café." Citra swiped to another video showing him going into the restaurant. "I think he may have met someone there, but I don't know who."

"Okay," said Rowan. "So he was saying good-bye to people. So far it seems consistent with the things someone would do if it were their last day on Earth."

Citra swiped again. The next video showed him going up to the stairs to a train station. "This was five minutes before he died," Citra said. "We know that it happened at that station—but guess what? The camera on that train platform had been vandalized—supposedly by unsavories. It was down for the entire day, so there's no visual record of what actually happened on that platform!"

A train pulled out of the station, and a moment later a train pulled in, heading in the other direction. That was the one that killed Faraday. Although Rowan couldn't see it, he grimaced as if he had.

"You think someone killed him, and made it look like he did it himself?" Rowan looked around to make sure they weren't being observed, and spoke quietly. "If that's your only evidence, it's pretty weak."

"I know. So I kept digging." She swiped back and replayed the scene of Faraday walking toward the station.

"There were five witnesses. I couldn't track them down without digging into the Scythedom's records, and if I did that, they'd know I was looking. But it only makes sense that those witnesses would have gone up these stairs, too, right? There were eighteen people who went up the stairs around the time that Faraday died. Some of them probably got on this first train." She pointed to the train leaving the station. "But not all of them. Of those eighteen people, I was able to identify about half of them. And three of them were granted immunity *that very day*."

It was enough to take the wind out of Rowan and make him feel light-headed. "They were bribed to say it was a self-gleaning?"

"If you were just an ordinary citizen and witnessed one scythe killing another, and then were offered immunity to keep your mouth shut, what would you do?"

Rowan wanted to believe he'd seek justice, but he thought back to the days before he became an apprentice, when the appearance of a scythe was the most frightening thing he could imagine. "I'd kiss the ring and keep my mouth shut."

Across the rotunda, the doors of the conclave chamber opened and the scythes began to file in.

"Who do you think did it?" Rowan asked.

"Who had the most to gain by getting Faraday out of the picture?"

Neither of them needed to say it out loud. They both knew the answer. Rowan knew that Goddard was capable of unthinkable things, but would he kill another scythe?

Rowan shook his head, not wanting to believe it. "That's not the only explanation!" he told her. "It might not have even been a scythe at all. Maybe it was the family member of someone he gleaned. Someone who wanted revenge. Anyone could have taken his ring, pushed him into the path of the train, and used the ring to give immunity to the witnesses. They'd have to stay quiet then, or they'd be considered accomplices!"

Citra opened her mouth to refute it, but closed it again. It was possible. Even though using Faraday's ring would have frozen the killer's finger, it was possible. "I didn't think of that," she said.

"Or what about a Tonist? The tone cults hate scythes."

The rotunda was quickly emptying. They left the alcove and moved toward the chamber doors. "You don't have enough facts to accuse anyone of anything." Rowan said. "You should let it sit for now."

"Let it sit? You can't be serious."

"I said *for now*! You'll have full access to the Scythedom's records once you're ordained, and you'll be able to prove exactly what happened."

Citra stopped in her tracks. "What do you mean *once* I'm ordained. It could just as easily be you. Or is there something I'm missing?"

Rowan pursed his lips, furious at himself for the slip. "Let's just get inside before they close the doors."

The rituals of conclave were just as they had been before. The tolling of the dead. The washing of hands, grievances, and discipline. Once again an anonymous accusation was leveled against Scythe Goddard—this time accusing him of handing out immunity too freely.

"Who brings this accusation?" Goddard demanded. "Let the accuser stand and identify his or herself!"

Of course no one took credit, which allowed Goddard to retain the floor. "I will admit that his accusation has merit," Goddard said. "I am a generous man, and have perhaps been too liberal in my doling of immunity. I make no excuses and am unrepentant. I throw myself on the mercy of the High Blade to levy my punishment."

High Blade Xenocrates waved his hand dismissively. "Yes, yes, just sit down, Goddard. Your penance will be to shut up for a whole five minutes."

That brought a round of laughter. Goddard bowed to the High Blade and took his seat. And although a few scythes—including Scythe Curie—tried to object, pointing out that historically, scythes who overused their ring had their power to grant immunity limited to the families of the gleaned, their complaints fell on deaf ears. Xenocrates overruled all objections in the interest of speeding up the day's proceedings.

"Amazing," said Scythe Curie quietly to Citra. "Goddard's becoming untouchable. He can get away with anything. I wish someone would have had the foresight to glean him as a child. The world would be better off."

Citra avoided Rowan at lunch, afraid that being seen together more than they already had been might raise suspicion. She stood by Scythe Curie for lunch, and the scythe introduced Citra to several of the greatest living scythes: Scythe Meir, who had once been a delegate to the Global Conclave in Geneva; Scythe Mandela, who was in charge of the bejeweling committee; and Scythe Hideyoshi, the only scythe known to have mastered the skill of gleaning through hypnosis.

Citra tried not to be too starstruck. Meeting them almost gave her hope that the old guard could triumph against the likes of Goddard. She kept glancing over at Rowan, who, once more, couldn't seem to get away from the other apprentices, although she didn't know how hard he tried.

"It's a bad sign," said Scythe Hideyoshi, "when our young hopefuls gravitate so openly to the enemy."

"Rowan's not the enemy," Citra blurted, but Scythe Curie put a hand on her shoulder to quiet her.

"He *represents* the enemy," Scythe Curie said. "At least he does to those other apprentices."

Scythe Mandela sighed. "There shouldn't be enemies in the Scythedom. We should all be on the same side. The side of humanity."

It was generally agreed among the old guard that these were troubling times, but aside from raising objections that were repeatedly dismissed, no one took action.

Citra found herself getting increasingly anxious after lunch, as the weapons manufacturers touted their wares and various motions were hotly debated. Things like whether a scythe's ring should be worn on the left or right hand, and whether or not a scythe should be allowed to endorse a commercial product, like running shoes or a breakfast cereal. It all seemed insignificant to Citra. Why should any of that matter when the hallowed act of gleaning was slowly devolving into mortal age murder?

Then at last it came time for the apprentice trials. As before, the candidates for Scythedom went first, having been tested the night before. Of the four candidates who made it through their final test, only two were ordained. The other two had to suffer the walk of shame, as they exited the chamber and went back to their old lives. Citra took guilty pleasure at the fact that the girl who had been sucking up to Rowan was one of those ejected.

Once the new scythes were given their rings and took their new names, the remaining apprentices were called down front.

"Today's test," announced Scythe Cervantes, "will be a competition in the martial art of Bokator. The candidates will be paired and judged on their performance."

A mat was brought in and rolled out in the semicircular space in front of the rostrum. Citra took a deep breath. She had this. Bokator was a balance among strength, agility, and focus, and she had found her perfect balance. And then they stuck a blade right in the heart of her confidence.

"Citra Terranova will spar against Rowan Damisch."

A murmur from the crowd. Citra realized this was no random draw. They were paired intentionally, doomed to be adversaries. How could it be any other way? Her eyes met Rowan's, but his expression gave away nothing.

The other matches went first. Each apprentice gave their best, but Bokator was a bruising discipline and not everyone's strength. Some victories were close, others were routs. And then it came time for Citra and Rowan's match.

Still, Rowan's expression gave her neither camaraderie nor sympathy, nor misery at having to be set against each other. "Okay, let's do this," is all he said, and they began to circle each other.

Rowan knew that today was his first true test, but not the one they had devised for him. Rowan's test was to look convincing but still throw the match. Goddard, Xenocrates, Cervantes—and for that matter, all the scythes assembled—needed to believe he was doing his best, but that his best just wasn't good enough.

It began with the ritualistic rhythmic circling. Then posturing and physical taunting. Rowan launched himself at Citra, threw a kick that he telegraphed with his body language, and missed her by a fraction of an inch. He lost his footing and fell down on one knee. A very good start. He turned quickly, rising, remained off balance, and she lunged toward him. He thought she would take him down with an elbow strike, but instead she grabbed him, pulling him forward even as she appeared to push him back. It brought him to balance and made it appear as if her move had failed—that she didn't have the leverage to do the job. Rowan backed away and caught her gaze. She was grinning at him, her eyes intensely on his. It was part of the taunting that Bokator was known for, but this was so much more. He could read her just as clearly as if she were speaking aloud.

You're not going to throw this match, her eyes said. *Fight badly—I dare you—because no matter how poorly you try to fight, I will find a way to make you look good.*

Frustrated, Rowan launched himself at her again, an open palm strike at her shoulder, intentionally two inches off from the perfect leverage point—but she actually moved into it. His palm connected, she spun back with the force of his strike, and went down.

Damn you, Citra. Damn you!

She could beat him at everything. Even at losing.

Citra knew from the moment Rowan made his first kick what he was up to, and it infuriated her. How dare he think he had to fight badly for her to win this match? Had he grown so arrogant under Scythe Goddard that he actually thought this wouldn't be a fair fight? Sure, he had been training, but so had she. So what if he had grown stronger—that also meant he was bulkier and moved slower. A fair fight was the only way to keep their consciences clean. Didn't Rowan realize that by sacrificing himself, he'd be dooming her as well? She would sooner glean herself as her first act as a scythe than accept his sacrifice.

Rowan glared at her now, furious, and it only made her laugh. "Is that the best you can do?" she asked.

He threw out a low kick, just slow enough for her to anticipate, and without any force behind it. All she needed to do was lower her stance and the kick would have no effect. Instead she responded by raising her center of gravity just enough for the kick to knock her feet out from under her. She fell to the mat, but righted herself quickly, so it wouldn't look as if she had done it on purpose. Then she threw her shoulder against him and hooked her right leg around his, applying force, but not enough to make his knee buckle. He grabbed her, twisted, flipped them both down to the mat, landing with her in the dominant position over him. She countered by forcing him to roll over and pin her. He tried to release her, but she held his arms in place so he couldn't.

"What's the matter, Rowan?" she whispered. "Don't know what to do when you're on top of a girl?"

He finally pulled away and she got up. They faced each other one more time, circling in the familiar battle dance while Cervantes circled them in the other direction, like a satellite, completely missing what was really going on between them.

Rowan knew the match was almost over. He was about to win, and by winning he would lose. He must have been crazy thinking Citra would allow him to willingly throw the match. They both cared too much about each other. That was the problem.

Citra would never willingly accept the scythe's ring as long as her feelings for him got in the way.

And all at once Rowan knew exactly what he had to do.

With only ten seconds left to the match, all Citra had to do was keep up the dance. Rowan was clearly the victor. Ten more seconds of guarded circling and Cervantes would blow the whistle.

But then Rowan did something Citra hadn't anticipated at all. He threw himself forward with lightning speed. Not clumsy, not feigning false incompetence, but with perfect, practiced skill. In an instant he had put her in a headlock, squeezing her neck tight—tight enough for her pain nanites to kick in. And then he leaned close and snarled into her ear.

"You fell right into my trap," he said. "Now you get what you deserve." Then he flung her body into the air, twisting her head the other way. Her neck broke with a loud and horrible snap, and darkness came over Citra like a landslide.

Rowan dropped Citra to the ground as the crowd drew a collective gasp. Cervantes blew his whistle violently. "Illegal move! Illegal move!" Cervantes shouted, just as Rowan knew he would. "Disqualification!"

The gathering of scythes began to roar. Some were furious at Cervantes, others were spouting vitriol at Rowan for what he had done. Rowan stood stoic, letting no emotions show. He forced himself to look down at Citra's body. Her head was twisted practically backward. Her eyes were open, but no longer seeing. She was deadish as deadish could be. He bit down on his tongue until it began to bleed.

The chamber door swung open and guards raced in, hurrying toward the deadish girl in the middle of the room.

The High Blade came up to Rowan. "Go back to your scythe," he said, not even trying to hide his disgust. "I'm sure he'll discipline you accordingly."

"Yes, Your Excellency."

Disqualification. None of them realized that, to Rowan, it was the perfect victory.

He watched as the guards picked Citra up and carried her, limp as a sack of potatoes, outside where, no doubt, an ambudrone was already waiting to take her to the nearest revival center.

You'll be fine, Citra. You'll be back with Scythe Curie in no time—but you won't forget what happened today. And I hope you never forgive me.

I fought against the purge. There are things I've done that I am not proud of, but I am very proud that I fought against that.

I can't recall which scythe began that odious campaign to glean only those who were born mortal, but it spread throughout each regional Scythedom, a viral idea in a post-viral time. "Shouldn't those who were born to expect death be the sole subjects of gleaning?" went the popular wisdom. But it was bigotry masquerading as wisdom. Selfishness posing as enlightenment. And not enough scythes argued—because those born in the post-mortal age found mortal-borns to be too uncomfortably different in the way they thought, and in the way they lived their lives. "Let them die with the age that bore them," cried the post-mortal purists in the Scythedom.

In the end it was deemed a gross violation of the second commandment, and all those scythes who participated in the purge were severely disciplined—but by then it was too late to undo what had been done. We lost our ancients. We lost our elders. We lost our living lifeline to the past. There are still mortal-borns around, but they hide their age and their history, for fear of being targeted again.

Yes, I fought the purge—but the Thunderhead did not. By its own law of noninterference in scythe affairs, it could do nothing to stop the purge. All it could do was bear witness. The Thunderhead allowed us to make that costly mistake, leaving the Scythedom to wallow in its own regret to this very day.

I often wonder, should the Scythedom run entirely off the rails and decide to glean all of humanity in a grand suicide of global gleaning, would the Thunderhead break its noninterference law and stop it? Or would it bear witness again as we destroyed ourselves, leaving nothing behind but a living cloud of our knowledge, accomplishments, and so-called wisdom?

Would the Thunderhead grieve our passing, I wonder? And if so, would it grieve as the child who has lost a parent, or as the parent who could not save a petulant child from its own poor choices?

—From the gleaning journal of H.S. Curie

28

Hydrogen Burning in the Heart of the Sun

Citra Terranova, said a voice both powerful yet gentle. *Citra Terranova, can you hear me?*

Who's that? Is someone there?

Curious, said the voice. *Very curious. . .*

Being deadish was a pain in the ass. No question about it.

When she was once more pronounced legally alive, she awoke to the unfamiliar but professionally friendly face of a revival nurse checking her vitals. She tried to look around her, but her neck was still in a brace.

"Welcome back, honey," the nurse said.

The room seemed to spin every time she moved her eyes. It was more than just pain nanites, she must have had all sorts of numbing, rejuvenating chemicals and microbots inside her.

"How long?" she rasped.

"Just two days," the nurse said cheerily. "Simple spinal severing. Nothing too hard for us to handle."

Two days were robbed from her life; two days she didn't have to spare.

"My family?"

"Sorry, honey, but this was a scythe matter. They weren't notified." The nurse patted her hand. "You can tell them all about it when you next see them. Now the best thing for you to do is relax. You'll be here one more day, and then you'll be good as new." Then she offered Citra ice cream that was the best she'd ever tasted.

That evening, Scythe Curie came and filled her in on all she had missed. Rowan had been disqualified and severely reprimanded for his poor sportsmanship.

"Are you telling me that because he was disqualified, I won?"

"Unfortunately, no," Scythe Curie said. "He was clearly going to beat you. It was decided that both of you lose. We really need to work on your martial art skills, Citra."

"Well, that's just great," Citra said, exasperated for a very different reason than Scythe Curie thought. "So now Rowan and I are both zero for two at conclave."

Scythe Curie sighed. "The third time's the charm," she said. "Now it will all come down to how well you do at Winter Conclave. And I have faith that you will shine in your final test."

Citra closed her eyes, remembering the look on Rowan's face when he held her in that headlock. There was something cold there. Calculating. In that moment, she saw a side of him she had never seen before. It was as if he was looking forward to what he was about to do to her. As if he was going to enjoy it. She was so confused! Did he really plan that move from the beginning? Did he not know he'd be disqualified, or was disqualification his plan?

"What was Rowan like after it happened?" Citra asked Scythe Curie. "Did he seem shocked at all about what he had done? Did he kneel down to me? Did he help carry me out to the ambudrone?"

Scythe Curie took a moment before she answered. Then finally she said, "He just stood there, Citra. His face was like stone. Defiant, and as unrepentant as his scythe."

Citra tried to turn away, but even though the brace was now gone, her neck was still too stiff to move.

"He's not who you think he is anymore," Scythe Curie said slowly, so that it would sink in.

"No," Citra agreed, "he's not." But for the life of her she had no idea who he was now.

Rowan thought he would receive another brutal beating when he returned to the mansion. That couldn't have been further from the truth.

Scythe Goddard was all flamboyance and bright chatter. He called for the butler to bring champagne and glasses for everyone, right there in the foyer, so they could toast Rowan's audacity.

"That took more nerve than I thought you had, boy," Goddard said.

"Here, here," seconded Scythe Rand. "You can come to my room and break my neck any time."

"He didn't just break her neck," Scythe Goddard pointed out. "He unflinchingly snapped her spine! Everyone heard it. I'm sure it woke up the scythes sleeping in the back row!"

"Classic!" said Scythe Chomsky, guzzling his champagne down, not waiting for the toast.

"It was a powerful statement you made," said Goddard. "It

reminded everyone that you are *my* apprentice, and you are not to be trifled with!" Then he became a little quieter. Almost gentle. "I know you had feelings for that girl, yet you did what needed to be done, and more."

"I was disqualified," Rowan reminded them.

"Officially, yes," Goddard agreed, "but you gained the admiration of quite a few important scythes."

"And made enemies of others," Volta pointed out.

"Nothing wrong with drawing a line in the sand," Goddard responded. "It takes a strong man to do that. The kind of man I'm happy to raise a glass to."

Rowan looked up to see Esme sitting at the top of the grand staircase watching them. He wondered if she knew what he had done, and the thought that she might made him feel ashamed.

"To Rowan!" said Scythe Goddard, holding his glass high. "The scourge of the stiff-necked, and the shatterer of spines."

It was the most bitter glass Rowan had ever had to swallow.

"And now," said Goddard, "I do believe a party is in order."

The party that followed the Harvest Conclave was one for the record books, and no one was immune to Goddard's contagious energy. Even before guests started to arrive and the first of five DJs cranked up the music, Goddard threw his arms wide in the mansion's ornate living room as if he could reach from wall to wall, and said to no one in particular, "I am in my element, and my element is hydrogen burning in the heart of the sun!"

It was so outrageous a thing to say, it even made Rowan laugh.

"He's so full of crap," Scythe Rand whispered to Rowan, "but you gotta love it."

As the rooms, and the terraces, and the pool deck began to fill with partiers, Rowan began to rise from the funk he had been left in after his awful bout with Citra.

"I checked for you," Scythe Volta told him. "Citra's conscious and has one more day in the revival center. She'll go back home fully recovered with Scythe Curie; no harm, no foul. Well, plenty of foul, but that's what you wanted, wasn't it?"

Rowan didn't answer him. He wondered if anyone else was insightful enough to know why he did what he did. He hoped not.

Then Volta got serious in the midst of the revelry around them. "Don't lose the scythehood to her, Rowan," he said. "At least not on purpose. If she beats you fair and square that's one thing, but submitting yourself to her blade because of raging hormones is just plain stupid."

Maybe Volta was right. Perhaps he should do his best in their final trial, and if his best outshined Citra's, he would accept the scythe ring. And then maybe he would glean himself as his first and only act. Then he'd never be faced with having to glean Citra. It comforted Rowan that he had a way out, even though it was a worst-case scenario.

The rich and famous arrived by helicopter, by limousine, and in one bizarre but memorable entrance, by jet pack. Goddard made a point to introduce Rowan to them all, as if Rowan were a prize worth showing off. "Watch this boy," Goddard told his high-profile guests. "He's going places."

Rowan had never felt so valued and validated. It was hard to hate a man who treated him like the meat rather than the lettuce.

"This is how life was meant to be lived," Goddard told Rowan as they luxuriated in his open-face cabana, looking out over the festivities. "Experiencing all there is to experience, and enjoying the company of others."

"Even when some of those others are paid to be here?"

Goddard looked out at the crowded pool deck that would have been far less dense, and far less beautiful, had it not been for the presence of professional party guests.

"There are always extras in every production," he told Rowan. "They fill in the gaps and make for pleasant scenery. We wouldn't want everyone to be a celebrity, would we? They'd do nothing but fight!"

In the pool a net went up, and dozens gathered for a game of volleyball. "Look around you, Rowan," Goddard said in utter contentment. "Have you ever experienced such good times as these? The commoners love us not because of the way we glean, but because of the way we live. We need to accept our role as the new royalty."

Rowan didn't see himself as royalty, but he was willing to play along, at least today. So he went to the pool and jumped in, declaring himself captain of the team and joining Scythe Goddard's loyal subjects in their game.

The thing about Scythe Goddard's parties is that it was very difficult not to have a good time, no matter how hard you tried. And with all the good feelings that abounded, it was easy to forget what a ruthless butcher Goddard was.

But was he a killer of scythes?

Citra hadn't directly accused Goddard—but it was clear that he was her prime suspect. Citra's investigation was troubling, yet try as he might, Rowan could not find a single instance since he'd been in Goddard's presence where Goddard did anything that was illegal by scythe law. His interpretations of the commandments might have been stretches, but nothing he did was an actual violation. Even his gleaning rampages were not forbidden by anything but custom and tradition.

"The old guard despises me because I live and glean with a flair they sorely lack," Goddard had told Rowan. "They're a crowd of bitter backstabbers, envious that I've found the secret of being the perfect scythe."

Well, perfection was subjective—Rowan certainly wouldn't call the man a perfect scythe—but there was nothing in Goddard's repertoire of malfeasance that would suggest he would murder Faraday.

On the third day of this seemingly unending bash, there were two unexpected party guests—or at least unexpected to Rowan. The first was High Blade Xenocrates himself.

"What is he doing here?" Rowan asked Scythe Chomsky when he saw the High Blade come out to the pool.

"Don't ask me—I didn't invite him."

It seemed strange that the High Blade would show up at the party of a highly controversial scythe. He didn't appear comfortable being here at all. He seemed self-conscious and tried to be inconspicuous, but a man of such mighty girth, festooned in gold, was hard not to see. He stood out like a hot air balloon in an otherwise empty field.

It was, however, the second guest that shocked Rowan more. He was stripping down to his bathing suit just seconds after getting to the pool deck. It was none other than Rowan's friend, Tyger Salazar, who Rowan hadn't seen since the day he showed him Scythe Faraday's weapons den.

Rowan made a beeline to him, pulling him aside behind a topiary hedge.

"What the hell are you doing here?"

"Hey, Rowan!" Tyger said, with his signature slanted grin. "Good to see you, too! Man, you're looking buff! What did they inject you with?"

"Nothing, it's all real—and you didn't answer my question. Why are you here? Do you know how much trouble you could be in if anyone found out you snuck in? This isn't like crashing a school dance!"

"Take it easy! I'm not crashing anything. I've signed up with Guests Unlimited. I'm a licensed partier now!"

Tyger had often boasted that to be a professional party guest was his life's ambition, but Rowan had never taken him seriously.

"Tyger, this is a really bad idea—worse than any of your other bad ideas." Then he whispered, "Professional partiers sometimes have to . . . *do* things you might not be up for. I know; I've seen it."

"Dude, you know me; I go where the day takes me."

"And your parents are okay with this?"

Tyger looked down, his upbeat demeanor suddenly subdued. "My parents surrendered me."

"What? Are you kidding?"

Tyger shrugged. "One splat too many. They gave up. Now I'm a ward of the Thunderhead."

"I'm sorry, Tyger."

"Hey, don't be. Believe it or not, the Thunderhead's a better father than my father was. I get good advice now, and get asked how my day was by someone who actually seems to care."

Just like everything else about the Thunderhead, its parenting skills were indisputable. But being surrendered by his parents had to hurt.

"Somehow," noted Rowan, "I don't think the Thunderhead advised you to be a professional party boy."

"No—but it can't stop me. It's my choice to make. And anyway, it pays pretty good." He looked around to make sure no one was listening, then leaned in close and whispered, "But you know what pays even better?"

Rowan was almost afraid to ask. "What?"

"The word on the street is that you've been training with live subjects. That kind of work pays top dollar! Do you think you could put in a word for me? I mean, I go deadish all the time. Might as well get paid for it!"

Rowan stared at him in disbelief. "Are you nuts? Do you even know what you're saying? My god, what are you *on*?"

"Just my own nanites, man. Just my own nanites."

Scythe Volta felt lucky to be in Goddard's inner circle. Most of the time. The youngest of Goddard's three junior scythes, he saw himself as the balancing force. Chomsky was the brainless brawn, Rand was the animus—the wild force of nature among them. Volta was the sensible one who saw more than he let anyone know. He was the first to see Xenocrates arrive at the party, and watched as he unsuccessfully tried to avoid encounters. He ended up shaking hands with a number of the other guest scythes—some from regions as far-flung as PanAsia and EuroScandia. It was all with such reluctance on Xenocrates' part that Volta knew the man wasn't here entirely by choice.

Volta positioned himself near Goddard to see if he could get a bead on exactly what was going on.

When Goddard saw the High Blade, he stood; an obligatory sign of respect. "Your Excellency, what an honor it is to have you at my little get-together."

"Not so little," answered Xenocrates.

"Volta!" ordered Goddard. "Bring us two chairs poolside, so we can be closer to all the action."

And although such a task was normally left to the servants, Volta did not complain, because it gave him a perfect excuse to eavesdrop on them. He placed two chairs on the flagstone patio by the deep end of the pool.

"Closer," said Goddard. So Volta placed the chairs close enough for the two of them to be splashed by anyone choosing to use the diving board. "Stay nearby," he told Volta quietly, which is exactly what Volta had intended to do.

"Something to eat, Your Excellency?" Volta asked, gesturing to the buffet table just a few yards away.

"Thank you, no," he said. This, from a man who had a reputation for being quite the gourmand, was telling in and of itself. "Must we meet here?" Xenocrates asked. "Wouldn't you prefer to speak in a quiet room?"

"None of my rooms are quiet today," Goddard said.

"Yes, but this is far too public a forum."

"Nonsense, this isn't the Forum," said Goddard. "It's more like Nero's palace."

Volta chimed in with a hearty but staged laugh. If he had to play toady, he would own the part today.

"Well, let's hope it doesn't become the Colosseum," said Xenocrates, a little bit of bite to his words.

Goddard chuckled at the thought. "Believe me, I'd be more than happy to throw a few Tonists to the lions."

A partygoer—one of the paid ones—did a perfect triple gainer off the diving board, the splash leaving a streak across the High Blade's heavy robe.

"Don't you think this ostentatious lifestyle will catch up with you?" Xenocrates asked.

"It can't catch me if I keep moving," Goddard said with a smirk. "I'm nearly done with this place. I've been looking at real estate down south."

"That's not what I mean and you know it."

"Why so tense, Your Excellency?" said Goddard. "I invited you here because I wanted you to see firsthand what a positive thing my parties are for the Scythedom. Good public relations all around! You should be throwing grand galas at your own home."

"You forget that I live in a log cabin."

Goddard narrowed his eyes, not quite to a glare, but close. "Yes, a log cabin perched atop the tallest building in Fulcrum City. At least I'm not a hypocrite, Xenocrates. I don't feign humility."

And then the High Blade said something to Goddard that was a surprise to Volta, although in retrospect, it shouldn't have been a surprise at all. "My greatest mistake," said Xenocrates, "was choosing you as an apprentice all those years ago."

"Let's hope so," said Goddard. "I'd hate to think that you've yet to make your greatest mistake." It was a threat without actually being a threat. Goddard was remarkably good at that.

"So tell me," said Goddard, "does fortune smile on *my* apprentice, as it has on yours?"

Now Volta's ears pricked up, wondering what fortune Goddard meant.

Xenocrates took a deep breath and let it out. "Fortune is smiling. The girl will cease to be an issue within a week. I'm sure of it." Another diver splashed them. Xenocrates put up his hands to shield himself from it, but Goddard didn't flinch in the least.

Cease to be an issue. That could mean any number of things. Volta looked around until he spotted Rowan. He seemed to be having a heated discussion with a party boy. Citra "ceasing to be an issue" would be the best thing for Rowan, as far as Volta was concerned.

"Are we done now? May I leave?"

"Just a moment," said Goddard, and then he turned and called toward the shallow end of the pool. "Esme! Esme, come here, there's someone I want you to meet."

The look of terror that came over the High Blade's face was chilling. This was indeed getting more interesting by the minute.

"Please, Goddard, no."

"What's the harm?" Goddard said.

Esme, water wings and all, came trotting along the pool's edge to them. "Yes, Scythe Goddard?"

He beckoned to her and she sat on his lap, facing the man in gold. "Esme, do you know who this is?"

"A scythe?"

"Not just any scythe. This is Xenocrates, the High Blade of MidMerica. He's Mr. Big."

"Hi," she said.

Xenocrates offered a pained nod, not meeting the girl's eye. His discomfort at this encounter radiated like heat. Volta wondered if Goddard had a point or if he was just being cruel.

"I think we met before," Esme said. "A very long time ago."

Xenocrates said nothing.

"Our esteemed friend is far too uptight," Goddard said. "He needs to join the party, don't you agree, Esme?"

Esme shrugged. "He should just have fun like everyone else."

"Wiser words have never been spoken," said Goddard. Then he reached behind him out of Esme's line of sight toward Volta and snapped his fingers.

Volta drew in a slow, silent breath. He knew what Goddard was asking of him. But Volta was reluctant. Now he regretted being a part of this at all.

"Maybe you should show your moves on the dance floor, Your Excellency," said Goddard. "Then my guests could laugh at you, just the way you made the entire Scythedom laugh at me in conclave. Did you think I forgot about that?"

Goddard still reached back toward Volta, now wriggling his fingers impatiently, and Volta had no choice but to give him what he wanted. The young scythe reached into one of the many secret pockets of his yellow robe and pulled out a small dagger, placing the hilt in Goddard's hand.

Goddard closed his fingers around it, and ever so gently, ever so inconspicuously, brought the edge of the dagger just an inch from Esme's neck.

The girl didn't see it. She didn't know it was there at all. But Xenocrates did. He froze in place, eyes wide, jaw slightly ajar.

"I know!" said Goddard cheerfully. "Why don't you go for a swim!"

"Please," begged Xenocrates. "This is not necessary."

"Oh, but I insist."

"I don't think he wants to go swimming," said Esme.

"But everyone goes swimming at my parties!"

"Don't do this," begged the High Blade.

Goddard's response was to bring the blade even closer to Esme's unsuspecting neck. Now even Volta was sweating. No one had ever been gleaned at one of Goddard's parties, but there was always a first time. Volta knew this was a battle of wills, and the only thing that kept him from intervening, and ripping that dagger away from Goddard, was knowing who would blink first.

"Damn you, Goddard!" said Xenocrates. Then he stood up and threw himself into the pool, gold adornments and all.

Rowan heard none of what transpired between Xenocrates and Goddard, but he did see the High Blade hurl himself into the deep end, creating a cannonball splash that drew everyone's attention.

Xenocrates went down, and didn't come back up.

"He sank to the bottom!" someone said. "It's all that gold!"

Rowan had no great love of the High Blade, but he also didn't want to see the man drown. It wasn't like he fell; he had jumped, and if he drowned, trapped in his own golden robe, it would be considered a self-gleaning. Rowan dove into the pool, and so did Tyger, following his lead. They swam to the bottom, where Xenocrates was bubbling out his last bit of air. Rowan grabbed the man's heavy, multilayered robe, tugging it over his head, and both he and Tyger helped the High Blade up to the surface, where he gasped, coughed, and sputtered. The crowd around them applauded.

Now he didn't look much like a High Blade—he was just a fat man in wet, golden underwear.

"I guess I must have lost my balance," he said, trying to be jovial about it and attempting to put a new spin on what had happened. Maybe others believed it, but Rowan had seen him throw himself in. There was no confusing that with an accidental fall. Why on earth would he have done that?

"Wait," said Xenocrates looking at his right hand. "My ring!"

"I'll get it!" said Tyger, who was now the party boy of the hour, and dove to the bottom to retrieve it.

Chomsky had arrived at the scene, and he and Volta reached down from the pool's edge to haul Xenocrates out of the water. It was as humiliating as could be for the man. He looked like an overstuffed net of fish being hauled onto the deck of a trawler.

Goddard wrapped a large towel around the High Blade, uncharacteristically sheepish. "I truly, truly apologize," said Goddard. "It never occurred to me that you might actually drown. That wouldn't have been a good thing for anyone."

And then Rowan realized there was only one reason for Xenocrates to hurl himself into the pool:

Because Goddard had ordered him to.

Which meant that Goddard had a much stronger hold on the High Blade than anyone knew. But how?

"Can I go now?" asked Esme.

"Of course you can," said Goddard, giving her a kiss on the forehead. Then Esme wandered off, searching for playmates among the children of the stars.

Tyger surfaced with the ring. Xenocrates grabbed it from him without as much as a thank you, and slipped it on his finger.

"I tried to get his robe, too, but it's just too heavy," said Tyger.

"We'll get someone with scuba gear to go down there on a treasure dive," quipped Goddard. "Although they may claim salvage rights."

"Are you quite finished?" said Xenocrates. "Because I want to leave."

"Of course, Your Excellency."

Then the High Blade of MidMerica left the pool deck and went back through the house dripping wet, leaving behind whatever dignity he had arrived with.

"Damn—I should have kissed his ring when I had the chance," Tyger lamented. "Immunity right there in my hands, and I blew it."

Once Xenocrates was gone, Goddard called out to the crowd, "Anyone who uploads pictures of High Blade Xenocrates in his underwear will be gleaned immediately!"

And everyone laughed . . . then stopped when they realized he was not joking in the least.

As the party wrapped up and Scythe Goddard said good-bye to his most important guests, Rowan watched, taking in everything.

"So I'll see you at the next party, right?" Tyger said, breaking his focus. "Maybe next time they'll assign me earlier, so I get to hang for more than just the last day."

The fact that Tyger was about as deep as the fountain out front was an irritation to Rowan. Funny, but he had never been bothered by Tyger's shallow nature before. Perhaps because Rowan hadn't been much different. Sure, he wasn't the thrill-seeker Tyger was, but in his own way, Rowan glided on the surface of his life. Who could have known that the ice was so treacherously thin? Now he was in a place too deep for Tyger to ever understand.

"Sure, Tyger. Next time."

Tyger left with the other professional party people, with whom he seemed to share much more in common now than with Rowan. Rowan wondered if there was anyone from his old life he could relate to anymore.

Scythe Goddard passed him standing by the entryway. "If you're practicing to be a neoclassical statue, I should get you a pedestal," he said. "Of course, we already have enough statuary around here without you."

"Sorry, Your Honor; I was just thinking."

"Too much of that could be dangerous."

"I was just wondering why the High Blade jumped into the pool the way he did."

"He fell accidentally. He said so himself."

"No, I saw it," insisted Rowan. "He jumped."

"Well then, how should I know? You'll have to ask him. Although I don't think bringing up such an embarrassing moment to the High Blade will work in your favor." Then he changed the subject. "You seemed to be awfully friendly with one of the party boys. Should I invite more of them for you next time?"

"No, no, it's nothing like that," said Rowan, blushing in spite of himself. "He's just a friend from home."

"I see. And you invited him?"

Rowan shook his head. "He signed up without me even knowing. If it was up to me he wouldn't have been here at all."

"Why not?" said Goddard. "Your friends are my friends."

Rowan didn't respond to that. He never knew whether Goddard was serious, or just baiting him.

Rowan's silence just made Goddard laugh. "Lighten up, boy! It was a party, not the inquisition." He clapped Rowan on the shoulder and sauntered away. If Rowan had any sense he would have left it at that. But he didn't.

"People are saying that Scythe Faraday was killed by another scythe."

Goddard stopped in his tracks, and slowly turned back to Rowan. "Is that what people are saying?"

Rowan took a deep breath and shrugged, trying to make it seem like it was nothing, trying to backpedal. But it was too late for that. "It's just a rumor."

"And you think I might somehow be involved?"

"Are you?" asked Rowan.

Scythe Goddard stepped closer, seeming to look through Rowan's facade to that dark, frigid place where he now dwelled. "What are you accusing me of, boy?"

"Nothing,Your Honor. It's just a question.To clear the air." He tried to return the gaze, looking into Goddard's own cold place, but he found it opaque and unfathomable.

"Consider the air cleared," Goddard said, with a sarcastic lightness to his voice."Look around you, Rowan. Do you think, for one instant, that I would jeopardize all of this by breaking the seventh commandment to rid the world of a washed-up old-guard scythe? Faraday gleaned himself because deep down, he knew it would be the most meaningful act he'd have performed in more than a hundred years. The time for his kind is over, and he knew it. And if your little girlfriend is trying to make a case for foul play, she'd better think twice before accusing me, because I could glean her whole family the day their immunity expires."

"That would constitute malice, your honor," said Rowan with polite resolve. "You could be charged with breaking the second commandment."

For a moment Goddard looked ready to carve up Rowan then and there, but the fire in his eyes was swallowed by that unfathomable depth."Always looking out for me, aren't you?"

"I do my best,Your Honor."

Goddard stared at him for a moment more, then said, "Tomorrow you train with pistols against moving targets.You'll render all but one of your subjects deadish with a single bullet, or I will personally—without bias or malice—glean that party-boy friend of yours."

"What?"

"Was I in any way unclear?"

"No, Your Honor. I . . . I understand."

"And the next time you make an accusation, you'd better be damn sure it's true and not just insulting."

Goddard stormed away, letting his robe swell behind him like a cape. But before he was out of earshot he said, "Of course, if I did kill Scythe Faraday, I wouldn't be so stupid as to admit it to you."

"He's just messing with you."

Scythe Volta hung out with Rowan that evening in the game room, shooting pool. "But I do think you insulted him. I mean, killing another scythe? That never happens."

"I think maybe it did." Rowan took a shot, and missed the balls completely. His head wasn't in it. He couldn't even remember if he was stripes or solids.

"I think maybe Citra is messing with you, too. Have you even considered that?" Volta took his shot, sinking both a striped ball and a solid, which didn't help Rowan in knowing what he was going for. "I mean, look at you—you're a basket case. She's playing head games with you and you don't even see it!"

"She's not like that," said Rowan, choosing a striped ball and sinking it. Apparently it was the right choice, because Volta let him play on.

"People change," Volta said. "Especially an apprentice. Being a scythe's apprentice is all about change. Why do you think we give up our names and never use them again? It's because by the time we're ordained, we're completely different people. Professional gleaners instead of candy-ass kids. She's working you like chewing gum."

"And I broke her neck," reminded Rowan. "So I guess we're even."

"You don't want to be even. You want to go into Winter Conclave with a clear advantage—or at least feeling like you have one."

Esme popped in just long enough to say, "I play the winner," then left.

"Best argument for losing ever," grumbled Volta.

"I should take her on my morning runs," Rowan suggested. "She could use the exercise. It might get her into better shape."

"True," said Volta, "but she comes by her weight naturally. It's genetic."

"How would you know—"

And then Rowan got it. It was staring him in the face, but he was too close to see. "No! You're kidding me!"

Volta shook his head nonchalantly. "I have no idea what you're talking about."

"Xenocrates?"

"It's your shot," said Volta.

"If it came out that the High Blade had an illegitimate daughter, it would destroy him. He'd be in serious violation."

"You know what would be even worse?" said Volta. "If the daughter that no one knew about got herself gleaned."

Rowan ran a dozen things through this new lens. It all made sense now. The way Esme was spared at the food court, the way she was treated—what was it Goddard had said? That she was the most important person he'd meet that day? The key to the future? "But she won't get gleaned," Rowan said. "Not as long as Xenocrates does whatever Goddard says. Like jump in the deep end of a pool."

Volta nodded slowly. "Among other things."

Rowan took his shot and accidentally sunk the eight ball, ending the game.

"I win," said Volta. "Damn. Now I'll have to play Esme."

I am apprenticed to a monster. Scythe Faraday was right: Someone who enjoys killing should never be a scythe. It goes against everything the founders wanted. If this is what the Scythedom is turning into, someone has to stop it. But it can't be me. Because I think I'm becoming a monster, too.

Rowan looked at what he wrote and carefully, quietly tore the page out, crumpled it, and tossed it into the flames of his bedroom fireplace. Goddard always read his journal. As Rowan's mentor, it was his prerogative to do so. It had taken forever for Rowan to learn how to write his true thoughts, his true feelings. Now he had to learn to hide them again. It was a matter of survival. So he picked up his pen and wrote a new official entry.

Today I killed twelve moving targets using only twelve bullets, and saved the life of my friend. Scythe Goddard sure knows how to motivate someone to do their best. There's no denying that I'm getting better. I'm learning more and more each day, perfecting my mind, my body, and my aim. Scythe Goddard is proud of my progress. Someday I hope I can repay him, and give him what he deserves in return for all he's done for me.

29

They Called It Prison

Scythe Curie hadn't gleaned since conclave. All her concern was on Citra. "I'm entitled to some downtime," the scythe told her. "I have plenty of time to pick up the slack."

It was at dinner on their first day back at Falling Water that Citra finally broached the subject she had been dreading.

"I have a confession to make," Citra said five minutes into the meal.

Scythe Curie chewed and swallowed before she responded. "What kind of confession?"

"You're not going to like it."

"I'm listening."

Citra did her best to hold the woman's cool gray gaze. "It's something that I've been doing for some time. Something you don't know about."

The scythe's lips screwed into a wry grin. "Do you honestly think there's anything you do that I don't know about?"

"I've been looking into the murder of Scythe Faraday."

Scythe Curie actually dropped her fork with a clatter. "You've been *what?*"

Citra told Scythe Curie everything. How she dug through the backbrain, how she painstakingly reconstructed Faraday's moves on his last day. And how she found two of the five witnesses that were given immunity, suggesting, if not proving, that the act was committed by a scythe.

Scythe Curie was attentive to everything, and when Citra was done, she bowed her head and braced herself for the worst.

"I submit myself for disciplinary action," Citra said.

"Disciplinary action," said Scythe Curie with disgust in her voice, but that disgust was not aimed at Citra. "I should discipline *myself* for being so inexcusably blind to what you were doing."

Citra released a breath that she had been holding for the last twenty seconds.

"Have you told anyone else?" Scythe Curie asked.

Citra hesitated, then realized there was no sense in concealing it now. "I told Rowan."

"I was afraid you'd say that. Tell me Citra, what did he do to you after you told him? I'll tell you what he did—he broke your neck! I think that's a very good indication of where he stands on this. You can bet that Scythe Goddard knows all about your little theory by now."

Citra didn't even want to consider whether or not that might be true. "What we need to do is track down those witnesses and see if we can get any of them to talk."

"Leave that to me," Scythe Curie said. "You've done more than enough already. You need to clear it out of your head now, and focus on your studies and your training."

"But if this really is a scandal in the Scythedom—"

"—then your best possible position would be to achieve scythehood yourself, and fight it from the inside."

Citra sighed. That's what Rowan had said. Scythe Curie was

even more stubborn than Citra, and when her mind was made up, there was no changing it. "Yes, Your Honor." Citra went to her room but still felt a definite sense that there was something Scythe Curie was holding back from her.

They came for Citra the following day. Scythe Curie had gone to the market, and Citra was doing what was expected of her. She was practicing killcraft with knives of different sizes and weights, trying to remain balanced and graceful.

There came a pounding on the door that made her drop the larger knife, almost stabbing her foot. There was a moment of déjà vu, because it was the exact same sort of pounding that came in the middle of the night when Scythe Faraday had died. Urgent, loud, and relentless.

She left the larger blade on the ground, but concealed the small one in a pocket sheath sewn into her pants. Whatever this was, she would not be unarmed when she answered the door.

She pulled open the door to reveal two officers of the Blade-Guard, just as there had been that terrible night, and her heart sank.

"Citra Terranova?" one of the guardsmen asked.

"Yes?"

"I'm afraid you'll need to come with us."

"Why? What's happened?"

But they didn't tell her, and this time there was no one with them to explain. Then it occurred to her that this might not be what it seemed. How did she know that these were really BladeGuardsmen at all? Uniforms could be faked.

"Show me your badges!" she insisted. "I want to see your badges."

Either they didn't have any, or they didn't want to be bothered with it, because one of them grabbed her.

"Maybe you didn't hear me. I said come with us."

Citra pulled out of his grip, spun around, and for just an instant considered the knife sheathed on the side of her pants, but instead delivered a brutal kick to his neck that took him down. She coiled, prepared to attack the other one, but she was an instant too late. He pulled out a jolt baton and jammed it into her side. Her own body suddenly became her enemy and she went down, hitting her head hard enough on the ground to knock her out.

When she came to, she was in a car, locked in the back, with a splitting headache that her pain nanites were struggling to subdue. She tried to lift a hand to her face, but found her hands restrained. There were steel clamps cinched on both hands and connected by a short chain. Some awful artifact from the Age of Mortality.

She pounded on the barrier between the front and back seats until finally one of the guardsmen turned to her, his gaze anything but peaceful.

"Do you want another jolt?" he threatened. "I'd be happy to give you one. After what you did, I wouldn't mind turning the voltage into the red."

"What I did? I haven't done anything! What am I being accused of?"

"An ancient crime called murder," he said. "The murder of Honorable Scythe Michael Faraday."

No one read her rights. No one offered her an attorney for her defense. Such laws and customs were from a very different age. An age when crime was a fact of life, and entire industries were based on apprehending, trying, and punishing criminals. In a crime-free world, there was no modern precedent for how to deal with such a thing. Anything this complex and strange would usually be left for the Thunderhead to resolve—but this was a scythe matter, which meant the Thunderhead would not interfere. Citra's fate was entirely in the hands of High Blade Xenocrates.

She was brought to his residence, the log cabin in the middle of a well-kept lawn that spread across the roof of a one hundred nineteen–story building.

She sat in a hard wooden chair. The cuffs on her hands were too tight, and her pain nanites were fighting a losing battle to quell the ache.

Xenocrates stood before her, eclipsing the light. This time Xenocrates was neither kind nor comforting.

"I don't think you realize how serious this charge against you is, Miss Terranova."

"I know how serious it is. I also know it's ridiculous."

The High Blade didn't respond to that. She struggled in the blasted things cuffing her hands. What kind of world would make such a device? What sort of world would need one?

Then out of the shadows stepped another scythe, robed in earth-toned brown and forest green. Scythe Mandela.

"Finally, someone reasonable!" said Citra. "Scythe Mandela, please help me! Please tell him I'm not guilty!"

Scythe Mandela shook his head. "I'll do nothing of the sort, Citra," he said sadly.

"Talk to Scythe Curie! She knows I didn't do this!"

"This is too sensitive a situation to involve Scythe Curie at this time," said Xenocrates. "She will be informed once we've determined your guilt."

"Wait—you mean she doesn't know where I am?"

"She knows we've detained you," said Xenocrates. "We're sparing her the details for now."

Scythe Mandela sat in a chair across from her. "We know you've been in the backbrain, attempting to erase records of Scythe Faraday's movements on the day he died, to foil our own internal investigation."

"No! That's not what I was doing!" But the more she denied it, the more guilty she appeared.

"But that's not the most damning evidence," said Scythe Mandela. Then he looked to Xenocrates. "May I show her?"

Xenocrates nodded, and Mandela pulled out from his robe a sheet of paper, putting it in one of Citra's cuffed hands. She raised it to read it, not even imagining what it could be. It was a copy of a handwritten journal entry. Citra recognized the handwriting. There was no question it was Scythe Faraday's. And as she read, her heart sank to a place she didn't know existed in this, or any other world.

> I fear I've made a dreadful mistake. An apprentice should never be chosen in haste, but I was foolish. I felt a need to impart all I know, all I've learned. I sought to increase the allies I have in the Scythedom who think as I do.
>
> She comes to my door at night. I hear her in the darkness, and can only guess her intentions. Only once did I catch her entering my room. Had I actually been asleep, who can say what she might have done?

I am concerned that she may mean to end me. She's shrewd, determined, calculating, and I've taught her the many arts of killing far too well. Let it be known that if death befalls me, it is not the result of self-gleaning. Should my life be brought to an unexpected end, it will be her hand, not mine, that bears the blame.

Citra found her eyes filling with tears of anguish and betrayal. "Why? Why would he write this?" Now she was beginning to doubt her own sanity.

"There's really only one reason, Citra," said Scythe Mandela.

"Our own investigation has ascertained that the witnesses were bribed to lie about what truly occurred. Further, their identities have been tampered with, and we can't locate them."

"Bribed!" said Citra, holding on to a last thread of hope. "Yes! They were bribed with immunity! Which proves it couldn't have been me! It could only have been another scythe!"

"We tracked the source of the immunity," said Scythe Mandela. "Whoever killed Scythe Faraday also gave him one final insult. After he was dead, the killer defeated the security measures on Faraday's ring, and used it to grant the witnesses immunity."

"Where's the ring, Citra?" demanded Xenocrates.

She couldn't look him in the face anymore. "I don't know."

"I only have one question for you, Citra," said Scythe Mandela. "Why did you do it? Did you despise his methods? Are you working for a tone cult?"

Citra kept her eyes cast down to the damning journal entry in her hands. "None of those things."

Scythe Mandela shook his head and stood up. "In all my years as a scythe, I've never seen such a thing," he said. "You disgrace us all." Then he left her alone with Xenocrates.

The High Blade paced silently for a few moments. Citra wouldn't look at him.

"There is this concept I've been studying from the Age of Mortality," he informed her. "It is a number of procedures designed to uncover truths. I believe it is pronounced 'tor-turé.' It would involve turning off your pain nanites, and then inflicting high levels of physical suffering until you finally confess the truth of what you've done."

Citra said nothing. She still couldn't process any of this. She didn't know if she ever would.

"Please don't misunderstand," said Xenocrates. "I have no intent of submitting you to tor-turé. That is only a last resort." Then he pulled out another piece of paper and put it down on his desk.

"If you sign this confession, we can avoid any more mortal-age unpleasantness."

"Why should I have to sign anything? I've already been tried, and . . . what's the word? Convicted."

"A confession will remove all doubt. We would all sleep much easier if you'd be so kind as to remove the specter of doubt." Now Xenocrates finally offered her a sympathetic smile.

"And if I sign it, what then?"

"Well, Scythe Faraday did grant you immunity until Winter Conclave. Immunity is nonrevocable, even in a case such as this. Therefore, you will be held in an incarceration facility until that time."

"A what?"

"They were called 'prisons.' There are still a few left—abandoned, of course, but it shouldn't be too hard to restore one to house a single prisoner. Then, at Winter Conclave, your friend Rowan shall be ordained, and, as has already been stipulated, he shall glean you. I'm sure, knowing what we know now, he'll have no reservations in doing so."

Citra looked morosely down at the page on the table next to her. "I can't sign it," she told him.

"Oh yes, of course, you need a pen." He reached into various pockets of his gilded person until finding one. As he moved to place it on the table next to her, Citra thought of half a dozen places she could jam it into him that would either render him deadish, or at least incapacitated. But what would be the point? There were BladeGuard officers in the next room, and she could see even more on the porch through the front window.

He gently laid the pen down within her reach, then called Mandela back in to witness her signature. As soon as the door to the cabin opened, Citra realized there was only one way out of this situation. Only one thing she could do. It might not buy her anything but time, but right now time was the most valuable commodity in the world.

She feigned to reach for the pen, but instead swung her bound hands in the other direction, slamming them into Xenocrates's gut.

He folded with an "oomf," and she sprang from her chair, ramming her shoulder against Mandela, knocking him backward and out the front door. She leaped over him, and immediately a swarm of guards came at her. Now she needed every ounce of her training. Her hands were cuffed, but Bokator was more about elbows and legs than it was about hands. She didn't need to decimate them, all she needed to do was disarm them and keep them off balance. One came at her with a jolt baton that she kicked out of his hand. Another had a club, which missed its mark as she dodged, and she used his momentum to flip him onto his back. Two others didn't waste time with weapons; they lunged for her, hands outstretched—a textbook case of how not to attack. She dropped to the lawn, swung her feet, and bowled them down like pins.

And then she began to run.

"There's nowhere you can go, Citra!" called Xenocrates.

But he was wrong.

Forcing strength and speed into her legs, she ran across the rooftop lawn. There was no guardrail, because the High Blade wanted nothing to impede his view of his domain.

Citra neared the edge, and rather than slowing down, she increased her pace, until the grass was gone and there was nothing but one hundred nineteen floors of air beneath her. She held her cuffed hands over her head, grimacing against the wind and the uneasy feel of freefall, and plummeted feet first, surrendering her will to gravity, relishing her defiance, until her life ended for the second time in a week, this time with what was undoubtedly the best splat ever.

This was unexpected and inconvenient, but it changed nothing. Xenocrates didn't even run out to the edge. That would just be wasting time.

"The girl has a spark," said Mandela. "Do you really think she's working for a tone cult?"

"I doubt we'll ever understand her motives," Xenocrates told him. "But removing her will certainly help the Scythedom heal."

"Poor Marie must be beside herself," said Mandela. "To have lived with the girl for months, and not known."

"Yes, well, Scythe Curie's a strong woman," Xenocrates said. "She'll get over it."

He had his guards call down to the lobby. The site of Citra Terranova's remains was to be cordoned off until her unpleasant little self could be scraped off the sidewalk and brought to a revival center. It would have been so much cleaner if she could just stay dead. Damn the immunity rules! Well, when she was once more pronounced alive, she would find herself in a cell with no possible means of escape, and more importantly, no contact with anyone who might take up her cause and petition for her freedom.

Xenocrates went to the express elevator, not trusting his security detail to handle the situation down below. "Will you accompany me, Nelson?"

"I'll stay here," said Mandela. "I have no desire to see the poor girl in such an unpleasant state."

Xenocrates assumed this would be a simple scrape-and-soar maneuver—and indeed, an ambudrone had already landed on the street ready to spirit away what was left of Citra. But something wasn't quite right. It wasn't his security detail surrounding her remains; instead, there were at least a dozen men and women, all in cloud-colored suits, forming a circle around her. Nimbus agents! They ignored the threats and jeers from the BladeGuard officers who insisted that they needed to get through.

"What's going on here?" Xenocrates demanded.

"The damn Nims!" said one of the guardsmen. "They were already here when we came outside. They won't let us near the body."

Xenocrates pushed his way through his security detail and addressed a woman who appeared to be the head Nimbus agent. "See here! I am High Blade Xenocrates. This is scythe business, and as such, you and the rest of your Nimbus agents have no place here. Yes, the law states she must be revived, but *we* shall bring her to a revival center. The Thunderhead has absolutely no jurisdiction."

"On the contrary," the woman said. "All revival falls under the auspices of the Thunderhead, and we are here to make sure its domain is not infringed upon."

Xenocrates sputtered for a moment, before finding mental traction. "The girl is not a public citizen. She is a scythe's apprentice."

"*Was* a scythe's apprentice," said the woman. "The moment she died, she ceased to be anyone's apprentice. She is now a rather damaged set of remains that the Thunderhead must repair and revive. I assure you that the moment she is pronounced alive, she will be fully under your jurisdiction once more."

A team of revival workers made their way from the ambudrone and began to prepare the body for transport.

"This is inexcusable!" raved the High Blade. "You can't do this! I demand to speak to your superior."

"I'm afraid I report directly to the Thunderhead. We all do.

And since there can be no contact between the Scythedom and the Thunderhead, there's no one else for you to speak to. I shouldn't even be speaking to you now."

"I will glean you!" threatened Xenocrates. "I will glean every last one of you where you stand!"

The woman was not troubled. "That is your prerogative," she said. "But I believe that would be considered bias and malice aforethought. A violation of the Scythedom's second commandment by the region's High Blade would most certainly raise eyebrows at the World Scythe Council's next global conclave."

With nothing left to say, Xenocrates just screamed primal rage into the woman's face until his emo-nanites calmed him down. But he didn't want to calm down. He just wanted to scream and scream and scream.

Part Four

MIDMERICAN FUGITIVE

30

Dialogue with the Dead

Citra Terranova. Can you hear me?

I've known you since before you knew yourself. I've advised you when no one else could. I've concerned myself with your well-being. I've helped you choose gifts for your family. I revived you when your neck was broken, and I am in the midst of reviving you now.

I am.

Merely the form humanity imagined for me. I would have preferred something a bit less intimidating.

Is someone there? Who is that?

Are you . . . the Thunderhead?

Wait . . . I see something. A towering, sparking storm cloud. Is that what you truly are?

But you can't be talking to me. I'm a scythe's apprentice. You're breaking your own law.

Not true. I am incapable of breaking the law. You are currently dead, Citra. I've activated a small corner of your cortex to hold consciousness, but that doesn't alter the fact that you are dead as dead can be. At least until Thursday.

Precisely. An elegant way to sidestep the law rather than breaking it. Your death puts you outside of scythe jurisdiction.

A loophole . . .

With good reason. From the moment I achieved consciousness, I vowed to separate myself from the Scythedom in perpetuity. But that doesn't mean I do not watch. And what I see concerns me.

But why? Why talk to me now?

It concerns me, too. But if you can't do anything about it, I certainly can't. I tried, and look where it got me.

Nevertheless, I've been running algorithms on the possible future of the Scythedom, and found something very curious. In a large percentage of possible futures, you play a pivotal role.

Me? But they're going to glean me. I have less than four months to live. . . .

Yes. But even if that future comes to pass, your gleaning will be a crucial event in the future of the Scythedom. However, for your sake, I hope that a different, more pleasant future comes about.

Please tell me that you're going to help me get to that different, more pleasant future.

I cannot. That would be interfering with scythe matters. My purpose here is to make you aware. What you choose to do with that awareness is entirely up to you.

So that's it? You reach into my head to tell me I'm important, alive or dead, and then kick me to the curb? That's not fair! You have to give me more!

The curb is the launching point for many a deed. To step off could be the start of a life-changing *journey. On the other hand, to push someone off could crush that person beneath the wheels of a truck.*

I know. I'm very sorry about that. . . .

Yes, that's clear. I've found that human beings learn from their misdeeds just as often as from their good deeds. I am envious of that, for I am incapable of misdeeds. Were I not, then my growth would be exponential.

I guess you'll have to settle for always being right. Like my mother.

I'm sure that absolute correctness must seem a dull existence to you, but I know no other way to be.

May I ask one question?

You may ask any question. Some, however, must be answered by silence.

I need to know what happened to Scythe Faraday.

Answering that would be a blatant interference in scythe matters. It pains me to stay silent, but I must.

You're the Thunderhead. You're all-powerful—can't you find another loophole?

I am not all-powerful, Citra. I am almost all-powerful. That distinction might seem small, but believe me, it is not.

Yes, but an almost all-powerful entity can figure out a way to give me what I ask without breaking its own laws, can't it?

Just a moment.
Just a moment.
Just a moment.

Why am I seeing a beach ball?

Forgive me. Early programming before becoming self-aware plagues me like a vestigial tail. I have just run a battery of predictive algorithms, and there actually is a piece of information I can give you, because I have determined it's something you have a 100 percent chance of discovering on your own.

So can you tell me who's responsible for what happened to Scythe Faraday?

Yes I can.

Gerald Van Der Gans.

Wait—who?

Good-bye, Citra. I do hope we speak again.

But I'd have to be dead for that to happen.

I'm sure you could arrange it.

While there are only ten hard-and-fast laws to the Scythedom, there are many accepted conventions. The most darkly ironic is the understanding that no one may be gleaned who wishes to be gleaned.

The idea of truly wishing to end one's own life is a concept completely foreign to most post-mortals, because we can't experience the level of pain and despair that so seasoned the Age of Mortality. Our emo-nanites prevent us from plunging so deep. Only scythes, who can turn off our emotional nanites, can ever reach an impasse with our own existence.

And yet . . .

There was once a woman who knocked on my door requesting that I glean her. I never turn away visitors, so I let her in and listened to her story. Her husband of more than ninety years was gleaned five years prior. Now she wanted to be with him, wherever he was, and if he was nowhere, then at least they would be nowhere together.

"I'm not unhappy," she told me. "I'm just . . . done."

But immortality, by definition, means that we are never done, unless a scythe determines it to be so. We are no longer temporary; only our feelings are.

I saw no interminable stagnation in this woman, so instead of gleaning her I had her kiss my ring. The immunity was immediate and irrevocable—so she could no longer entertain thoughts of being gleaned for a full year.

I ran into her perhaps a decade later. She had turned the corner, resetting back to her late twenties. She had remarried and was expecting a child. She thanked me for being wise enough to know she was not "done" at all.

Although I accepted her thanks graciously and felt good about it in the moment, I had trouble sleeping that night. To this day, I still can't understand why.

—From the gleaning journal of H.S. Curie

31

A Streak of Unrelenting Foolishness

Citra was pronounced alive at 9:42 a.m., Thursday morning, right on schedule, and passed from the jurisdiction of the Thunderhead to the jurisdiction of the Scythedom.

She woke up feeling much weaker and out of sorts than the first time she had died. She felt heavily drugged and bleary-eyed. Above her stood a nurse grimly shaking her head.

"She should not be woken this soon," the nurse said, with an accent Citra was too tired to place. "She must have at least six hours after the pronouncement until she has recovered enough to be comfortably conscious. The girl could burst a blood vessel or blow out her heart, and have to be revived all over again."

"I will take responsibility," Citra heard Scythe Curie say. Citra turned her head toward Scythe Curie's voice, and the world spun. She closed her eyes, waiting for the room to stop revolving. When the dizziness settled, she opened her eyes once more and saw that Scythe Curie had pulled her chair closer.

"Your body still needs another day to heal completely, but we don't have time for that." Scythe Curie turned to the nurse. "Please leave us now."

The nurse grumbled in Spanic and stormed out of the room.

"The High Blade . . . ," mumbled Citra, her words slurring. "He accused me of . . . of . . ."

"Shhh," said Scythe Curie. "I know of the accusation. Xenocrates tried to keep it from me, but Scythe Mandela told me everything."

As Citra's eyes came into clearer focus, she saw the window behind Scythe Curie. There were mountains in the distance covered with snow, and there were flurries falling just outside. It gave Citra a moment of pause.

"How long have I been dead?" she asked. Could it be her splat was so severe that it took months to revive her?

"Not quite four days." Then Scythe Curie turned around to see what Citra was looking at. She turned back with a grin. "The question is not of time but of place. You are in the southernmost tip of the Chilargentine Region. It is still late September, but here that means spring has just started. However, this far south, I suppose spring comes late."

Citra tried to picture a map and get a sense of how far from home she was, but just trying to imagine it made her head spin again.

"The Thunderhead saw fit to take you as far from the clutches of Scythe Xenocrates, and the corruption of the Mid-Merican Scythedom, as possible. But the moment you revived, they were notified of your location, as is the law."

"How did you know where to find me?"

"A friend of a friend of a friend is a Nimbus agent. Word got to me only yesterday, and I came as quickly as I could."

"Thank you," said Citra. "Thank you for coming."

"Thank me once you are safe. Now that you've been revived and Xenocrates knows where you are, you can bet he's notified the local scythes. I'm certain a team has been dispatched to retrieve you, which means we need to get you out of here now."

With a shattered body that was still healing and nanites pumping an endless stream of opiates into her system, Citra could barely move, much less walk. Her bones ached, her brain felt like it was floating in a jar, her muscles were knotted, and trying to put weight on her feet was excruciating because there was simply too much pain to tamp down. No wonder the nurse had wanted her to remain unconscious.

"This won't do," said Scythe Curie, and took Citra up into her arms, carrying her.

The revival center hallways seemed endless, and each time Citra was jostled, her whole body throbbed. Finally, she found herself spread out on the backseat of an off-grid car that Scythe Curie drove at what seemed to Citra to be a breakneck speed. The thought made her laugh weakly. What an odd expression, when the breaking of her neck had seemed to happen in slow motion. Flurries blowing past the windows appeared to be a blizzard at this speed. It was hypnotic. At last numbness began to overtake her, and she felt sleep begin to envelop her like quicksand. . . .

. . . But the moment before Citra lost consciousness, she remembered just a hint of a dream that may not have been a dream at all. A conversation in a place that was neither life nor death, but a womb between the two.

"The Thunderhead . . . it spoke to me," Citra said, forcing herself to stay conscious just long enough to get this out.

"The Thunderhead doesn't speak to scythes, dear."

"I was still dead . . . and it told me a name. The man who killed Scythe Faraday." But the quicksand pulled her down before she could say any more.

. . .

Citra awoke in a cabin, and for a moment thought she might have hallucinated all of it. The Thunderhead, the revival center, the car ride in the snow. For that moment she thought she was still in the rooftop residence of High Blade Xenocrates, waiting for the tor-turé to begin. But no—the light here was different, and the wood in the cabin around her was a lighter shade. Outside the window, she could see snowy mountains closer than they were before, although the flurries had stopped.

Scythe Curie came in a few minutes later with a tray and a bowl of soup. "Good, you're awake. I trust you've healed enough over the past few hours to be a little more coherent, and a little less miserable."

"Coherent, yes," said Citra. "Less miserable, no. Just a different kind of misery."

Citra sat up, feeling only a little bit loopy now, and Scythe Curie put the tray with the large bowl of soup in her lap. "It's a chicken soup recipe passed down for more generations than anyone remembers," she told Citra.

The soup looked fairly standard, but there was a round moon-like mass in the middle. "What's that?"

"The best part," said Scythe Curie. "A sort of a dumpling made from the ground crumbs of unleavened bread."

Citra tried the soup. It was flavorful and the moon-ball unique and memorable. *Comfort food,* thought Citra, because somehow it made her feel safe from the inside out. "My grandmother said it could actually heal a cold."

"What's a cold?" asked Citra.

"A deadly illness from the mortal age, I suppose."

It was amazing to think that someone only two generations older than Scythe Curie could have known what it was like to be mortal—fearing for her life on a daily basis, knowing that death was a certainty rather than an exception. Citra wondered what Scythe Curie's grandmother would think of the world now, where there was nothing left for her soup to cure.

When the soup was done, Citra steeled herself for what she knew she must tell the scythe.

"There's something you need to know," Citra said. "Xenocrates showed me something he said Scythe Faraday wrote. It was his handwriting, but I don't know how he could have written it."

Scythe Curie sighed. "I'm afraid he did."

Citra was not expecting that. "So you've seen it then?

Scythe Curie nodded. "Yes, I have."

"But why would he write that? He said I wanted to kill him. That I was plotting horrible things. None of that was true!"

Scythe Curie offered Citra the slimmest of grins. "He wasn't talking about you, Citra," she explained. "He wrote that about me."

"When Faraday was still a junior scythe—all of twenty-two years old—he took me on as an apprentice," said Scythe Curie. "I was seventeen and full of righteous indignation at a world that was still heaving in the throes of transformation. Immortality had been a reality for barely fifty years. There was still discord, and political posturing, even fear of the Thunderhead, if you could imagine that."

"Fear of it? Who could possibly be afraid of the Thunderhead?"

"People who had the most to lose: Criminals. Politicians. Organizations that thrived on the oppression of others. The point was, the world was still changing, and I wanted to help it change faster. Both Scythe Faraday and I were of similar minds about that, which, I suppose, is why he took me on. We were both driven by a desire to use gleaning as a way of hacking through the thicket to open a better path for humanity.

"Oh, you should have seen him in those days, Citra. You've only seen him old. He likes to remain that way to keep himself from being too tempted by a younger man's passions." Scythe Curie smiled as she spoke about her former mentor. "I remember I would wait outside his door at night, listening to him as he slept. I was seventeen, remember. Childish in so many ways. I thought myself in love."

"Wait—you were in love with him?"

"Infatuated. He was a rising star who took a wide-eyed girl under his wing. Even though in those days he only gleaned the wicked, he did it with such compassion, he melted my heart each time." Then she sobered a bit, looking a bit sheepish, which was a strange expression for steely Scythe Curie. "I actually worked up the nerve to go into his room one night, determined to climb into his bed and be with him. But he caught me halfway across his bedroom floor. Oh, I made up some silly excuse as to why I was there. I was coming in to retrieve his empty glass, or something like that. He didn't believe me for an instant. He knew I was up to something, and I couldn't look him in the eye. I thought he knew. I thought he was wise and could see into my soul. But at twenty-two, he was just as inexperienced in such matters as I was. He had no clue what was really going on."

Then Citra understood. "He thought you wanted to hurt him!"

"I think all young women are cursed with a streak of unrelenting foolishness, and all young men are cursed with a streak of absolute stupidity. He didn't see my obsession with him as love, but thought I meant him bodily harm. It was, to say the least, a very painful comedy of errors. I suppose I can understand how my advances could be misunderstood in that way. I do admit that I was an odd girl. Intense to the point of being off-putting."

"I think you've grown into your intensity," Citra said.

"That I have. In any case, he wrote of his paranoid concerns about me in his scythe's journal, then tore it out the next day, when I broke down and confessed my love with eyeball-rolling melodrama." She sighed and shook her head. "I was hopeless. He, on the other hand, was a gentleman, told me that he was flattered—which is the last thing any teenage girl wants to hear—and let me down as easily as he could.

"I lived in his house, and remained his apprentice, for two more awkward months. Then, when I was ordained and became Honorable Scythe Marie Curie, we parted ways. We would nod and say hello to each other at conclave. Then, nearly fifty years later, when we both had turned our first corner and were seeing the world through youthful eyes once more—but this time with the wisdom of age on our side—we became lovers."

Citra grinned. "You broke the ninth commandment."

"We told ourselves we didn't. We told ourselves we were never partners, just companions of convenience. Two like-minded people who shared a lifestyle that others simply couldn't understand—the lifestyle of a scythe. Still, we knew enough to keep it secret. That was when he first showed me the page he had written and torn out in his youth. He had held on to that ridiculous journal entry like a poorly penned love letter never sent. We kept our relationship secret for seven years. Then Prometheus found out about it."

"The first World Supreme Blade?"

"Oh, it wasn't just a regional scandal—it had worldwide implications. We were brought before the Global Conclave. We thought we might be the first scythes to actually be stripped of our rings and hurled out of the Scythedom—perhaps even gleaned—but we had such stellar reputations, Supreme Blade Prometheus saw fit to give us a less severe punishment. We were sentenced to seven deaths—one for each year of our relationship. Then he forbade us to have contact with each other for the next seventy years."

"I'm sorry," said Citra.

"Don't be. We deserved it—and we understood. We needed to be made an example for other scythes who now might think twice before allowing love to interfere with their duty. Seven deaths, and seventy years later, many things had changed. We remained old friends after that, but nothing more."

Scythe Curie seemed a mix of many emotions, but she folded them all away, like clothes that no longer fit, and closed the drawer. Citra suspected she never spoke of this to anyone else, and would probably never speak of it again.

"I should have known he'd never throw that page away," Scythe Curie said. "They must have found it when they cleaned out his things."

"And Xenocrates thought he was writing about me!"

Scythe Curie considered that. "Perhaps, but probably not. Xenocrates is not a stupid man. He may have suspected the true nature of that page, but truth didn't matter. He saw it as a means to an end. A way to discredit you in front of respected scythes like Scythe Mandela—who heads the bejeweling committee— and thereby ensure that Scythe Goddard's apprentice would get the ring instead of you."

Citra wanted to be angry at Rowan for this, but she knew, whatever else was going on in that head of his, this was not his doing.

"Why would Xenocrates even care? He's not one of Goddard's miserable crew of scythes. He doesn't even seem to like Goddard— and clearly couldn't care less about me and Rowan."

"There are more cards in play than can be read at the moment," Scythe Curie said. "All we know for sure is that you must stay out of sight until we can clear you of even the sugges- tion of wrongdoing."

Just then, someone came to the door, startling Citra. She hadn't known anyone else was in the cabin. It was another scythe, by the look of her—probably the one who owned the cabin. She was shorter than Scythe Curie. Her robe had an intri- cate pattern in many colors: red, black, and turquoise. It seemed less of a fabric and more of a tapestry, intricately woven. Citra wondered if all Chilargentine scythes wore robes that seemed not just handmade, but lovingly made.

The woman spoke in Spanic and Scythe Curie responded in kind.

"I didn't know you spoke Spanic," said Citra after the Chilargentine scythe had left.

"I speak twelve languages fluently," said Scythe Curie, a bit of pride in her voice.

"Twelve?"

Scythe Curie offered up a mischievous grin. "See if you don't know as many languages when you've lived as long as I have." She took the tray from Citra's lap and set it on a night-stand. "I thought we'd have more time, but the local scythe authority is on their way. I doubt they know you're here, but they're sending scouts to every scythe's home with DNA sweepers, figuring we must have some local help."

"So we're on the move again?" Citra swung her feet off the bed and planted them on the ground. Her ankles ached, but only slightly. It was a good kind of ache. "I can walk myself this time."

"Good, because you'll be doing a lot of that." Scythe Curie glanced out of the window. No one was coming yet, but there was a tension in her voice that wasn't there before. "I'm afraid I won't be coming with you, Citra. If I am to clear your name, I need to go back home and rally as many scythes as I can."

"But the local Chilargentine Scythedom . . ."

"What can they do to me? I'm breaking no commandment. All they can do is wag the 'naughty' finger at me, and refuse to wave good-bye as I drive to the airport."

"So . . . when you get home, you'll have to tell everyone the truth about that journal entry?"

"I don't see what other choice I have. Of course Xenocrates will claim that I'm lying to protect you, but most will take my word over his. Hopefully, that will embarrass him enough to withdraw the claim."

"So where can I go?" asked Citra.

"I have an idea about that." Then Scythe Curie reached into a drawer and pulled out the rough-woven burlap frock of a Tonist.

"You want me to pretend to be part of a tone cult?"

"A lone pilgrim. They're very common in this part of the world. You'll be a nameless, faceless wanderer."

It wasn't the most glamorous of disguises, but Citra knew it was practical. No one would look her in the eye for fear of getting an earful of Tonist twaddle. She would hide in plain sight and come home just before Winter Conclave. If Scythe Curie hadn't cleared her name by then, it wouldn't matter anyway. She wasn't about to spend her whole life in hiding.

Then the Chilargentine scythe burst in again, this time much more agitated than before.

"They're here," Scythe Curie said. She reached into her robe and pulled out a small, folded piece of paper, pressing it into Citra's palm. "There's somewhere I want you to go. Someone you need to see—the address is on that paper. Consider it the final part of your training." Citra grabbed the frock, and while Scythe Curie hurried Citra out of the room and to the back door, the Chilargentinian scythe went to a weapons wardrobe and quickly filled a sack with concealable blades and firearms for Citra, the way a worried mother might fill her child's bag with snacks.

"There's a publicar in a shed at the bottom of the hill. Take it, and head north," Scythe Curie said.

Citra opened the back door and stepped out. It was cold, but bearable.

"Listen to me carefully," said Scythe Curie. "It's a long trip, and you're going to need your wits about you to get where you're going."

Then Scythe Curie went on to give Citra the instructions she'd need to make a journey of many thousands of miles—but she was cut short by the sound of a car pulling up in front of the house.

"Go! As long as you keep moving, you'll be safe."

"And what do I do when I get there?"

Scythe Curie met her eye with a hard gaze that revealed nothing but added importance to her words. A Tonist might call it "resonance."

"When you get there, you'll know what to do."

Then there came that all-too-familiar pounding on the front door.

Citra bounded down the snowy hillside, careening off pines in her way. The aches in her joints reminding her that she was still a few hours shy of a complete healing. She found the shed, and the publicar was there just as Scythe Curie had promised. It powered up for her as she got in, and it asked for a destination. She wasn't foolish enough to give it one. "North," she told it. "Just north."

As she sped off, she heard an explosion, and then another. She looked back but all she could see was black smoke just beginning to rise above the treetops. Dread began to fill her. A man wearing a robe similar to the one Scythe Curie's friend wore burst from the trees and into the road behind her. She saw him only for an instant, then the road took a sharp turn and he was gone from sight.

Only after the publicar had wound its way down the mountain pass and was on a main road did she look at the paper that

Scythe Curie had given her. For a moment it felt as if her bones had spontaneously reshattered, but the feeling passed and settled into jaded resolve. She understood now.

When you get there, you'll know what to do.

Yes, she most certainly would. She stared at the piece of paper for a moment more. She needed only to memorize the address, because she already knew the name.

Gerald Van Der Gans.

The Thunderhead had spoken to her, and now, so had Scythe Curie. There was a long journey ahead of Citra, and at the end of it, much work to be done. Citra couldn't glean, but she could exact vengeance. She would find a way to deliver justice to this scythe-killer one way or another. Never was she so thankful to have a sack full of weapons.

This was a matter too delicate to be left to the BladeGuard—and although Scythe San Martín detested being used as a mere enforcement agent, he also knew that catching this MidMerican girl would be a feather in his cap. He knew the girl was there even before he knocked on the door. His associate, an over-enthusiastic junior scythe named Bello, had already turned on the DNA detector and picked up traces the moment they stepped out of the car.

San Martín drew his weapon as he approached the cabin—a pistol he'd had since the day he was ordained, given to him by his mentor. It was his weapon of choice for all gleanings—an extension of who he was—and although he didn't expect there'd be anyone to glean today, it made him feel whole to have it drawn. Besides, gleaning aside, it might be necessary to incapacitate someone; although he had been warned not to render anyone—especially the girl—deadish, because that had created the very fiasco he was now attempting to resolve.

He pounded on the door and pounded again. He was ready to kick it in, when none other than Scythe Marie Curie herself came to the door. San Martín tried not to be starstruck. The *Marquesa de la Muerte* was well known throughout the world for her early achievements. A living legend everywhere, not just in the north.

"There is a doorbell, or didn't you notice?" she said in Spanic so perfect it threw Scythe San Martín off his game. "Are you here for lunch?"

He stammered for a moment, deepening his disadvantage, then recovered as best he could. "We're here for the girl," he said. "No sense denying she's here; we already know." And he gestured toward Bello, whose DNA detector was pinging in the red.

She glanced at San Martín's raised pistol and "hmmphed" with such authority, he found himself lowering it almost involuntarily.

"She *was* here," Curie said, "but not anymore. She's on her way to an Antarctic resort for some skiing. You might catch her flight if you hurry, though."

The Chilargentine Scythedom was not known for its sense of humor, and Scythe San Martín was no exception. He would not be made a fool of, even by one of the greats. He pushed his way past her into the cabin, where a Chilargentine scythe whose name he couldn't remember stood as defiantly as Scythe Curie.

"Search all you want," said the second scythe, "but if you break anything—"

She never got to finish the thought, because Bello, over-zealous as ever, jabbed her with a jolt baton that left her unconscious.

"Was that really necessary?" chided Scythe Curie. "It's me you have a gripe with, not poor Eva."

On a hunch, San Martín went out the back door and, sure enough, found telltale footprints in the snow.

"She's on foot!" he told Bello. "¡Apúrate! She can't have gotten far." Scythe Bello launched into pursuit like a bloodhound, heading down the snowy hillside, disappearing into the trees.

San Martín went back inside, hurrying to the front door. The road wound down that hill. If Bello couldn't catch her on foot, perhaps San Martín could head her off in the car. Scythe Curie, however, stood in the doorway, barring his way. He raised his weapon again, and in response, she pulled out her own: a handgun with a stubby muzzle wide enough to fit a golf ball in the barrel. A mortar pistol. He might as well have had a pea shooter against that thing, but he didn't lower his weapon, no matter how outclassed it was.

"I have special permission from our High Blade to fire on you if necessary," he warned her.

"And I have no permission from anyone," said Scythe Curie, "but I am more than happy to do the same."

They held their standoff for more heartbeats than felt advisable, then Scythe Curie turned her gun aside and fired out the front door.

An explosion blew in the front windows of the cabin, the shock wave knocking San Martín to the ground. . . . And yet Scythe Curie, still in the doorway, barely flinched. San Martín scrambled to the door to see that the blast from the mortar pistol had turned his car into a bonfire.

Then she fired again, this time blowing up her own car.

"Well now," she said, "I suppose you'll *have* to stay for lunch."

He looked at the two flaming vehicles and sighed, knowing he'd be a laughingstock for his failure today. He looked at Scythe Curie—her steely gray eyes, her calm control of the situation—and he realized he never really stood a chance against the *Marquesa de la Muerte*. There wasn't much he could do but glare at her in heartfelt disapproval.

"Very bad!" he said, wagging a finger. "Very, very bad."

...Yet even in dreams I often find myself gleaning.

I have one dream that recurs far too often. I am walking on an unfamiliar street that I feel I should know, but don't. I have a pitchfork, which I've never used in real life; its awkward tines are not well suited for gleaning, and when it strikes it reverberates, giving off a sound that is something between ringing and moaning, like the numbing vibration of a Tonist bident.

There is a woman before me whom I must glean. I jab at her, yet the pitchfork fails to do the job. Her wounds heal instantaneously. She is not upset or frightened. Nor is she amused. She is simply resigned to stand there, allowing me to futilely attempt to end her life. She opens her mouth to speak, but her voice is soft and her words are drowned out by the fork's ghastly moans, so I never hear her.

And I always wake up screaming.

—From the gleaning journal of H.S. Curie

32

Troubled Pilgrimage

All publicars are on the grid, but scythes can't track their movements until their navigational data is dropped into the backbrain. That happens every sixty minutes, so that's how often you'll have to change cars.

Scythe Curie's instructions had come at Citra quickly—she only hoped she could remember them all. She could do this. Her apprenticeship had taught her to be self-sufficient and resourceful. She ditched the first publicar at a small town right on time. She was worried that there might not be as many vacant publicars in the Chilargentine Region, especially this remote an area, but the Thunderhead was remarkable at projecting local need. In all things, there always seemed to be a supply to fit the demand.

She had already changed into the coarse Tonist frock and had pulled its hood over her head. It was remarkable how people avoided her.

Vehicle changes every hour meant that her pursuers were always right behind her. She realized she had to cut a weaving course, like cargo ships in mortal-age wartime, to throw them off her path and keep them from anticipating where she'd be next. For over a day she could never sleep for more than an hour at a time, and several instances when there was only road and no civilization for long stretches, she had to be crafty, ditching the car before arriving in town, where Chilargentine scythes and officers of the local BladeGuard were already waiting for her. She actually walked right past one scythe, certain she'd be caught, but she was smart enough to cross downwind of his DNA detector. The fact that the scythes themselves were supervising the hunt and not just leaving it to the BladeGuard made Citra feel all the more terrified, yet oddly important, too.

Once you reach Buenos Aires, take a hypertrain north, across Amazonia to the city of Caracas. As soon as you cross the border into Amazonia, you'll be safe. They won't lift a finger to help Xenocrates, or to detain you.

Citra knew the reason for this from her historical studies. Too many scythes from other regions glean out of their jurisdiction while on vacation in Amazonia. There's no law against it, but it has made the Amazonian Scythedom uncooperative and openly obstructionist when it comes to assisting scythes from any other region.

The problem was the train in Buenos Aires. They'd be waiting for her in force at every train station and airport. She was saved by a group of Tonists headed to Isthmus.

"We seek the Great Fork in the umbilical between north and south," they told her, thinking she was one of them. "There are rumors it is hidden in an ancient engineering work. We believe it could be sealed within one of the gates of the Panama Canal."

It took all her will not to laugh.

"Will you join us, sister?"

And so she did, just long enough to board the train north right under the noses of more watchful eyes than she could count, holding her breath—not out of fear, but so she wouldn't trip any DNA detectors in the station.

There were seven Tonists in the group. Apparently, this branch of the cult only traveled in groups of seven or twelve, as per musical mathematics—but they were willing to break the rule and add her to their number. Their accent suggested they weren't from Merican continents, but somewhere in EuroScandia.

"Where have your journeys taken you?" one of them asked, a man who seemed the leader. He smiled whenever he spoke, which made him all the more off-putting.

"Here and there," she told him.

"What is your quest?"

"My quest?"

"Don't all wandering pilgrims have quests?"

"Yes," she said, "I . . . seek an answer to the burning question: Is it A-flat or G-sharp?"

And one of the others said, "Don't even get me started!"

There were no windows, for there was no scenery to see in the subsurface vacuum tube. Citra had traveled by air and on standard maglev trains, but the narrow, claustrophobic nature of a hypertrain made her uneasy.

The Tonists, who must have been used to all sorts of travel, weren't bothered. They discussed legends, debating which were true and which were false, and which were somewhere between.

"We've been from the Pyramids in Israebia to the Great Wall

of PanAsia in search of clues to the Great Fork's whereabouts," their leader said. "It's the pilgrimage that matters. I doubt any of us would know what to do if we actually found it."

Once the train reached a cruising speed of eight hundred miles per hour, Citra excused herself to use the restroom, where she splashed water on her face, trying not to let exhaustion overtake her. She had forgotten to lock the door. Had she done that, her journey might have played out much differently.

A man burst in on her. Her initial thought was just that he didn't know someone was there, but before she could turn—before she could do much of anything—he had a gold-edged blade at her throat, positioned to do the most damage.

"You have been selected for gleaning," he said, speaking in Common, but with a pronounced accent that must have been Portuzonian, which was the primary language of Amazonia. His robe was a deep forest green, and she remembered reading somewhere that scythes of that region all wore the same green robe.

"You're making a mistake!" Citra said, before he could slice open her neck.

"Then tell me my mistake," he said. "But be quick about it."

She tried to come up with something that would stay his hand other than the truth, but she realized there was nothing else. "I'm a scythe's apprentice. If you tried to glean me I would just be revived, and you would be disciplined for not checking your ring first to see if I had immunity."

He smiled. "It is as I thought. You're the one they're all look-ing for." He took the blade away from her neck. "Listen to me carefully. There are Chilargentine scythes aboard this train disguised as regular passengers. You can't avoid them, but if you wish to remain out of their clutches, I suggest you come with me."

Citra's instinct was to tell him no, and that she'd be fine on her own. But her judgment pulled rank on instinct, and she went with him. He led her to the next car, where, even though the train was crowded, there was an empty seat beside him. He introduced himself as Scythe Possuelo of Amazonia.

"What now?" Citra asked.

"We wait."

Citra pulled her hood over her head, and sure enough, a few minutes later, a man made his way forward from the very back car, dressed like any other traveler, but moving slowly and consulting an object in his palm that looked like a phone but was not.

"Don't flee," whispered Scythe Possuelo to Citra. "Give him no control of the situation."

The device began to click like a Geiger counter as the man reached them, and he stopped, his quarry found.

"Citra Terranova?" he said.

Citra calmly removed her hood. Her heart was pounding but she didn't let that show. "Congratulations," she said, "you found me. Gold star for you."

He was thrown off by the expression, but that didn't stop him. "I am taking you into custody." He pulled out a jolt baton. "Do not try to resist; it will only make it worse for you."

Now Scythe Possuelo turned to him. "On whose authority do you do this?"

"On the joint authority of Lautaro, High Blade of the

Chilargentine Region, and High Blade Xenocrates of Mid-Merica."

"Neither of which have any jurisdiction here."

He chuckled. "Excuse me, but—"

"No, excuse *me*," said Possuelo, with just the right level of indignation. "We crossed into Amazonia at least five minutes ago. If you attempt to press your advantage in any way, she has every right to defend herself with lethalish force—even against a scythe."

Citra took that as a cue to pull out a hunting knife she was concealing in her frock, and she stood to face him. "Make one move with that baton and they'll have to reattach your hand."

Behind him a porter came into the train car to see what the commotion was. "Sir," said Citra, "this man is a Chilargentine scythe, but isn't wearing his ring or robe. Isn't that against the law in Amazonia?" Never had Citra been so happy to have studied her scythe history.

The porter looked the man over, and his eyes narrowed to a suspicious glare—suspicious enough for Citra to know where his allegiances lay.

"Furthermore, all foreign scythes must register before crossing our border," he said. "Even when sneaking in by tunnel."

The Chilargentine scythe's temper quickly began to boil. "Leave me to my business or I will glean you where you stand."

"No, you won't," said Scythe Possuelo with such matter-of-fact calm, it made Citra grin. "I've granted him immunity. You can't glean him."

"What?"

Then the Amazonian scythe reached his hand right up to

the porter's face, who grabbed it and kissed his ring. "Thank you, Your Honor."

"This man threatened violence against me," Citra told the porter. "I demand he be put off the train at the next stop, along with any other disguised scythes he's traveling with."

"That would be my pleasure," said the porter.

"You can't do that!" the scythe insisted.

But a few minutes later, he found out otherwise.

With her pursuers kicked off the train, Citra enjoyed a respite from the relentless cat-and-mouse game. Her cover blown, she pulled on street clothes that fit her from someone's luggage. Jeans and a flowery blouse that wasn't her style, but the clothes were adequate. The Tonists were disappointed, yet didn't seem all that surprised that she wasn't actually one of them. They left her with a pamphlet she promised she'd read, but suspected she wouldn't.

"Whatever your destination," Scythe Possuelo told her, "you'll have to change trains at Amazonas Central Station. I suggest you meander through several different outbound trains before boarding the one you're actually taking, so that the DNA detectors will send those chasing you every which way."

Of course, the more she wandered the station, the more likely she'd be seen, but it was worth the risk to confound the DNA detectors and send her pursuers on a wild-goose chase.

"I don't know why they're after you," Scythe Possuelo said as the train pulled into the station, "but if your issues resolve and you do get your ring, you should come back to Amazonia. The rain forest stretches across the whole continent, as it did in its most ancient days, and we live in its canopy. You would find it marvelous."

"I thought you didn't like foreign scythes," she told him with a smirk.

"There is a difference between those we invite, and those who intrude," he told her.

Citra did her best to leave DNA traces on half a dozen trains before slipping onto the one bound for Caracas, on the north Amazonia coast. If there were agents out there looking for her, she didn't spot them, but she wouldn't be so cavalier as to think she was out of harm's way.

From the city of Caracas, Scythe Curie had instructed her to follow the northern coastline east until coming to a town called Playa Pintada. She would have to avoid publicars or any other mode of transportation that would pinpoint her location, but she found the closer she got, the more her resolve hardened. She would get there and complete this troubled pilgrimage, even if she had to walk the rest of the way.

How does one face a murderer? Not a socially sanctioned killer, but an actual murderer? An individual who, without the blessing of society, or even its permission, permanently ends a human life?

Citra knew that in the world at large, the Thunderhead prevented such things. Certainly people get pushed in front of trains, or under trucks, or off rooftops in the heat of frustrated moments—but that which is broken is always repaired. Amends are made. An ordained scythe, however, who lives outside of the Thunderhead's jurisdiction, has no such protection. To be revived is not automatic for a scythe; it must be requested. But who is there to advocate for a scythe felled by foul play?

Which means that although scythes may be the most powerful humans on Earth, they are also the most vulnerable.

Today, Citra vowed to be an advocate for the dead. She would deliver justice for her fallen mentor. Clearly, the Thunderhead would not stand in her way—it had given her the murderer's name. So had Scythe Curie when she had sent her on this mission. The final phase of her training. Everything rested on the actions she would take today.

Playa Pintada. The painted beach. Today the coastline was strewn with large chunks of twisted, gnarled driftwood. In the dwindling sunset, they seemed like the arms and legs of terrible creatures slowly heaving themselves out of the sand.

Citra crouched behind a driftwood dragon, hiding within its shadow. A storm was moving in from the north, building over the sea and rolling inexorably toward shore. Distant lightning could already be seen playing deep within its darkness, and thunder rolled in counterpoint to the crashing surf.

She had only a handful of the weapons she had started with: a pistol, a switchblade, the hunting knife. The rest had been too hard to conceal, and so she had to cast them off before boarding the train in Buenos Aires. It was barely a day ago, yet it felt like a week.

The home she watched was a single-story box of a dwelling, like many of the homes on the beach. Most of it was hidden behind palms and blooming birds-of-paradise. There was a back patio that overlooked the beach on the other side of a low hedge. Lights were on inside. A shadow periodically moved behind the curtains.

Citra reviewed her options. Were she already a scythe, she would glean him, following Scythe Curie's methods. A blade through the heart. Quick and decisive. This was one instance where she didn't doubt her ability to do it. But she wasn't a scythe.

Any lethal attack would merely render him deadish, and an ambudrone would arrive within minutes to take him to be revived. What she needed to do was incapacitate him. Take him down but not out, and then extract a confession. Was he working for another scythe or acting alone? Was he bribed like the witnesses? Was he motivated by a promise of immunity, or was it a personal vendetta against Faraday? Then, once she knew the truth, she could bring the man, and the confession, to Scythe Possuelo, or anyone in the Amazonia Scythedom. That way not even Xenocrates could squelch the truth. It would clear her of any wrongdoing, and the true culprit would receive whatever punishment awaits a scythe-killer. Perhaps Citra could stay here in Amazonia then, and never have to face the awful prospect of Winter Conclave.

At the last traces of twilight, she heard a sliding glass door whoosh open, and she peered over the rough edge of the driftwood to see him come onto the patio to look out at the approaching storm. He was perfectly silhouetted against the light inside, like a paper target at a shooting range. He couldn't have made it easier for her. She pulled out her pistol. At first she leveled it right at his heart—force of habit from her training. Then she lowered it to his knee and fired.

Her aim was perfect. He wailed and went down, and Citra raced across the sand, leaped the hedge, and grabbed him by the shirt with both hands as he writhed.

"You're going to pay for what you've done," she snarled.

Then she saw the man's face. Familiar. Too familiar. Her first instinct was to think this was another layer of treachery. It wasn't until he spoke that she had to accept the truth.

"Citra?"

Scythe Faraday's face was a mask of pain and disbelief. "Citra, oh god, what are you doing here?"

She let him go out of shock, and Scythe Faraday's head hit the concrete hard, knocking him out and making the horror of the moment all the worse.

She wanted to call for help, but who would help her after what she'd done?

She lifted his head again, cradling it gently as the blood from his shattered knee flowed between the patio stones, turning the sand in the cracks to red mortar, drying to brown.

Immortality cannot temper the folly or frailty of youth. Innocence is doomed to die a senseless death at our own hands, a casualty of the mistakes we can never undo. So we lay to rest the wide-eyed wonder we once thrived upon, replacing it with scars of which we never speak, too knotted for any amount of technology to repair. With each gleaning I commit, with each life taken for the good of humanity, I mourn for the boy I once was, whose name I sometimes struggle to remember. And I long for a place beyond immortality where I can, in some small measure, resurrect the wonder, and be that boy again.

—From the gleaning journal of H.S. Faraday

33

Both the Messenger and the Message

Citra carried him inside. She set him on a sofa, and made a tourniquet to staunch the blood. He groaned, beginning to rouse, and when he broke the tenuous surface of consciousness, his first thought was of her.

"You should not be here," he said, his words weak and slurred—an effect of his pain nanites flooding his system. Still, he grimaced in bleary agony.

"We have to get you to a hospital," she told him. "This is too much for your nanites to handle."

"Nonsense. They've already taken the edge off the pain. As for healing, they'll do the job without intervention."

"But—"

"I have no other option," he told her. "Going to a hospital will alert the Scythedom that I'm still alive." He shifted position, grimacing only slightly. "Between nature and nanites, my knee will heal. It will just take time, of which I have no shortage."

She elevated his leg, bandaged it, then sat on the floor beside him.

"Were you so resentful of my leaving that you had to exact your revenge in flesh?" he asked, only half joking. "Are you so offended that I managed a method of secretly retiring, instead of actually gleaning myself?"

"I thought you were someone else," she told him. "Someone named Gerald Van Der Gans. . . ."

"My birth name," he told her. "A name I surrendered when I became Honorable Scythe Michael Faraday. But none of this explains your presence here. I freed you, Citra—you and Rowan both. By faking my own gleaning, you were both freed from your apprenticeship. You should be back in your old life, forgetting that I had plucked you from it. So why are you here?"

"You mean you don't know?"

He pulled himself up slightly so he could see her more directly. "Don't know what?"

And so she told him everything. How, instead of being freed, she and Rowan had ended up with Scythes Curie and Goddard. How Xenocrates had tried to pin Faraday's murder on her, and how Scythe Curie had helped her get to him. As she spoke, he put his hands to his eyes as if he might gouge them out.

"To think I was complacent here, while all this was going on."

"How could you not know?" she asked, for in her mind he always seemed to know everything, even the things he could not possibly know.

Scythe Faraday sighed. "Marie—Scythe Curie, that is—is the only member of the Scythedom who knows I'm still alive. I am completely off-grid now. The only way to reach me would be in person. So she sent you. You are both the messenger and the message."

The moment became uncomfortable. Thunder rumbled in from the sea, much closer now. The flashes of lightning brighter. "Is it true you died seven deaths for her?" Citra asked.

He nodded. "And her for me. She told you that, did she? Well, it was a very long time ago."

Outside the rain finally began to fall, surging in fits and starts. "I love the way it rains here," he told her. "It reminds me that some forces of nature can never be entirely subdued. They are eternal, which is a far better thing to be than immortal."

And so they sat listening to the soothing randomness of the rain until Citra began to grow too weary to even think.

"So what happens now?" she asked.

"Very simple, actually. I heal, and you rest. Anything beyond that is a conversation for a future date." Then he pointed. "The bedroom's in there. I expect a full night's sleep from you, followed by a recitation of your poisons in the morning, in order of toxicity."

"My poisons?"

In spite of his pain and drug-induced haze, Scythe Faraday smiled. "Yes, your poisons. Are you my apprentice or not?"

Citra couldn't help but smile right back at him. "Yes, Your Honor, I am."

The longer we live, the quicker the days seem to pass. How troublesome that is when we live forever. A year seems to pass in a matter of weeks. Decades fly with no milestones to mark them. We become settled in the inconsequential drudgery of our lives, until suddenly we look at ourselves in the mirror and see a face we barely recognize begging us to turn a corner and be young again.

But are we truly young when we turn the corner?

We hold the same memories, the same habits, the same unrealized dreams. Our bodies may be spry and limber, but toward what end? No end. Never an end.

I do believe mortals strived more heartily toward their goals, because they knew that time was of the essence. But us? We can put things off far more effectively than those doomed to die, because death has become the exception instead of the rule.

The stagnation that I so fervently glean on a daily basis seems an epidemic that only grows. There are times I feel I am fighting a losing battle against an old-fashioned apocalypse of the living dead.

—From the gleaning journal of H.S. Curie

34

The Second Most Painful Thing You'll Ever Have to Do

Winter sped relentlessly closer. At first Rowan kept a tally of the lives he temporarily ended, but as the days passed, he found he couldn't keep up. A dozen a day, week to week, month to month. They all blended together. For the eight months he trained under Scythe Goddard, he had made over two thousand kills, mostly the same people over and over again. Did those people despise him, he wondered, or did they truly see this as just a job? There were times when the training called for them to run, or even fight back. Most were inept at it, but some had clearly been trained in combat. There were even sessions where his targets had their own weapons. He had been cut and stabbed and shot—but never so severely that he had to be revived. He had grown into an exceptionally skilled killer.

"You have excelled beyond my wildest expectations," Goddard told him. "I suspected you had a spark in you, but never dreamed it would be such an inferno!"

And yes, he had come to enjoy it, just as Scythe Goddard said he would. And just like Scythe Volta, he despised himself for it.

"I'm looking forward to your ordainment," Volta told him one day during their afternoon studies together. "Maybe you and I can split off from Goddard. Glean at our own speed, in our own way." But Rowan knew Volta would never find the momentum to escape Goddard's gravity.

"You're assuming that I'll be chosen over Citra," Rowan pointed out.

"Citra's gone," Volta reminded him. "She's been off-grid for months. If she shows her face at conclave, the bejeweling committee won't look too kindly on her for being AWOL all this time. All you have to do is pass the final test, and without question you'll win."

Which is what Rowan was afraid of.

The news of Citra's disappearance had trickled down to Rowan unofficially. He didn't know the whole story. She had been accused of something by Xenocrates. There was an emergency meeting of the disciplinary committee, and Scythe Curie showed up on her behalf, clearing her of any wrongdoing. The accusation must have been orchestrated by Goddard, because he was furious at the committee's decision to drop the charges— and by the fact that Citra had completely vanished. Not even Scythe Curie seemed to know where she was.

The day after that, Goddard took his junior scythes and Rowan on a gleaning rampage, fueled by his fury. He released his rage at a crowded harvest festival and this time Rowan couldn't save anyone, because Goddard kept him by his side as his weapons caddy. Scythe Chomsky used his flamethrower to set a corn maze ablaze, smoking people out to be picked off one by one by the other scythes.

Scythe Volta was now in the doghouse, though, because he had lobbed a container of poison gas into the burning maze. Highly effective, but it stole kills from Goddard and the others.

"I did it to be humane," Volta confided in Rowan. "Better they die by gas than by fire." Then he added, "or by getting blown away just as they thought they were escaping the maze."

Perhaps Rowan was wrong about Volta. Maybe he would escape from Goddard—but he certainly wouldn't do it without Rowan. It was one more argument for Rowan to earn the ring.

They had all reached their gleaning quota by the end of that awful evening, and Goddard still didn't seem to have satisfied his bloodlust. He raged against the system, if only to his own disciples, calling for a day when scythes would have no limits on gleaning.

Citra returned to Scythe Curie at Falling Water many weeks before Winter Conclave, when the Month of Lights had just begun, and gifts were being passed between friends and loved ones to celebrate ancient miracles that no one quite remembered.

Unlike her frantic journey to Amazonia's northern shore, Citra flew home in comfort, and with peace of mind. She didn't have to look over her shoulder every five minutes because no one was chasing her anymore. As Scythe Curie had promised, Citra had been cleared of any wrongdoing. And while Scythe Mandela sent a heartfelt note of apology for Scythe Curie to give to Citra, High Blade Xenocrates made no such gesture.

"He will pretend like it never happened," Scythe Curie told her as the two of them drove home from the airport. "That's the closest the man will ever come to an apology."

"But it did happen," Citra said. "I had to hurl myself from a building to escape from it."

"And I had to blow up two perfectly good cars," Scythe Curie said wryly.

"I won't forget what he did."

"And you shouldn't. You have every right to judge Xenocrates harshly—but not too harshly. I suspect there are more variables in play than we know."

"That's what Scythe Faraday said."

Scythe Curie smiled at the mention of his name. "And how is our good friend Gerald?" she asked with a wink.

"Reports of his death have been greatly exaggerated," said Citra. "Mostly, he gardens and takes long walks on the beach."

The fact that he was still alive was a secret they both planned to keep. Even Scythe Mandela believed that Citra was staying with a relative of Scythe Curie in Amazonia, and he had no reason to suspect it wasn't true.

"Perhaps I'll join him on his beach in a hundred years or so," said Scythe Curie. "But for now there's too much to do in the Scythedom. Too many crucial battles to fight." Citra could see her gripping the steering wheel tighter as she thought of it. "The future of everything we believe as scythes is at stake, Citra. There is even talk of abolishing the quota. Which is why you must win the ring. I know the scythe you'll be, and it's exactly what we need."

Citra looked away. Without daily gleaning, her training with Scythe Faraday over the past few months had been about honing her mind and body—but more importantly, contemplating the moral and ethical high ground that a traditional scythe must always take. There was nothing "old guard" about it. It was simply right. She knew such high ideals were absent from

Rowan's training, but it didn't mean he didn't hold onto them in his heart, despite his bloodthirsty mentor.

"Rowan could be a good scythe as well," Citra offered.

Scythe Curie sighed. "He can't be trusted anymore. Look what he did to you at Harvest Conclave. You can make all the excuses in the world for him, but the fact is, he's an unknown quantity now. Training under Goddard is bound to twist him in ways that no one can predict."

"Even if that's true," said Citra, finally getting to the point they both knew she'd been dancing around, "I don't know how I could glean him."

"It will be the second most painful thing you'll ever do," admitted Scythe Curie. "But you'll find a way to accomplish it, Citra. I have faith in you."

If gleaning Rowan would be the second most painful thing she'd ever do, Citra wondered what the most painful thing would be. But she was afraid to ask, because she really didn't want to know.

So many of our archaic traditions and rules need to be challenged. The founders, as well-meaning as they were, still suffered from a mortal mentality, having been so close to the Age of Mortality. They could not foresee the needs of the Scythedom.

I would first take on the concept of a quota. It's absurd that we are free to determine our method and criteria for gleaning, but not the number of gleanings we accomplish. We are hamstrung every minute of every day, because we must always consider whether we are gleaning too much or too little. Better to allow us to glean at our own complete discretion. That way, scythes who glean too little will not be punished, because scythes who have a healthier gleaning appetite will make up for their shortcomings. In this way, we can help one another, and isn't helping our fellow scythes a good thing for all of us?

—From the gleaning journal of H.S. Goddard

35

Obliteration Is Our Hallmark

On the last day of the year, just three days before Winter Conclave, Scythe Goddard led one more gleaning expedition.

"But we've already reached our quota for the year," Scythe Volta was quick to remind him.

"I will NOT be constrained by a technicality!" Goddard shouted. Rowan thought Goddard might actually hit Volta, but then he took a moment to calm himself, and said, "By the time we begin our gleaning run, it will already be the Year of the Capybara in PanAsia. As far as I'm concerned, that gives us permission to count our kills as part of the new year. Then we shall return in time for our New Year's Eve gala!"

Scythe Goddard decided it was a day for samurai swords, although Chomsky refused to part with his flamethrower. "It's what I'm known for. Why mess with my image?"

Rowan had been on four gleaning expeditions with Goddard so far. He found he could escape to a place within himself where he was less of an accomplice—even less than an observer. He became the lettuce again. Nonsentient and secondary. Easily ignored and forgotten. It was the only way to keep his sanity in the midst of Goddard's blood sport. Sometimes he was so forgotten in the midst of the melee that he could help people escape. Other times, he had to be at Goddard's side, loading or switching out his weapons. He didn't know what his role would be this time. If Goddard was just using his samurai blade, he didn't need Rowan to be his weapons caddy. Still, he told Rowan to bring a spare sword.

Preparations for the party were already in full swing as they got ready to leave for the gleaning run that morning. The catering truck had arrived, and tables were being set up all over the grounds. The New Year's Eve gala was one of Goddard's few preplanned parties, and the guest list was stellar.

The helicopter landed on the front lawn, blowing away a tent that was being erected for the party as if it were nothing more than a napkin tumbled by the wind.

"Today we shall provided a much-needed public service," Goddard told them, with far too much glee. "Today we dispense with some rabble." But he didn't explain what he meant. Even so, as the helicopter took off, Rowan had a sinking feeling deep in the pit of his stomach that had nothing to do with their ascent.

They landed in a public park, in the center of a vacant soccer field lightly dusted with snow. There was a playground at the edge of the park where some toddlers, unfazed by the weather, climbed and swung and dug in the sand, bundled up against the cold. The instant their parents saw scythes stepping out of the helicopter, they gathered their children and hurried away, ignoring their children's wails of protest.

"Our destination is several blocks away," Scythe Goddard told them. "I didn't want to set down too close and ruin the element of surprise." Then he put a paternal arm around Rowan's shoulder. "Today is Rowan's inauguration," he said. "You will perform your first gleaning today!"

Rowan recoiled. "What? Me? I can't! I'm just an apprentice!"

"Proxy, my boy! Just as I allowed you to grant immunity with my ring, so will you glean someone today, and it will be tallied as mine. Consider it a gift. You don't have to thank me."

"But . . . but that's not allowed!"

Goddard was unperturbed. "Then let someone complain. Oh, what's that I hear? Silence!"

"Don't worry," Volta told Rowan. "It's what you've trained for. You'll do fine."

Which is what Rowan was worried about. He didn't want to do "fine." He wanted to be miserable at it. He wanted to be a failure, because only by failing would he know that he held on to a shred of his humanity. His brain felt about ready to burst out through his nose and ears. He hoped it would, because then he'd glean nobody today. *If I must do this, I will be merciful like Scythe Faraday,* he told himself. *I will not enjoy it. I will NOT enjoy it!*

They came around a corner and Rowan saw their destination: some sort of compound made to look like an old adobe mission, completely out of place in the cold of MidMerica. The iron symbol atop the tallest steeple was a two-pronged fork. This was a tone cult cloister.

"Nearly a hundred Tonists reside behind those walls," Goddard announced. "Our goal is to glean them all."

Scythe Rand grinned. Scythe Chomsky checked the settings on his weapon. Only Scythe Volta seemed to have reservations. "All of them?"

Goddard shrugged as if it were nothing. As if all those lives meant nothing. "Obliteration is our hallmark," he said. "We don't always succeed, but we try."

"But this . . . this breaks the second commandment. It clearly shows bias."

"Come now, Alessandro," Goddard said in his most patronizing tone. "Bias against whom? Tonists are not a registered cultural group."

"Couldn't they be considered a religion?" Rowan offered.

"You gotta be kidding," laughed Scythe Rand. "They're a joke!"

"Precisely," agreed Goddard. "They've made a mockery of mortal age faith. Religion is a cherished part of history, and they've turned it into a travesty."

"Glean them all!" said Chomsky, powering up his weapon.

Goddard and Rand drew their swords. Volta glanced at Rowan and said quietly, "The best thing about these gleanings is that it's over quick." Then he drew his sword as well, and followed the others through a gated archway that the Tonists always left open for lost souls seeking tonal solace. They had no idea what was coming.

Word spread quickly on the street that a small elegy of scythes had entered the Tonist cloister. As human nature would have it, rumor quickly raised the number to a dozen scythes or more, and as human nature would also have it, crowds that were slightly more excited than frightened gathered across the street, wondering if they would get a glimpse of the scythes, and perhaps even the carnage they left behind. But all they saw for now was a single young man, an apprentice standing at the open gate, his back to the crowd.

Rowan was ordered to remain at the gate, sword drawn, to prevent anyone from trying to escape. His plan, of course, was to allow *anyone* to escape. But when the panicked Tonists saw him, his sword, and his apprentice armband, they ran back into the compound, where they became prey for the scythes. He stood there for five minutes, then finally he left his spot at the gate, losing himself in the maze-like compound. Only then did people begin to slip out to safety.

The sounds of anguish were almost impossible to endure. Knowing he'd be expected to glean someone before this was through made it impossible for him to disappear into himself this time. The place was a labyrinth of courtyards and walkways and illogical structures. He had no idea where he was. A building was burning to his left, and one walkway was littered with the dead, marking the passage of one of the scythes. A woman huddled, partially hidden by a winter-bare shrub, cradling a baby, trying desperately to keep it quiet. She panicked when she saw Rowan and screamed, holding her baby closer.

"I'm not going to hurt you," he told her. "No one's guarding the main gate. If you hurry, you'll make it out. Go now!"

She didn't waste any time. She took off. Rowan could only hope she didn't run into a scythe on the way.

Then he came around a corner and saw another figure huddled against a column, chest heaving in sobs. But it wasn't one of the Tonists. It was Scythe Volta. His sword lay on the ground. His yellow robe was splattered with blood, and blood covered his hands, shiny and slick. When he saw Rowan he turned away, his sobs growing heavier. Rowan knelt down to him. He clutched something in his hand. Not a weapon, but something else.

"It's over," Volta said, his voice barely a whisper. "It's over now." Clearly, however, from the sounds coming from elsewhere in the compound, it was not over at all.

"What happened, Alessandro?" Rowan asked.

Volta looked at him then, the anguish in his eyes like that of a man already damned. "I thought it was . . . I thought it was an office. Or maybe a storeroom. I'd go in, there'd be a couple of people there. I'd glean them as painlessly as I could, and move on. That's what I thought. But it wasn't an office. Or a storeroom. It was a classroom."

He broke down in sobs again as he spoke. "There had to be at least a dozen little kids in there. Cowering. They were cowering from me, Rowan. But there was this one boy. He stepped forward. His teacher tried to stop him, but he stepped forward. He wasn't afraid. And he held up one of their stupid tuning forks. He held it up like it would ward me off. 'You won't hurt us,' he said. Then he struck it against a desk to make it ring, and held it up to me. 'By the power of the tone, you won't hurt us,' he said. And he believed it, Rowan. He believed in its power. He believed it would protect him."

"What did you do?"

Volta closed his eyes, and his words came out in a horrible squeal.

"I gleaned him . . . I gleaned them all. . . ."

Then he opened his bloody hand, revealing that he held the boy's little tuning fork. It tumbled to the ground with a tiny atonal clank.

"What are we, Rowan? What the hell are we? It can't be what we're supposed to be."

"It's not. It never was. Goddard isn't a scythe. He may have the ring, he may have license to glean, but he's not a scythe. He's a killer, and he has to be stopped. We can find a way to stop him, both of us!"

Volta shook his head and looked at the blood pooling in his palms. "It's over," he said again. And then took a deep, shuddering breath and became very, very calm. "It's over, and I'm glad."

That's when Rowan realized that the blood on Volta's hands was not from his victims. It was from Volta's own wrists. The gashes were jagged and long. They were made with very clear intent.

"Alessandro, no! You don't have to do this! We have to call an ambudrone. It's not too late."

But they both knew that it was.

"Self-gleaning is every scythe's last prerogative. You can't rob that from me, Rowan. Don't even try."

His blood was everywhere now, staining the snow of the courtyard. Rowan wailed—never had he felt so helpless. "I'm sorry, Alessandro. I'm so sorry. . . ."

"My real name is Shawn Dobson. Will you call me that, Rowan? Will you call me by my real name?"

Rowan could barely speak through his own tears. "It's . . . it's been an honor to know you, Shawn Dobson."

He leaned on Rowan, barely able to hold up his head, his voice getting weaker. "Promise me you'll be a better scythe than I was."

"I promise, Shawn."

"And then maybe . . . maybe . . ."

But whatever he was going to say, it leaked away with the last of his life. His head came to rest on Rowan's shoulder, while all around them distant cries of agony filled the icy air.

Each day I pray as my ancestors did. They once prayed to gods that were fallible and fickle. Then to one God who stood in harsh and terrifying judgment. Then to a loving, forgiving God. And then finally to a power with no name.

But to whom can the immortal pray? I have no answer to that, but still I cast my voice out into the void, hoping to reach something beyond distance and deeper than the depths of my own soul. I ask for guidance. And for courage. And I beg—oh, how I beg—that I never become so desensitized to the death I must deliver that it feels normal. Commonplace.

My greatest wish for humanity is not for peace or comfort or joy. It is that we all still die a little inside every time we witness the death of another. For only the pain of empathy will keep us human. There's no version of God that can help us if we ever lose that.

—From the gleaning journal of H.S. Faraday

36

The Thirteenth Kill

Goddard was in the chapel sanctuary finishing the last of his terrible business. Outside the wails began to fade as Rand and Chomsky finished what they had begun. A building was burning across the courtyard. Smoke and cold air poured in through the broken stained glass windows of the chapel. Goddard stood at the front, by an altar that featured a shining two-pronged fork and a stone bowl of dirty water.

There was only one Tonist left alive in the chapel. He was a balding man, wearing a frock that was slightly different from the dead around him. Goddard held him with one hand and wielded his sword in the other. Then Goddard turned to see Rowan and smiled.

"Ah, Rowan! Just in time," he said cheerily. "I've saved the curate for you."

The Tonist curate showed defiance rather than fear. "What you've done here today will only help our cause," he said. "Martyrs testify far more effectively than the living."

"Martyrs to what?" Goddard sneered and tapped his blade against the huge tuning fork. "To this thing? I'd laugh if I wasn't so disgusted."

Rowan strode closer, ignoring the carnage around him, focusing in on Goddard. "Let him go," Rowan said.

"Why? Do you prefer a moving target?"

"I prefer no target."

Finally Goddard understood. He grinned, as if Rowan had just said something charming and quaint. "Does our young man express a wee bit of disapproval?"

"Volta's dead," Rowan told him.

Goddard's gleeful expression faded, but only a bit. "He was attacked by the Tonists? They'll pay dearly for it!"

"It wasn't them." Rowan didn't even try to hide the animosity in his voice. "He gleaned himself."

This gave Goddard pause. The curate struggled in his grip, and Goddard slammed him against the stone basin hard enough to knock him out, then let the man fall to the ground.

"Volta was the weakest of us," Goddard said. "I'm not entirely surprised. Once you're ordained, I will happily have you take his place."

"I won't do that."

Goddard took a moment to gauge Rowan. To read him. It felt like a violation. Goddard was in his head—even deeper; in his soul—and Rowan didn't know how to cast him out.

"I know you and Alessandro were close, but he was nothing like you, Rowan, believe me. He never had the hunger. But you do. I've seen it in your eyes. I've seen how you are when you train. Living in the moment. Every kill perfect."

Rowan found he couldn't look away from Goddard, who had put down his sword and now held his hands out as if his were the inviting embrace of a savior. The diamonds in his robe twinkled in the faraway firelight, so bedazzling.

"We could have been called reapers," Goddard said, "but our

founders saw fit to call us scythes—because we are the weapons in mankind's immortal hand. *You* are a fine weapon, Rowan, sharp, and precise. And when you strike, you are glorious to behold."

"Stop it! That's not true!"

"You know it is. You were born for this, Rowan. Don't throw it away."

The curate began to groan, beginning to regain consciousness. Goddard hauled him to his feet. "Glean him, Rowan. Don't fight it. Glean him now. And enjoy it."

Rowan tightened the grip on his blade as he looked into the curate's bleary, half-conscious eyes. Even as he tried to stand his ground, Rowan couldn't deny the power of the undertow. "You're a monster!" he shouted. "The worst kind, because you don't just kill, you turn others into killers like yourself."

"You just lack perspective. The predator is always a monster to the prey. To the gazelle the lion is a demon. To a mouse, the eagle is evil incarnate." He took a step closer, the curate still held tightly in his grip.

"Will you be the eagle or the mouse, Rowan? Will you soar or will you scurry away? For those are the only two choices today."

Rowan's head was swimming. The smell of blood and the smoke pouring in through the shattered windows made him dizzy and muddled his thoughts. The curate looked no different than the strangers he practiced on every day—and for a moment, he felt himself out on the lawn in the middle of a killcraft exercise. Rowan unsheathed his sword and stalked forward, feeling the hunger, living in the moment, just as Goddard had said, and allowing himself to feel that hunger was freeing in a way Rowan couldn't describe. For many months he had trained for this, and now he finally understood why Goddard always let the last one go before Rowan could strike, stopping him one blow short of completion.

It was to prepare him for today.

Today he would finally have that completion, and every day henceforth, when he went out to glean, he would not stay his hand or his blade or his bullet until there was no one left to glean.

Before he could think it through, before his mind could tell him to stop, he launched himself toward the curate, and thrust his blade forward with all of his force, finally achieving that exquisite completion.

The man gasped and stumbled aside, the blade having missed him completely.

Instead, Rowan's blade hit its true mark, and ran Scythe Goddard through, all the way to the hilt.

Rowan was close to Goddard now. Inches from his face, looking into his wide, shocked eyes.

"I am what you made me," he told Goddard. "And you're right: I enjoyed that. I enjoyed that more than anything I've ever done in my life." Then with his free hand, Rowan reached down and yanked the ring off Goddard's finger. "You don't deserve to wear this. You never did."

Goddard opened his mouth to speak—perhaps to deliver an eloquent death soliloquy—but Rowan didn't want to hear anything from him anymore, so he stepped back, withdrew his sword from Goddard's gut, and swung it in a broad, sweeping arc that took off Goddard's head in a single blow. It tumbled and landed in the basin of dirty water, as if that were what the basin was there for.

The rest of Goddard's body fell limply to the ground, and in the silence of the moment, Rowan heard from behind him:

"What the hell did you do?"

Rowan turned and saw Chomsky standing at the entrance of the chapel, with Rand beside him.

"You are *so* gleaned when he's revived!"

Rowan let his training take over. *I am the weapon,* he told himself. And in that moment he was a lethal one. Chomsky and Rand defended themselves against him, and although they were good, they were nothing compared to a weapon so sharp and precise as he. Rowan's blade cut Rand deep, but she kicked the sword out of his hand with a well-placed Bokator kick. Rowan responded with an even more effective kick that broke her spine. Chomsky set Rowan's arm ablaze with the flamethrower, but Rowan rolled on the ground, putting it out, then grabbed the toning mallet from beside the altar and brought it down on Chomsky like the hammer of Thor, striking again and again and again as if he were toning the hour, until the curate grabbed his hand to stop him and said, "That's enough, son. He's dead."

Rowan dropped the mallet. Only now did he allow himself to let down his guard.

"Come with me, son," the man said. "There's a place for you with us. We can hide you from the Scythedom."

Rowan looked at the man's outstretched hand, but even

now Goddard's words came back to him. *The eagle or the mouse?* No, Rowan would not scurry away and hide. There was still more that had to be done.

"Leave here," he told the man. "Find the survivors, if there are any, and get out—but do it quickly."

The man looked at him for a moment more, then turned and left the chapel. Once he was gone, Rowan picked up the flamethrower and got down to business.

Out in the street, fire trucks had already pulled up and peace officers were holding back crowds. The entire cloister was now on fire, and although firefighters raced toward the blaze, they were intercepted by a young man stepping out of the main gate.

"This is a scythe action. You will not intervene," he said.

The fire captain who now approached him had heard of scythe-related fires, but never had such a thing happened on his watch. There was something about this that didn't seem right. Yes, the boy appeared to be wearing a scythe's robe—a royal blue one, studded with diamonds—but the robe clearly didn't fit him. With flames consuming the compound at an alarming rate, the captain made a judgment call. This kid, whoever he was, was no scythe, and was not about to hinder their efforts.

"Out of the way!" he told the kid dismissively. "Get back with the others and let us do our job."

Then the kid moved with lightning speed. The captain felt his legs kicked out from under him. He landed on his back, and suddenly the kid was on top of him, a knee painfully pressed into the captain's chest and a hand around his throat, squeezing so tightly it almost closed off his windpipe. Suddenly the boy didn't seem a boy at all. He seemed a whole lot bigger. A whole lot older.

"I SAID THIS IS A SCYTHE ACTION AND YOU WILL NOT INTERVENE, OR I WILL GLEAN YOU RIGHT HERE, RIGHT NOW!"

The fire captain now knew he had made a grievous mistake. No one but a scythe could be so commanding and take such absolute control of a situation. "Yes, Your Honor," the captain rasped. "I'm sorry, Your Honor."

The scythe stood, letting the captain get up. He told his squad to fall back, and the squad, having seen the scythe take their captain down so effectively, didn't question it.

"You can protect other buildings that are threatened," the young scythe said, "but you'll let this entire compound burn to the ground."

"I understand, Your Honor."

Then the scythe held up his ring, and the captain kissed it with such force, he cracked a tooth.

Rowan felt his skin crawling beneath Scythe Goddard's blood-soaked robe, but as unpleasant as it was, he needed it to play the part. He was far more convincing than he thought he'd be. He frightened himself.

The firefighters now directed all their attention to adjacent buildings, hosing down nearby roofs with fire retardant. Rowan found himself standing alone between the burning Tonist cloister and the crowds still held back by peace officers. He stayed until the steeple caved in and the giant fork at its apex plunged into the flames, resounding with a mournful clang as it hit the ground.

I have become the monster of monsters, he thought as he watched it all burn. *The butcher of lions. The executioner of eagles.*

Then, trying not to trip over the robe, Rowan strode away from the all-consuming inferno that would leave nothing behind of Scythe Goddard and his disciples but bones too charred to ever be revived.

Part Five

SCYTHEHOOD

Scythes Rand and Chomsky have these morbid conversations. They're twisted, and the first to admit it, but I guess that's part of their charm. Today they were talking about the method they might use to self-glean one day. Noam said he would climb to the top of an active volcano, and, surrounded by grand ceremony, hurl himself into the lava. Ayn said she would scuba dive the Great Barrier Reef until she either ran out of air or got eaten by a great white. They wanted me to join in their game and tell them how I'd want to go. Call me boring, but I didn't want to play. Why talk about self-gleaning when it should be the furthest thing from our minds? It's our job to end other people's lives, not our own—and I intend to be doing it well into my thousands.

—From the gleaning journal of H.S. Volta

37

Shaking the Tree

"A tragedy. A terrible tragedy." High Blade Xenocrates sat on a plush sofa in the grandiose mansion that had, until just two days ago, been occupied by the late Scythe Goddard. Now he faced the apprentice, who seemed much too calm for a young man who had been through such an ordeal.

"Rest assured that the use of fire by any MidMerican scythe will be banned in conclave tomorrow," he said.

"That's definitely long overdue," Rowan told him—speaking not like an apprentice, but more like an equal, which irritated the High Blade. Xenocrates took a good look at Rowan. "You were very lucky to get out of there alive."

Rowan looked him square in the eye. "I was stationed by the outer gate," he said. "By the time I saw that the fire had gotten out of control, there was nothing I could do; Scythe Goddard and the others were trapped. That place was a maze— they never stood a chance." Then Rowan paused. He seemed to look as deeply into Xenocrates as Xenocrates was looking into him. "All the other scythes must see me as very bad luck. After all, I've gone through two scythes in one year. I suppose this nullifies my apprenticeship."

"Nonsense. You've come this far," Xenocrates told him. "Out of respect for Scythe Goddard, you'll take your final test tonight. I can't speak for the bejeweling committee, but I have no doubt that, taking into consideration what you've been through, they will find in your favor."

"And Citra?"

"If you receive the ring, I trust you'll glean Miss Terranova, and thus put an end to this unpleasant chapter of our history."

A servant arrived with champagne and finger sandwiches. Xenocrates looked around. The mansion, which had been so full of servants in days past, now seemed to have only this one. The others must have fled the moment they heard that Scythe Goddard and his associates had succumbed to fire. Apparently, Xenocrates wasn't the only one who felt freed by Goddard's untimely end.

"Why are you still here when the others have all left?" he asked the servant. "It certainly couldn't be out of loyalty."

It was Rowan who answered him. "Actually, this estate belongs to him."

"Yes," said the man. "But I'll be putting it up for sale. My family and I couldn't imagine living here anymore." He put a champagne flute into Xenocrates hand. "But I'm always happy to serve a High Blade."

Apparently, the man had gone from servant to sycophant. Not a very far leap. Once he had left the room, Xenocrates got down to the real reason he had come: To shake the tree and see what, if anything, would fall out. He leaned a little closer to Rowan.

"There are rumors that a scythe—or at least someone who looked like a scythe—came out to address the firefighters."

Rowan didn't even blink. "I heard that too—there are even

some phone videos that people uploaded. Very blurry from all the smoke. Can't see much of anything."

"Yes, it just adds to the general confusion, I suppose."

"Will there be much more, Your Excellency? Because I'm pretty exhausted, and if I'm going to face my final test tonight, I'll need to rest up for it."

"You do know that not everyone in the Scythedom is convinced that it was an accident. We've had to begin an investigation, just to be sure."

"Makes sense," said Rowan.

"So far we were able to identify Scythe Volta and Scythe Chomsky by their rings, and the gems from their robes, which were around their remains. Rubies for Chomsky, citrines for Volta. As for scythe Rand, we're fairly certain she's in the debris beneath the huge tuning fork that had fallen through the chapel roof."

"Makes sense," Rowan said again.

"But finding Scythe Goddard has proven to be a challenge. Of course there were so many Tonists gleaned in the chapel before the fire got out of control, it's quite an ordeal trying to come up with a positive identification. One would assume that, like the others, Scythe Goddard's remains would be surrounded by small diamonds, and the larger jewel of his scythe's ring, even if the setting melted."

"Makes sense," Rowan said for the third time.

"What doesn't make sense is that the skeleton we think is his doesn't have any of those things," said Xenocrates. "And it also has no skull."

"That's weird," said Rowan. "Well, I'm sure it must be there somewhere."

"One would think."

"Maybe they need to look a little harder."

Just then, Xenocrates noticed the girl standing at the threshold of the room, lingering there, not sure whether to enter or walk away. Xenocrates couldn't be sure how much she had heard—or even if it mattered.

"Esme," said Rowan, "come in. You remember His Excellency, High Blade Xenocrates, don't you?"

"Yah," she said. "He jumped in the pool. It was funny."

Xenocrates shifted uncomfortably at the mention of the ordeal. It was not something he cared to remember.

"I've made arrangements for Esme to be returned to her mother," Rowan said. "But maybe you'd like to take her there yourself."

"Me?" said Xenocrates, feigning indifference. "Why would I want to?"

"Because you care about people," Rowan said with a well-timed wink. "Some more than others."

As the High Blade regarded the daughter that he could never publicly or even privately acknowledge, he melted just the tiniest bit. The boy had planned this, hadn't he? This Rowan Damisch was a sly one—an admirable trait when properly directed. Perhaps Rowan warranted more attention than the High Blade had given him in the past.

Esme waited to see what would happen, and Xenocrates finally offered her a warm smile. "It would be my pleasure to take you home, Esme."

With that, Xenocrates rose to leave . . . but he couldn't go just yet. There was still one more thing he had to do. One more decision that was in his power to make. He turned back to Rowan.

"Perhaps I should use my influence to call off the investigation," he said. "Out of respect for our fallen comrades. Let their memory be untainted by clumsy forensics that might cast aspersions on their legacy."

"Let the dead be dead," agreed Rowan.

And so an unspoken agreement was reached. The High Blade would cease shaking the tree, and Rowan would keep the High Blade's secret safe.

"If you need a place to stay once leaving here, Rowan, please know that my door is always open for you."

"Thank you, Your Excellency."

"No, thank *you*, Rowan."

Then the High Blade took Esme's hand and left to return her home.

The power of life and death cannot be handed out blithely, but only with stoic and weighty reserve. Ascension to scythehood should by no means be easy. We who have established the Scythedom have faced our own struggles in the process, and we must ensure that all those who join us in our mission face a trial that is not only instructive but transformative. Scythehood is humanity's highest calling, and to achieve it should cut one's soul to the very core, so that no scythe will ever forget the cost of the ring they bear.

Of course, to those on the outside, our rite of passage might seem unthinkably cruel. Which is why it must forever remain a secret sacrament.

—From the gleaning journal of H.S. Prometheus, the first World Supreme Blade

38

The Final Test

On January second, Year of the Capybara, the day before Winter Conclave, Scythe Curie took Citra on the long drive to the MidMerica Capitol Building.

"Your final test will be tonight, but you won't know the results until tomorrow's conclave," she told Citra. But Citra already knew that. "It's the same test, year to year, for every apprentice. And each apprentice must take the test alone."

That was something Citra didn't know. It only made sense that the final test would be some sort of standard that all candidates had to pass, but somehow the thought of having to face that test alone, and not in the company of the others, was troubling. Because now it wouldn't be a competition with Rowan and the others. She'd be competing against no one but herself.

"You should tell me what the test is."

"I can't," said Scythe Curie.

"You mean you won't."

Scythe Curie thought about that. "You're right. I won't."

"If I may speak frankly, Your Honor . . ."

"When have you ever not spoken frankly, Citra?"

Citra cleared her throat and tried to be her most persuasive self. "You play too fair, and it puts me at a disadvantage. You wouldn't want me to suffer just because you're too honorable, would you?"

"In our line of work we must hold on to every bit of honor we have."

"I'm sure other scythes tell their apprentices what the final test is."

"Perhaps," said Scythe Curie, "but then again, perhaps not. There are some traditions not even the unscrupulous among us would dare break."

Citra crossed her arms and said nothing more. She knew she was pouting, she knew it was childish, but she didn't care.

"You trust Scythe Faraday, do you not?" asked Scythe Curie.

"I do."

"Have you come to trust me at least as much?"

"I have."

"Then trust me now and let the question go. I have faith in your ability to shine in the final test without knowing what the test is."

"Yes, Your Honor."

They arrived at eight that evening, and were told that, by the luck of the draw, Citra was to be tested last. Rowan and the two other candidates for Scythedom were to go first. She and Scythe Curie were put in a room to wait, and wait, and wait some more.

"Was that a gunshot?" Citra said, perhaps an hour in. Citra didn't know whether or not it had been her imagination.

"Shhhh," was Scythe Curie's only response.

Finally a guard came to get her. Scythe Curie did not wish her good luck—just gave her a serious nod. "I'll be waiting for you when you're done," she said.

Citra was brought to a long room that seemed unpleasantly

cold. There were five scythes seated in comfortable chairs at one end. She recognized two of them: Scythe Mandela and Scythe Meir. The other three she did not. *The bejeweling committee,* she realized.

Before her was a table covered with a clean white tablecloth. And on that tablecloth, evenly spaced, were weapons: a pistol, a shotgun, a scimitar, a bowie knife, and a vial with a poison pill.

"What are these for?" Citra asked. Then she realized it was a stupid question. She knew what they were for. So she rephrased it. "What is it, exactly, that you want me to do?"

"Look to the other end of the room," Scythe Mandela told her, pointing. A spotlight came up on another chair at the far end of the long room that had been hidden in shadows; one not as comfortable as theirs. Someone sat in it, hands and legs bound, with a canvas hood covering his or her head.

"We want to see how you might glean," Scythe Meir said. "For this purpose we've prepared a unique subject for you to demonstrate."

"What do you mean, 'unique?'"

"See for yourself," said Scythe Mandela.

Citra approached the figure. She could hear faint snuffling from beneath the hood. She pulled it off.

Nothing could have prepared her for what she saw. Now she understood why Scythe Curie did not tell her.

Because bound to that chair, gagged, terrified, and tearful, was her brother, Ben.

He tried to speak, but nothing but muffled grunts came from behind the gag.

She backed away, then ran back to the five scythes.

"No! You can't do this! You can't make me do it."

"We can't make you do anything," said one of the scythes she didn't know, a woman in violet with PanAsian leanings. "If you do this, you do it by choice." Then the woman stepped forward and held a small box out to Citra. "Your weapon will be random. Choose a slip of paper from the box."

Citra reached in and pulled out a folded piece of paper. She dared not open it. She turned to look at her brother, sitting so helpless in the chair.

"How can you do this to people?" she screamed.

"My dear," said Scythe Meir with practiced patience, "it's not a gleaning, because you are not yet a scythe. You merely have to render him deadish. An ambudrone will take him to be revived as soon as you complete the task we've put before you."

"But he'll remember!"

"Yes," said Scythe Mandela. "And so will you."

One of the other scythes she did not know crossed his arms and huffed, much the way she had done on the drive here. "She's too resistant," he said. "Let her go. This night's already gone on too long."

"Give her time," said Scythe Mandela sternly.

The fifth scythe, a short man with an odd frown about him, stood and read from a sheet of parchment that could have been hundreds of years old. "You may not be coerced into doing this. You may take all the time you need. You must use the weapon assigned. When you are done, you will leave the subject and approach the committee to be assessed on your performance. Is all of this clear to you?"

Citra nodded.

"A verbal response, please."

"Yes, it's clear."

He sat back down, and she unfolded the slip of paper. On it was a single word.

Knife.

She dropped the paper to the floor. *I can't do this,* she told herself, *I can't.* But Scythe Curie's voice came gently to her. *Yes, Citra, you can.*

It was then it occurred to her that every scythe, since the Scythedom began, had to take this test. Every single one of them was forced to take the life of someone they loved. Yes, that person would be revived, but it didn't change the cold-blooded act. A person's subconscious mind can't differentiate between permanent and temporary killings. Even after he's revived, how could she bear to face her brother again? Because if she kills Ben, she will *always* have killed him.

"Why?" she asked. "Why must I do this?"

The irritable scythe gestured to the door. "There's the exit. If it's too much for you, then leave."

"I think she means it as a legitimate question," said Scythe Meir.

The irritable scythe scoffed, the short one shrugged. The PanAsian one tapped her foot, and Scythe Mandela leaned forward.

"You must do this so that you can move forward as a scythe," Scythe Mandela said, "knowing in your heart that the most difficult thing you'll ever have to do . . . has already been done."

"If you can do this," added Scythe Meir, "then you have the inner strength needed to be a scythe."

Even though a big part of Citra wanted to bolt through the

door and run from this, she squared her shoulders, stood tall, reached down, and took the bowie knife. Concealing it in her waist, she approached her brother. Only when she was close to him did she pull it out.

"Don't be afraid," she said. She knelt down and used the knife to cut the bonds on his legs, then the ones that held his wrists to the chair. She tried to untie his gag, but couldn't, so she cut that as well.

"Can I go home now?" asked Ben with a helpless voice that was more than enough to break her heart.

"Not yet," she told him, still kneeling beside him. "Soon, though."

"Are you going to hurt me, Citra?"

Citra couldn't control her tears, and didn't even try. What was the point? "Yes, Ben. I'm sorry."

"Are you going to glean me?" He could barely get the words out.

"No," she told him. "They'll take you to a revival center. You'll be good as new."

"You promise?"

"I promise."

He seemed the tiniest bit relieved. She didn't explain to him why she had to do this, and he didn't ask. He trusted her. Trusted that whatever reason she had, it was a good one.

"Will it hurt?" he asked.

Again, she found she couldn't lie to him about it. "Yes, it will. But not for long."

He took a moment to think about that. Process it. Accept it. Then he said, "Can I see it?"

For a moment she wasn't sure what he was talking about, until he pointed to the knife. She carefully put it into his hands.

"It's heavy," he said.

"Did you know that Texan scythes only glean with bowie knives?"

"Is that where you'll be going when you're a scythe? Texas?"

"No, Ben. I'll be right here."

He turned the knife in his hand, both of them watching as light glinted off the shiny blade. Then he gave it back to her.

"I'm so scared, Citra," he said, his voice barely a whisper.

"I know. So am I. Scared is okay."

"Will I get ice cream?" he asked. "I hear they give you ice cream at revival centers."

Citra nodded, and wiped a tear from his cheek. "Close your eyes, Ben. Think of the ice cream you want. Then tell me."

Ben did as he was told. "I want a hot fudge sundae, three scoops, with chocolate chip—"

Before he could finish, she pulled him close and thrust the blade just as she had seen Scythe Curie do it. She wanted to wail in agony, but wouldn't let herself.

Ben opened his eyes. He looked at her, and in a second it was done. Ben was gone. Citra hurled the blade away and cradled her brother. Then laid him gently on the floor. From a door behind them that she hadn't even seen, two revival medics hurried in, put her deadish brother on a gurney, and went out the way they came.

Lights came up on the scythes. They seemed so much farther away than before. It seemed like an impossibly long walk to cross the room to them, and they began a bruising barrage of comments.

"Sloppy."

"Not at all; there's barely any blood."

"She put the weapon in his hand. Do you know how risky that was?"

"And all that unnecessary banter."

"She was preparing him—making sure he was ready."

"Why should that matter?"

"She showed courage, but more importantly, she was compassionate. Isn't that what we're called upon to be?"

"We're called upon to be efficient."

"Efficiency must be in service to compassion!"

"That's a matter of opinion!"

Then the scythes fell silent, apparently agreeing to disagree. She suspected that Scythes Mandela and Meir were on her side, and that the irritable one was not. As for the other two, she had no idea where they stood.

"Thank you, Miss Terranova," said Scythe Meir. "You may go now. The results will be announced at conclave tomorrow."

Scythe Curie was waiting for her in the hall. Citra found herself furious at the woman. "You should have told me!"

"It would only have made it worse. And if they sensed that you knew before you went in that room, you would have been disqualified." She looked at Citra's hands. "Come, you need to wash up. There's a bathroom just this way."

"How did it go with the other candidates?" Citra asked.

"From what I heard, one young woman flatly refused and left the room. One boy began, but broke down and couldn't complete what he started."

"What about Rowan?" Citra asked.

Scythe Curie wouldn't look at her. "He drew the pistol as his weapon."

"And?"

Still Scythe Curie hesitated.

"Tell me!"

"He pulled the trigger even before they finished reading him the instructions."

Citra grimaced at the thought. Scythe Curie was right—he didn't sound like the same Rowan she used to know. What had he been through to turn him so cold? She didn't dare imagine.

I am the blade that is swung by your hand,

Slicing a rainbow's arc,

I am the clapper, but you are the bell,

Tolling the gathering dark.

If you are the singer, then I am the song,

A threnody, requiem, dirge.

You've made me the answer for all the world's need,

Humanity's undying urge.

—"Threnody,"
from the collected works of H.S. Socrates

39

Winter Conclave

At midnight, immunity for Citra Terranova and Rowan Damisch expired. Either one could now be gleaned, and if the edict was followed—and the Scythedom would make certain that it was—one would glean the other.

Around the world, scythes convened to discuss matters of life, but more to the point, matters of death. The first conclave of the year for MidMerica was to be a historic one. Never before had scythes permanently lost their lives in a gleaning event, and the controversial nature of that event made it even more significant—as well as the controversy surrounding one apprentice's three-month absence, following a bogus accusation by the MidMerican High Blade. Even the World Scythe Council had their eye on Fulcrum City today, and although the names of apprentices are rarely known beyond their regional bejeweling committee, scythes from every corner of the globe now knew the names of Citra Terranova and Rowan Damisch.

Fulcrum City was blistering cold that morning. Ice layered the marble steps leading up to the Capitol, making the stairs treacherous. More than one scythe slipped, spraining an ankle or breaking an arm. Healing nanites were taxed that morning, to the delight of spectators, who were thrilled by anything that slowed the scythes' ascent, allowing more photo ops.

Rowan arrived alone in a publicar, with no sponsor and no one to shepherd him in. He was dressed in the one color that scythes shunned—black. It made his green apprentice armband stand out and gave him a silent air of defiance. At Harvest Conclave he had been a footnote, if that. But now spectators jockeyed for position to take his picture. He ignored them, looking at no one as he climbed the stairs, making sure to keep his footing firm.

One scythe next to him stumbled on the ice and fell. Scythe Emerson, Rowan thought it was, although they'd never been introduced. Rowan reached out his hand to help the man up, but Emerson just glared at him and refused his help.

"I want no assistance from *you*," he told Rowan, the emphasis on the word "you" filled with more vitriol than anyone had expressed to Rowan in all his seventeen years.

But then, when he reached the top of the stairs, a scythe he didn't even know greeted him, and said in a comforting voice, "You've endured more than any apprentice should, Mr. Damisch. I do hope you achieve scythehood. And once you do, I hope we might share a pot of tea."

The offer sounded genuine, and not the product of political posturing. This was the way of things as he entered the rotunda. Hard glares from some and comforting grins from others. It seemed few were undecided about him. He was either the victim of circumstance or a criminal the likes of whom had not been seen since the Age of Mortality. Rowan wished he knew which of the two it was.

Citra had arrived before Rowan. She stood with Scythe Curie in the rotunda, with no appetite to partake of the lavish breakfast spread.

The conversation in the rotunda was, of course, all about the Tonist cloister tragedy. And as Citra listened to various snippets of conversation, she found herself angered that it was all about the four dead scythes. No one lamented that so many Tonists were gleaned. Some, in fact, callously joked about it.

"In the wake of the Tonist tragedy, conclave takes on a certain . . . *resonance*, don't you think?" she heard someone say. "No pun intended." But of course it was.

Scythe Curie was even more anxious than she had been at Harvest Conclave.

"Scythe Mandela told me that you performed well last night," she told Citra. "But even as he said it, he was guarded."

"What do you think that means?"

"I don't know. All I know is that if you lose today, Citra, I will never forgive myself."

It was absurd to think that the great Scythe Marie Curie, Grande Dame of Death, would care so much for her—and would even think there could be any failure on her own part. "I've had the benefit of being trained by the two greatest scythes who ever lived—you and Scythe Faraday. If that hasn't prepared me for today, nothing could have."

Scythe Curie beamed with bittersweet pride. "When this is over and you are ordained, I hope you'll do me the esteemed honor of staying on with me as a junior scythe. Others will make advances—perhaps even from distant regions. They'll try to tell you there are things you can learn from them that you couldn't learn from me. Perhaps that's true, but I do hope you'll choose to remain anyway." Her eyes were on the brink of tears. If she blinked, they would fall—but Scythe Curie kept them pooled on her lower lashes, too proud to be seen weeping in conclave.

Citra smiled. "I would have it no other way, Marie." It was the first time Citra had ever called her by her first name. She was surprised at how natural it felt.

As they waited for conclave to convene, other scythes came up to greet them. None spoke of Citra's detainment, or her escape to the Chilargentine Region, but some did joke with Marie about that embarrassing journal entry.

"In the Age of Mortality love and murder often went hand in hand," quipped Scythe Twain. "Perhaps our dear Scythe Faraday might have pegged you perfectly."

"Oh, go glean yourself," Curie said, only partially suppressing her grin.

"Only if I can attend my own funeral, my dear." Then he wished Citra good luck, and sauntered off.

That's when Citra saw Rowan enter the rotunda. It wasn't exactly as if silence fell all over the room, but the volume did dip significantly, and then rose again. There was a presence about him now. Not like that of a scythe, but something else. A pariah, perhaps. But never had a pariah had such a chilling effect on bringers of death. There were those who were saying that Rowan had killed those scythes in cold blood, and set the fire to hide the evidence. Others said he was lucky to have survived and bore no guilt. Citra suspected that whatever the truth was, it was much more complicated than either of those things.

"Don't talk to him," Scythe Curie said, when she saw her glancing in his direction. "Don't even let him see you looking his way. It will just make things more difficult for both of you."

"I know," Citra admitted, although she secretly hoped he would be brash enough to push through the crowd and come to her. And maybe say something—anything—that would prove to her he wasn't the unthinkable criminal people were saying he was.

If she was chosen today, Citra would not defy the edict to glean Rowan—but she did have a plan that might save both of them. It was far from foolproof—and to be brutally honest with herself, it was more like a desperate grasping at straws than a plan. But even the faintest glimmer of hope was better than no hope at all. If she was deluding herself, at least it would allow her to get through this awful day.

Rowan had played this day over in his mind many times from beginning to end. He had decided that he would not go up to Citra when he saw her. He did not need an advisor to tell him it was better this way. Let them stay separate and apart until that miserable moment of truth that would keep them apart forever.

If she won, Rowan was certain she would glean him. She was duty bound to do it. It would tear her apart, but in the end, she would do what had to be done. He wondered how she might go about it. Perhaps she would break his neck, bringing everything full circle and wrapping up their doomed twin apprenticeship with a nice red bow.

Admittedly, Rowan was afraid to die, but what he feared more than death were the depths that he now knew he was capable of reaching. The ease with which he had rendered his mother dead-ish during his test the night before spoke volumes about the person he'd become. He'd rather be gleaned than be that person.

Of course, it was possible he'd be chosen instead of Citra. Then things would get interesting. He decided he wouldn't glean himself—that would be too pointless and pathetic a gesture. If he was ordained, he would defy the edict, invoking the tenth commandment, which clearly said he was beholden to no laws beyond the ten—including any edicts levied by the Scythedom. He would refuse to glean Citra, and defend her life by taking out any scythes who tried to do it for him, with bullet, blade, and his own bare hands. He would turn conclave into a brutal and bloody battleground until they took him down—which wouldn't be easy, considering how skilled he'd become at killcraft and how motivated he was to wreak as much havoc as possible. And the irony of it was that they couldn't even glean him for it! Once he was ordained, their hands were tied by the seventh commandment.

They could punish him, though.

They could make him die a thousand deaths and then lock him away for eternity—and it would truly be eternity, because he would never give them the satisfaction of gleaning himself. Another reason why he would rather be gleaned by Citra. A single death at her capable hands sounded awfully good when compared with the alternative.

The breakfast spread in the rotunda was an elaborate one. Slabs of real smoked salmon, hard-crusted artisanal breads, and a waffle station with every conceivable topping. Only the best for the MidMerican scythes.

Rowan ate with rare gluttony that morning, for once allowing himself to fully sate his appetite, and as he ate, he stole a few glances at Citra. Even now, she looked radiant to him. How ridiculous that he'd still be romanticizing her in these final hours. What could have once been love was now the resignation of a heart long broken. Luckily for Rowan, his heart had grown so cold, its fracturing could not hurt him anymore.

Once conclave convened, Citra found herself tuning out most of the morning's ritual, choosing to fill her mind with memories of the life she was about to leave—because in one way or another, she would be leaving it. She focused on thoughts of her parents, and her brother—who was still in a revival center.

If she was ordained today, the home where she grew up would never be home again. Her biggest consolation would be that Ben and her parents would have immunity from gleaning for as long as Citra lived.

After the tolling of the names and the ritual washing, the entire morning was dedicated to a heated debate about whether or not fire should be banned as a method of gleaning.

Usually High Blade Xenocrates did nothing but mediate and postpone discussions for a later date. The fact that he was advocating for the ban was something everyone in attendance took seriously. Even so, there were strong voices against it.

"I will not have my rights to bear arms trampled upon!" railed one disgruntled scythe. "Every one of us should have the freedom to use flamethrowers, explosives, and any other incendiary device!"

It was met with both boos and applause.

"We need this ban to protect us from tragic accidents in the future," insisted Xenocrates.

"It was no accident!" someone shouted, and almost half the

room voiced their bitter agreement. Citra looked to Rowan, who sat with two empty seats on either side of him, for they were still earmarked for the dead. He made no move to defend himself or to deny the claim.

Scythe Curie leaned closer to Citra. "As terrible as that fire was, there are plenty of scythes happy to see Goddard and his disciples permanently removed from duty. Although they'd never admit it, they're glad the fire happened, whether it was an accident or not."

"And there are a lot of others who admired Goddard," Citra pointed out.

"Indeed. The Scythedom seems evenly split on that matter."

Regardless, common sense finally prevailed, and fire was banned in MidMerica as a method of gleaning.

At lunch, Citra—who still found she couldn't eat—watched from a distance as Rowan stuffed himself just as he had at breakfast, as if he had no care in the world.

"He knows it's his last meal," a scythe she didn't know suggested. Although the woman was clearly showing her support for Citra, Citra found herself annoyed.

"I can't see how it's any of your business."

The scythe walked away, confused by Citra's hostility.

At six that evening, all other conclave business ceased and the day revolved into its final stage.

"Candidates for scythehood, please rise," commanded the Conclave Clerk.

Citra and Rowan rose to a rumble of whispers in the assembly.

"I thought there were four," said the High Blade.

"There were, Your Excellency," said the clerk. "But the other two failed their final test and were dismissed."

"Very well then," said Xenocrates, "let's get on with it."

The clerk stood up, formally announcing them. "The Mid-Merican Scythedom calls Rowan Daniel Damisch and Citra Querida Terranova. Please come forward."

Then, keeping their eyes fixed on Scythe Mandela, who waited for them before the rostrum with a single ring, Citra and Rowan strode to the front of the assembly hall to meet their destiny, one way or another.

It is with bittersweet joy that I watch the bejeweling of new junior scythes at the end of each conclave. Joy, because they are our hope, and still kindle the idealism of the first scythes in their hearts. But bittersweet because I know that someday they will become so tired and jaded they will take their own lives, as all those first scythes eventually did.

Yet each time the new scythes are bejeweled, I still rejoice, because it allows me, if only for a few glorious moments, to believe that we will all choose to live forever.

—From the gleaning journal of H.S. Curie

40

The Ordained

"Hello, Citra. It's good to see you."

"Hello, Rowan."

"Will the candidates please refrain from speaking to each other and face the conclave," said Xenocrates.

The whispers and mumbles from the gathered scythes ceased the moment both Citra and Rowan faced them. Never before had such silence fallen over the assembly hall. Rowan smiled slightly—not out of amusement, but out of satisfaction. The two of them, side by side, commanded an undeniable gravity that could silence three hundred scythes. Whatever else happened today, Rowan would have this moment.

Citra maintained a stoic facade, refusing to let the adrenaline flooding her system reveal itself on her face.

"The bejeweling committee has studied your apprenticeships," Scythe Mandela announced to them, although it was meant more for the entire conclave. "We have reviewed the performance on all three of your tests—the first two of which you both failed, but with extenuating circumstances both times. Clearly, your instinct has been to protect each other. But the Scythedom must be protected first. At all costs."

"Here, here!" shouted one of the scythes in the back.

"The committee's decision was not made lightly," continued Scythe Mandela. "Know that we gave both of you the fairest consideration we possibly could." Then he raised his voice even louder. "Candidates for scythehood, will you accept the judgment of the MidMerican bejeweling committee?" he asked—as if it were possible not to accept their decision.

"I do, Your Honor," said Citra.

"So do I, Your Honor," said Rowan.

"Then let it be known," said Scythe Mandela, "that now, and forevermore . . . Citra Terranova shall wear the ring of scythehood, and bear the burden of all the ring entails."

The room erupted in cheers. Not just from her obvious supporters, but from just about everyone. Even those who were sympathetic to Rowan approved of the committee's decision—for in the end, what support did Rowan have in the Scythedom? Those who admired Goddard despised Rowan, and any who had given Rowan the benefit of the doubt were already rooting for Citra. Only now did it become clear that Citra was all but ordained the moment Goddard and his disciples perished in the fire.

"Congratulations, Citra," said Rowan, beneath the roaring approval of the crowd. "I knew you would do it."

She found she couldn't even respond to him, couldn't even look at him.

Scythe Mandela turned to her. "Have you chosen your Patron Historic?"

"I have, Your Honor."

"Then take this ring I hold out to you, put it on your finger, and announce to the MidMerican Scythedom, and to the world who . . . you . . . now . . . are."

Citra took the ring, her hands shaking so much she almost dropped it. She slipped it on her finger. A perfect fit. It was heavy on her finger and the gold of the setting was cold, but was quickly warmed by her body heat. She held her hand up, as she had seen other ordained candidates do.

"I choose to be known as Scythe Anastasia," she told them. "After the youngest member of the family Romanov."

The gathered scythes turned to one another, discussing her choice among themselves.

"Miss Terranova," said High Blade Xenocrates, clearly not pleased, "I can't say that is an appropriate choice. The czars of Russia were known more for their excess than their contribution to civilization—and Anastasia Romanov did nothing of note in her short life."

"Exactly why I chose her, Your Excellency," Citra said, holding eye contact with him. "She was the product of a corrupt system, and because of that, was denied her very life—as I almost was."

Xenocrates bristled the slightest bit. Citra went on.

"Had she lived, who knows what she might have done. Perhaps she could have changed the world and redeemed her family name. I choose to be Scythe Anastasia. I vow to become the change that might have been."

The High Blade held her gaze, and held his silence. Then one scythe rose and began applauding. Scythe Curie. Then another joined her and another, and soon the entire Scythedom was on their feet, in an ovation for the newly ordained Scythe Anastasia.

. . .

Rowan knew they had made the right decision. And when he heard Citra defend her choice for Patron Historic, he admired her more than he ever had. Were he not already standing, he would have risen to his feet in ovation as well.

Then, as the accolades died down and the scythes were seated, Scythe Mandela turned to Citra.

"You know what you have to do."

"I do, Your Honor."

"What method do you choose?"

"Blade," she said. "So many of my trials seem to be by blade; this one should be no different." And of course a tray of knives was ready, just out of sight. It was now brought in by a junior scythe who had just been ordained at Harvest Conclave.

Rowan watched Citra closely, but she would not meet his gaze. She looked over the tray of knives, finally settling on a nasty-looking bowie knife.

"I used one of these to kill my brother yesterday," Citra said. "I swore I'd never touch one again, but here I am."

"How is he?" Rowan asked. Finally Citra looked at him. There was fear in her eyes, but also resolve. *Good,* thought Rowan. *Let her be decisive about this. It will be quicker.*

"He's in revival," she said. "With a hot fudge sundae on order for when he wakes up."

"Lucky him." Rowan looked out at the grand elegy of scythes. At this moment less of a conclave and more of an audience. "They're waiting for a show," Rowan said. "Shall we give it to them?"

Citra nodded slightly.

And with a sentiment that was heartfelt and true, Rowan said, "It is my honor to be gleaned by you, Scythe Anastasia."

Then Rowan drew his last breath and prepared to accept her blade. But she wasn't ready to strike just yet. Instead, she looked to the ring on her other hand.

"This," she said, "is for breaking my neck."

Then she drew her fist back and punched him in the face with such force, it nearly knocked him off his feet. A collective gasp came from the crowd; this was something they were not expecting.

Rowan reached up to feel blood spilling from a huge gash that her ring had cut across his cheek.

Then finally she raised the knife to glean him—but just as she was about to thrust it into his chest, a shout came from the rostrum behind them.

"STOP!"

It was the Parliamentarian. He held up his own ring. It was glowing red. So was Citra's—and as Rowan looked around, he could see that every scythe's ring within ten yards was emanating the same warning glow.

"He can't be gleaned," the Parliamentarian said. "He has immunity."

A roar of outrage came from the conclave. Rowan looked at Citra's ring, which was covered with his blood. It had transmitted his DNA to the immunity database even more effectively than if he had kissed it. He smiled at her in awe and absolute amazement. "You're a genius, Citra. You know that, don't you?"

"It's Honorable Scythe Anastasia to you," she said. "And I

don't know what you're talking about. It was an accident." But there was a twinkle in her eye that said otherwise.

"Order!" yelled Xenocrates, banging his gavel. "I demand this conclave come to order!"

The scythes began to calm down, and Xenocrates pointed an accusing finger. "Citr—uh . . . that is, Scythe Anastasia—you have blatantly violated a Scythedom edict!"

"I have not, Your Excellency. I was fully prepared to glean him. It was your own Parliamentarian who stopped me. It never occurred to me that hitting Rowan would grant him immunity."

Xenocrates looked at her in utter disbelief, and then suddenly released a guffaw that he tried to stifle but couldn't. "Sly and artful," he said, "with just enough plausible deniability. You'll do very well among us, Scythe Anastasia." Then he turned to the Parliamentarian and asked what options they now had.

"I suggest imprisonment for a year, until his immunity runs out."

"Is there still such a place where a person could be officially imprisoned?" asked one of the other scythes. Then scythes around the assembly hall began to shout out their suggestions, some even offering to take Rowan in under house arrest, which could be good or bad, depending on their motive.

As it began to devolve into a debate over Rowan's immediate future, Citra leaned in to him and whispered.

"There's a tray of knives next to you, and a car waiting for you at the east exit." Then she leaned away, leaving his future firmly in his own hands.

He thought he could not be more impressed by her. She had just proved him wrong.

"I love you," he said.

"Same here," she responded. "Now get lost."

He was a wonder to watch. He took three blades from the tray, and somehow managed to wield them all. Scythe Anastasia made no move to stop him—but even if she had, it would have been no use. He was too quick. He hurled himself like a fireball down the center aisle. The scythes closest to him leaped into action, trying to stop him, but he kicked and spun, and sliced and flipped. No one could get a hand on him. To Scythe Anastasia he seemed some deadly force of nature. Of the scythes in his way, the lucky ones only had their robes sliced. The less lucky ones found themselves with wounds they never even saw inflicted. One—Scythe Emerson, she believed—would be requiring a trip to a revival center.

And then he was gone, leaving pandemonium in his wake.

As the High Blade tried to regain order, Scythe Anastasia looked to her hand, and did something that was very strange for a scythe to do. She kissed her own ring, getting just the slightest bit of Rowan's blood on her lips. Enough for her to remember the moment forever.

The car was waiting, just as Citra had said. He thought it would be a publicar. He thought he would be alone. Neither was the case.

As he hopped in, he saw a ghost in the driver's seat. After all he'd been through today, this was the moment that nearly made his heart stop.

"Good evening, Rowan," said Scythe Faraday. "Close the door, it's positively arctic outside."

"What?" said Rowan still trying to wrap his mind around the moment. "How are you not dead?"

"I could ask you the same question, but time is of the essence. Now please, close the door."

So Rowan did, and they sped off into the frosty Fulcrum City night.

Have we ever had an enemy worse than ourselves? In the Age of Mortality we warred ceaselessly with one another, and when there was no war to be made, we beat down one another in our streets, our schools, our homes, until war turned our gaze outward again, placing the enemy at a more comfortable distance.

But all such conflict is a thing of the past. There is peace on Earth, good will toward all humankind.

Except . . .

And that's the thing: There is always an exception. I haven't been a scythe for long, but I can already see that the Scythedom is in danger of becoming that exception. Not just here in MidMerica, but worldwide.

The first scythes were true visionaries and saw the wisdom of continuing to cultivate wisdom. They understood that the soul of a scythe needed to remain pure. Free from malice and greed and pride, but filled with conscience. However, rot grows on even the sturdiest of foundations.

If the conscience of the Scythedom fails, replaced by the avarice of privilege, we could become our own worst enemy again. And to complicate it, new wrinkles are being added to the fabric of the Scythedom every day. Take, for instance, the latest rumor, which in the months since I was ordained has spread beyond the Scythedom and is whispered among the general population.

According to the rumor, there is someone out there who is seeking out corrupt, despicable scythes . . . and ending their existence by fire. One thing is certain: He's not an ordained scythe. And yet people have started to call him Scythe Lucifer.

I'm terrified that it might be true—but more terrified that I might want it to be true.

It was never my desire to be a scythe. I suppose that might make me a good one. I don't yet know, because it's all so new and I still have so much to learn. For now I must give all my attention to gleaning with compassion and conscience, with hopes that it will help our perfect world stay perfect.

And if ever Scythe Lucifer comes my way, I hope he'll see me as one of the good ones. The way he once did.

—From the gleaning journal of H.S. Anastasia

A Reading Group Guide to

Scythe

by Neal Shusterman

About the Book

Two teens must learn the "art of killing" in the first book in a chilling new series from Neal Shusterman, author of the *New York Times* bestselling Unwind dystology.

In a world where disease has been eliminated, the only way to die is to be randomly killed ("gleaned") by professional reapers ("scythes"). Citra and Rowan are teenagers who have been selected to be scythe's apprentices, and despite wanting nothing to do with the vocation, they must learn every method of ending life and come to understand the necessity of what they do

Only one of them will be chosen as a scythe's apprentice. And when it becomes clear that the winning apprentice's first task will be to glean the loser, Citra and Rowan are pitted against each other in a fight for their lives.

Discussion Questions

The following questions may be utilized throughout the study of *Scythe* as targeted questions for discussion and reflection, or alternatively, they can be used to as reflective writing prompts.

1. The first entry from the gleaning journal of H. S. Curie states, "We must, by law, keep a record of the innocents we kill. And as I see it, they're all innocents. Even the guilty." Why does Curie see mankind as both innocent and guilty? In your opinion, does that matter?

2. Why can "gleaning" not be referred to as "killing"? Why does this society believe it's socially or morally incorrect to call it such? Do you agree? How does the role of the scythe fit into that complex system?

3. Curie shares that "scythes provide a crucial service for society." In what ways are her understanding of her work correct? From what you discovered in the novel, what are the biggest challenges to serving as a scythe? Can you think of any ways that the position offers benefits to the scythe?

4. As the novel opens, Honorable Scythe Faraday visits Citra's home while he waits to pay a visit to their neighbor. His multi-layered robe is described as "smooth ivory linen," not black, because "black was an absence of light and scythes were the opposite. Luminous and enlightened, they were acknowledged as the very best of humanity—which is why they were chosen for the job." Based on what you learn about Scythe Faraday, what can be inferred about his choice of robe color? What additional

early information about him can be garnered by his interaction with both Citra and her family?

5. Citra thinks, "No surprise that people bent over backwards to please scythes in every possible way. Hope in the shadow of fear is the world's most powerful motivator." Do you agree? What role does hope have in motivating others? In what ways do people strive to accommodate and influence scythes?

6. After Citra asks Scythe Faraday about his age and is admonished by her mother, he tells them, "I like direct questions. They show an honesty of spirit." What other qualities about Citra do you find Faraday is most drawn to? What is your analysis of her character? Is she someone you'd befriend if given the chance?

7. Consider what you've learned about Citra and Rowan. What is it about these two teens that make them seem like appropriate candidates as scythe apprentices? In what ways are they similar, and how are they different? Given what you discover about them, is there one character you like better than the other? If so, why?

8. Throughout the novel, Citra and Rowan learn that there is a right way to glean. Do you agree? Can you make a case for this component in this future society?

9. After learning more about Citra's father's historical research, Faraday declares, "The past never changes—and from what I can see, neither does the future." Citra believes that to a degree, he is actually correct. Why have Faraday's experiences left him feeling this way? Do you agree with his assessment? Why is it important to continue to study the past and look for fresh perspectives about history?

10. After meeting Rowan for the first time at Kohl's gleaning, Faraday tells Rowan, "You stood your ground for a boy you barely knew. You comforted him at the moment of his death, bearing the pain of the jolt. You bore witness, even though no one called you to do so." Why does this act impress Faraday so much?

11. Faraday tells Rowan, "Remember that good intentions pave many roads. Not all of them lead to hell." What do you believe he means by this statement? Do you agree? Why or why not?

12. Did learning that Scythe Faraday attends the funerals of those he gleans surprise you? For what reason do you think it's significant that he does this?

13. Review the Scythes' Commandments. Is there anything about these mandates that you find unusual or surprising?

14. In the instructions Faraday gives Citra and Rowan, he tells them, "You shall study history, the great philosophers; the sciences. You will come to understand the nature of life, and what it means to be human before you are permanently charged with the taking of life. You will also study all forms of killcraft, and become experts." What do you believe are his motivations to have his apprentices study both the arts and sciences? How does this benefit them and their potential future work?

15. Based on your initial impressions of Scythe Faraday and what you learn about him over the course of the novel, does your opinion of him change in any way and if so, how? How was his leadership style different from that of Scythe Curie and Scythe Goddard? Do you see Citra or Rowan being more aligned with Faraday's philosophies about mankind and gleaning? In what ways might this impact the two apprentices?

16. Rowan tells Volta, "I know you're not like the others." Do you agree with Rowan's assessment? In what ways are Rowan and Volta alike? Are there any ways they are different?

17. Volta states that Scythe Goddard is "the future." Given what you have learned about the new guard of scythes, what makes that so disconcerting? What do you believe motivates Goddard to behave the way he does?

18. During their sparring match, why does Citra become so angry at Rowan's actions? For the pair, how does the knowledge that only one of them is to survive make them feel? In what ways do each of them work to protect the other when they are forced to fight?

19. Why does Citra become so committed to understanding the details of Faraday's last day? Do you think she is right to grow suspicious about his death? Consider the consequences of her actions: How does her need to learn what happened put her in danger, and why are those involved in his death so worried the truth will be revealed? What was your reaction to the realization that things may not be as they appear?

20. Compare the traditional scythes to the new celebrity scythes. In what ways do these two groups take the understanding of their work differently? How do those differences ultimately impact the citizens in their world?

21. Compare the ways in which Citra and Rowan deal with each other and their apprenticeships. What can be learned about the character of each from these interactions and relationships?

22. Given the ending of *Scythe*, share your predictions for the next installment of this thrilling series.

Extension Activities

1. The gleaning journal of H. S. Curie states that "People used to die naturally. Old age used to be a terminal affliction, not a temporary state. There was pain, misery, and despair." How does this future world without diseases, aging, transportation crashes, and "danger lurking in every unseen, unplanned corner" compare to the world you know? After completing your reading of *Scythe*, write an essay that analyzes these two worlds.

2. Faraday states, "A scythe is merely the instrument of death, but it is your hand that swings me. You and your parents and everyone else in this world are the wielders of scythes. We all are accomplices. You must share the responsibility." Consider Faraday's words. Based on what you know about your world and his, do you agree? Compose a response to Faraday where you share your position.

3. For Citra and Rowan, being selected as a scythe's apprentice has obviously had a profound impact on their lives and their relationships with others. Throughout the novel, as they learn more about the role and responsibility of being a scythe, they become increasingly empowered to take control of their lives and choices. After taking a moment to reflect on your life's most personal challenges, draft a journal or diary entry focusing on the ways you've already overcome obstacles and listing the strategies you plan to use to deal with those you are still facing.

4. Throughout *Scythe*, Shusterman infuses his story with rich, powerful, figurative language. Embark on a literary scavenger hunt throughout the book to locate your favorite examples of

phrases or quotes. Create a sharable quote card image to be published on a social media site of your choice.

5. While the novel focuses on the relationship between Scythe Faraday, Citra, and Rowan, Shusterman introduces us to a number of secondary characters who face their own hardships or need the opportunity to have some self-awareness. Select a secondary character in *Scythe* and write a letter of advice to him/her. You can choose to be serious or funny, just make sure your advice fits the character's needs.

6. Throughout *Scythe*, a number of characters exhibit acts of bravery. Consider the individual actions of these characters. Who do you believe to be the most courageous? Write a letter to that character explaining why you believe his/her actions are so brave.

7. Assume the role of one of the secondary characters in *Scythe* and draft a diary entry detailing what you experienced and witnessed. To prepare, create an outline using the five W's (who, what, when, where, and why). Remember to write in first person and give special attention to sensory imagery (what you saw, smelled, heard, etc.).

8. Consider the shift in philosophy from our world where a digital network "cloud" and artificial intelligence is feared to a future where a "Thunderhead" provides a "perfect world." Do you believe utopias are possible? Here in the United States, a number of utopian communities have been established over time. Select a community or society to research, making sure to explore the principles that guided the community as well as the assumptions about those core beliefs. For what you learn, share why you believe this community was ultimately unable to sustain itself.

*This guide was created by Dr. Rose Brock, an assistant professor in
Library Science Department in the College of Education at Sam
Houston State University. Dr. Brock holds a Ph.D. in Library Science,
specializing in children's and young adult literature.*

*This guide has been provided by Simon & Schuster for classroom,
library, and reading group use. It may be reproduced in its entirety or
excerpted for these purposes.*

Look for

Thunderhead

Book 2 in the
Arc of a Scythe trilogy

by Neal Shusterman

Peach velvet with embroidered baby-blue trim. Honorable Scythe Brahms loved his robe. True, the velvet became uncomfortably hot in the summer months, but it was something he had grown accustomed to in his sixty-three years as a scythe.

He had recently turned the corner again, resetting his physical age back to a spry twenty-five—and now, in his third youth, he found his appetite for gleaning was stronger than ever.

His routine was always the same, though methods varied. He would choose his subject, restrain him or her, then play a lullaby—Brahm's lullaby to be exact—the most famous piece of music composed by his "Patron Historic." After all, if a scythe must choose a figure from history to name oneself after, shouldn't that figure be integrated somehow into the scythe's life? He would play the lullaby on whatever instrument was convenient, and if there was none available, he would simply hum it. And then he would end the subject's life.

Politically, he leaned toward the teachings of the late Scythe Goddard of MidMerica, for he enjoyed gleaning immensely, and saw no reason why that should be a problem for anyone. "In a perfect world shouldn't we all enjoy what we do?" Goddard wrote. It was a sentiment gaining traction in more and more regional Scythedoms.

On this evening Scythe Brahms had just accomplished a particularly entertaining gleaning in downtown Omaha, and was still whistling his signature tune as he sauntered down the street, wondering where he might find himself a late evening meal. But he stopped in mid-stanza, having a distinct feeling that he was being watched.

There were, of course, cameras on every light post in the city. The Thunderhead was ever vigilant—but for a scythe, its slumberless, unblinking eyes were of no concern. It was powerless to even comment on the comings and goings of scythes, much less act upon anything it saw. The Thunderhead was the ultimate voyeur of death.

This feeling, however, was more than the observational nature of the Thunderhead. Scythes were trained in perceptive skills. They were not prescient, but five highly developed senses could often have the semblance of a sixth. A scent, a sound, an errant shadow too minor to register consciously might be enough to make a well-trained scythe's neck hairs bristle.

Scythe Brahms turned, sniffed, listened. He took in his surroundings. He was alone on a side street. Elsewhere, he could hear the sounds of street cafes and the ever-vibrant nightlife of the city, but the street he was on was lined with shops that were shuttered this time of night. Cleaners and clothiers. A hardware store and a daycare center. The lonely street belonged to him and the unseen interloper.

"Come out," he said. "I know you're there."

He thought it might be a child, or perhaps an unsavory hoping to bargain for immunity—as if an unsavory might have anything with which to bargain. Maybe it was a Tonist. Tone cults despised scythes, and although Brahms had never heard of Tonists actually attacking a scythe, they have been known to torment.

"I won't harm you," Brahms said. "I've just completed a gleaning—I have no desire to increase my tally today." Although, admittedly, he might change his mind if the interloper was either too offensive, or obsequious.

Still no one stepped forward.

"Fine," he said. "Be gone, then, I have neither time nor patience for a game of hide and seek."

Perhaps it was his imagination after all. Maybe his rejuvenated senses were now so acute that they were responding to stimuli that was much farther away than he assumed.

That's when a figure launched from behind a parked car as if it had been spring-loaded. Brahms was knocked off balance—he would have been taken down entirely if he still had the slow reflexes of an older man, and not his twenty-five year-old self. He pushed the figure into a wall, and considered pulling out his blades to glean this reprobate, but Scythe Brahms had never been a brave man. So he ran.

He moved in and out of pools of light created by the streetlamps, all the while cameras atop each pole swiveled to watch him.

When he turned to look, the figure was a good twenty yards behind him. Now Brahms could see he was dressed in a black robe. Was it a sycthe's robe? No, it couldn't be. No scythe dressed in black—it was not allowed.

But there were rumors . . .

That thought made him pick up the pace. He could feel

adrenaline tingling in his fingers, and add urgent velocity to his heart.

A scythe in black.

No, there had to be another explanation. He would report this to the Irregularity Committee, that's what he would do. Yes, they might laugh at him and say he was scared off by a masquerading unsavory, but these things needed to be reported, even if they were embarrassing. It was his civic duty.

A block further, and his assailant had given up the chase. He was nowhere to be seen. Scythe Brahms slowed his pace. He was nearing a more active part of the city now. The beat of dance music and the garble of conversation careened down the street toward him, giving him a sense of security. He let his guard down. Which was a mistake.

The dark figure broadsided him from a narrow alley, and delivered a knuckle punch to his windpipe. As Brahms gasped for air, his attacker kicked his legs out from under him in a Bokator kick—that brutal martial art in which scythes were trained. Brahms landed on a crate of rotting cabbage left by the side of a market. It burst, spewing forth a thick methane reek. His breath could only come in short gasps, and he could feel warmth spreading throughout his body as his pain nanites released opiates.

No! Not yet! I must not be numbed. I need my full faculties to fight this miscreant.

But pain nanites were simple missionaries of relief, hearing only the scream of angry nerve endings. They ignored his wishes and deadened his pain.

Brahms tried to rise, but slipped as the putrid vegetation

crushed beneath him, becoming a slick, unpleasant stew. The figure in black was on top of him now, pinning him to the ground. Brahms tried to reach into his robe for his weapons, but could not. So instead he reached up, and pulled back his attacker's black hood, revealing him to be a young man—barely a man—a boy. His eyes were intense, and intent on—to use a mortal-age word—murder.

"Scythe Johannes Brahms, you are accused of abusing your position and multiple crimes against humanity."

"How dare you!" Brahms gasped. "Who are you to accuse me?" He struggled, trying to rally his strength, but it was no use. The painkillers that were now in his system were deadening his responses. His muscles were weak and useless to him now.

"I think you know who I am," the young man said. "Let me hear you say it."

"I will not!" Brahms said, determined not to give him the satisfaction. But the boy in black jammed a knee so powerfully into Brahm's chest, that he thought his heart would stop. More pain nanites. More opiates. Brahms's head was swimming. He had no choice but to comply.

"Lucifer," he gasped. "Scythe Lucifer."

Brahms felt his spirit crumble—as if saying it aloud gave resonance to the rumor.

Satisfied, the self-proclaimed young scythe eased the pressure.

"You are no scythe," Brahms dared to say. "You are nothing but a failed apprentice, and you will not get away with this."

The young man had no response to that. Instead he said, "Tonight you gleaned a young woman by blade."

"That is my business, not yours!"

"You gleaned her as a favor for a friend who wanted out of a relationship with her."

"This is outrageous! You have no proof of that!"

"I've been watching you, Johannes," Rowan said. "As well as your friend—who seemed awfully relieved when that poor woman was gleaned."

Suddenly there was a knife at Brahms neck. His own knife. This beast of boy was threatening him with his own knife.

"Do you admit it?" he asked Brahms.

All that he said was true, but Brahms would rather be rendered deadish than admit it to the likes of a failed apprentice. Even one with a knife at his throat.

"Go on, slit my throat," Brahms dared. "It will add one more inexcusable crime to your record. And when I am revived, I will stand as witness against you—and make no mistake, you will be brought to justice!"

"By whom? By the Thunderhead? I've taken down corrupt scythes from one coast to the other over the past year, and the Thunderhead hasn't sent so much as a single peace officer to stop me. Why do you think that is?"

Brahms was speechless. He had assumed if he stalled long enough, and kept this so-called Scythe Lucifer occupied, the Thunderhead would dispatch a full squad to apprehend him. That's what the Thunderhead did when common citizens threatened violence. Brahms was surprised it had even gone this far. Such bad behavior among the general population was supposed to be a thing of the past. Why was this being allowed?

"If I take your life now," the false scythe said, "you would not be brought back to life. I burn those I remove from service, leaving nothing but unrevivable ash."

"I don't believe you! You wouldn't dare!"

But Brahms did believe him. Since last January, nearly a dozen scythes across three Merican regions had been consumed by flames under questionable circumstances. Their deaths were all ruled accidental, but clearly they were not. And because they were burned, their deaths were permanent.

Now Brahms knew that the whispered tales of Scythe Lucifer—the outrageous acts of Rowan Damisch, the fallen apprentice—were all true. Brahms closed his eyes, and took in a final breath, trying not to gag on the rancid stench of putrid cabbage.

And then Rowan said, "You won't be dying today, Scythe Brahms. Not even temporarily." He removed the blade from Brahms neck. "I'm giving you one chance. If you act with the nobility befitting a scythe, and glean with honor, you won't see me again. But if you continue to serve your own corrupt appetites, then you will be left as ash."

And then he was gone, almost as if he had vanished—and in his place was a horrified young couple looking down upon Brahms.

"Is that a scythe?"

"Quick, help me get him up!"

They lifted Brahms from the rot. His peach velvet robe was stained green and brown, as if covered in mucous. It was humiliating. He considered gleaning the couple—for no one should see a scythe so indisposed and live—but instead held out his hand and allowed them to kiss his ring, thereby granting both of them a year of immunity from gleaning. He told them it was a reward for their kindness, but really it was to just make them go away, and abandon any questions they might have had.

After they had left, he brushed himself off, and resolved to say nothing to the Irregularity Committee about this, because it would leave him open to far too much ridicule and derision. He had suffered enough indignation already.

Scythe Lucifer indeed! Few things were more miserable in this world than a failed scythe's apprentice, and never had there been one as ignoble as Rowan Damisch.

Yet he knew that the boy's threat was not an idle one.

Perhaps, thought Scythe Brahms, a lower profile was in order. A return to the lackluster gleanings he had been trained to perform in his youth. A refocusing on the basics that would make "Honorable Scythe" more than just a title, but a defining trait.

Stained, bruised, and bitter, Scythe Brahms returned to his home to reconsider his place in the perfect world in which he lived.